Shaughnessy Brothers

Always My Girl

MVFOL

Also by Samantha Chase

The Montgomery Brothers
Wait for Me
Trust in Me
Stay with Me
More of Me
Return to You
Meant for You
I'll Be There

The Shaughnessy Brothers
Made for Us
Love Walks In
Always My Girl
This Is Our Song

Holiday Romance
The Christmas Cottage
Ever After
Mistletoe Between Friends
The Snowflake Inn

Life, Love and Babies
The Baby Arrangement
Baby, I'm Yours
Baby, Be Mine

One
More
Kiss

SAMANTHA CHASE

sourcebooks
casablanca

Published by Sourcebooks Casablanca, an imprint of Sourcebooks, Inc.
P.O. Box 4410, Naperville, Illinois 60567-4410
(630) 961-3900
Fax: (630) 961-2168
www.sourcebooks.com

Printed and bound in Canada.
MBP 10 9 8 7 6 5 4 3 2 1

Frank—the man who keeps music in my life, even if it's music I don't want, and is one of the most gifted musicians I know. Thank you for always being there and encouraging me to keep going when the fight seems too hard. I love you.

Nicholas—the one who makes me laugh more than any human being alive. What an inspiration you are, reminding me every day to go after my dreams even when no one else believes in them.

And Michael—the one who reminds me that there are good people in this world. Your heart and your outlook on life—even when it's negative— always help keep things in perspective.

I am a blessed woman, indeed.

Prologue

Two years ago

THE NOISE LEVEL BACKSTAGE WAS ALMOST AS DEAFENING as it had been while they took their final bow. Not that it was much of a surprise. The fans always went wild after the encore, always wanting more. But that's how you're supposed to leave them. It guaranteed they'd come back and see you the next time you were in town.

Matt Reed wasn't sure that was going to happen.

Shaughnessy, the band he'd cofounded and played lead guitar in for over ten years, was going on hiatus. It was a good thing. A necessity. A chance to check out other creative outlets. And he was going to spend the next year exploring those options.

Someone shoved a bottle of Jack Daniels into his hands as he made his way through the crowd to his dressing room. He readily took it, opened it, and was drinking from it before he was behind closed doors. Not that it was a shock to anyone—he was a rock star; he drank. The two seemed to go hand in hand. Only… he was getting tired of it. It was no longer fun getting drunk. It make him feel…sad. Weak.

Alone.

He was just about to strip off his shirt when there was a loud knock on the door behind him. "Fifteen minutes, Matty!"

Hell, he was ready for a break—from the band and the persona. For a little while, it was going to be nice to be just Matt Reed again. Cursing, he took another pull from the bottle, downing a good portion of it before slamming the bottle down.

So. Damn. Ready.

It wasn't that he didn't love playing with Riley, Dylan, and Julian—he did. It was just that it was time to do something new. Something different. Something that put him in the spotlight and center stage. For years, Matt had dreamed of breaking out a bit, but he hadn't found the right avenue to do it until now.

Only a few weeks ago, Matt's agent had presented him with the opportunity to be the lead in a new rock opera that was being written for Broadway. The timing had been perfect—Dylan was joining the lineup of one of those rock-legends tours, and Julian was getting ready to cowrite the music for his girlfriend Dena's debut album.

"Dena," Matt grumbled as he searched for a clean change of clothes. "She is going to be the death of him. Doesn't he realize she's only using him for his connections? She has zero talent! Why is he wasting his time on something like that?" While he knew no one was there to answer him, it still helped him to vent about the situation his friend was putting himself in.

He wasn't stupid. Matt knew exactly why Julian was doing what he was doing. But it still seemed a bit ridiculous. "Because he's in love," he said with a derisive snort. "One day, he'll realize she's all wrong for him, but the more we keep telling him, the more determined he is to prove us wrong."

None of this was new information, so he had no idea why he was even thinking about it. What he really needed to focus on was getting cleaned up and out of here. After the party, they were all going to sit down with Riley, who had been blindsided by the fact that they were all moving on to do solo projects rather than taking a short break. Matt felt bad about it—he really did—but it was time for him to put his life first, rather than the band.

Pushing that thought aside, he quickly finished stripping and changed into clean clothes. One more party to show up at, one more night of flirting and drinking and dancing, and then he'd be able to head off and start this new chapter of his life.

"This could finally be my turn," he mumbled as he packed up his clothes, stuffing them into his bag. With a final look around the room, he checked his reflection and grimaced. "Time for a shower would have been nice."

Wishing for that time was pointless, so with nothing left to do, he grabbed the almost-empty bottle, strode across the room, and pulled open the door.

And froze.

Standing there was his every fantasy come to life.

Wide, chocolate-brown eyes; long, wavy dark-brown hair; red lips; and a body that was lovingly encased in faded denim jeans and a black T-shirt. Black looked good on her. The only question he had was: *Who is she?* His agent Mick and their security team made sure no one got backstage. Especially when they were on a tight schedule.

"Matt?" she asked nervously.

Matt? That stopped him because his stage name was

Matty—something he hated but the fans loved—and every groupie he'd ever met referred to him as such. If this woman was calling him Matt, he had to know her from somewhere else. Taking a closer look, he then stepped back in shock.

"Vivienne?"

She nodded and gave a small wave as she sighed with relief. "Hey," she said quietly, a small smile crossing her face. "How are you?"

Holy shit! His best friend Aaron's little sister was here and looking...hot! How was *he*? At the moment, he felt like he was having a stroke!

"Um...Matt?"

"Oh, right. Right. Come on in!" Matt took another step back and motioned for Vivienne to step into his dressing room. He closed the door and watched as she looked around the space.

After a few seconds, she turned back to him and smiled. "It's not quite what I imagined."

He smiled sheepishly. "Yeah. Not glamorous at all."

"So how are you?" she asked.

"I'm good. I'm good," he replied. "How...how did you get back here? No one is supposed to get backstage."

She blushed, looking embarrassed. "Oh. Sorry. I know the head of security here at the arena, and then I spotted Riley, so..." She shrugged. "I'm sorry. I should probably go. I just wanted to stop and say hello." Vivienne ducked her head and started to walk to the door when Matt stopped her. She looked up at him, those big, brown eyes filled with regret.

Matt cursed himself under his breath. "Hey, I'm not mad you're here. I'm just surprised. Like I said, security never lets this happen. Sometimes fans get a little…overzealous, so we have a policy that no one gets backstage without clearance." He had his hand gently wrapped around her upper arm and she was close.

Very close.

When the hell had Vivienne grown up? The last time Matt had seen her, she had been fourteen and wore braces. But this woman standing in front of him was… *Wow*. He took a deep breath before speaking again. "It's really good to see you."

She seemed to relax visibly. "Oh. Good. Me too." She shook her head and murmured something to herself. "I mean it's good to see you too."

Matt knew he should step back, move away, but he couldn't. He couldn't take his eyes off her face. She was beautiful.

"I…I wasn't sure if you'd even recognize me or remember me," she said softly.

"It took me a minute," he admitted, his tone equally soft. It hit him how quiet everything had gotten. The loud hum of activity on the other side of the door seemed to have died away, and the only thing he could hear was the two of them breathing.

He knew he should ask about her brother and stick to safe topics, but he was feeling a little buzzed from the liquor and his thinking was slightly skewed. In that moment, he didn't really care about talking or making idle chitchat. Her lips—all soft and red and glossy— were beckoning him. When he began to lower his head, it registered that she wasn't pulling away. If anything, she was slowly meeting him halfway.

The moment his lips captured hers, Matt was lost.

He dropped his bag and the bottle to the floor, the latter hitting with a loud crash neither of them noticed. Vivienne's arms slowly came up and looped around his shoulders as Matt's banded around her waist.

She tasted so sweet he simply forgot where they were.

The door behind them crashed open. "Matty! Let's go! The car's waiting!"

Matt lifted his head and looked behind him to see Mick's angry face staring back at him.

"What the hell?" Mick growled. "How did this one get by security?" He called out to someone in the hallway, and he stalked over, grabbed Matt's bag off the floor, and then Matt by the arm. "Let's go!"

"Mick…wait!" Matt stammered, doing his best to break free.

"Take him to the car," Mick snapped, shoving Matt toward three security guys. "And you," he said firmly to Vivienne, "I suggest you leave now, or I'll have you escorted out and press charges!"

"No!" she cried. "You don't understand. I'm—"

"Save it!" Mick turned back toward where Matt was struggling with the security guards. "Go!"

There seemed to be hundreds of people lining the hallway, and no matter how much Matt struggled to free himself from the security guys, he couldn't. He called back toward where he last saw Vivienne, but it was no use. He could barely hear himself shout, how was she supposed to hear him?

Maybe it was for the best. There was no way it was a good idea to mess around with her. Aaron was one of his best friends and would probably kick his ass for even thinking about Vivienne.

Once he was in the limo with the door firmly shut behind him, Matt sagged into the seat. Yeah, maybe it was all for the best. He wasn't going to ruin a friendship over a one-night stand.

Even if there was the merest possibility of her being more.

Chapter 1

"MATTY! HOW DOES IT FEEL TO KNOW YOU KILLED THE SHOW?"

"Matty! Are you going to reimburse the investors?"

"Matty! Is it true you were drunk on opening night?"

"Matty! Does this mean the end of Shaughnessy too?"

Every. Day.

Every damn day, it was the same thing. Every time Matt stepped out of his condo, there was a crowd of vultures just waiting to taunt and torment him about the epic failure that was his Broadway debut.

Three nights. Two years in the making and the damn show had only run three nights before getting axed.

Dammit.

Now he was the laughingstock of…well, pretty much everything. The media was having a field day with him. His picture was all over blogs and newspapers and tabloid magazines with phrases like "disappointing" and "no talent" and, his personal favorite, "fake."

There was no way he believed any of it, but it was getting harder and harder to ignore. In a city of eight million plus people, it should be easy to walk around undetected. Clearly that was only the case when you weren't in the spotlight for being a failure.

Everybody's a critic, especially when you're down.

With his cap firmly in place, Matt made his way through the crowd of people, doing his best to get to the curb. Ducking into the car waiting for him, he sighed with relief when the door closed and the driver immediately took off without asking any questions. Mick had sent the car to get Matt across town and to Mick's office. He almost wished it was winter, so he could bundle up more in a disguise. The spring weather didn't offer as many options.

Closing his eyes, Matt rested his head against the seat cushion and tried to scrape off the negative feelings. It wasn't easy to do. It had been two weeks, and there hadn't been any other scandals to get the focus off him. He had thought he'd be over it by now—or that they would—but it wasn't happening. Cheryl, his publicist, had done her best to put out statements with positive spins; she'd done as much damage control as she possibly could, but Matt was unwilling to speak to the press directly. At least until some of the ugliness died down.

Maybe that was what Mick wanted to talk to him about—a way to get over this nightmare. Although, wouldn't Cheryl have called first? A one-on-one meeting with Mick was never good. Riley Shaughnessy, lead singer and cofounder of the band, didn't mind having them back when they were still functioning as a group, and maybe—now that Matt thought about it—it had been intentional. Riley obviously knew how to handle Mick and took it on so the rest of them didn't have to.

Unfortunately, this was a situation Riley couldn't handle for him. He had to do this on his own since it was a situation of his own doing.

Dammit.

With nothing left to do and refusing to get himself worked up even more, Matt leaned forward, pulled a bottle of water from the stocked bar, and decided to let his mind go blank for a little while.

At least, that was the plan until his cell phone rang.

Looking down at the screen, he smiled. Since the debacle of the show, he had decided to keep his phone turned off as much as humanly possible. Right now, he was glad it was on.

"Hey, man! What's going on?"

There was a brief chuckle on the other end. "I'm calling to check on you and see how you're doing."

Matt took a quick drink of the bottled water before answering. "I'm not gonna lie, Aaron, it pretty much sucks to be me at the moment."

"Yeah. I know." He sighed. "So why are you still in New York? Get out of there for a while. Without the show, there's no reason for you to stay."

Matt had been struggling with that idea himself. Leaving meant running, and he didn't want to appear to be a coward—which was exactly what he told Aaron.

"You're not being a coward, Matt," Aaron replied. "New York wasn't your home before the show; no one expects you to make it your home now. Seriously, it's time to move on. You can't tell me you're enjoying being harassed every time you open the door."

"Hell no," Matt said with a mirthless laugh. "The thing is…I don't even really have a home base anymore. I'm used to living out of hotels. I sold my place in Los Angeles because I was never there and I thought I'd be here for a while. Where would I go?"

"Anywhere. Pick a spot on the map if you've got to."

How could he possibly explain that as much as he hated the harassment he was currently getting, it was easier than dealing with the unknown? Right now, Matt knew what to expect when he went out in public. But if he moved someplace else, he had no idea what the reaction would be. What if the media was worse at an unknown location? What if he was followed? What if—

"You could come here," Aaron suggested, interrupting Matt's thoughts.

"What?"

"You could totally come back to North Carolina. My property is pretty secluded. No one would have to know you were here."

Matt's immediate reaction was to say yes, but he reconsidered almost as fast. "I couldn't do that to you, man. You have no idea what it's been like. I'd hate to have the paparazzi climbing all over your house and property. It's not fair to you."

"I wouldn't have offered if I wasn't sure. I have a ten-foot privacy fence around the property and a gate at the driveway. There are security cameras all over, and I'd make sure the place was stocked so you wouldn't have to go out for a while."

"Dude…paranoid much? What's with all the privacy?"

Aaron chuckled. "I'm making a healthy living now, and this house is an investment for me. I put every bell and whistle into it that I ever dreamed of, and I want to protect it. And besides that, I really do enjoy the privacy. It's kind of fun making the locals wonder what's behind the fence. And it looks like it will work to your advantage too."

"You're talking as if you wouldn't be there."

"I'm getting ready to head over to London for a couple of weeks for business. I figured you might enjoy a change of scenery in a place no one really knows you."

Matt chuckled. "You forget we both grew up in the same town. The same town you're currently living in. People know me."

"You haven't been back here since the day after we graduated high school. No one's expecting to see you here." Aaron paused. "Come on, Matt. My offer stands. You find a way to get here undetected, and I'll make sure you have peace and privacy for a couple of weeks. What do you say?"

It was so tempting. He was about to say that when he realized the car had pulled up to Mick's building and was heading to the underground parking garage. "Listen, Aaron, can I call you back in a little while? I'm just pulling up to Mick's, and I need to know my options before I pull a disappearing act."

"Okay," Aaron agreed. "But promise me you'll think about it."

"I will," he replied and then paused. "And, Aaron?"

"Yeah?"

"Thanks."

Matt shut the phone down and slid from the car as soon as it came to a stop. He was immediately whisked up in a private elevator to Mick's office on the twenty-fourth floor. It was late in the day, and only Mick's assistant was in the office.

"He's waiting for you," she said softly with a smile— the kind of smile that said *I'm so sorry*.

He was beginning to hate that smile.

Closing the door behind him, Matt strode across the room toward Mick's desk and sat in the chair facing him.

"Did anyone give you trouble downstairs?" Mick asked.

Matt shook his head. "I don't think anyone followed us here, so—"

Before he could say anything more, Mick slid a newspaper across his desk toward Matt. "This isn't good."

Great. More bad news. Picking up the paper, he scanned the article, his ire growing with every word. "This is bullshit!"

Mick nodded.

"So...do something!" Matt yelled. "Get Cheryl on the line! Release tapes! Do whatever you have to do to prove these bastards wrong!"

"Already working on it," Mick said calmly. Almost too calmly.

"But...?"

"But," he began, "this just means you're going to be thrust into the spotlight even more around here. You need to leave town and lay low for a while."

His conversation with Aaron immediately sprang to mind. And while he hated the thought of having to pack up and leave like a thief in the night, obviously it was his only option.

"Look, Matty, I know this all sucks, but it is what it is. It's been hard enough trying to reel in this media circus when it was just about you. Now they're going after the band and trying to screw up your reputation as musicians. I can't allow it. It's not fair to the guys."

"What about me?" Matt snapped. "So because this stupid show flopped, it's okay to call me out as a fraud in every aspect of my life? How the hell is that fair?"

"Okay, let me rephrase that," Mick said patiently. "It's not fair to any of you. You know we dealt with similar bullshit when Riley was working on his solo album. The press had a field day with him for a while, claiming he had no talent without the band." He shrugged. "Now it's your turn."

"Yeah, but—"

Mick cut him off. "We're already working on releasing tapes to prove you *can* sing, that no one's singing or playing for you. The producers of the Broadway gig aren't being cooperative, but luckily we had people there recording you and taking video during a lot of your rehearsals, so we can show you were the one singing the whole time. We're going to say it was just…stage fright or an illness that made you sound…"

"Like shit?" Matt finished for him.

Mick grinned. "There's no point in calling it anything else, is there? The fact is, you sucked. You know it, I know it, and everyone who saw the damn thing during those three days knows it. So why sugarcoat it?"

He hated when the man threw logic at him.

"All I know is that I don't want anyone questioning the integrity of Shaughnessy." He held up a hand to stop Matt before he could say anything. "I hate that you're going through this, kid, I really do, but you guys worked your asses off for far too long to let something like this take you down. I need to do damage control, and to do it quickly and shut down the rumors, I need you out of the way. You're a distraction right now."

Again. Logic.

Matt waited a minute and let his knee-jerk hissy fit calm down before he spoke. "Have you talked to the guys? What are they saying?"

"Riley's going to do the late-night talk show circuit

starting next week. You know it's a topic that's going to come up, so he'll do what he can there. We're putting out press releases, and I have people who owe me favors. This whole thing should die down in the next couple of weeks."

Matt jumped to his feet. "You have favors and you've waited until now to call them in? What about when it all hit the fan for me? Why the hell weren't you doing anything about it then?"

Mick nearly leveled him with a glare. "You wanna know?"

Matt held his ground. "I wouldn't have asked if I didn't."

Slowly Mick came to his feet. "Because this Broadway thing was your own fault. I warned you not to do it. You're not an actor, Matty. You're a guitar player. You're great at backup vocals, but you're not a front man." He threw out his hands. "You did this for your ego and you weren't going to listen to anyone who didn't think it was a good idea. This was all on you."

It was on the tip of Matt's tongue to tell Mick to go to hell, but he refrained.

It was obvious Mick knew exactly what he was thinking. "You can cast me as the bad guy all you want, but it's not going to change anything. I want you to get out of town for a while. Let's say a month. I'll call you when the smoke's cleared. Okay?"

"Like I have a choice?"

"Sure, you have a choice. Stay in town and keep getting harassed. Become more of a joke than you already are." He shrugged. "And know you're the reason your bandmates are going to go down with you."

It was one thing to be defiant when he was only

hurting himself. There was no way he was going to take Riley, Dylan, and Julian down with him. No matter how much he wanted to stick it to Mick.

Raking a hand through his hair, Matt nodded. "Fine." He turned and headed toward the door.

"Where are you gonna go?"

He stopped with his hand on the doorknob and faced his agent. "Probably better if you don't know. The fewer people who know, the better. Right?"

Mick gave him a sympathetic look. The first one he'd ever seen on the man. "It's not forever, Matt. You know that."

"Yeah" was all he could say. Pulling open the door, he stepped out and shut it quietly behind him.

Now he just had to figure out how he was going to get out of the city and to Aaron's without anyone knowing.

Vivienne Forrester was on top of the world. Spinning in her office chair, she giggled with pure glee at the current turn of events in her life. For years, she had been blogging and freelance writing for any online site that would let her, and now all of her hard work had finally paid off.

As of ten minutes ago, she was officially an assistant editor for *Modern Lifestyle*, an online lifestyle magazine. All of the food and restaurant trends, reviews, and blog posts were now her domain, and she couldn't be happier. No more doing it all on her own and hoping for a site to pick up her work; now Vivienne was in charge of picking the topics and which posts were going to be used.

"Yay me!" she squealed and gave herself a final

spin. When she stopped, the room was still seemingly in motion, so she gave herself a moment to let it all come to a stop before she stood. "Aaron," she said and immediately turned to pick up her phone. "I need to call Aaron."

When her parents retired and decided to move back to her mother's birthplace, Paris, Vivienne had been thrilled for them. What she didn't realize was how they were pretty much retiring from being active in their children's lives too. It had bothered her a lot at first, but Aaron had pointed out that it was only fair for them to live the life they wanted and that he would always be there for her.

And he was.

Honestly, she couldn't have asked for a better brother.

Scanning her phone, she pulled up his number, hit Send, and then waited, bouncing on her feet the entire time.

"Hey, you've reached Aaron. Leave me a message and I'll get back to you…"

It was the third time this week she'd gotten that message and she was starting to get concerned. She knew he was leaving for London next week, but he hadn't mentioned he'd be unreachable until then. "Hey, it's me again," she said cheerily. "You're starting to freak me out. Please call me back. I have exciting news for you!"

She hung up the phone and looked around her office—her home office. It was another perk to the new position. As a freelance writer and blogger, she was able to write from home; with her new position, she'd get to keep doing so. Although right now it didn't feel very perkish. There was no one there to celebrate with her, no one to laugh and smile and jump up and down with.

Although, if she were honest, there wasn't very much room for jumping up, down, or anywhere right now. There were boxes lining all of the walls of her home, and in another week, she'd be loading them onto a truck and moving across town to her new place. This was all part of the new beginning she'd been hoping for, and it just sucked that she had no one readily available to share in her excitement.

While trying to decide what to do about her brother, she checked the day's news online. Local stuff wasn't really of interest, but checking out sites like *USA Today* and MSN helped her see what was trending and what she could use for *Modern Lifestyle*.

Where in the World Is Matty Reed?

The headline rang out above a picture of Matt shielding his face as he walked into what Vivienne assumed was his apartment building. Scanning the article, she saw that no one had seen him coming or going in three days. Some reports were claiming he was simply hiding out in shame, while another source was stating that he was brutally depressed because of all the negative publicity.

Vivienne shook her head. "Seriously? This is all over a failed musical?"

She couldn't easily comprehend it. Being in the public eye the way Matt was had never been something she'd aspired to. No, thank you. Working behind the scenes was more her style. That's why the magazine was the perfect job for her—even if it meant she worked alone a lot and sometimes didn't see people for days.

"Okay, no pity-partying for me," she murmured. "I'll just make a couple of calls and organize a girls' night out to celebrate."

Vivienne was scanning her favorite contacts when the phone rang. A big smile crossed her face as she answered. "Hey! You're alive!"

Aaron chuckled. "Was there any doubt about it?"

"Well, you haven't returned my calls, so I was beginning to wonder."

"Yeah, sorry about that. I had some…stuff to take care of before I leave next week. So what's the good news?"

Stuff? It was so unlike Aaron to be vague. She'd address it later; right now, she wanted to share her news. "I got the assistant editor job!" she said excitedly.

"Viv, that's awesome! I knew you would get it! They would have been crazy to give it to anyone else. I'm so proud of you!"

"So how about dinner? I was thinking we could go to that seafood place you like so much—you know the one where they have the lobster tails as big as your head?"

"Oh…um…tonight's not good for me. Can I get a rain check?"

"What's going on, Aaron?" she quickly demanded.

"What… I don't know what you mean."

"Don't be like that," she snapped. "First you disappear for a few days without telling me why or where you went, and now you're passing on dinner. You never do that. Ever. So tell me what's going on or I'm coming over there and—"

"No!" he shouted and then instantly softened his tone. "I mean—"

"Okay, clearly something is going on, so you can

either tell me, or I'll be there in no time to find out for myself."

"Hold on," he said, and for a minute, she could hear the muffled sound of him talking to someone. Aaron came back on the line with a sigh. "Pick up enough Chinese food for three and come over."

"But…why can't we go out and celebrate? Who's the third person?"

"Viv, will you just trust me on this one? Pick up the food and we'll talk when you get here."

"You're freaking me out, Aaron. Why are you so secretive?"

"Look, it will all make sense when you get here. I'll call in the order, and I'll see you soon."

"But…" She never got to finish. Aaron had hung up. For a solid minute, Vivienne looked at her phone, unable to comprehend what had just happened. She and Aaron had no secrets from one another, and the fact that there was something going on with him was beyond infuriating.

"Fine," she said, tossing her phone in her purse. "Enjoy the last thirty minutes of your secret because once I get there, I'm going to give you hell for it."

Taking a few minutes to freshen up, she did her best not to let this get her down. There was a new job to celebrate, and no matter what was going on with her brother, Vivienne was going to keep her cheerful mood.

No matter how much she wanted to strangle Aaron.

Within minutes she was locking up and heading out to her car. Looking at her town house, she sighed. It wasn't going to be a hardship to leave this place behind. Aaron's property included a fabulous guesthouse that Vivienne had been renovating in a French country decor to make it her own. She was moving in next week while Aaron was away. If she were a more suspicious person, she'd say he'd planned it that way. But it didn't matter. The house was amazing, and it was finished exactly as she wanted it.

It took less than ten minutes to reach Panda Gardens, and because she and Aaron were regulars and it was a Tuesday night, their order was waiting when she walked in. The drive to Aaron's took only another fifteen minutes, and when she pulled into the driveway, Vivienne looked around to see if anything was out of place. Aaron had mentioned dinner for three, but there were no other cars in front of the house.

"No time like the present to find out," she murmured as she grabbed the bag and climbed from the car. The weather was perfect, she observed as she walked to the front door. Coastal Carolina in the spring was—as far as Vivienne was concerned—the best. Maybe she could convince Aaron to eat outside.

At the door, she didn't bother knocking—she never did—but when she went to open it, she found it locked. "Okay, this better be huge." With her hands full of Chinese takeout, Vivienne had no choice but to ring the doorbell with her elbow. It didn't take long for Aaron to answer, an apologetic look on his face.

"I know, I know," he said immediately. "I forgot to leave it unlocked."

Without a word, Vivienne stepped around him and walked into the house.

"Viv! Wait!"

She glared at him over her shoulder but kept on walking.

Aaron caught up and stepped in front of Vivienne to stop her. "I don't want you to be upset with me. I want to celebrate your new job, and it's kind of hard to do that if you're all mad at me." He gave her a smile that usually guaranteed she'd forgive him anything. "Please."

Rolling her eyes, Vivienne could only laugh. "Okay, fine. I'm not mad at you. But I am hungry, and there's a lot of food here. It feels like we're feeding a small army. So what's going on? Who's here?" As she walked into the kitchen, she looked around for signs of who was visiting.

Vivienne put the food down and immediately went to work getting out plates and silverware while Aaron got drinks for them. "Can we eat out back on the porch?" she asked. "It's so beautiful out tonight."

"Sure," Aaron agreed.

Together they set the food up outside, and when there was nothing left to do, Vivienne looked at him expectantly. "Well?"

"Well, what?"

"Aaron," she groaned with exasperation. "Enough now. I picked up the food, I came over, and we're ready to eat. Can you please just tell me who's here?"

Behind her, someone cleared their throat.

A male someone.

Vivienne turned around and froze.

Matt Reed was standing in the open doorway.

How? Why? A million questions began to race through her mind, but there was no way she could get her voice to work.

There he stood, in all his sexy-rock-star glory, and she had to force herself not to react like a groupie, flinging herself at him or asking him to sign her bra.

He looked just as good as he always did—six-feet-plus of lean muscle, his sandy-brown hair in sexy disarray, and mossy-green eyes she could stare into all day long. Another quick glance at him and she noticed the dark circles under those eyes and how exhausted he looked. And yet Matt somehow still managed to look better than any man she had ever seen.

Dammit.

How was it possible that ripped, faded denim and a T-shirt looked better on him than a suit on a *GQ* model?

"Viv?" Aaron asked, concern lacing his tone. "Are you okay? You look a little…"

Sick? Horrified? Vivienne could only imagine. It had been two years since she had seen and kissed Matt, and she had secretly hoped she'd never have to see him again. After security had escorted her from the arena that fateful night, she had stood in the parking lot and asked herself just what in the world she had done. Going to see Matt on a whim was one thing. Kissing him as if her life depended on it was quite another.

And now he was here.

Standing five feet away and looking at her like… *What the hell is that expression on his face?* she wondered. It wasn't a smile; it wasn't a scowl. It was more like he was trying to figure out who she was.

Son of a bitch! Was it possible he didn't even remember her? Kissing her? Seriously?

Forget about feeling sick or horrified. Now she was just mad! "Hey, Matt," she said coolly. "Nice to see you." *Not.*

Matt nodded and walked down the two steps onto the porch. "You too, Viv. How've you been?"

She hated mindless chitchat. "Good. I'm good," she said and then turned back to her brother. "Shall we eat?" Without waiting for either man, she walked around the table and took her seat. When she was ready to start serving, she looked up at both of them, surprised that neither had sat down. "Well?"

Aaron stammered an apology and took a seat to her left while Matt took the chair to her right. They each took turns helping themselves to the variety of dishes, and it wasn't until they had taken a few bites that Aaron asked, "Aren't you curious why Matt's here?"

Vivienne looked at him as if he were crazy. "To visit?"

Rolling his eyes, Aaron grunted. "Seriously? Have you been living under a rock? When was the last time Matt came back home for a visit?"

Twelve years, three months, and six days.

But who's counting?

She shrugged and glanced at Matt before answering. "No idea."

Her brother and Matt exchanged looks before Matt spoke. "So I'm sure you heard about my Broadway disaster," he began.

"Yes. Contrary to my brother's earlier question, I haven't been living under a rock," Vivienne replied.

Matt nodded. "Yeah, well…things were getting a little out of hand, and I needed to leave the city and find someplace to go for a while to…you know…lie low."

She couldn't help the snort that came out, and she immediately put her hand over her mouth. "Sorry," she mumbled and then straightened. "But come on…seriously? Lie low? Isn't that just a bit dramatic?"

"The press has been relentless," Matt continued. "I

couldn't leave my apartment without being harassed. Then the rumors started flying about how the band was a bunch of frauds too. So while my PR team is doing damage control, everyone thought it would be best for me to be out of sight."

"For how long?" Vivienne asked.

"About a month."

She looked over at Aaron. "But...you're leaving for London in a few days."

He nodded. "I know. Matt's going to stay here. It's private, and no one would think to look for him here in North Carolina. It's been well documented that he never comes back to his hometown."

"This is crazy," she said. "Why would you wait to bring him here when you're going to be gone? What is he supposed to do with himself if you're not here?"

Matt cleared his throat, and both Forresters turned to look at him. "I believe I can answer that for myself," he said with a grin. "Aaron's made sure the house is stocked, so I shouldn't need to go into town or leave the property for anything. While I'm here, I'm going to work on writing some new music and just...relax."

"Don't you have houses all over the world?" she asked. "Wouldn't it have been more convenient to go to one of them?"

"Viv..." Aaron warned.

"It's okay," Matt said, his eyes never leaving Vivienne's. "In fact, I don't have houses all over the world. Whenever we toured, I stayed in hotels. And, as your brother pointed out, this is more private than any-place else. No one knows I'm here."

"How can you be so sure? You mentioned how

relentless the press was being. How can you be sure no one saw you fly in here?"

"He didn't fly," Aaron responded. "I flew up to New York, rented a car, and we left in the middle of the night. No one saw us leave."

"Right," she said sarcastically. "Because no one's awake in the middle of the night in the city that never sleeps. Even you can't be that gullible."

"I left my place during the day and went to my agent's office. He sent a decoy back to my apartment, and I stayed at the office until Aaron showed up. We went out the delivery exit and drove through the night."

She looked between the two of them with disbelief. "All of this over a failed Broadway show?"

"I know it seems extreme—"

"Ya think?" she cried and then turned to her brother. "So while you're over in London, I'm supposed to move in here and deal with paparazzi climbing the trees to get a glimpse of Matty Reed? No, thank you!"

"It's not going to be like that if—"

"If what?" she demanded. "If I move all of my furniture by myself? You know I've got movers coming onto the property, Aaron! If this is supposed to be so hush-hush, what am I supposed to do while I'm moving in?"

"Wait," Matt said. "You're moving in here?"

Vivienne glared at him. "Into the guesthouse. I just finished the renovations and I'm moving in next week."

"I still don't see a problem, Viv," Aaron said. "No one's going to go near the house—this house—only yours. Matt will make sure he stays out of sight, and as soon as the movers are gone, you set the security system up again. No big deal."

She supposed he had a point and forced herself to relax. After all, the movers wouldn't have any reason to be in Aaron's house, and once she was moved in, it would... Her stomach gave a funny little kick. After she moved in, it would just be her and Matt on the property.

"Maybe I'll wait to move in until you get back. I'd feel better about the whole thing if you were here too," she told Aaron, her gaze never leaving her plate.

It was crazy, she realized while eating, to think that someone like Matt Reed would even remember her or their impulsive kiss. Hell, they'd barely had any interactions with one another when they were younger because of their age difference. And now he was part of one of the biggest rock bands in the world. He probably had women kissing him all the time—she was just one of the masses.

Unfortunately, that just depressed her even more.

And on top of that, Vivienne hated that just sitting next to him was enough to make her want to move closer and kiss him again. *Yikes*. Not a good sign. Who knew what she'd do if left to her own devices? There was no way she was going to take that risk. It would be better if she didn't let herself be alone with Matt. So she'd wait until Aaron was back and then, even if Matt was still staying there, she'd have the safety net of her brother being around to stop her from doing something crazy.

The night she had gone to see Matt had been the biggest risk she had ever taken. Vivienne had used every contact and connection she had to get a ticket to the show and then to get backstage with a press pass. Spotting Riley had been pure luck. Having grown up in the same town as the Shaughnessys and knowing Riley and Aaron had been friends in school, she used it to her advantage when she'd spotted him. She had been beyond relieved when he'd remembered her and even helped her get past security and see Matt.

That had been as far as she had let herself plan—getting backstage and saying hi to Matt. No way had she imagined that within minutes of being in the same room as him that he'd kiss her.

Liar, liar, liar!

Okay, maybe in her wildest fantasy, it had happened that way. But how often did fantasies come to life?

What would have happened if they hadn't gotten interrupted? Lord, she could only imagine. Reverting back to her fantasy version, they would have continued to kiss and then Matt would have whisked her back to his luxurious hotel room and made love to her all night long.

Which would have made this meeting even more awkward than it already was—especially if he still didn't remember her.

Vivienne held no illusions—she would have had one night with the legendary Matty Reed, and then he would have left to move on to the next stop on the tour, and she wouldn't have seen him again.

Until now.

The buzz of excitement from her promotion earlier was gone. With a sigh, she pushed her food around on her plate. She chanced a look at her brother and saw he was watching her intently. "What?" she asked.

"We're supposed to be celebrating, and I feel like I kind of ruined your night."

Bingo! Rather than make him feel bad—after all, he

had no idea why exactly she was suddenly so quiet—she decided to try to turn it all around. "You didn't, Aaron. Really. I just never expected this turn of events. I know how important it is for Matt to have his privacy and I don't want to be the one to jeopardize it. I can wait a couple of weeks to move. I'm sure my landlord won't mind."

Aaron reached out and covered one of her hands with his. "Viv, it's not necessary. I don't leave until Monday—that gives us five days to get things done. I'll make all the arrangements, and we'll move you in this weekend. This way it will all be done with me here, so you won't have anything to worry about."

Her eyes went wide. "What? I mean… Um… No! I don't want you to do that. I'm…I'm not ready. I still have more packing to do and I know you have a lot to do before your trip. I don't want you wasting your time on me. I can wait. Really."

He chuckled. "I know how anxious you are to move in, Viv. You hated having to wait as long as you have. All the work is done, so why continue to wait? Why inconvenience your landlord and pay to stay for a few more weeks when you don't have to?"

Why indeed? She swallowed hard and tried to come up with a reasonable excuse, but none came to her.

Dammit.

"And I know you—you have been packing for months. It wouldn't be hard for you to power through and pack up the rest of your stuff. And, if you wanted to, we could start moving stuff over now. I have the pickup in the garage, and we could start bringing boxes over tonight if you want." He smiled at her. "Come on. You know you want to."

She did. She really did. This house had been a labor of love, and the thought of moving in had been consuming her for weeks. If it weren't for the fact that she wanted it to be perfect, she would have moved in during the renovations. The thought of all the dust and how much she would have to clean up her belongings afterward had convinced her to wait.

Now the only thing standing between her and her beautiful new home was her own silly insecurity and Matt Reed.

"I don't know, Aaron. You know I hate rushing."

He rolled his eyes and laughed. "You are extremely organized; you can't tell me you don't have a to-do list sitting on your kitchen counter with everything you have to pack noted and the order in which you want it packed listed. All you have to do is start packing those things up a little sooner. It's not going to be difficult." He cut her off when she started to argue. "Plus, by doing it this way, we can move a couple of boxes a night, and Matt and I will even help you unpack as you go, so when the big stuff gets here, you won't have to deal with the little stuff. Right, Matt?" He looked over at his friend for approval.

"Absolutely," Matt said, smiling at Vivienne. "It will give me something to do."

She almost snorted at the absurdity of it all. Matt Reed was going to help her move into her house and be useful? Somehow she doubted it. He probably hired people to unpack his suitcase.

"I can see you're doubting me," Matt said, as if reading her thoughts. "I'll admit it's been a while since I had to move or do anything like this, but I'm not a complete moron." He winked. "You tell me what to do and I'll do it."

Now there was a statement to make her overactive imagination go wild. Only it had nothing to do with moving boxes and unpacking, and everything to do with them kissing and being alone and continuing the fantasy of years ago.

"Come on, Viv," Aaron said, instantly bringing her back to the present. "We'll finish up our dinner, and you and I will go over and pick up the first load of boxes. What do you say?"

There wasn't a good reason not to. She was going to have to suck it up and be a big girl and do the only thing she could—let Matt and Aaron help her move into the guesthouse and then, once her brother was gone, do everything she could to avoid the one and only Matt Reed.

Chapter 2

MATT PACED BACK AND FORTH IN AARON'S LIVING ROOM, his mind spinning.

Vivienne Forrester was stunning.

And somewhat familiar.

The first thing that went through his mind when he'd seen her earlier was that he'd seen her somewhere before. Then he kicked himself because of course he'd seen her before—he and Aaron had been friends since elementary school, so they'd practically grown up together. But the longer they'd sat together over dinner, the more Matt couldn't shake the feeling he'd seen her someplace recently.

Or somewhat recently.

It was possible they might have crossed paths at some point while he was touring, but for the life of him, he couldn't pinpoint where. And no matter how many hints he'd dropped, Vivienne hadn't seemed too anxious to fill in the blanks or mention the last time they'd seen one another. It was beyond maddening.

He continued to pace and began to wonder about this plan for him to stay at Aaron's for the month. He'd been here for only a day and already he was getting antsy. The place wasn't familiar, and Matt knew it wouldn't be long before the walls started to close in on him. A month was a long time to have to stay in one place and not go out and socialize.

And then there was Vivienne.

She was going to be a distraction for sure. And it didn't take a genius to realize that she not only wasn't impressed with him and who he'd become, but she didn't seem to like him very much either. It was going to make things difficult when she was the only person around for him to talk to. He was either going to have to confront her about why she didn't like him, or he was going to have to turn on the charm and hope she'd eventually warm up to him.

Dangerous territory, dude, he admonished himself. There was no way he could possibly charm her without it turning to flirtation and him wanting something more. And it wasn't just because he was a natural flirt or because it was his go-to response around a beautiful woman.

It was because it was Vivienne.

Those dark, exotic eyes drew him in like nothing he'd ever experienced before. If she were anyone else and it were any other circumstances, he would have certainly made a move on her already. But it wasn't the time, it certainly wasn't the place, and he'd never disrespect Aaron—especially after he had taken Matt in and given him a place to stay when he quite literally had no place else to go. How shitty would he have to be to go and hit on the man's sister right under his own roof?

So where did that leave Matt? With nowhere to go and nothing to do and no other distractions, how was he supposed to see Vivienne and hang out with her without wanting her?

"I guess there's my project during my downtime," he murmured.

He roamed to the kitchen and then the dining room. The house was impressive. Aaron had custom designed the place and had Riley Shaughnessy's brother Aidan build it. If Matt were to ever take the leap into home ownership again, a place like this was definitely to his liking.

It was a sprawling ranch on five acres and everything inside was high-tech—from the remote-controlled window shades to the heated floors, everything was top-of-the-line and designed for convenience as far as Matt could tell. Aaron had always been a numbers man. He had graduated from Duke University in the top ten percent of his class in economics and finance, meaning it was a piece of cake for him to become a top investment banker. Matt had always been in awe of his friend's financial skills and even sought out his help in managing his own investments and finances, so it was little wonder the house was damn near a masterpiece with every cutting-edge upgrade you could imagine. The room Aaron had set him up in could rival any luxury resort—king-size bed, a private bath, and a seventy-two-inch flat-screen TV. Staying there wasn't going to be a hardship.

All of the amazing designs flowed as you stepped outside too—from the outdoor kitchen and sitting area with a fireplace to the pool, and then across the yard was Vivienne's cottage. According to Aaron, the cottage had been his idea, but it had originally been intended for guests. When Vivienne had moved back to North Carolina two years ago, after living in Denver for several years, he'd given her the option of taking over the guesthouse. She had readily agreed but decided it needed a complete overhaul before she would move in.

Apparently overhauls take two years, he thought with a chuckle. If it had taken two years to renovate a guest cottage, he could only imagine how long a full-sized house would take her. He was intrigued, however, to see the results. For something to take that long, he had to imagine the interior was going to be just as fantastic and high-end as the main house.

Matt hadn't asked what Vivienne did for a living, so maybe the cottage had been more of a hobby to her and that's why it had taken so long. He made a mental note to ask about it when she and Aaron returned.

He hated having to stay here and wait. No doubt he could have given them a hand at Vivienne's place and they could have moved twice as much, but it was too soon for him to be driving around town and risk someone recognizing him and leaking it to the press. He was already on edge as it was, waiting to see when they'd notice he wasn't in New York anymore. He'd seen today's headlines and knew there was already some speculation as to his whereabouts, but for now, the consensus seemed to be that he was still holed up in his condo. Hell, he hoped they held on to that thought for a little while longer so he could start to relax.

It was a toss-up how much he wanted to follow the news. No doubt Mick would keep him up-to-date on what was going on, and Matt already had plans to put in calls to Riley, Dylan, and Julian. He'd been putting it off, but now that he was settling in for the month, he figured it would be the perfect time to call his bandmates and make sure they all didn't hate him.

Tomorrow.

～～～

"Okay, that last box in the corner should do it for tonight," Vivienne said, scanning the room for any other items she could live without temporarily. "Once it's loaded, we will have officially made a big dent in my packing and moving list."

Aaron picked up the box and walked out to the truck. When he came back in a minute later, he took the bottle of water Vivienne was holding out for him and thanked her. After a long drink, he put the bottle down on the counter and studied his sister.

"What?" she asked with a chuckle. "You're looking at me funny."

He smiled and shook his head. "What's going on with you? You were borderline rude to Matt earlier."

Crap. Clearing her throat, she reached for her water and took a sip before replying. "What do you mean?"

"I mean I know it was a shock to see him there, but you pretty much sounded like you wouldn't move into the cottage because of him."

She rolled her eyes. "Geez, dramatic much?"

"Come on, Viv. Don't deny it."

She sighed. "Okay, fine. Yes, it was a bit of a surprise to see him there, and after seeing all the media stuff about what he's going through, I kind of felt overwhelmed. If they were harassing him like that in New York, who's to say it won't happen here?"

"But no one knows he's here," Aaron countered.

"Yeah, for now. I'm used to being able to come and go as I please. Now I have to worry about making sure everything is locked down so no one can see Matt's here. It's intimidating, and I would have appreciated a heads-up."

He looked a bit bashful. "I wanted to tell you—I did. But after Matt and I talked, we just knew the fewer people in the know, the better. Even his agent doesn't know he's here."

"How is that even possible?"

"Simple. He told Matt he needed to get out of town and lay low, so he did."

"I'm just not comfortable with all of this, Aaron. I enjoy my privacy as much as the next person, but with you out of the country for a couple of weeks, it leaves all the responsibility for Matt's privacy on me. I'd hate to be the reason someone got into your house simply because I was careless with the security system."

"You're not going to have to do anything, Viv. He's a grown man who can take care of himself. I'm stocking the house with enough food to get him through the month."

"It seems a bit excessive. Surely he doesn't think he can stay inside the entire time," she argued.

Aaron shrugged. "Maybe. Maybe not. But I want him to have that option. I'm sure he's used to donning disguises when he's on tour so he can go out."

"You do realize this is Matt we're talking about? He was pretty much a media whore before this whole thing hit. The band was always in the tabloids because of their partying. I don't think he would understand the concept of putting on a disguise."

"Well, that's neither here nor there. If he wants to go out, then he's going to have to take some precautions or risk someone tipping off the press." He sighed. "Look, he just needs a break—a chance to be out of the public eye for a little while and have people around him who aren't going to screw him. I'm not saying you have to like him or be his biggest fan, but could you please just be nice to him at least?"

If only he realized just what he was asking of her.

"I'm not making any promises…"

Coming around the kitchen island, Aaron hugged her. "You're the best!" When he stepped away, he took another look around the room. "Are you sure there isn't anything else you want to take tonight?"

Vivienne shook her head. "I think we're off to a good start. We'll get these boxes over to the cottage and unpack them, and then I can bring the boxes back with me to reuse. It will be a great way to keep track of how much we can realistically get done in a night."

"So you want to do this every night?" he asked.

She glanced at him suspiciously. "You said that's what we'd do!"

He grinned. "Just checking."

She swatted his arm playfully. "I just hope you can get the movers to come this weekend. I'm not sure how you're going to pull that one off."

"Don't worry about it. I'll make it happen. And as overwhelmed as you're feeling, you are going to be so happy when you get to sleep in your new home."

Vivienne couldn't help but smile because he was totally right.

"And you'll be even happier because we moved all these boxes beforehand and you'll be almost completely unpacked. It will be like moving perfection." Then he stepped back and took a dramatic bow. "You're welcome."

"You're a doofus." She laughed, and together they made their way out of the town house. Vivienne locked the door and then followed Aaron out to the truck. "You know this isn't going to be a quick and easy process, right?"

"What do you mean?"

"Well, coming here and loading the boxes was easy because they were all piled up and ready to go. Unloading them will take longer—especially since I didn't have time to prep the cottage and may not have everything I need to unpack the way I want to."

"So why don't we just put the boxes inside while you make a list of what you'll need, and then tomorrow we'll tackle the unpacking?"

He did have a point, she thought. "What time can you meet me tomorrow to pick up the next load?"

"I have to go into the office for a while, but I can probably be to you by four. I'll swing by and pick up the next load, and we'll order pizza for dinner and eat at the cottage while we unpack. How does that sound?"

She couldn't help but grin. Things were falling into place and they had a plan. "Perfect."

***

"This is the last box."

Vivienne looked around the room and then pointed to the far corner. "You can put it over there." She stopped and paused when she noticed Matt standing and looking at her, but not moving. "Please."

He grinned. "There. That wasn't so hard, was it?" Walking across the room, he placed the box where she requested and then stretched. Apparently he was a little more out of shape than he'd realized. Moving a dozen boxes should have been a breeze, but he was beginning to feel a couple twinges of pain.

And he was going to keep that information to himself.

Aaron strode back into the house and looked around. "Okay, kiddo. That's everything for tonight. Are you going to unpack any of them, or are we waiting for tomorrow night?"

"I think I'll wait until tomorrow night so I can have some time to think about what I'm going to need to get started. How about—" Her words were cut off by the sound of Aaron's phone ringing.

"Damn," he muttered and then looked up at Matt and Vivienne. "Sorry. I need to take this. I'll see you tomorrow, Viv, and I'll see you back at the house," he said to Matt. He walked out as he answered the phone.

Matt took a moment and considered his options—he could stay and try to break the ice between him and Vivienne, or he could follow Aaron back to the house and do...nothing. He sighed. He seriously had nothing to do. Dammit.

"So tell me again why you're not unpacking anything tonight?" he asked casually, moving across the room toward her.

Vivienne was standing next to the marble-topped island in the center of the kitchen. Matt didn't know a whole lot about cooking, but even he could tell that this kitchen was a chef's dream. Done in a French country decor, the cabinets were a muted green with ornate crown molding along the top. White subway tile lined the backsplash, and the white marble countertops flowed along to one of the largest kitchen sinks he'd ever seen.

He'd heard Aaron and Vivienne talking about the stainless steel appliances and how the eight-burner stove was a thing of beauty. Matt wasn't sure about that, but every time he caught Vivienne looking at it, she would smile and sigh happily. He shrugged. It was a stove. Why did people get emotional over inanimate objects?

His gaze lingered on Vivienne. Now there was a thing of beauty, and he knew he had to be careful not to stop, smile, and sigh whenever he looked at her—dark eyes; long, dark, curly hair; and a curvy body he would love to explore. She wasn't tall—well, at least not compared to his own six-foot frame, but her head came up to his shoulder. Which was the perfect height difference in his mind.

No! he silently reminded himself. There was no thinking of Vivienne in terms of *perfect*. She was Aaron's sister. Aaron—the only person in the world who seemingly cared about him and was willing to open his home up so Matt could have a haven until this whole stupid media circus was over.

Forcing himself to focus, he realized Vivienne had been talking the entire time he'd been lost in his own thoughts. Now he had no idea why she was doing things the way she was. Great. He'd either have to pretend he was paying attention and hope for the best, or admit he hadn't been listening and look like a jerk.

"Matt?"

Yeah, she knew he wasn't listening based on the annoyed look on her face. He supposed it was better if she stayed annoyed at him and kept her distance—less likely for him to do something stupid, like make a move on her and piss everyone off.

"Why French country?" he quickly asked.

"Excuse me?" Her brows furrowed as she asked the question.

"The place," he began, motioning to the kitchen and the living area. "What made you go with French country?"

Vivienne eyed him suspiciously. "Because I like it,"

she said simply. "I think the color palette is lovely, and the textures give the place character." She shrugged. "The cottage was a blank space, so I was able to pick out every little thing from countertops to light fixtures and paint colors."

He nodded and leaned against the island. "So you must enjoy cooking."

She seemed to relax a little, her posture a little less stiff. "I do."

"What's your favorite dish to make?"

With a nervous chuckle, Vivienne shook her head. "You don't want to know any of this. It's late, and I'm sure you've got better things to do than stand here listening to me yammer on about cooking."

Her laughter made him join in. "Believe it or not, I have nothing else to do." Then he stopped and laughed a little harder. "I know that didn't sound quite the way I meant it. I mean I would like to know about what you like to cook. Honestly, I'd like to hear all about what you've been up to for the last…"

Secretly he was hoping for her to fill in the blank, and then maybe he could figure out where he'd last seen her.

But she didn't take the bait.

"Twelve years?" she supplied with a grin. "That's a lot of time to fill in."

"As you can tell, I've got nothing but time on my hands. I'm going to be living in veritable isolation for the next month so…"

Vivienne's expression turned serious. "Can I ask you something?"

"Anything."

"What is the big deal?"

"I'm not sure I'm following."

"So you got a bad review," she said. "So what? It happens to people all the time. Why are you taking this to such an extreme?"

Matt sighed and looked around for someplace to sit. He might as well tell her all about it, so they wouldn't have to tiptoe around the subject for the next month. It was either boxes or the floor, so he opted for the floor and was surprised when Vivienne came and sat beside him. She was quiet, and Matt had to figure out how to explain the whole thing without sounding like some diva having a hissy fit.

Which is where he decided to begin.

"This isn't just about me getting pissy because of some bad reviews."

"Okay," she said, her voice sounding completely neutral.

He sighed and rested his head back against the wall. "I put everything I had into that show. Hell, it was my idea to begin with."

That seemed to take her by surprise. "Really?"

"Yeah." He nodded. "I was getting burned out touring, and I felt like the band was getting a little stagnant, and I wanted a change. Broadway seemed like a good way to go—I'd still get to perform onstage, in front of an audience, and honestly, I thought I could handle it."

"So what changed?"

He gave a mirthless laugh. "Apparently I'm only good when I'm playing with the band. I was able to get through rehearsals without it being such a big deal. Everyone knew I was nervous, and I kept saying I needed the energy of the crowd to put me at ease." He shrugged. "I guess I was wrong. It was worse once there were people in the seats. And I crashed and burned."

Rather than offer empty platitudes, Vivienne remained quiet.

"When they decided to shut down the show, I was relieved. I don't think I could've kept going. By the third night, I was completely freaking out."

"What about the previews? Don't shows normally run for a few weeks before doing the—what's it called?—opening night?"

"Everyone thought it best to limit the previews because I wasn't performing well enough. It seemed like a good idea at the time, but now I see we probably could have used the feedback."

"Would it have changed anything?" she asked carefully.

"Probably not. I was arrogant and didn't want to admit I was overwhelmed." He shook his head. "I've performed for audiences ten times the size of that theater, maybe more, and I have never felt so completely out of my element before."

"They're two completely different things."

Turning his head, Matt looked at her as if she were crazy.

"It's true," she said. "When you play with the band, you are a unit. Sure, Riley's the front man, but you're all playing together. It takes the four of you to make it work. It seems to me, with the show, the spotlight was solely on you. That's enough to freak anyone out."

Could it be that easily explained? "Yeah, but—"

"So you got stage fright and you weren't very good at acting. It's still not enough to make you go into hiding. Or at least...it shouldn't be."

He had a feeling she knew all of this, but he was finding it helpful to say it all out loud. "Yeah well…I thought it was all going to finally die down—all the negative media stuff. Then someone started spouting off about how if I sucked that bad, what did it mean for Shaughnessy—the band. If I sounded that bad live, was it me singing or playing on our albums? Then it started people speculating about whether any of us in the band were playing or if we were just some hacks with no talent." He sighed again. "That's when Mick, my agent, finally said enough. He's got our PR team working overtime to get people off the idea that the band is a bunch of phonies. I'm telling you, Viv, it's exhausting."

"I'm sure it is," she agreed. "So…what are you supposed to do while the PR people are doing their thing?"

He shrugged. "Rest. Wait." He chuckled. "I have no idea. I've never had to do this before. Even when we were on breaks from touring and recording and I was supposed to be on vacation, I never rested. It's just not who I am. I hate not having a purpose. It annoys the shit out of me that I can't do anything to make this right."

"Maybe it won't be so bad. Maybe something will come up and take the media attention off of you and the band."

"That's the thing—Riley's got a great tour going on right now for his solo stuff, and this nonsense is marring it. He's going on the talk show circuit, and rather than promoting his own stuff, he's going to have to clean up my mess."

"What are your options? Would you want to go out there and face the media yourself?"

Hell no. The press was brutal. There was no way he

would be able to stay calm and not cause more of a PR nightmare if it were up to him to face everyone. Rather than answer her, he simply shook his head.

"What does Riley have to say?"

"I haven't talked to him yet. I was planning on tackling that task tomorrow, calling him and Dylan and Julian. I should have done it a week ago but…"

"I'm sure they'll all understand. You'd be understanding if the roles were reversed, right?"

Would he? Matt would like to think so, but he knew he could be a hard-ass sometimes when things didn't go according to his plan. "Maybe. I don't know," he replied honestly. "We've never had to deal with a situation like this."

Vivienne nodded and then yawned loudly. "Well, I hope for your sake that they all stand behind you. I don't think Riley's the type of guy to hold a grudge, but I don't know the other guys, so…" She shrugged and then slowly came to her feet. Matt immediately did the same. "Thanks for helping me tonight."

"I really didn't do much of anything except carry in some boxes."

She chuckled. "Don't worry. There will be a lot more of them coming in and then the unpacking can begin. I'll have it all mapped out tomorrow so we can get started."

"You have to map out how to unpack?" he asked with a grin. "I mean, the boxes say what room they go in. How much more information do we need?"

She frowned at him. "Some things aren't as cut-and-dried. I have a system."

"Ah," he said and took a step back.

"*Ah?* What does that even mean?"

"It means you're a bit OCD. I get it."

"I am not OCD," she countered. "I just like things organized."

"No," he said as he took another step back. "You like everything organized and you like to be in control of it—OCD."

She rolled her eyes as she huffed. "Do you even *know* what OCD means?"

"Obsessive *controlling* disorder," he said with a grin. Then he winked at her as he turned and made his way to the door. "I'll see you—and your map and directions on how to unpack the silverware—tomorrow."

"It's not like that!" she called after him.

Matt was almost out the door when he turned and met her irritated gaze. "Prove it."

Crossing her arms over her chest, she snapped, "Prove what?"

"That you don't have OCD," he replied.

"I don't."

"Yeah, yeah, yeah," he teased. "Show up here tomorrow without a list or a map or instructions or whatever it is you were planning on, and let Aaron and me unpack."

Her dark eyes went huge. "Are you crazy? I'll have to tell you—"

"Uh-uh. The boxes are labeled, so we won't need you telling us where they need to go."

"And what am I supposed to be doing while you and my brother are randomly dumping my stuff all over the house?"

Matt stepped back inside and faced her while making a tsking sound. "Oh, ye of little faith. Aaron and I are perfectly capable of unpacking a couple of boxes. You can pick one room for yourself but the rest we'll do. Deal?"

She immediately went back to frowning. "This is ridiculous. I don't see why I can't—"

"Because you're OCD," he said, enjoying this playful banter. Although, to be fair, he was pretty sure he was the only one thinking of it in those terms. The look on Vivienne's face was proof she was most definitely *not* amused.

"Fine," she finally said.

"Fine?"

She nodded. "Fine. No instructions. You and Aaron can handle the bulk of the unpacking while I work on one room myself."

"And you won't try to micromanage us?" he asked.

"Not even a little bit."

He had a niggling feeling he was missing something—she agreed too easily all of a sudden. But for now, he'd take it.

"Okay then. I'll see you tomorrow night." With another wink and a wave, he was out the door.

It wasn't even noon and Matt was already on the verge of losing his mind.

He had left Vivienne's the previous night and come back and hung out with Aaron until almost midnight. He'd slept fine, and so far this morning, he had avoided his phone as if it were the plague.

Make the call.

It wasn't as if anyone was expecting his call—not really—but still he couldn't seem to make himself take the first step and just do it. Riley had to be first. Matt owed it to him. And yet no matter how much he rationalized with himself, it didn't make him spring into action.

Make the call.

Part of him wanted to call Mick first and find out the initial reactions of all the guys. Matt knew Mick had been planning on talking to all of them, and he had secretly hoped his agent would simply call and give him the heads-up before Matt called them. No such luck.

Make the damn call!

"What the hell," he muttered and stalked across the room and picked up his phone. It was late enough on the East Coast that even if Riley was back on the West Coast, it was still a decent time to call.

Two minutes later, with his heart pounding in his chest, Matt listened and waited for Riley to answer the phone.

"Ah, so you *do* remember how to use the phone," Riley joked rather than going for a typical greeting. "I was beginning to wonder if all the years of people helping you caused you to forget basic life skills."

Instantly Matt relaxed. "Ha-ha," he deadpanned. "Thank God for the ease of having numbers programmed into the phone and being able to swipe the screen. I don't know if I could have handled more than that." They both laughed, and Matt realized how much he'd been missing his friend. "How's the tour going?"

"Better than I ever expected," Riley replied. "I honestly thought it was going to be weird being on the road without…you know…you guys…but it's been great."

"I'm sure having Savannah with you helps too."

Riley chuckled. "I still can't believe how lucky I am. Hell, I still can't believe I'm married!"

"Neither can your fans," Matt teased. "I'm sure there are thousands of women who are still crying over that one."

"Yeah, well…I guess you'll have to take up the cause."

"If only."

"So how are you doing, man? Seriously," Riley said, his tone filled with concern. "I talked to Mick, and obviously I've seen the reports, but…"

Matt sighed. "I cannot even believe it all hit the fan like this."

"You know how the press can be. You remember how they tormented the hell out of me while I was struggling with the album? I thought I was going to lose my mind!"

"Look, Riley, you have to know how sorry I am that I brought all this negative attention on you and the guys. I hate that it's going down like this."

"It's not your fault, Matt. This is how it goes—people like to kick you when you're down, and when it's a slow news week, it's not unusual for them to start making up shit to keep people interested in a fizzling story."

"I just can't believe how it turned so damn fast!" Matt snapped, finally relieved to be able to talk about this with someone he knew fully understood how it felt. "Broadway shows close down all the damn time! Why did the media have to latch on to this one?"

"Like I said," Riley said reasonably, "slow news week."

"It's not right."

"No, it's not. I totally agree with you. Where are you? What are you doing with yourself?"

"I'd rather not say," Matt said miserably. "It's probably better if no one knows."

"Okay, now I'm worrying about you. Are you sure you're all right?"

Matt gave a mirthless laugh. "Yeah. I'm fine. Really. I just hate being the butt of the joke and being forced to hide out—not that I have anything else to do. I had no fallback plans. In my mind, the show was going to run for a while, and then you'd come crying to me about wanting to get the band back together." Another laugh. "Joke's on me there too, I guess."

Riley groaned. "It's not like that, Matt. I'm having a great time on this tour, don't get me wrong, but it's not the same as playing with you and Dylan and Julian. We're like brothers. I couldn't imagine never playing music with you guys again. It's just—"

"Yeah I know," Matt interrupted. "It's gonna be a while."

"Have you talked to Dylan and Jules?"

"No. I wanted to talk to you first. And believe me, it was harder than I thought possible to find the balls to pick up the phone and call you."

"Dude, we've been friends since we were twelve. You never have to be afraid to call me. Ever."

Matt grew silent for a minute. "I feel like I let you down, Ry. You're always the one taking care of everything, and the one time I branch out on my own, I screw up."

"We all screw up," Riley corrected. "I'm sure you haven't been paying too much attention to what else is going on in the world, but believe me when I say we're all guilty of it."

"What do you mean?"

"Other than my nightmare of a year? I mean…prior to the tour and Savannah? I was the subject of all kinds of ridiculous speculation and none of you guys came down on me for it. Dylan's partying a little too hard, and if he's not careful, he's going to hurt himself or someone else. He's one bottle of tequila away from a stint in rehab."

Matt nodded. "I thought he was starting to calm down."

"Apparently not. I don't know what caused this latest bender he's on, but he's not returning my calls."

"Has he talked to Mick?"

"Like he had a choice," Riley said with a chuckle. "There's no avoiding that man. If you don't answer the phone, he'll show up at your house or your hotel room and force you to talk to him."

"And?"

"And," Riley continued, "he swears he's just letting off steam. It's been a while since he's had this much free time on his hands—unsupervised free time—and he's just…being Dylan."

"At least Julian's got his shit together."

"Well…"

"Oh, come on!" Matt huffed. "I'm not that out of the loop! What's going on with him?"

"The usual. He's so wrapped up in being Dena's puppet, he's totally losing himself."

"I thought he was going to move on from that."

"So did I. She has no chance of ever making it in the business and yet she somehow keeps convincing him to work on projects with her. I'm telling you, Matt, it's like everyone can see it but him."

"She's going to kill his spirit if nothing else."

"Exactly."

"So what do we do?"

"Honestly?" Riley asked. "I don't think there's anything we can do. He's a grown man, and if he hasn't listened to any of us by now, he's not going to."

"So we're supposed to sit back and let him crash and burn?"

"Isn't it what we've all been doing in one form or another?"

Shit. Riley had a point. They were all stubborn bastards who had to learn their lessons the hard way and on their own. "I guess."

"Look, for what it's worth, all this crap with you is dying down. Mick is doing damage control and the tapes they're releasing seem to be the key to shutting down the rumors."

"I hope so, Ry. I really do. I'm going out of my mind."

"So use the time wisely."

"What the hell does that even mean?"

"Use the time to write some music. Think of the future. We'll all end up back in the studio together eventually. It would be great if we had some well-planned-out music ready to go."

"You know that's not my strong suit. That was all you and Julian."

"Bullshit," Riley quickly said. "You contributed just as much as any of us. Don't sell yourself short. Don't let these reviewers get in your head. You're a kick-ass musician and a talented songwriter. Go do what you do best!"

Matt laughed. "Ease up with the pom-poms. Sheesh. That was a little too 'go, team, go!' for me."

"Hey," Riley said with a laugh of his own, "it's what I do."

Matt waited a few seconds before he said, "Thanks, man. Seriously."

"I wish there was more I could do."

"You're doing plenty—more than I did when you were the one down."

"Yeah, well...it's partially my fault too. I didn't want to reach out to anyone. I'm glad you called me, Matt."

"Do you think I should call the guys?"

"I don't think it can hurt, but I don't think it's going to help much either. It may make you feel better just knowing you tried but...just don't put too much hope in them responding. They're both dealing with their own crises."

"I hear ya."

"Listen, Matt, I gotta go. Savannah and I have a plane to catch and the car's going to be here to pick us up in about twenty minutes and I'm nowhere near ready to go."

"How'd you convince her to fly again? I thought she hated it."

Riley chuckled. "It's a short flight and a private plane. Every once in a while she agrees to it, but once we land, it's back to ground transportation for a while."

"You're a good man," Matt said, and he truly meant it. "Be safe out there, Ry. And again, thanks."

"Anytime," Riley said, and Matt could hear the smile in his voice. "Don't hesitate to call me again if you need me. I'm always here to listen, even if you just need to vent."

"I will. Now go. I don't want you to get in trouble with the wife for not being ready on time."

"Such an ass," Riley teased before he said good-bye.

Matt stared at the phone in his hand for a solid minute, smiling the entire time. It was good to know he had friends supporting him.

For the first time in weeks, he felt mildly optimistic.

———

"You're joking, right?"

Vivienne suppressed a grin as she shook her head. "Nope."

"But…this is…"

"A closet," she finished for him.

Matt eyed her warily. "So these four boxes are all for this one closet?"

She nodded. "If you need me, I'll be unpacking in the kitchen." Turning to walk away, she stopped when she heard Matt laughing softly. "What's so funny?"

"You."

She turned and faced him fully. "Me? What did I do?"

"You just thought you'd toss some ridiculous task at me like a closet and get yourself off on a technicality."

Rolling her eyes, she crossed her arms and did her best to seem bored and unaffected. "There is no technicality. You asked me to trust you with a task and I did. You're unpacking the linen closet while Aaron unpacks my office. I chose the kitchen. That is what you asked me to do, right?"

"You're something else," he said, laughing a bit harder now. "You chose the biggest task, with the most boxes because you didn't trust me or Aaron with it."

Damn. Vivienne hadn't realized how transparent she was. All day she had been feeling so smug about her plan, and it had taken all of three minutes for Matt to see through it. "Are you saying you can't handle unpacking a closet?" she asked, hoping to distract him.

"I think I can handle a closet," he said, mildly defensive. "Linens. Towels. Whatever. It's not exactly brain surgery."

"Good," she replied. "Then if you'll excuse me, I have my own boxes to attend to."

"If I get done before you do, I'm coming in there to help," he taunted as she walked away.

Doing her best not to react, she simply called out a word of thanks as she made her way down the stairs and to the kitchen.

Looking at all of the boxes stacked against the wall had Vivienne smiling. Rubbing her hands together, she was anxious to get started. This was her thing—organizing and unpacking and making sure everything had its place. Its *perfect* place.

She cast a wary glance over her shoulder, wondering what kind of havoc Matt was wreaking on her poor linen closet. Forcing herself to focus on her own task, she reminded herself that whatever he did, she could fix after he was gone and no one would be the wiser.

"Okay, let's do this," she murmured as she opened the first box. Cabinet liners and racks and organizers. This was the key to making everything work. Every drawer, every cabinet had to be lined for protection. That in and of itself was a big task, but the end result would be well worth it.

Music began to play from somewhere in the cottage, and she wasn't sure if it was from Matt or Aaron but either way, she was thankful for it. It was the perfect background for her task. Carefully, she measured and cut and placed the liner everywhere it was needed. Once that was done, she moved on to putting her new flatware bins in their drawers and then all of the new racks for lids and baking sheets in their rightful places.

A look at the clock showed it had been an hour already. She looked around and realized she hadn't heard a peep out of her brother or Matt. Aaron she could understand. He was hooking up all of her electronics—computer, phone, Internet—in her office and around the house, but Matt only had a closet. A giggle escaped her at the thought of one of the biggest rock stars in the world sitting upstairs folding towels and sheets.

It was probably a good thing for his ego to remind him of what it was like to be a regular person again.

"Okay, next box," she said and turned and moved it across the room.

Baking pans. Just the sight of them made her smile. As someone who had been food blogging for years, it was important for her to have top-of-the-line cookware and bakeware. Out of the two, she preferred cooking, but every once in a while she would test out her baking skills and was pleasantly surprised with the results.

Each piece was placed lovingly in its new spot so that if anyone were to open the cabinet, it would look neat, clean, and organized. Stepping back, Vivienne smiled with satisfaction. "And that's how it should be." Closing the doors, she immediately went and carefully cut the tape lines on the box and collapsed it so she could transport it easily back to her town house and put it back together for the next load.

And that was her pattern for the next six boxes. Every pot, every pan, every lid had its place. And it was glorious.

Another hour had passed. Where the heck were the guys? After quickly and neatly stacking all of the collapsed boxes by the front door, Vivienne went in search of them. In her office, everything seemed to be completed. All that was needed was her furniture. The same was true for the equipment in the living area. How had she not even heard Aaron in there? The main floor was one open room; only her office was separate. Walking up the stairs, she found a stack of collapsed boxes and still no sign of Matt or her brother. *What in the world?*

Unable to suppress her curiosity, she opted to check out the linen closet before continuing to search for the guys. Pulling open the door, she stopped and stared with wonder.

Towels were folded neatly and color-coordinated—just as neatly as she'd packed them.

The bedsheets were folded perfectly and separated by set—just as she'd placed them in the box.

Spare pillows were on the top shelf beside her two spare blankets. The pillows were fluffed and the blankets stacked with the same precision.

On the bottom shelf were three bins with cleaning supplies, and they were all lined up by size, their labels facing forward. On the floor were her humidifier and air purifier—both still in their boxes with pictures facing forward, so anyone searching for them could see what they were.

She was impressed.

Seriously impressed.

Maybe Matt wasn't quite as useless as she had pegged him to be. True, this hadn't been a difficult task, but she'd imagined him sort of tossing things haphazardly on the shelves and calling it a day.

"Aaron?" she called out. "Matt?" No answer. Vivienne walked into her bedroom and bathroom and saw no sign of them. With no other choice, she went back down the stairs and then stepped out of the house and noticed the two men walking toward her. "Where were you?"

Aaron chuckled and then looked at Matt. "I told you she didn't even notice us leaving."

Vivienne looked at them both curiously. "When did you leave?"

"About an hour and a half ago," Matt said. "You were so engrossed in talking to yourself about the wonders of cookware that you didn't hear us calling out that we were going to order dinner and would be back soon."

"Soon? It took you an hour and a half to get dinner?" she asked rather than admit she hadn't heard a word either of them had said earlier.

Aaron shrugged and then motioned to the boxes in his hands. "Pizza. I would have been back sooner, but a bunch of football players from the high school came in and they were running behind."

She looked at Matt. "Did you go with him?"

He shook his head. "Uh…no. I hung out and waited for Aaron to get back." He looked uncomfortable admitting that. He paused. "So, you're hungry, right?"

As if on cue, her stomach rumbled. Vivienne blushed. "Does that answer your question?"

Both men chuckled.

"You want to eat at your place or mine?" Aaron asked.

"Why don't we eat outside again, on your porch? I still don't have any furniture."

With nods, they all turned and walked back over to Aaron's. Matt went into the house to retrieve drinks and napkins.

Once he was out of earshot, Aaron asked, "So? Did the closet and the electronics meet with your approval?" He was teasing her and had a grin on his face as he set up the pizza boxes.

"Well...I haven't tested any of the computers or televisions yet, so I can't really say."

Aaron laughed. "That's my girl. No need to overdo the praise." He shook his head. "And the closet? Was it all done to your satisfaction?"

Vivienne looked beyond Aaron and into the house to make sure Matt wasn't nearby. She lowered her voice. "I was impressed. I figured he'd dump stuff and run. But everything looked perfect." When Aaron started to comment, she immediately put her hand over his mouth. "But if you tell him I said that, I will deny it!"

When she lowered her hand, they both laughed. "What's wrong with letting him know he got it right?"

"I don't think your friend needs to have his ego stroked. It might be good for him to get used to doing things without praise." It wasn't meant to be snarky, but she had a feeling that was exactly how it came off.

"Or," Aaron quickly said, "it might be nice to tell him how happy and thankful you are because he's been getting kicked around a lot these last few weeks."

Well, damn. She hadn't thought of that, and she immediately felt bad. "You're right. I can't believe I didn't think of that myself. I'm normally a pretty compassionate person."

"Pretty compassionate? Viv, you are the queen of

compassion. That's why I can't understand why you're so antagonistic toward Matt. He's a good guy, and we've been friends for what seems like forever. He's not a stranger, and he's always been nice to you. So what gives?"

Hell, there was no way she could tell her brother her attitude was a defense mechanism because she was embarrassed over something that happened years ago and was a nonevent, if she were being honest. So she'd kissed Matt—and so he didn't remember.

Okay, that still burned, but she was working on it.

"I...I don't know," she said evasively. It was rare that she kept any secrets from her brother. With parents who were essentially absent, each was all the other had. But this was just something she felt she needed to keep to herself. Aaron was a good man—a good friend and a good brother—and the last thing she wanted to do was put him in the middle of an awkward situation. "I guess I'm just a little out of sorts and—"

Just then, Matt stepped back outside, his arms full of a variety of drinks. He looked at the two of them as if he suspected he was interrupting something. "Um...sorry."

"For what?" Aaron asked, his tone light again. "It looks like you grabbed one of everything in the refrigerator!"

Matt smiled and stepped closer, putting the bottles on the table. "Well, I wasn't sure who would want a beer or who would want soda, and then I saw the bottled water..." He shook his head. "I figured it would be safe if I just brought out a few of everything and let you all decide what you want."

"Thanks, man," Aaron said and then motioned for them all to sit down.

For the next few minutes, they were all too busy eating to talk, and Vivienne took the time to chastise herself. She was a grown woman and she was behaving like a child. A lot of it was because of her own bruised ego. Just because she remembered their kiss and it had rocked her world didn't mean it meant the same thing to Matt.

Although it would have been nice if he had at least remembered.

Or would it have made things even more awkward right now?

The gasp she took at the question had her choking on her pizza and Aaron immediately jumped up to pat her on the back and make sure she was all right. When she was finally able to stop coughing, she thanked him.

"Just went down the wrong way," she said breathlessly. "Thanks."

He eyed her carefully as he sat back down, and after assuring him again she was fine, Aaron went back to eating. "Try taking smaller bites," he teased.

She smiled at him and took a minute before she started eating again. And that's when it hit her. She realized she was looking at this situation entirely the wrong way. Matt didn't remember—he had no clue she had essentially come on to him and then gotten herself thrown out of the arena. This was seriously great news! She didn't have to feel embarrassed or ashamed because no one knew about that small blip in her judgment except for her!

Holy crap is that freeing, she thought excitedly. It was all in how she looked at it. It was going to continue to sting a little bit if she obsessed about it, but if she put the right spin on it, this was all good. Matt would be here for a month, and she could act as if this were the first time she was seeing him since she was a kid.

No harm, no foul.

Of course, there was still the fact that he was incredibly handsome and sexy and the object of most of her fantasies, but…as a mature adult, she could handle that too.

He was off-limits.

There was a lot of work to be done to settle into her new place and she was going to be busy with her new position at the magazine, so really, there shouldn't be any lingering issues. She could totally control herself.

And if there was one thing Vivienne had come to pride herself on—especially after the night in Matt's dressing room—it was her self-control. She was the queen of it. Her world was carefully and systematically organized. She was starting a new job and moving into her new home, and even if Matt weren't her brother's best friend, she was too busy to think about getting involved with anyone.

Even one of the sexiest men alive.

In all fairness, it had been a while since she'd been in a relationship. Her job was her top priority and really, she was fine with it. Or she had been. The men in her life had all been business professionals who led fairly regular lives just like her. It was what Vivienne was comfortable with. And yet now she was wondering what it would be like to date a man who traveled, who was charismatic and charming and sexy and—

Stop it! First of all, if he didn't remember the kiss, it probably meant it was because Matt wasn't attracted to her. Not that that bit of information did a whole heck of a lot for her self-esteem, but it did cement the fact that getting involved with him wasn't going to happen. It wasn't in the cards. It wasn't part of anyone's plan.

And that was a good thing.

Yes. She nodded. It was a very good thing. Now was the time to focus on her career and getting settled, not on sexy rock stars. Taking a bite of her slice of pizza, she felt the last remnants of tension leave her body. Looking up, she couldn't help but smile as Matt and Aaron engaged in a playfully heated debate about where to get the best pizza.

Food. That was a safe topic, and one she loved to indulge in as well.

Just then, Matt let out a hearty laugh, and when Vivienne looked at him, all she could think was, *Yum*.

Look but don't touch, she reminded herself. *You can do this*.

And again, it was a good thing.

Wasn't it?

Chapter 3

FIVE DAYS LATER, AARON LEFT ON HIS TRIP OVERSEAS AND Matt was alone in the house.

And he was slowly losing his mind.

At least he used to have Aaron coming home and the two of them helping Vivienne move to distract him. Now? He had nothing. Vivienne was completely unpacked—the woman was the definition of efficiency—and Aaron was going to be gone for weeks. So now what was he supposed to do?

Walking back into his bedroom, Matt went to the closet and pulled out his guitar. There was a time when just touching the Les Paul was enough to energize and inspire him. But right now there wasn't any music in him, and he wasn't sure if he was disappointed to admit it.

Back in the living room, he sat on the sofa and strummed a few chords. It sounded flat to him, and he figured maybe it had more to do with his mood. All of the blinds were drawn and he felt a little bit like he was living in a cave. There was almost no way anyone would be able to see into the house from the street—not with the mature trees that surrounded the property and the privacy fence—but Matt wasn't feeling too secure in his environment yet. He'd have to think about it for a little bit longer before he'd be comfortable having the house more open or even stepping outside while the sun was out.

God, he admonished himself, *paranoid much?*

And the thing that bothered him the most was that there seemed to be a total lull in entertainment industry scandals. Seriously, there hadn't been a drunken brawl, a divorce, or a young actress flashing the paparazzi in weeks. How was that even possible? And while he wasn't in the headlines, there was still enough mention of him to keep him from wanting to go out.

Forcing his attention back on what he was doing, he looked around the room and sighed. Aaron had a magnificent baby grand piano in the corner of the room. He'd admitted to Matt that he bought it more for the look than for practical purposes, and at the time, Matt had laughed. Leave it to Aaron to choose something so big and expensive that he had no intention of using.

After a few minutes of mindless melodies, Matt put the guitar down and walked over to the piano and pulled out the bench. As someone who loved to play all kinds of music, he had grown up learning to play any instrument he could get his hands on. The piano was something that had always drawn him, but it was also the instrument he'd had the hardest time learning.

Or maybe it was hard to find the time to learn on a quality piano.

He touched the keys reverently. Aaron had mentioned how, even though he rarely touched it, he did maintain it and keep it tuned. For that, Matt was thankful because until Aaron got back, there wouldn't have been a damn thing Matt could have done about it otherwise.

For almost half an hour, he went through the basic drills he had managed to learn years ago. He even felt a little bit giddy when he remembered a few scales and arpeggios. There were plenty of mistakes, and it didn't feel natural at first, but Matt was fairly confident that if he worked at it a bit, he'd readily improve.

"Finally," he murmured, "a purpose!"

When his fingers began to cramp, he stood and stretched and then opened the bench seat to see if Aaron had any sheet music inside. He felt like he'd won the lottery when he found a stack of it. Taking his find over to the sofa, Matt sat down and sifted through it, seeing if there was anything in the pile that called out to him.

There was such an eclectic variety to choose from—classical, pop, rock, and even show tunes. Matt instantly tossed the show tunes to the side. The last thing he wanted or needed now that he was feeling inspired was to be reminded of his recent failure. After almost thirty minutes of analyzing his options, he decided he would focus on learning four songs during the week: "Stairway to Heaven" because, well, Led Zeppelin, "Imagine" because it was one of John Lennon's best songs, "Your Song" by Elton John because the man had been an inspiration to Matt when he was growing up, and finally "Piano Man" by Billy Joel because obviously the man knew how to play piano.

There were many classical sheets in the bunch, but Matt wasn't looking to play on that level. He wanted songs he had connections to, songs that had inspired him and songs he could relate to and maybe incorporate into his future work.

With his decision made, he went and placed the four songs at the piano and tucked the rest back in the bench before making himself a sandwich. He felt like he had been up for days when in reality he'd slept until ten and it was only a little before one in the afternoon.

This was another thing he was having to get used to: preparing meals for himself. Although putting a sandwich together wasn't a hardship, it certainly had been a while since he'd done it. For so long, he'd been staying at hotels and had a staff on hand to handle things like this, and he felt like he was all thumbs as he put together a simple ham and Swiss sandwich.

"Thank God no one is here to witness this," he said with a chuckle. "I can just imagine if the damn paparazzi were lurking in the bushes and took pictures. 'Matt Reed too incompetent to make a sandwich. Story below.'" And the sad thing was, it wasn't all that unbelievable. Over the years, he had read plenty of stories that were similar to that one, where pictures that were simply taken at an inopportune time were turned into a media field day. It was somewhat funny when you weren't the subject. Now that Matt had experienced it firsthand, he knew he'd never look at anything like that the same way again.

Sandwich in hand, he grabbed a can of soda and went back out to the living room. He sat down and picked up the television remote, figuring watching a little mindless TV would be okay while he ate. It didn't take long for him to realize that daytime programming was definitely not geared for him.

"Okay, dining in silence," he said as he shut it off. With a long-suffering sigh, he ate his sandwich— probably quicker than he should have—and cleaned up. Returning to the living room, he looked at the piano and decided there was no time like the present to get started.

It should have been fairly easy—after all, he wasn't

a complete novice—but his first few attempts at the intro to "Imagine" had him feeling completely out of his element.

"It's not supposed to be easy," he quickly reminded himself. "You're a guitar player, and most pianists take years of lessons to feel completely at ease with the music. It's okay if this takes some time. Rome wasn't built in a day." Then he groaned at how he was at the point in his life where he had to offer up pep talks to himself.

With a muttered curse, he stopped, took a deep breath, and then…his fingers began to glide with a little more ease. Every time he stopped due to a mistake, he'd made it a little bit further into the song. Granted, even without the mistakes, the music was rough, crude, but it still managed to fill Matt with a sense of pride and accomplishment.

Eventually, he stopped relying so much on looking at the sheet music and let his memory of the song take over. His eyes closed as the music washed over him, and while he wasn't anywhere near ready to go for a round of dueling pianos with Sir Elton himself, Matt knew it wouldn't take long for him to have the confidence to incorporate playing piano into his original music.

He played through the afternoon, and since the blinds were closed, he had no idea what time it was when he finally stopped from exhaustion. But it was the good kind of exhaustion—the kind that even though your muscles ached, you knew you had accomplished something. And really, considering how his past several weeks had gone, it was exactly the kind of thing Matt needed.

Standing, he stretched. His stomach rumbled and his throat was dry. "Doesn't matter what time the clock says, it's time to eat," he murmured, walking across the room to the kitchen. He opened the blinds on the window over the sink and looked out toward Vivienne's cottage. Was she even home from work yet? In all their interactions over the last week, he never did ask what her work schedule was like.

As if he'd conjured her up, Vivienne stepped outside and began walking toward the house. Matt grinned and tried not to think so hard about how his heartbeat sped up a little and how just the sight of her made him feel happy.

"You're just happy to have someone to talk to," he said to himself.

A minute later, Vivienne lightly knocked on the back door before letting herself in. "Hello?" she tentatively called out.

"In here," he replied and then walked over to her.

"Hey," she said softly. "How was your day?"

He chuckled.

"What? What's so funny about that?"

"It just sounded a little domesticated. Like, 'Hey, honey, how was your day?'" He shook his head and chuckled again. "I didn't think people actually did that."

She frowned slightly and Matt knew he had offended her.

"Sorry," he said, his tone and expression turning serious. "I was just going to see about making some dinner."

"Oh. That was what I was coming over about."

He arched a brow at her.

A light blush covered her cheeks. "I, um…I was playing around with a recipe and I have enough for two if you're interested. I mean…you don't have to. I know

Aaron stocked the house with food for you, and you may just want to be alone and—"

"Viv?" he interrupted and waited for her to look at him. "You're rambling."

She let out a breath and seemed to relax. "Sorry. I guess I just wasn't sure if you would even want to…" She looked beyond him into the kitchen. "Did you already start making dinner?"

Matt looked over his shoulder and cringed. There were cabinets open and plates and silverware and open condiments all over the kitchen counter. "Um…no."

The look on her face clearly showed she didn't believe him.

"It was from lunch."

"Oh, good grief," she murmured, walking around him and into the kitchen, where she promptly began to clean up. "What in the world did you make?"

"A sandwich."

Vivienne stopped and stared at him. "How many?"

He shrugged. "Just one."

Her eyes widened. "All of this is from one sandwich? Are you kidding me?"

Another shrug. "I don't mind cooking for myself; it's the cleanup that does me in."

A loud sigh came out as she put dishes in the dishwasher and walked around closing cabinets. "I have a feeling I'm going to be spending a lot of time cleaning up after you."

The idea of Vivienne hanging around was pretty damn appealing, and he had to kick himself to remember his earlier resolutions to keep a safe distance from her. But what harm could having dinner together be?

"So…dinner, huh?"

Smiling, she looked at him and nodded, and Matt felt like he had been punched in the gut. Her smile lit up her entire face, and it just made him feel warm and good and…happy.

"Like I said, I was trying out a new recipe I want to feature on the site, and I think it turned out quite well. Do you like salmon?"

"Absolutely." His mouth was already watering.

"It's a butter-lime-glazed salmon I paired with risotto and a Greek salad." She shrugged, almost as if she was shy. "The risotto and salad aren't a big deal, but the salmon was something I wanted to try. Are you up for it?"

Matt couldn't help but chuckle. Putting his hands in his pockets—because he was tempted to walk over and hug her or touch her—he nodded. "You saw what happens when I put some sandwich meat and bread together. I'd be extremely grateful for the chance to have a meal I didn't have to make and don't have to clean up after."

"Hey, now," she teased, "no one said you're not going to have to help clean up."

That made him laugh. "As long as it's not completely up to me, I think we'll be safe."

"Good," she said with a nod. "Do you want me to bring everything over here or do you want to come across the yard to the cottage?"

After being isolated in Aaron's house all day, Matt was ready for a change of scenery and a little fresh air. "The cottage would be great."

Vivienne must have sensed the reason for his choice

because she chuckled. "The walls starting to close in on you?"

"I didn't think it was possible, but yes. Maybe it's because I've kept the blinds and curtains closed. It's sort of like a cave in here."

They walked to the back door and outside. Vivienne turned to him as they made their way across the yard. "You know you're overly paranoid now, right? I think it's safe to open the blinds. I haven't seen anyone lurking in the trees."

"Yeah but you're at work all day."

"So? I work from home, and I think I would notice if someone was climbing over the fence or sitting perched in one of the trees."

Matt stopped. "You work from home?"

By this time Vivienne was at the front door of her house, her hand on the doorknob. "Um…yeah. I thought you knew that."

He shook his head. "I…guess I didn't realize."

"You mean you weren't paying attention," she teased and walked into the house.

Following her inside, he shut the door behind him. "What's that supposed to mean?" It was impossible to hide his irritation. For as long as he could remember, going back to when they were kids, he and Vivienne never had a problem with one another. But ever since he'd shown up here at Aaron's, she'd been giving him a bit of a hard time and he decided he'd had enough.

She gave him a look over her shoulder that conveyed her own annoyance. "I mean you're so used to talking about yourself and your career that you don't spend time listening to anyone else talk about themselves. The night we first started unpacking, you stood right here and listened to me and Aaron talk about setting up my office and I know we talked about my job." Now she turned and faced him, crossing her arms across her chest. "So you want to stand here now and tell me I'm wrong?"

He wanted to argue, but she kind of had a point. It just happened to be one that made him look like a completely self-absorbed jackass. When he looked at her, he noticed the satisfied grin on her face.

"Thought so," she said and turned toward the kitchen.

Matt knew he could handle this two ways—try to prove her wrong or just move on.

"The dishes are in the cabinet over there. Can you grab two plates and two bowls, please?"

Moving on it is, he thought and immediately went to do as she asked. "So are you feeling settled in yet?"

Vivienne shrugged and then bent to take the salmon from the oven. "I think so. It wasn't a hard transition— I've been working on the place for years, so it's a relief to finally be moved in. And the fact that everything is unpacked and all traces of the move are already gone makes things easier too."

"I have to admit, it was impressive how organized you were. The last place I moved into I had about a dozen people helping and it still took over a month to get unpacked."

She shook her head and tsked. "Lack of organization, my friend. Lack of organization."

"Well, no one had an outline or a map." He placed the dishes beside her on the counter.

"Like I said—"

"Yeah, yeah, yeah."

"Plus, I kind of have a feeling your house was a lot bigger than this one," she said, and Matt realized there was no condescension there. She was simply stating a fact.

And for a minute, he felt kind of ashamed at the excessive lifestyle he had been living. He shrugged and let out a nervous laugh. "Just a little." Looking around, he noticed the place had a very comfortable, lived-in feel. If he hadn't been there helping her do it, he would never have guessed she had just moved in. "What else can I do?"

"Um…" Vivienne stopped and glanced at the table. "If you can grab some silverware from the drawer on the end, that would be great."

Nodding, Matt went to the drawer and got the utensils. "What about drinks? What are you having?"

"I've got water, soda, sweet tea, or wine." When he didn't move, she looked at him. "Oh, I'll have wine."

"Okay." He was more of a beer guy and even that was in moderation nowadays. His drink of choice in the last year or so had been water, but for tonight, he'd join her in a glass of wine. He noticed the wine fridge and walked over to it. "Any preference?"

"I believe there's a pinot noir on the top rack that would go great with this." Rather than watch him, she was busy plating their food and making sure it was all perfect.

Matt grinned before grabbing the bottle. When he turned around, there was an electronic opener on the counter.

"It makes things easier," she said. Again, without watching him to make sure he was doing what she'd asked, Vivienne walked over and put their plates on the table and then went back for their salad bowls. Matt joined her a minute later and put the opened bottle of wine on the table, rather than pouring it right away.

Then, in a move that surprised even him, he walked over and held out Vivienne's chair for her so she could sit.

"Wow," she said softly. "Thank you."

He grinned. "Believe it or not, I do have manners." Stepping away from the chair after he gently tucked her in, he stepped around and took a seat. "This all looks and smells amazing."

"Thanks." She blushed.

Taking his first bite, he moaned with delight. "Holy shit is this good."

Beside him, Vivienne burst out laughing.

"What?" he asked with a grin. "What did I say?"

"That was probably the best compliment I've ever had on my cooking."

"Probably not the most eloquent thing I've ever said, but it's the truth, Viv. Seriously, this is fantastic." He took another bite and then motioned to the wine. "Want me to pour?"

She nodded.

"So you work from home and you cook for it. I know I'm only confirming what you pointed out a few minutes ago, but what kind of job allows you to do this?"

With a smile, she took a taste of her dinner before answering. "I'm an assistant editor for an online lifestyle magazine."

He paled for a moment. "A…a magazine?"

Vivienne shook her head. "It's not an entertainment magazine, per se. It's a lifestyle publication. I deal with all of the food. For years, I was a food blogger, but it wasn't paying the bills. Now I can combine the things I love without worrying so much about finances."

Matt picked up his glass and studied her. "Okay, this

time you are going to have to cut me some slack because I have no idea what you're talking about."

She rolled her eyes—not with annoyance, but amusement. "You've heard of the Internet right?"

"Ha-ha. Very funny," he deadpanned.

"Okay, well, nowadays people read their magazines online. Food blogging was a way for me to get my thoughts and ideas and recipes out there to share with people. I had sponsors for the blog and it was fun, but it was a lot of pressure on me because you have to be... amazing to get noticed."

"Amazing how?"

"Well, for starters, you have to love food. I mean like seriously love it and be passionate about it."

"People are passionate about their food?" he asked, not convinced there was such a thing.

Vivienne nodded. "Oh yeah. You have to have an appreciation for it and the presentation."

He leaned forward. "So, how it looks on the plate, right?"

"Very good." She nodded and picked up her own glass and took a sip. "Ooh, that's good. It's more than just looking right on the plate, though. It's about colors and textures and making people who are seeing it in a picture feel like they can taste it."

"Sounds like a lot of effort."

"It is. I've always enjoyed cooking, but I haven't gone to culinary school or anything. I'm pretty good at following recipes though. I majored in journalism in college, and photography was always a hobby so...it's kind of cool how I can combine all those things together."

"You take the pictures yourself?"

She nodded. "Have to. To keep costs down, I had to

be a one-woman show. I didn't mind. With everything being digital now, it's not too hard to do. Believe me, I couldn't compete with professionals on any level, but I think I do okay."

"If this is the kind of stuff you're putting together, you're doing more than okay." He took another bite of his food. "I'd love to see some of the photos you've done." Then it hit him—he glanced around and saw the all of the framed photos on the wall. Some were of family, some were of nature, but the ones closest to the kitchen were of food. His gaze returned to hers. "You took all of these?"

"Sure did," she proudly replied. "I invested in a quality printer—one that can handle some of the larger sizes—and do most of the printing myself. Sometimes I let the professionals handle the matting and framing, but only on the big ones, like the picture of the lake over above the sofa."

He turned and couldn't help but be impressed. "Damn, Viv. That's stunning." He turned back to her. "And you do all of this from home? By yourself?"

She nodded.

Matt continued to look around the room. "You've got serious talent. Have you ever thought of displaying your stuff anywhere? A gallery? Or online for people to purchase?"

"Oh…that's not for me," she said a bit shyly. "The pictures I take are more for my own pleasure. I don't think there's anything I can create that people would want to hang in their homes."

"That's where you're wrong," he said, turning back around to face her. "I could totally see some of your food pictures that you've got in the kitchen in some fancy restaurant. Or the picture over there of the sunset on the beach? It would look fabulous in anyone's house." He paused and took a sip of his wine. "You should think about it."

She shook her head. "I think I've got enough on my plate with the job. Working from home means I have to be very disciplined. I can't afford to take on too many side projects."

"But you do like it, right? Working from home?"

"It's great. No one breathing down my neck, I make my own deadlines, and I have creative control." She paused. "Well, now I have a little more pressure since taking the assistant editor position, but I still get to set the schedule."

"I don't think I'd be able to work for myself," he said with a chuckle.

"How come?"

"I'm not disciplined enough," he admitted honestly.

"Oh, come on," she said softly. "I would think you'd have to be disciplined to live the lifestyle you do."

Matt shook his head. "People tell me where I'm supposed to be, what I'm supposed to do and say, what to wear..." He shrugged. "I didn't notice it until now, when I have some downtime and everything around me is going to shit because I have no idea what I'm supposed to be doing."

She looked like she was about to say something and then thought better of it and went back to focusing on her meal. They ate the remainder of it in silence. When they were done, Matt stood and began clearing the table. "You don't have to do that," Vivienne said, coming to her feet.

"No, no, no. You cooked. I can clean up." Then he looked around the kitchen. "Besides, it looks like you cleaned up as you went along because the only things out here are the things we used." He smiled. "Even I can handle that."

Picking up her wine and taking a sip, she smiled and relaxed in her seat. "Then I'm going to let you." For a moment, she simply let him do his thing. "So have you been online today?"

"Uh-uh," he replied from across the room. "Why?" He had a feeling she'd seen something about him and was testing the waters.

"No reason," she said quickly and returned her focus to her drink.

"Viv…"

"It's nothing. Really."

He shut the dishwasher with a little too much force and cringed for a moment. *Screw it*, he thought. Stalking across the kitchen, he came to stand in front of her. "Come on. Out with it. You saw something online. What was it?"

When she didn't answer right away, Matt's stomach sank. *Shit*. Things were supposed to be getting better. He'd stayed out of sight and done nothing to draw any attention to himself. Why the hell couldn't he catch a break here? He huffed with agitation and raked a hand through his already unkempt hair. "Viv?"

She looked up at him, brown eyes filled with pity, and he wanted to curse. He wanted to throw something. But more than that, he wanted to demand she not pity him.

"Matt, just…let it go. It was nothing. I shouldn't have said anything." Jumping to her feet, Vivienne put her glass down and walked to the kitchen. "I have some apricot tartlets for dessert. Would you like to try one? I may even have some vanilla ice cream to go with them."

He was practically on top of her in the blink of an eye, spinning her around to face him. "Tell me, dammit! What did you see? What did you read? What are those vultures saying now?"

For a minute, he couldn't believe he even cared. The vultures had been circling and picking at him for weeks. He should have been used to it. He shouldn't want to know, because it didn't matter; he knew the truth. And yet...

"They're speculating about where you are and about...your mental health," she said quietly, refusing to look him in the eye. Busying herself with the dessert, she put some distance between them. "I had read something about it when you first got here, but I thought they had let it go. Today...well...it was on one of the entertainment sites."

Cursing loudly and colorfully, Matt stalked across the room and began to pace. "My mental health? What the hell does that even mean? Do they think I'm depressed? Am I on suicide watch?" He didn't wait for her to respond. "Oh, they'd love that! The world likes nothing more than to watch people on their way down. Bastards!"

"Matt."

Out of the corner of his eye, he saw Vivienne walking toward him, but he was too upset at the moment—too raw—to have a rational conversation. Without a word, he spun and stalked out the door.

"Well, that went just great," Vivienne murmured to herself. With a sigh, she went back to the kitchen and put the tartlets on one plate and covered them.

What was she supposed to do? Maybe she shouldn't have brought up the rumors swirling about him, but… it had just slipped out! At some point, Matt was going to have to stop hiding and face the fact that he wasn't immune to gossip and speculation, and one day, he was going to have to go out in public again and deal with it.

Obviously, he wasn't at that point yet.

She hated how dinner had ended. With a weary sigh, she figured since she'd been the one to start this, she might as well see it through to the end. Matt clearly needed a friend, needed to know someone was in his corner and believed in him—someone to help him see things were going to get better.

It felt like she was walking to her own execution.

Halfway across the yard, she stopped to consider her actions. Maybe it was wrong to go in there and push. Maybe Matt needed to blow off some steam.

Or maybe he really was suicidal and the reports were right.

"Dammit. Now I'm believing the nonsense," she huffed and continued making her way to Aaron's back door. She didn't bother to knock, and as soon as she stepped inside, she found him flat on his back on the floor in the middle of the living room. "Oh my God! Matt!" she cried and ran to his side, dropping to her knees beside him. "Please be okay! Please be okay!"

Her hands were on his face and fear had her by the

throat when he opened his eyes. Green eyes blazed with anger as they met hers. Matt smacked her hand away as he sat up. "You believed them!" he shouted accusingly, coming to his feet. "You freaking believed what you read today! Dammit, Viv! What the hell?"

It took a moment for her heart rate to return to normal as she sat back on her heels. It was foolish to believe he would harm himself—or that he had managed to do it in the five minutes since she'd last seen him.

But he had scared the hell out of her for a brief moment.

Slowly, she came to her feet and stood her ground. "You know what? Yes. For one second, I did. I came in here and found you on the floor, not moving, with your eyes closed. What was I supposed to think?"

"I don't know, maybe that I was just trying to calm down? Geez! Do you honestly think I'd kill myself over a stupid show? Over bad reviews?"

"Why not?" she yelled back. "You're locked up here having a damn pity party over them! And I don't know you well enough to know what your state of mind is. For all I know, you're holed up in here all day drinking or taking stuff to numb the pain. It's what guys like you do, isn't it?"

His eyes went wide and then narrowed significantly. "*Guys like me*?" he snarled.

Okay, not the best thing to say when trying to calm someone down, she told herself, but there was no way to take it back. "Oh please. Don't even try to tell me you don't drink or never did drugs because it would be insulting to us both."

He took a menacing step toward her. "Sweetheart, you don't know anything about me."

"You're a drinker. Jack Daniels. Right out of the bottle," she spat at him accusingly.

And then it hit her what she'd done. There was no way she could know that—at least not that Matt was seemingly aware of. She looked at him and tried to keep her expression neutral, but she saw the suspicion on his face.

"I've seen pictures of you," she said quickly, defiantly. "So don't bother denying it." *Plus, I've been alone with you in your dressing room and tasted it on your breath when you kissed me into oblivion.*

"Fine. I drink," he sneered and then stopped and let out a ragged sigh. "At least…I used to. I haven't had a bender in…two years." He paused and took several deep breaths before he continued. "I'm not going to apologize or explain my actions to you, Vivienne. It's not a crime to drink. When I realized it was becoming a crutch, a problem, I stopped. Not completely," he quickly added. "I just know my limitations now. I can have a beer or a glass of wine and stop there. It's a choice, and I'm very lucky I don't have an addiction."

She nodded as understanding dawned on her. On top of the weight of this scandal—or semi-scandal— hanging over him, he was also struggling with other demons. He was strong and wanted to remain so, but sooner or later, he was going to break. Taking a tentative step toward him, she sighed. "I'm sorry."

"It's not your fault," he said gruffly. "And it's not your battle. I shouldn't have taken it out on you."

"No, but…I shouldn't have brought it up. We were having a nice evening, and I ruined it. Again, I'm sorry."

Matt's gaze remained hard for a moment longer,

and then he seemed to relax a bit. A long sigh was his immediate response, but Vivienne had a feeling he was searching for something to say. "You'd think I'd be used to it by now. And I can't figure out why I'm not."

I don't want to touch that statement with a ten-foot pole was the first thing to enter her mind. And as much as it pained her, she remained silent.

"It's ego," he said and then walked over and flopped down on the sofa. "And I hate it. I always hated guys who were so damn wrapped up in themselves they thought they could do no wrong." He gave a mirthless laugh. "Turns out I'm one of them."

Another statement she was biting her tongue on.

"How can I make it go away?" Matt shook his head. "Not the rumors and speculation—I can't stop people from talking—but the feelings. How the hell do I stop letting those things get to me? How do I stop taking it personally?"

"By proving them wrong," she said before she could stop herself. Her hand instantly went up to cover her mouth and she mumbled, "Sorry."

Matt studied her for a moment and then held out his hand to her. Vivienne had no idea what to do because she had a feeling touching him was the worst thing she could do—it might crumble her resolve, or he'd be able to see how much she was attracted to him. So she simply stared at his hand.

"Um…Viv?"

"Oh…right," she mumbled and forced herself to sit down at the opposite end of the sofa—without touching him.

He frowned. Deeply. Almost scowled. Then he threw

his head back against the cushions and growled. "See? Even you think I'm scum."

Great.

"No I don't," she said, but it sounded weak even to her ears.

"Right. That's why you're sitting practically on the other side of the room and looked at my hand as if touching me was repulsive." He cursed. "When did I become this guy? This...completely self-absorbed jackass?"

Two years ago, she wanted to say, and then stopped herself from rolling her eyes. Her inner dialogue was almost getting too hard to control.

"Look, Matt," she began casually, "most of us don't realize we're changing. You spent a lot of years with people catering to your every whim. I'm sure, given the chance, most people would change. You now have the opportunity to see the change and decide which version of yourself you want to be. I bet a lot of people wish they could have done that before they were too far gone."

"What if I'm already too far gone?"

"You're not," she replied softly. "You're sitting here telling me what you see in yourself. If you were really too far gone, we wouldn't be having this conversation." She paused. "Now you can be whatever kind of guy you want. It's up to you."

He straightened and looked her directly in the eye, his expression less angry and more pleading. "I'd like to be the kind of guy you don't cringe away from."

Well, damn. "I didn't cringe," she said, going for light and teasing. She even forced herself to grin.

Rather than speak, he simply held out his hand again. His gaze held hers as he waited.

There wasn't an option. Doing her best to have no reaction at all, Vivienne stood and walked toward him and placed her hand in his.

And felt more alive than she had in years.

His hand was large, his skin rough and warm. Her eyes met his, and if she wasn't mistaken, he looked just as shaken as she was. Her lips parted and she took a slow, shaky breath. Matt's hand closed around hers and he gently tugged her down onto the sofa beside him. She sat stiffly for a moment and then—as if of one mind—they relaxed against each other. Vivienne's head was on his shoulder, his arm around her, and it felt...nice.

Natural.

Like everything she'd been waiting for.

Now what? How was she supposed to act? What was she supposed to say that wouldn't come out as her begging Matt to kiss her? Touch her?

She should have stayed in the cottage and let him have his meltdown and recovery on his own. Now she was stuck here with no way to get up and leave without it being completely obvious that she was no better than the hundreds of girls he'd been with over the years.

She visibly shivered even as the proverbial bucket of cold water was dumped on her with that thought.

"You okay?" he murmured, his voice low and gruff in her ear.

Not trusting her voice, she nodded.

They sat in somewhat companionable silence for several minutes. Vivienne's mind wasn't quiet for even one second. When she noticed the sheet music out on the piano, she twisted slightly and looked up at him. "You play the piano?"

He chuckled softly and placed a light kiss on her temple. "Sort of."

"What does that mean?" she asked, forcing herself to laugh even though all she could think about was the fact that his lips had just touched her.

"I've tried it several times over the years, but while I was sitting here today doing nothing, I decided to give it a try. It was a little intimidating and I still basically suck at it, but I'm better at it than I was yesterday."

"I was forced to take lessons for years. My mother was obsessed with me learning. I was relieved when I moved out on my own and didn't have room for a piano in my apartment. Then Aaron went and built this house and bought one. Every time our parents come to visit, I'm obligated to play a little. If I'm not mistaken, that's their old sheet music you're using."

"That would explain why there isn't anything from the last decade or two."

She chuckled. "Aaron really didn't even need it. I think it was just something my parents passed on to him. Lord knows I didn't want it."

"Sounds like you hate it."

She shrugged. "I think hate is a strong word for it, but it's very different when you play for pleasure than when you're doing it because you're expected to. I used to love to play the popular songs—I have an ear for it now and can play a lot of them without sheet music—and it used to make my mother crazy." She couldn't help but laugh at the memory. "Whenever she was nearby, I'd play Mozart or Beethoven, but as soon as she would leave, I would break into some NSYNC or Backstreet Boys."

"Ugh! Not the boy bands!" he cried in mock disgust.

"What can I say?" she said, unable to control her laughter. "It's the music I was listening to."

"Please tell me you don't still listen to it?" he begged. "If you could sit down and play anything right now, what would you play?"

"Oh, don't do that."

"Why not?"

"Because now I feel like I'm under the microscope, like you're going to criticize my choice in music, especially if I pick something that's not one of your songs or something."

Matt pulled back and shifted so they were fully facing one another. She immediately missed the heat of his body pressed up against hers.

"No pressure. Just honesty. I'm genuinely curious. If no one were here, what would you play?"

"Classic Elton John," she said without hesitation. "I love his music. All of it. But his earlier stuff is my favorite."

"I was working on one of his songs earlier, and I have to admit, it didn't sound half bad."

"Prove it," she challenged, a grin on her face and a twinkle in her eye.

"No way," he replied, shaking his head. "That's not fair."

"How is it not fair? You're a musician. You play music in front of tens of thousands of people all the time. Why can't you play one song on the piano for me?"

"Because I barely know how to play it." Then he stopped, and Vivienne did not like the look on his face. Matt stood and held out his hand to her again. "Play it with me." His voice was so soft, as was his expression, and this time, she fit her hand into his without hesitation.

Together they sat on the piano bench and Matt set up the sheet music and started to play.

Only...he couldn't.

At least, that's how it seemed to Vivienne.

He seemed stiff and uncomfortable, and finally, she placed her hand over his and stopped him. "You need to play a little. You're still too new at this just to jump in. I always had to do warm-up exercises before my instructor would let me play."

"I always thought that seemed like a waste of time," he said. "You think it's necessary?"

"Technically, you're a beginner. So I would say yes, just to loosen your hands up and get you comfortable with the keyboard." Then she started playing some exercises she remembered from when she was a kid and encouraged Matt to do them. Then, they easily moved on to "Chopsticks." And from there, she moved on to "Twinkle, Twinkle, Little Star." They both laughed as she played it and Matt sang along, and then he played it back for her, teasing that she needed to sing it to him.

She declined but laughed the entire time. There was no way she was singing for him—she knew her strengths, and singing was not one of them.

"What about this one?" he asked and started the very basic beginnings of "Heart and Soul."

"Oh," she sighed, "this is one of my favorites." She joined in, with Matt doing the A section and Vivienne doing the chords. Their shoulders bumped together as they played, and she couldn't help the tingles she got as Matt quietly sang the lyrics beside her.

When she turned her head and caught him watching her with an odd expression on his face, she began to wonder if maybe he was remembering the way he'd held her that night and kissed her…and let her go.

She jumped up from the bench so quickly she stumbled and almost fell on her butt. When she righted herself, Vivienne looked at him with wide eyes, her heart beating madly. "Sorry."

"You okay?" he asked, obviously concerned.

"Um…yeah. I had a…a, um…leg cramp and I needed to get up and move." *Way to sound like an eighty-year-old woman, Viv*, she cursed herself. Trying to prove she wasn't lying, she limped around a bit and then sat back down on the very edge of the bench, effectively putting space between the two of them. "So…I think you should be good to go. Why don't you play something for me?" Her voice sounded weird even to her own ears.

Matt was still looking at her funny, but he didn't say a word. He cleared his throat as he turned, put his focus on the keyboard, and began to play. It was slightly off and riddled with mistakes, but he kept going. Vivienne was learning more and more about him. For instance, she could tell he was tempted to stop and start over again with every mistake. But he didn't. He kept on playing and singing.

He opted for the Elton John tune, and as he had before, he sang as he played. Vivienne could only sit and listen, his voice washing over her. She knew he hadn't purposely chosen this song—the lyrics weren't his—but for one brief moment, she let her imagination run wild. A small sigh escaped her lips as she imagined it was her own sweet eyes he was singing about.

Matt was looking at her again, and Vivienne felt hot all over. She was feeling things she shouldn't. He was making her feel things she shouldn't. Or maybe he was just singing lyrics, and she was reading too much into them. When he turned back to the piano and continued to sing, she told herself that was all it was—her imagination.

Her stupid, overactive imagination.

With her mind somewhat made up, she allowed herself to relax a little and just enjoy the music. As the last note faded and the room became silent, she knew he was waiting for her to give him feedback. Forcing herself to smile, she turned her head and looked at him. "That was pretty good. I would never know you were new to playing the piano."

"Really?" he asked, and she could tell he didn't fully believe her. "Because it was riddled with mistakes."

"Matt, you know you have talent."

"I used to."

"That's a bunch of bull and you know it," she said a bit harshly. "You can't be good at everything. It sucks, but there it is. You're a very talented musician. So you can't act? Big deal. So you're better at backup vocals than lead? There are worse things that could happen! Seriously, you have more skill and musical ability than most people. Why can't you just be happy with that?"

His answer wasn't immediate. Instead, he got up and went to the kitchen and grabbed them each a bottle of water. When he walked back over and handed Vivienne hers, he smiled sadly. "I hate to fail."

She couldn't help but smile back. "It's natural. We all do. You have to cut yourself some slack. If I were to get up on a stage and try to do what you do, I'd fail too. But it doesn't mean I'd beat myself up over it. You just have to know your limitations."

He sat back beside her and nudged her playfully with his shoulder. "Oh, come on, you can't tell me you haven't tried to play the guitar a time or two. Or sang into a hairbrush while looking in the mirror. Or in the shower—everyone does that one."

"Oh, I sing all the time," she quipped. "Just not well. And I'm okay with it."

"Normally I am. I learned a long time ago it was better just to prove people wrong. But lately—"

"Okay, so what is it going to take for you to get over this?" she interrupted. "Because it seems like you are refusing to move on."

"Move on? It just happened!"

"Weeks ago, Matt!" she cried. "I mean, I could see the first week, even the second, but now? It's time to move on. You're giving the press and the haters all the power. And, personally, I think you're making it worse by hiding out."

His eyes went wide. "Excuse me?"

Okay, insert foot in mouth. Once again, there was no backing down. "Look, I'm not belittling what you're feeling—"

"Um…yes, you are."

She chose to ignore him. "All I'm saying is maybe it's time to stop hiding and go on with your life. Clearly the hermit thing isn't helping. The only thing it seems to be doing is making you obsess about it and doubt yourself. How is that a good thing?"

Stammering and partial thoughts tumbled out of his mouth for a minute before he stopped. "I'm just doing what I'm supposed to do! I'm lying low to help the band, so I don't jeopardize our credibility. It's not like I'm going to live in seclusion forever!"

"Says you," she mumbled and took a drink of her water.

"What do you expect me to say, Viv?" he asked wearily. "What is it I'm supposed to be doing? Have you ever lived your life in a fishbowl?"

She shook her head.

"Then I guess it's real easy for you to pass judgment. You have no idea what it's like." He sounded tired, defeated. "This is all new to me because it's never been this intense, so I'm handling it the only way I know how. And it's not fair for you to stand there as judge and jury and tell me I'm doing it wrong."

Carefully, she put the cap back on the bottle and stood. "Okay, maybe I don't know exactly what you're going through, but I can see how it's affecting you. And I know I don't know you that well, but it doesn't mean I can't see what's right in front of me."

"Really?" he asked incredulously.

"Yes, really."

He made a snorting sound and walked away.

Vivienne eyed the back door and seriously considered just calling it a night. Clearly she wasn't helping him in any way, shape, or form and was only serving to bring up an already-sensitive subject. Besides, she wasn't good with confrontations. It was one of the reasons she enjoyed working from home—no drama.

So without a word, she simply made her way across the room to the door. Her hand had barely touched the doorknob when she felt Matt's hands on her shoulders as he spun her around to face him. She gasped in surprise. "Matt? What—?"

"What do you see right now, Vivienne?" he asked, his voice low, a near growl.

"I don't… What do you mean?" There was a tremor in her voice and it was breathy and very unlike her.

He stepped closer and her back came in contact with the wall. "You said you can see what's right in front of you. So tell me, what do you see?"

It was a loaded question, she thought. And if she wasn't careful, she'd blurt out how she saw a sexy-as-hell man who turned her on simply by being in the same room. But there was no way she could admit to that, and she knew it certainly wouldn't help the situation.

"I see a man who is struggling with his identity," she said, swallowing hard.

His eyes narrowed. "Seriously? That's what you see? That's *all* you see?"

There was something in his tone that warned her this was going in a completely different direction than she thought and all she could do was nod.

"Then you honestly can't see what's right in front of you." Now his voice was gruff and so deep and so close that Vivienne almost purred from the sound of it. "Because I'm not struggling—I'm a bastard. I'm selfish. And you know what? I don't even care."

She shook her head.

"Trust me. I know what I want, and it's right in front of me."

Her eyes went wide as she softly gasped.

And then he pressed against her fully and kissed her.

Chapter 4

HOLY SHIT.

He was kissing Vivienne.

And she was kissing him back.

Damn.

Matt couldn't believe he had made the move and yet now that he had and she was slowly wrapping her arms around him, he was glad. Slowly, he lowered his hands from her shoulders and skimmed down her arms and then moved to her waist. She was soft and warm and curvy, and as he banded his arms around her, he marveled at just how right she felt.

And familiar.

Wait... *What?*

Vivienne sighed as his tongue teased her lips and she seemed to press impossibly closer to him. He could feel her from head to toe, and he wanted more. Her hands raked up into his hair. His head angled so he could take the kiss deeper, and when he felt the soft swipe of her tongue against his, Matt's knees went weak. Over and over, his lips claimed hers with a need that threatened to overwhelm him.

How was this even possible? Hell, he knew from the first moment he'd seen her a week ago he was attracted to her. A man would have to be dead not to want her—she had incredible curves and was beautiful and had an amazing smile and laugh... There wasn't a thing about Vivienne that Matt would change. It seemed like fate that she had come back into his life at this point, at a time when he needed someone like her—someone with her light and gentle spirit and fiery determination. He sent a silent prayer heavenward that she hadn't seen him at his worst, when he had been drinking heavily and partying and...

Holy. Shit.

Matt roughly broke the kiss and lifted his head and looked down at her with equal parts embarrassment and horror. "We've done this before."

Her eyes snapped open, and it seemed to take a moment for his words to sink in. When they did, she moved out of his arms and took a few steps away before turning her back on him.

"Vivienne?" he asked impatiently. "Am I right? This isn't our first kiss."

"I should go," she murmured and tried to open the door, but Matt slapped his hand against it to stop her. He waited for her to turn around, but she wouldn't. Instead, she rested her head against the door and sighed. "I really should go," she said quietly.

"Why didn't you say anything? I've been back here for a week—we've seen each other *every day*, and you never mentioned it had only been...two years since we'd seen one another. Why?"

Slowly, she turned around. "To what end, Matt? Why would I bring it up, especially in front of my brother?"

Crap. He hadn't thought of that. "You left that night—"

"I was escorted out of the building," she corrected. "And none too gently, thank you very much."

"Viv, I had no idea—"

She held up a hand to stop him. "It was a long time

ago, and it doesn't matter." A flush crept up her cheeks, and she wouldn't meet his gaze. "I…I really should go."

"No," he said. "Not yet. I think we need to talk about this."

She looked ready to spit nails. Seriously? He wanted to talk about this when she was clearly hostile? Did he have a death wish?

"There's nothing to talk about," she said firmly. "I went to the concert and came backstage to say hello. You'd obviously been drinking, and we kissed. It's not a big deal." And then she mumbled, "Clearly."

Before she could move away, Matt grasped her arm and pulled her close. "Clearly?"

"Oh please! You didn't even remember it happened up until a minute ago. So yeah…I'm going with it not being a big deal."

"That's where you're wrong. It was a big deal. It *is* a big deal!"

"Why?" she cried, her frustration at this conversation difficult to ignore. "Do you carry on like this over every woman you've ever kissed?"

Matt reeled back as if she'd slapped him. He released her arm and then took a step back. He noticed a glint of satisfaction in her eyes as she too took a step back.

Without another word to him, she turned and reached for the doorknob again.

That was it? He was just going to let her leave like that? Like hell he'd beg her—even though it was exactly what he wanted to do.

"This isn't over, Viv. Sooner or later, we're going to talk about it. I'm not going anywhere for another couple of weeks. You can't avoid me the entire time."

She didn't comment, and she didn't look at him. She simply walked out the door and closed it behind her.

And left Matt standing there, wondering if she was stubborn enough to stay away.

He cursed and slammed his hand against the door before turning and walking away. He wasn't sure what was bothering him more—the fact he had crossed the line and kissed Vivienne tonight or that he'd done it before and hadn't remembered it until now.

Collapsing on the couch, he let his head fall back against the cushions as he sighed. It was all coming back to him.

The concert.

How disillusioned he was at that point with the band and how much he had been looking forward to taking his career in a whole new direction.

And...kissing Vivienne.

Seeing her standing in the doorway that night had struck him as odd, especially since he hadn't recognized her right away. But once he had, he'd been pleased. Unfortunately, he was more than a little buzzed, and by the time Mick had barged in and had Vivienne escorted out, Matt's reflexes were too slow to stop it all from happening.

He remembered being pissed off, yelling at Mick for throwing her out and for stepping in at all. But in typical Mick fashion, he had found a way to distract Matt, and by the time he'd been ushered to the waiting limo, it was hard to say if he had even been aware of what had just happened.

Hell, he remembered questioning if it had happened at all.

One minute she was there and he was kissing her and

feeling like the missing piece of the puzzle of his life was finally in place, and the next she was gone.

Between Mick's incessant chatter all the way to the after party, the party itself, and all of the media attention they were getting for it being the end of the tour, the end of Shaughnessy before they took a break, Matt didn't have time to think. And by the time he came out of his alcohol-induced haze, he thought he'd imagined it all.

That's when he'd realized he had to quit drinking so hard. When you hit a point when you aren't sure what is reality and what isn't, it's time to call it quits.

So the first three months of his preparations for Broadway had been spent doing a little self-imposed rehab. There was no way he was going to go away for it—not when he and the band were still in the public eye. So he'd spent a lot of time with private counseling. It was grueling and brutal, and there were so many times when he'd just wanted to quit, but in the end, he'd stuck it out and was glad he did.

Now he could have a beer and know he didn't have to drink the six-pack. Or he could have one glass of wine without finishing the bottle. And really, he only drank when he was with others—and even then, Matt primarily limited it to social occasions. In the past few weeks, he'd been tempted to go back to his old ways—it would offer him a bit of oblivion from everything that was going on. But now that he'd had this revelation with Vivienne, he was even happier he hadn't.

Vivienne.

What the hell was he supposed to do now?

The obvious answer for tonight was nothing. It was clear she had been upset and couldn't get away from him fast enough. It stung his pride for sure. But what about tomorrow? Or the next day? Or the one after that? He was staying at Aaron's, and there was no way he was going to leave just because things might be awkward.

"Might," he murmured with disgust. "Good one."

The thing that seemed to have him by the throat was that, in any other circumstances, he would have been more than happy to let a woman walk away. Matt didn't do relationships, and he certainly didn't like drama.

"Only this time, it's *you* creating the drama, dumb ass."

Yeah. This was quite possibly the first time he was the one who was looking to cling, looking to push for more, looking to… Hell, he was looking to see where this all could go.

The timing sucked.

The circumstances sucked.

And Vivienne's opinion of him certainly sucked.

Matt couldn't remember the last time he'd had to put in an effort to win a woman over. Seduction was easy because, in most cases, he didn't have to do a damn thing. Women were thrilled just to say they'd been with Matty Reed. That wasn't going to be the case with Vivienne and, if he was being completely honest, he didn't want this to be like anything he'd done before. It was Vivienne, and she was special.

She wasn't one of his groupies, and she wasn't someone easily swayed by his charm.

And there was a very distinct possibility she was going to be the first woman who had the ability to break his heart.

She had to hand it to herself—walking away from Matt had taken Herculean effort, but she'd managed it.

Now, as she stripped and changed into a pair of comfortable pajamas—the silky, lounging kind—and made her way to her bed, she realized just how out of her element she felt. Again. Thanks to Matt.

Dammit.

Tossing back the comforter, she scolded herself. She was an intelligent, levelheaded adult. Dating never made her nervous or stupid, and she was somebody who enjoyed a healthy sex life when the opportunity presented itself. So why was it that Matt Reed only had to kiss her to turn her mind to complete mush and make her jittery like a virgin? It was annoying as hell, and she had no idea what to do about it.

Avoiding him would be the perfect solution, but unless she started coming and going from her home through a back window, she was bound to see him. Or maybe she'd take a page from his book and just hole up in her house and vow not to be seen in public. Well... maybe if she hadn't gone on and on all night about how ridiculous he was being about isolating himself. With her luck, he'd probably take her up on her little pep talk and start venturing outside more and more, and then she'd have to see him all the damn time.

"Why couldn't I just keep my mouth shut?" she questioned with a sigh, climbing into bed. Reaching over to her bedside table, she grabbed her tablet and made herself comfortable. It was a nightly ritual—a little reading, a little downtime—and after the night she'd had, Vivienne most definitely needed it.

Her library of ebooks was overwhelming, even to her,

and since she had finished the latest romantic best seller the night before, she wasn't sure what to start on next.

"Bad boys, bad boy CEO, billionaire, the boss, the hockey player, biker dude," she murmured as she scanned the titles. "Geez, can't a regular girl meet a regular guy anymore?" A little farther down, she found one that stopped her. "The rock star."

Interesting.

"When bad-boy rocker Max Adams stumbles on prim and proper Hailey Noelle in an elevator during a blackout, sparks fly. Their all-too-brief encounter leaves Hailey running for cover and Max hot on her heels…"

A snort of disgust came out before Vivienne could stop it. "Seriously? How prim and proper could she be if she's doing him in an elevator? Come on!" Deciding it wasn't the book for her, she started to scroll down the page but somehow ended scrolling right back up and clicking on it.

"There's nothing wrong with being curious," she said out loud, as if needing to justify her choice of reading material to her collection of decorative pillows. "Maybe poor ole Hailey has her reasons for letting the bad boy get up close and personal in that darkened elevator. We don't know." She paused. "And now I have to know."

Two hours later, Vivienne wanted to throw her tablet across the room in frustration.

Sexual frustration.

Good Lord the book was explicit. And the entire time she'd been reading, it hadn't been the least bit difficult to picture herself and Matt in the roles of Max and Hailey. Now she was wide awake and even more turned on than she had been in Matt's arms earlier, and there wasn't a damn thing she could do about it.

It was just a book. A really sexy book.

Filled with the kind of sexual escapades she wished she could be experiencing right now.

"Gah!" she cried out and kicked the blankets off of her before jumping from the bed. With a loud sigh, Vivienne stalked from her bedroom and went down the stairs, to the kitchen, to get something to drink. "This is ridiculous," she murmured, pouring herself a glass of water.

Glass in hand, she walked over to the front window and noted that the lights were still on at her brother's house. Maybe Matt was awake, or maybe he just left them on. She didn't know. But for some reason, she really wanted to know. What was he doing? Was he still beating himself up over the fact that she had called him a coward for not moving on, or was he maybe, just maybe, beating himself up because he had forgotten about their kiss?

Maybe he wasn't beating himself up at all, she realized. For all she knew it was a normal, everyday occurrence for him—kissing random women and then just forgetting about it.

With a curse, Vivienne turned away from the window, walked to the kitchen, and put her glass in the dishwasher. Well, this little detour did manage to do something—piss her off enough that she was no longer feeling the sexual frustration of moments ago.

Anger she could work with.

Stomping back up to her bedroom, she shut the door, crawled into bed, and punched her pillow a few times.

It didn't really make her feel any better but it seemed like the thing to do. Once she was lying down and comfortable, Vivienne forced herself to relax, taking a couple of deep breaths. There had been a blog post in the magazine not too long ago that had talked about deep breathing exercises to help you sleep, and she tried some of them. Within minutes, the tension had started leaving her body and she felt herself begin to relax.

Probably for the first time in a week.

With her mind cleared and her body pliant, she took another deep, cleansing breath and rolled over onto her belly.

And finally fell asleep.

He couldn't sleep.

Correction, he couldn't go *back* to sleep. Damn dreams. Damn vivid, terrifying dreams. They should be gone by now. Over. Done with. Matt ran a shaky hand over his throat and did his best to keep reminding himself that it was over. It was just a dream.

Even if it was one based on reality.

How long was he going to have to suffer from those memories? And what was it going to take to make them stop?

He shook his head to clear it. Why couldn't he be having sex dreams about Vivienne? Kissing her? Stripping her? Making love to her? But no. He was stuck in his own private hell that, no matter how much time went by or how far he traveled, he couldn't get away from.

Lying in the dark, he did everything he could to push

the images aside and fill his mind with something else.
Something good. Something positive.

Something a lot less horrifying.

He knew why he was having them now. There was
logic to it. But it still pissed him off. He tossed, he
turned, and yet he couldn't shake the images from his
mind, could still feel the pain. The panic. Could still
hear the voice.

With a muttered curse, he reached over to the bedside table, turned on the light, and reached for the television remote.

Another sleepless night.

—⁓—

Two days later, Matt decided he'd had enough. He'd
given Vivienne space the previous day because he
thought it was only fair. After the way she had practically sprinted away from the house after they'd kissed, it
seemed like the right thing to do. But now? After having
way too much time alone to think about it, he decided
she was right—hiding out wasn't helping anything.

True, she had said it in reference to his situation with
the press, but he still felt pretty strongly that it applied
in this situation too.

He was just stepping out of the shower—which was
where he'd finally come to this conclusion—when he
heard his cell phone ring. The sound momentarily para-
lyzed him. No one other than Aaron had called him in
weeks. And with the time difference, Matt had a feeling
Aaron was deep in work mode and not up for a casual
conversation to catch up on how Matt was doing.

Wrapping a towel around his waist, he walked out

of the bathroom and into his room and glanced down at the screen.

Riley.

The breath he hadn't realized he'd been holding whooshed out of him as he swiped the screen to answer it.

"Hey," he said. "What's up?"

"I was beginning to wonder if you were going to answer," Riley said with a chuckle. "You doing okay?"

Matt sat down on the bed and reclined against the pillows. "Bored out of my damn mind, but other than that, I'm dealing."

Riley chuckled again. "Just dealing? That doesn't sound good."

"It's all I've got right now," Matt admitted. "I've been messing around on the piano, but nothing new or original. Just sort of teaching myself to play."

"That's awesome, Matt. And it sounds like a decent distraction." He paused. "So that kind of tells me you're not at a hotel or resort. Because if you were, people would see and hear you playing and possibly leak the information to the press. So, come on. Where are you?"

Matt laughed. "Nice. I already told you, man. It's not a big deal. I've got a place to stay that's private."

"Private? So there's no one around to talk to? That would make me crazy."

"I seem to recall you spending some time alone when you were writing the music for your album."

"Yeah and I hated it," Riley admitted. "I think I spent more time with my family during that experience than I had in years. Between them and Mick and the studio musicians and then Savannah, they're what kept me sane. Especially my time with Savannah."

Matt smiled. It hit him in that instant how jealous he was of Riley—not professionally, although maybe that wasn't the complete truth. Riley had overcome his obstacles and the bad press and turned it into one of the biggest successes of his life. But what Matt was really jealous of was that Riley had found Savannah. Matt hadn't even been around the two of them all that much, but he could simply hear it in his friend's voice how happy he was.

"But seriously, Matt, is there anyone around for you to talk to? I hate the thought of you sitting by yourself for freaking weeks. It's not healthy. You'll start to lose your mind."

Too late, Matt wanted to say. He sighed, raking a hand through his damp hair. "I've got a house to myself and there's someone else on the property."

"Oh," Riley said, sounding relieved. "Well that's good. And you're...you're good? Things are all right? Are you feeling better?"

"Why do I get the feeling you're checking up on me for a specific reason? Has something happened?"

Riley let out a breath. "I don't suppose you're going online or reading newspapers."

"No," he said firmly. "I've been avoiding anything media related like the plague. Why? What's going on?" A sense of dread began creeping over him, and for a minute, Matt wished he had simply ignored his friend's call.

"Mick was going to call you, but...I thought it would be better coming from me."

"What the hell, Riley? Just say it!" he shouted, sitting straight up.

"Dylan was in an accident last night," Riley said. "It was pretty bad."

"Was he driving?"

"Yeah."

Shit. That meant… "Had he been drinking?"

"Yeah," Riley wearily replied.

"So…what happened? Was anyone hurt? Is Dylan all right?"

"He was alone in the car—that ridiculous Lamborghini. He slammed into another car just off the Vegas Strip. Totaled both cars."

Matt's stomach knotted. "Please tell me no one was hurt."

"The car had four men who were in Vegas on business. They're all pretty messed up, but they survived."

Relief washed over him. "Okay. Okay," he said as he took a deep breath. "That's good. And Dylan?"

"He's banged up but nothing's broken. After getting checked out at the hospital, they arrested him. It's all over the news. I barely recognized him in the mug shot. Mick's ready to bust a vessel, he's freaking out so bad. He was screaming about how none of this shit happened when we were all together as a band."

It sounded exactly like something their manager would say. "When did this happen?"

"It hit the press this morning. I've been doing damage control as much as I can, but—"

"It's not your mess, Riley," Matt said adamantly. "Dylan's been on this path for a while now. We both said it the other day. I hate that this happened, but I'm so damn thankful he didn't kill anyone."

"Yeah," Riley sighed. "Small miracles."

"So…what now? Do we need to make statements for Mick to release? Talk to the media? What?"

"Matt…you…you'd be willing to do that?"

It hit Matt in that instant that he would. Even though Dylan's current situation was one hundred percent his own doing and preventable, they were brothers. Maybe not by blood, but that didn't make it any less true. It also hit him how much it would have meant to him to have Dylan and Julian stand up and defend him when his own shit hit the fan.

Just as it probably would have helped Riley a year ago.

Lesson learned.

"Yeah," he said firmly. "I'd be willing to do it. Dylan's got a rough road ahead of him, and he's going to need some friends in his corner."

"Yes, he will."

"Listen, Riley… I'm sorry."

"For what?"

"I wasn't there for you. You were struggling and I wasn't—"

Riley cut him off. "Matt, we already covered this. It's the past. It's over and done with, and at the time, I don't think anything anyone could have done would have helped. It was all in my own head. What you went through? And what Dylan's going through? Those are things where having someone there beside you means the most."

Riley was always the gracious one.

"So my original question stands—what do we need to do?"

Riley sighed. "Well, I'll call Mick and see if he wants

a statement from us and Julian or if the PR team is simply putting one out there. Personally, I'd feel better knowing it was one that was legitimately from us. And then…" He paused. "Then we might want to take a trip to see Dylan. If we can."

"I'll get on a plane today if that's what we need to do."

A low chuckle was Riley's first response. "I don't doubt it for a minute, Matt. I'm just not sure we'd even be allowed to see him right now. We should probably wait a day or two to figure out where he's at and what charges are going to be filed and what his legal team and Mick think we should do."

"Man, this is a nightmare," Matt murmured. "I can't even imagine what Dylan's feeling."

They fell silent for a moment.

"Matt?"

"Yeah?"

"I'm proud of you."

What? "Me? Why?"

"Because you've been dealing with your own shit for a few weeks and struggling with your own demons, and yet…you're willing to step out and help a friend. I know Dylan hasn't exactly been the greatest friend to you… or any of us—"

"Doesn't matter," Matt interrupted. "He had his own battle going on. I just hope this is the wake-up call to get the help he desperately needs."

"I guess that's one silver lining."

"Hey, if one's all we get, I'll take it."

"Well," Riley began and Matt could hear the smile in his voice, "there is another one."

Matt frowned. "There is?"

"Uh-huh. This story isn't going to go away anytime soon, unfortunately."

"I thought you said there was a silver lining."

"For you there is."

What the…?

"Matt, the spotlight is off of you. You don't have to stay in hiding. You can take your life back."

It took a minute for those words to sink in. Riley was right. It didn't particularly make Matt feel good—he was getting a reprieve because his friend and bandmate was in trouble. Real trouble.

"I'm scum," Matt cursed.

"What?" Riley asked incredulously. "What are you even talking about?"

"Dude, I'm sitting here feeling relieved because the vultures found someone else to go after. How shitty is that? I mean, if you compare the two situations, how dare I sit here for as long as I did wallowing in self-pity. Dylan's life is forever going to be changed because of this! Those guys in the other car? Their lives are going to be changed because of this. My life, my struggles were nothing compared to that. My ego got bruised. God," he spat, disgusted with himself. "I'm so damn ashamed!"

"Matt—"

"It's true, Riley. Dylan's no doubt facing criminal charges. Those four guys in the car could be dealing with horrific injuries and rehab. What did I have to face? The fact that I wasn't as talented as I thought I was? Big freaking deal. I always knew I wasn't good enough," he murmured. "I should have listened—"

"Hey!" Riley snapped. "It isn't true. It never was

true! I thought you had gotten over that. It was a long time ago."

"Some things never really go away. You just get better at pushing them aside."

"Matt…"

There was so much more he wanted to say, but he had already been a selfish prick for weeks. Probably longer. Now wasn't the time to keep the focus on him. It was time to do something for somebody else for a change.

"Talk to Mick and get back to me. Let me know what we need to do."

Riley was silent for a long moment. "Okay. I'll call him and get back to you. It probably won't be until later tonight. I've got a sound check to do, and I promised Savannah we'd have an actual dinner date before the show, so it will be kind of late when I call. I'm on Central Time. Where are you?"

Matt chuckled. "East Coast, man. I'm pretty close to home. Well, where we grew up."

"Seriously?" Riley cried. "You swore you'd never go back there and now you're…"

Matt knew the instant Riley figured it out.

"Aaron."

"Yeah."

"Good. I'm glad you're there. I think it's the best place for you to be. Maybe now that this nightmare is behind you, you can put some other ghosts to rest."

Doubtful, Matt thought but didn't argue. "Call me tonight. I don't care how late it is. I'll be here."

"Tell Aaron I said hello. Maybe once all this craziness dies down, we can all get together. The tour is going to be doing a stop in Myrtle Beach next month.

I know it's not really close by, but my whole family is coming, and it would be great if you and Aaron did too. Maybe you could even come up and play a song or two with me."

The thought made Matt smile. It was exactly what he longed for, but his insecurities were still a little too close to the surface and raw. "Maybe. Let's get through this media circus first."

"Sounds good, Matt. I'll talk to you later."

Hanging up the phone, Matt placed it on the table and sighed. He should feel happy. This was what he'd been wishing for—someone else to take over the spotlight so he could have his life back. He just hated that it was Dylan.

He was beginning to think the band was cursed.

He stood up and let the towel that had been wrapped around him drop to the floor. He strode to the closet and grabbed a pair of jeans before walking naked across the room to grab a pair of boxer briefs. Hastily, he threw them both on before walking out to the kitchen. It was lunchtime and he was hungry, but his mind was still reeling from all of the information he'd been given this morning.

With a curse, he pulled open the refrigerator and was looking around for the makings of a sandwich when he heard a soft knock on the back door. He'd locked it last night and hadn't been out there since, but he knew it could only be one person.

Vivienne.

Thirty minutes ago, he had been more than ready to storm across the yard and talk to her. But now? Now he wasn't so sure he was ready.

"Matt?" he heard her call through the door. "Are you there?"

With a sigh of resignation, he closed the refrigerator and walked over to the door. He pulled it open and then turned and walked away. He wasn't ready to look at her. Hell, he wasn't even sure he'd be able to look at himself. He'd meant what he said to Riley only moments ago. He was scum. And selfish.

And he was ashamed of himself.

Vivienne had been right the other night when she'd called him out on his behavior. And it wasn't that he was angry about her being right, but it just meant he really wasn't someone who was particularly likable at the moment.

"Are you okay?" she asked softly.

Matt shrugged, figuring she was referring to their awkward encounter the other night. "I was just about to make a sandwich. You want something?" he asked.

Vivienne closed the door and followed him into the kitchen. "No. Thanks. I'm good."

Unable to help himself, he glanced over his shoulder and looked at her. She was dressed casually in a pair of black yoga pants and a snug, pink T-shirt. Her long hair was pulled back into a ponytail, and she wasn't wearing makeup.

And she was the most beautiful woman he had ever seen.

Cursing himself and his thoughts, he returned his attention to the food in the refrigerator. Without a word, he pulled out a package of sliced turkey breast, some cheese, and a jar of mayo. Slamming the door shut, he put the food down on the granite countertop and then grabbed the bread from the pantry. He knew Vivienne was watching him, but he forced himself to stay focused on making his lunch.

Out of the corner of his eye, Matt saw Vivienne move closer, taking a seat at the kitchen island. "Matt, I saw a story on the news about Dylan. I…I wasn't sure if you knew or if anyone called you but—"

"I just got off the phone with Riley," he said quietly, putting the finishing touches on his sandwich.

"Oh. Okay."

Matt wasn't sure what else to say. His mind was racing in a dozen different directions, and he had no idea which topic of conversation he was ready to discuss with her—if any—at the moment. When he remained silent, he heard the stool she had been sitting on move. Glancing over his shoulder, he saw that she was walking toward the back door.

"Viv?"

She turned back and looked at him, a sad smile on her face. "I just thought you should know. Just in case no one had reached out."

Forgetting all about the small meal he had just put together, Matt walked toward her. Taking one of her hands in his, he led her to the living room, where they sat on the couch. And then, in a move that surprised even him, he completely opened up and shared with her all of his fears for Dylan and how guilty he felt because now this meant the media spotlight was off him.

"That makes me a horrible person, doesn't it?" he asked, his voice gruff.

Vivienne shook her head. "No. It makes you human. Which is what I've been trying to tell you all along."

"Are you sure? Because it pretty much feels like I'm a horrible person."

She chuckled softly. "Again, it just means you're a normal person. You have feelings, Matt, and remorse. If you were as selfish as you seem to think you are, it wouldn't even occur to you to feel bad about being relieved." She playfully nudged him with her shoulder. "There's hope for you yet."

He laughed. A real, honest laugh. "Maybe I should have you write some of my PR stuff—Matty Reed: There's hope for him yet!"

Vivienne laughed with him and then shifted on the sofa to face him. "Okay, all kidding aside, what happens now? It sounds to me like you're completely free to go and resume your normal life—move back to your own place and do your own thing. Have you thought about what you're going to do?"

"I'm waiting to hear back from Riley—or Mick. I'm not ready to jump back out there. This is a pretty serious situation, and I don't want it to look like I'm using it as an excuse to get my life back."

"I doubt anyone's going to think that, Matt. But you also have to realize that just because Dylan is in the news, it doesn't mean everyone will have forgotten about you and the show. Are you sure you're going to be able to handle the questions and comments now?"

He shrugged. "I honestly don't know. But as you pointed out to me, I'm also not going to know by hiding out."

She grimaced. "Look, that was completely insensitive of me. I never should have—"

He stopped her. "Viv, you were right. I guess it's

kind of been a while since anyone's just been that blunt with me, and it sort of took me by surprise. I should have addressed the media scrutiny right from the start—maybe then they wouldn't have started with the rumors and speculation. My publicist was doing everything she could to try and make things right and downplay it, but the reality is, I sucked." He shrugged. "Cheryl could only do so much, but the proof was out there. I wasn't good."

"Matt—"

"The press was pretty blunt, I know," he added quickly. "But it was different. I mean, the people around me aren't normally like that. Everyone tries to find a nice way of saying things to soften the blow. Even Mick. He's a hard-ass most of the time, but for all his gruff exterior, he still coddles us in his own way."

He looked at Vivienne and saw she didn't believe him. "It's true."

"If you say so."

They sat for a moment in companionable silence before Matt stood. "I really am hungry," he began, looking toward the kitchen. "I know it's nothing gourmet or blog worthy, but you're welcome to join me for a sandwich."

Standing, Vivienne smiled. "Thanks, but I have some soup simmering next door." She paused. "Why don't you bring your sandwich over and you can try the soup."

"What kind?" he asked, a slow grin spreading across his face.

"A good one."

He laughed out loud again. "That tells me it's something I'm probably not going to want to try!"

She grinned at him. "Well...some people aren't very adventurous."

"I am very adventurous," he replied, all teasing gone. His voice was gruff, serious, and he heard Vivienne's soft intake of breath.

"I...I meant with food," she said nervously.

Clearing his throat, Matt did his best to sound a little less intense. "I can do that too."

She seemed to hesitate for a moment and then bit her bottom lip before responding. Matt almost groaned because she made even that simple gesture look sexy.

"It's an autumn vegetable soup. It's creamy, so you really don't even see the specific vegetables, and then it's topped with fried prosciutto. It's crispy and makes a wonderful, savory topping."

"Sort of like bacon," he commented and smiled when she nodded, clearly pleased he understood what she was going for. "Okay, I'm game."

"Really?"

Matt continued to smile at her, glad they were seemingly all right with one another. If she was still holding a grudge from the other night, there was no way she would have invited him to join her for lunch. He took this as a good sign.

Walking across the kitchen, he grabbed his sandwich and was about to wrap it up in a napkin, but then threw it in the trash.

"Matt!" Vivienne cried. "Why'd you do that?"

He shrugged. "There was no way I was going to insult your... What did you call it? Your autumn vegetable soup with that poor excuse for a sandwich. It just seemed wrong." He strode toward her and opened the back door. "And I have a feeling you're not just serving soup. I'm sure there's going to be something to go with it."

She blushed. "You don't know that."

He looked at her expectantly.

"Fine. I baked some whole-grain rolls and made a field greens salad with a honey balsamic dressing." Then without another word, she walked out the door and started to make her way across the yard.

Matt hung back for a minute and watched her, unable to help the smile on his face. He was getting to know Vivienne more than he'd ever really known any other woman, and the more he learned and discovered about her, the more he found he genuinely liked her.

And while she may not have been willing to admit it just yet, Matt had a feeling she was starting to like him too.

Why, oh why, had she gone over and talked to him? Vivienne asked herself as she calmly walked across the yard. Why hadn't she just called her brother and had Aaron check on Matt? She knew her initial instinct was to find out if Matt had heard the news about his bandmate and make sure he was all right. But as soon as she'd seen him, every pep talk she'd given herself about keeping her distance had been shot to hell. He'd looked...sad. Lost.

Alone.

She was playing with fire. She knew it, and yet there didn't seem to be a way for her to keep her distance.

Without waiting for Matt to catch up, Vivienne walked into her house and went to work frying up the prosciutto and taking the rolls out of the warming oven.

"What can I do to help?"

She almost screamed when Matt spoke so closely behind her. He was seriously like a ninja because she never even heard him come in. When he chuckled, she glared at him. "What's so funny?"

"You," he said simply. "I've never met anyone who just completely zones out like you do. I think bombs could go off around you and you wouldn't even notice. When you're cooking, it's like you're in your own world."

He had her there—she knew it was exactly what she did. Normally it was just her in the house, so it wasn't a big deal, but if this was going to keep up and they were going to share meals, she was going to have to keep her head in the game and pay more attention to her surroundings.

"I kind of am," she admitted. "I tend to get caught up in what I'm cooking and then looking at it while trying to imagine if it's something I should be taking pictures of or if it's something I can describe with just my words." Looking down at the prosciutto—which was nearing the perfect level of crispiness—she quickly stepped around Matt and reached for her camera. Within seconds, she was clicking away. Then, just as quickly as she had started, she stopped.

"That was it?" he asked. "How many pictures did you take?"

"It only takes a few. But I took about a dozen and I'll look at them after lunch and decide if any of them will work."

Matt shook his head and stepped aside, leaning against the counter to watch her. "So do you ever just, you know, eat?"

Vivienne looked over at him in confusion.

"I mean I know you eat, but do you just ever eat a normal meal? Like a burger or a sandwich? Or is every meal up for consideration for your blog?"

Nodding with understanding, she shut off the burner and moved around to start ladling the soup into bowls. "Oh, I totally just eat. You'll never see my morning cereal on the blog." She grinned at him before adding, "Cheerios."

"Nothing gourmet about that," he said with a chuckle.

"Exactly. Although every once in a while I'll crave something with a little more substance and I've whipped up some truly beautiful omelets." She stopped and winked playfully. "And those did make it onto the blog."

With the efficiency she was known for, Vivienne sprinkled the crispy prosciutto over the soup and then carried the bowls over to the table before turning around to grab the rolls and salad. "There's a small bowl of dressing in the refrigerator. Can you grab it for me?"

Matt did as she requested and joined her at the table.

Vivienne watched him stir the soup around for a minute. "It's totally okay if you don't like it. You look like you are definitely a heartier eater than this. You really should have brought your sandwich over with you."

He immediately stopped stirring and gave her a lop-sided grin. "I'm not going to lie to you, soup is not something I tend to gravitate toward, but that doesn't mean I'm not going to like it." He looked down at the bowl. "It's just very...orange."

She laughed. "Well, yeah. What's wrong with orange?"

He shrugged and began stirring again. "It's just not a color I associate with soup. To me it's normally more like a broth or a white, creamy consistency. This is just a little…" He stopped and dropped the spoon again. "It's orange. And it's not something I'm used to."

Deciding not to take offense, Vivienne shifted in her chair and faced him a little more head-on. "Let me ask you something. Do you eat sweet potatoes?"

Matt nodded.

"Do you eat carrots?"

Another nod.

"So it's not that you're opposed to orange-colored foods," she began logically, "just orange-colored soups."

He frowned. "Well, when you say it like that, it seems a bit ridiculous." Then he picked up his spoon and stirred again before lifting some to his lips. He stared at it before Vivienne reached out to stop him. "What? What did I do? I'm going to taste it."

"If you could see the look on your face, you wouldn't." With her hand on his arm, she guided him until the spoon was back in the bowl. She stood up and walked over to the refrigerator. "I have some leftover ham in here and some Swiss cheese. I'll make you a sandwich on one of the rolls. Do you like spicy brown mustard or do you prefer honey Dijon?"

"Holy shit," Matt swore softly behind her.

Vivienne spun around. "What? What's the matter?"

"This is freaking delicious!"

Leaning back against the refrigerator door, she watched in amazement as Matt took another spoonful of the soup. She couldn't help but be pleased.

"The prosciutto is still crisp! How is that even possible?" Another spoonful. "It's like the perfect consistency—not too thick, not too thin—and the fla-vors are amazing together!" He looked over at her, smiling. "Seriously, Viv. This is incredible. Seriously incredible." Without waiting for her to respond, Matt reached across the table and grabbed one of the rolls and cut it open. "Do you have any butter?"

Grabbing the butter, she shut the refrigerator and walked back over to the table to join him. Wordlessly, she served their salads and then finally took a taste of her own soup. "Oh, that is good," she said with a happy sigh. "I tasted it while it was cooking, but now with the prosciutto in there, it's even better."

When she looked up, Matt was already done with his. "Is there more?"

"Help yourself," she said, feeling ridiculously proud of herself. "There's more prosciutto in the pan to top it with."

Within minutes, Matt was back at the table and digging into his second bowl. "Okay, I have a proposition for you."

She almost choked on her food. After coughing and trying to catch her breath, she straightened and looked at him. "A proposition?" Part of her feared what he was referring to. She knew they hadn't even remotely touched on the topic of the kiss—the one two years ago or the one from the other night—but that didn't mean Matt wasn't ready to bring it up now.

He nodded. "Aaron stocked the house with all kinds of foods for me, mostly stuff that's prepackaged and requires little effort to heat up. It's all fine and well, but…knowing you can cook like this, it's kind of hard to work up any enthusiasm for a microwave meal." He paused to take a couple of bites of his salad. "This dressing is amazing."

Vivienne wasn't sure if she could handle all the compliments—especially as he was speaking them with his mouth full of food—but she did appreciate his enthusiasm for her cooking.

Swallowing, he reached over and took a quick sip of the sweet tea she had put out before continuing. "I'd like to be your test subject."

She looked at him quizzically. "Test subject?"

He nodded. "Seems to me like you do this blog stuff and it's all simply your opinion. And while there's nothing wrong with it, I think it could be interesting to almost make it a 'he said, she said' kind of thing. You know, get the guy's perspective on some of these recipes."

It was an interesting idea. Maybe they could...

"Take this soup, for instance," he began. "If you were here alone and made this and took pictures and put it on your blog, chances are your readers, who are probably primarily female, would see it and think *ooo, pretty* and maybe make it. But...they would probably be wondering if the guys in their lives would want to eat some creamy orange...stuff."

Vivienne rolled her eyes and chuckled. "I don't think it would be quite like that."

"Trust me. If I were out with a woman and she put this in front of me, I would have reacted exactly as you saw me react, only worse. I didn't want to hurt your feelings, and I was trying to be tactful."

"That was you trying to be tactful?" she asked incredulously. "It was a little childish, getting squeamish because of the color of the food."

He laughed and took another bite of his roll. "Okay, maybe. But I'm a guy, and I know how guys think. Most of us aren't gourmets. We enjoy simple food—steaks, burgers, pizza."

"Not all guys are like that!"

"Oh, I know, I know," he quickly interjected. "But the majority are. So if you could say, or confirm, that this was the response of a guy who is not a gourmet—he loved it and went back for..." He stopped and looked at his bowl and then back at the pot on the stove. "Thirds, then you'll know your readers are going to take that into consideration before they try this recipe." He shrugged and reached for his glass. "It's worth a shot."

She considered him for a long moment. "So basically you get free food, you don't have to cook, and I'm getting the male perspective to use on my blog."

"Exactly."

While it really was a great idea, it would mean she'd be spending a lot of time with Matt—something she still wasn't sure she could handle.

"I don't cook like this every single day, Matt. There are going to be times when you're going to have to fend for yourself."

He looked disappointed. "You mean like breakfast?"

Laughing, she shook her head. "I mean there are days I just eat leftovers or get takeout or...just make a peanut butter and jelly sandwich." She shrugged. "Now that I'm settling in to this assistant editor position, I don't have to cook as much. I mainly do it now for the pleasure and an occasional blog post—you know, just in case someone doesn't hand in a post on time, I can have some logged away. I really do enjoy cooking. But now I do it for myself more than for the blog."

Now he really looked disappointed. "So if I'd shown

up here a month ago, this would have been a great idea."

She nodded. "Afraid so."

"Well, damn." With a sigh, he finished up his bowl of soup and then got up to get another one. "So I'm stuck with the microwave meals."

"That's not what I said," she replied. "I'm just saying it's not going to be an everyday occurrence. I'm happy to share a meal with you a couple of times a week, and I really like your idea about being able to put the male perspective on a recipe."

Stopping abruptly, inspiration hit. Vivienne stood up and walked across the room to grab her tablet and pulled up the app to jot down some notes. "What if…what if we sort of put together some classic 'guy' meals, your burgers and steaks and pizzas, and glammed them up a bit? I can do a spotlight for the magazine. We can promote it as guy-friendly gourmet!" She looked up at him excitedly. "We can play around with of your favorite choices and make them into something couples would enjoy together. What do you think?"

Matt eyed her skeptically. "I don't know, Viv. I mean I seriously don't know a thing about cooking. How the hell am I supposed to be of any help?"

"What's your favorite meal?" she asked simply.

He thought about it for a minute. "There's this phenomenal steak house in Denver we always eat at when we perform there. They do steaks that are to die for."

Vivienne shook her head. "Okay, let me rephrase that. What's one of your favorite everyday meals? You mentioned burgers and pizza. Let's start with the pizza. What's your favorite topping?"

"Pepperoni. Isn't it everyone's?" he asked with a wink.

"I'd say it's probably the number-one choice. But what if we played around with some different toppings?"

With a shrug, he replied, "I know I'm not up on the latest food trends, but even I know gourmet pizza isn't that big of a deal. People put all kinds of crap on as toppings. I don't think you'll get a big response from something like that."

Hmmm… He had a point. "Okay, then maybe we don't go for the obvious. Maybe we play around with snacks and appetizers, things we can make look fun to prepare and eat. What do you think?"

"So now we're just snacking?"

"Matt…"

"So I still have to eat sad sandwiches to tide me over until we can create snacks. Is that what you're saying?"

She rolled her eyes and laughed. "You are seriously all about your stomach!"

"A man can't live on snacks alone," he countered playfully.

"I'll tell you what, we'll work on this concept and I promise you one solid meal a day. How does that sound?"

His grin was broad and made her tingle all over. "Sweetheart, I think this sounds like the beginning of a beautiful arrangement."

Yeah. That's what she was afraid of.

Chapter 5

MATT HAD TO ADMIT THIS ARRANGEMENT WITH VIVIENNE was damn near perfect. She might have originally agreed to one meal, but he'd managed to get two every day. Sometimes the meal she was preparing was for lunch and he'd just hang around talking about it and how she would present it on the blog until it was time for dinner. And she always took pity on him and invited him to stay for whatever she was making.

When her featured meal was for dinner, he pretended he'd forgotten and would show up at lunchtime and play on her sympathies. So far she hadn't called him out on it and he took it as a good sign. Plus, he was beginning to see she was becoming a lot more relaxed around him.

They still hadn't addressed the one topic he really wanted to—the kiss—but he was trying to earn her trust first.

Knocking lightly on her door, he let himself in. "Viv?"

"In my office," she called out.

Last night she had mentioned needing to get some editorial work done this morning, but he knew she was an early riser, and since it was nearing lunchtime, he was hoping she'd be ready for a break.

He stepped into her office and stopped. Her long hair was piled in a messy knot on top of her head, and she had on glasses and looked like she was still in her pajamas—an oversized T-shirt and flannel pants.

And she was breathtaking.

Vivienne looked up at him and smiled. "You're up early."

"It's almost noon," he replied with a grin.

She looked at him in confusion and then looked at her computer screen. "Oh! Wow, I completely lost track of time!" Standing up, she stretched.

"Did you get all of your work done?"

"Just about," she said, coming out from behind the desk. "I just need to send out the schedule to my bloggers, and then we should be good through the end of next week."

Matt stepped aside as she walked by, heading toward the kitchen. He quickly followed and found her pouring herself a glass of juice. "You want some?" she asked.

"No. I'm good." He watched her for a minute, finding her more and more intriguing by the minute.

When she noticed him watching her, she froze. "What?"

How could he possibly explain to her what he was seeing? He'd rarely been around a woman who was just so completely at ease in everything she did. She wasn't fussy or obsessed about how she looked or what she was wearing, and it was like a foreign concept to him. In the past five years or so, ever since they'd hit it big, most of the women he'd come in contact with were self-conscious and more than a little self-absorbed. But not Vivienne.

"I'm just standing here thinking that you are an incredible woman," he said honestly and noticed that she blushed.

She looked like she was going to say something but then didn't. She simply finished her drink and moved around the kitchen, putting the juice back in the refrigerator and the glass in the dishwasher. When she had nothing else to do, she turned and looked at him.

"It's true," he said, his voice a little gruff. "You're amazing. I look around and it's like there's nothing you can't do."

"That's not true," she protested softly.

"Not from where I'm standing. I saw the way you put this place together not so long ago and now look at it—it could be featured in one of those home decor magazines. You cook these amazing meals, you're an assistant editor of a popular online magazine, and on top of that, you're beautiful."

Vivienne's eyes went wide at his admission. "Matt…"

He stepped in close and noticed his hand shake as he reached up to caress her cheek. "You are." Her eyes slowly drifted closed as he touched her. "When I walked in, I was just… It's staggering to me how beautiful you are."

She reached up and held his hand against her cheek, her dark eyes opening and meeting his gaze.

Words simply escaped him. Looking at her face, staring into her eyes, felt more powerful to Matt than anything else he could possibly say. He already knew he was attracted to Vivienne—he had been from the first time he saw her the night she'd shown up at Aaron's for dinner. Hell, thinking back to the night she'd shown up backstage after the concert, he remembered how he'd thought she was his every fantasy come to life. But standing here and touching her now? It confirmed it all and Matt had no idea what to do about it.

Kiss her.

Yeah, that was the main thing screaming in his mind right now. To lower his head and claim her lips like he'd been dying to do all along would be his first choice, but unfortunately, he needed to think with his brain and not his—

"Matt." Slowly, Vivienne lowered her hand from his and took a step back. Clearing her throat, she turned her head and looked back toward the kitchen. "Um…I was just planning on making some tuna for lunch. I need to grab a shower and go food shopping, so I can stock the pantry for the week and get some last-minute ingredients for tonight's meal. So…why don't you come back in about a half an hour? I'll be showered by then and we can have lunch. Is that all right?"

She was nervous and rambling, and it made Matt smile. He could tease her or push her to acknowledge there was something simmering between them, but he was willing to wait it out. When the time came, he wanted Vivienne to be comfortable enough with him to admit it without him prompting her.

With a deep breath, he forced himself to smile and take his own step back. "That sounds good. I'm going to give Mick a call and see how things are going with Dylan."

"I thought you talked to Riley about that the other night. Do you think anything's changed?"

He shrugged. "He was arraigned and released on bail. Now they're looking into rehab facilities. I'm just curious where it's all at and to see if Dylan's all right. He hasn't been willing to talk to any of us, but I'm sure that didn't include Mick."

"How come?"

Matt let out a low chuckle. "Mick is a force of nature. You don't say no to him, and if you do, he finds a way to make you do what he wants anyway." He shook his head. "It's not always a bad thing. We may not like it at the time, but the man has a serious gift about knowing what we need even before we do."

"Yeah, right," she mumbled.

That's when it hit him—Vivienne had had her own run-in with Mick that night two years ago and it didn't go well. It would have been easy to simply pretend he hadn't heard her comment, but maybe it was the perfect segue. "He had no idea who you were that night, Viv. And while I'm definitely not condoning the way he handled things, I'm just as much to blame."

She almost looked shocked at his statement.

Matt took a cautious step toward her. "I should have stopped him. I should have reacted faster. In my defense, I was kind of messed up." Then he realized how pathetic he sounded. "I knew what I was doing with you, Vivienne. Don't ever doubt that. But when Mick barged in, I feel like everything happened so fast, and at the same time, I felt like I was walking in quicksand. Does that make sense?"

"It does," she said, nodding. "I hated the way it all happened. I was scared and embarrassed, and…I never told anyone about it."

His eyes went wide. "No one?"

"No one."

"I wanted to go after you—at the very least I was going to call Aaron and see if you were all right—but Mick kept me distracted, and by the next day, I started questioning if it had even happened at all, if you had really been there or if I'd imagined it."

Looking down at the floor, she nodded. "I don't even know what I was thinking, going there like that."

Closing the distance between them, he tucked a finger under her chin and gently guided her to look up at him. "I was glad you did. Seeing you…kissing you— it was amazing."

She let out a mirthless laugh. "Right. That's why you remembered it so well."

He immediately dropped his hand. "You have to know I was pretty much at my lowest when you saw me—with my partying and drinking. I started counseling a week later and other than an occasional beer or glass of wine, I don't drink anymore. I know it's not an excuse, and it doesn't make me look good, but there it is."

"I'm glad you got help, Matt. I really am. It's just…" She paused and sighed loudly. "It's really kind of humiliating to know I did that—which is so completely out of character for me—and then you didn't even remember it. I thought I was okay with it, that I was over it, and then you showed up here, and it brought it all back. Only…I couldn't say anything. First, because of Aaron, and second because…well…what was the point?" She shrugged.

"I am so sorry, Vivienne. Believe me, if I could, I would change everything about that night. I would have…locked the door. Or stood up to Mick and taken you with me. Hell, there are probably a dozen things I'd do differently, but I can't. The only thing I can do is apologize and hope we can move on from it." Frustration had his voice rising and with a sound of disgust, he stepped away and raked a hand through his hair. "I honestly don't know what else to say."

Vivienne studied him for a long time before letting out a loud, shaky breath of her own. "When you go back to Aaron's, can you see if he has any mayo? I'm running a little low." And then she turned and walked out of the room and Matt heard her footsteps going up the stairs. He stood rooted to the spot until he heard her bedroom door close.

With a muttered curse, he did the only thing he could do—went back across the yard into Aaron's house, and waited.

Standing under the hot spray, Vivienne had to keep reminding herself to breathe. Not only had Matt finally acknowledged their kiss, but he'd even gone so far as to apologize. For everything. She had sworn all along that it was what she was waiting for, what she needed so she could have some form of closure, but now that she did, it didn't feel nearly as satisfying.

What would have happened if Matt had locked the door and his manager hadn't gotten in? What if they hadn't been interrupted? What if she hadn't been physically escorted out of the building?

She shook her head—it was too late for all of those what-ifs. What was the point anyway? There was no way to go back and change anything, no matter how badly she wanted to. But oh…if she could. A long sigh came out before she could stop it, and she let her head fall back as the hot water cascaded over her. There wasn't a doubt in her mind she would have let Matt do whatever he wanted to with her that night.

Hell, she was just about ready to let him do whatever it was he wanted with her now.

"This is crazy," she murmured, forcing herself to focus on the shower. Grabbing her shampoo, she quickly washed her hair and applied conditioner. Taking another look around her large shower, she grabbed the bottle of body wash and lathered up from head to toe before rinsing and shutting off the water.

This bathroom was like her own mini-retreat, and she had done a ton of upgrades to make it that way—heated floors, heated towel racks—and at times like this, she appreciated those upgrades all the more. Wrapping herself in a towel, she made fast work of drying off and applying moisturizer everywhere before stepping into her bedroom to get dressed.

Jeans and a soft, jade-colored sweater were what she had already been planning on wearing. With or without having lunch with Matt, she was going out to go shopping and she felt it was important to put in at least a small effort to look put together. Not that she was one of those women who obsessed about her hair and makeup or wardrobe, but it was still important to Vivienne that she look nice.

Once dressed, she applied minimal makeup and pulled out the blow-dryer to get the bulk of the dampness out of her hair. With it being so long, it was a lengthy task. But today she was just going to let it go with as little fuss as possible and was thankful for its natural curl.

Looking at the clock, Vivienne knew Matt would be back any minute and she wanted to be downstairs when he arrived. She needed to be busy, to at least give the appearance of being busy, so she didn't do anything stupid like reaching out and touching him again. God, it had felt so good to have his hand caressing her cheek earlier. He had great hands.

"Oh sure, there's a way to stay focused on not touching him," she mumbled as she walked down the stairs. "Keep imagining his hands on you. Perfect."

Walking with purpose, she immediately went into the kitchen and sprang into action. Grabbing the tuna from the pantry, she quickly opened the cans and emptied them out into a strainer to drain. Next she grabbed some celery from the crisper and began chopping it. Normally she enjoyed a little onion in her tuna salad but opted against it this once. There was a fresh loaf of multigrain bread in her bread box she knew would be perfect for their sandwiches once it was toasted, and she grabbed it and cut several thick slices from it.

Right on time, Matt knocked on the door and walked in. Honestly, she wasn't even sure why he bothered knocking—he never waited for her to ask him in or even open the door herself.

"Aaron did have mayo, and I also brought over some chips. I know it's probably not something you'd pair with one of your sandwiches, but it's a personal favorite of mine."

She laughed and felt some of the tension leave her body. "I think it's perfect. It's been a long time since I had chips on the side." Glancing toward her refrigerator, she added, "Do me a favor and look in there and see if I have any pickles. We'll make these plates up like you would find in a traditional deli or diner."

"Yes!" Matt walked over and claimed victory as he lifted the glass jar over his head. "Although, if you didn't have any, I know Aaron does. I just saw them over there."

"Yes, but mine are going to be better," she teased.

Matt laughed with her and put the jar down on the counter. "Why? Because you buy better quality foods than your non-cooking bachelor brother?"

She smiled and winked. "Exactly."

"Maybe you should take pity on him and teach him how to do all of this."

"Are you kidding? And give away all my secrets?" she cried, feigning offense. "It's bad enough that you're getting to peek behind the curtain. I can't let everyone know how it's done."

Reaching over, Matt grabbed one of the unchopped celery stalks and took a bite out of it. "Don't worry. Your secrets are safe with me."

"Thank you."

They worked together to finish putting the sandwiches together, Matt toasting the bread while Vivienne seasoned and mixed the tuna. Within minutes, they were seated at the table and eating. Vivienne carefully considered her next words.

"So…would you like to come food shopping with me?"

Matt immediately choked on his food and began to cough. Vivienne reached over, patting his back until he was okay.

"You said you were free to go back to your regular life," she said nervously, even though she was going for light and breezy. "I know food shopping isn't something you would do in your normal life—you know, pre-Broadway—but it might be a nice way to ease yourself back out into the public eye."

He shook his head. "No."

"Why not?" She was seriously perplexed. To her, it

was the perfect plan. He'd be able to get out for a little bit without it being a major media event.

"I…I'm just not ready."

Vivienne put her sandwich down and stared at him. "Matt, I'm asking you to go to the grocery store, not a red-carpet event."

Meanwhile, he continued to eat as if she hadn't spoken a word.

"You can put on a baseball hat and glasses. If you try, I'm sure no one will even recognize you."

"Not gonna happen, Viv," he said around a mouthful of chips.

It was beyond frustrating, but she just wasn't sure what she could say to convince him to go. Rather than argue, she decided to let it go and change the subject. "Did you talk to Mick?"

Matt looked over at her with surprise, no doubt wondering why she let the argument go so quickly. Slowly, he nodded. "I did."

"And?"

He took a long drink from the can of soda he had brought over with him before responding. "Well, for starters, Dylan's in rehab."

"I thought that was a given."

Matt shook his head. "It was what was going to happen eventually, but there was a possibility of it taking some time to get him there."

"What changed?"

"I figured it was just Mick putting his foot down like he normally does, but he said Dylan didn't put up a fight at all. They found him a facility that is known to cater to celebrities—"

"That's just wrong," Vivienne muttered with disgust.

"I agree, but...that's the way it is. This place is secluded, has high security, and will guard Dylan's privacy while he's there."

"Sounds to me like it's probably a glorified spa." She threw down the chip she was about to eat. "So the guys in the car he hit are in the hospital and dealing with their injuries, and the big rock star gets to go and get coddled and massaged. Nice."

Matt rested his elbows on the table and glared at her. "Okay, first of all, that's a pretty big assumption you're making." His tone was firm and just a little bit hostile. "You have no idea what it's like to go through rehab for an addiction. Just because the place is upscale doesn't mean it's a damn cakewalk."

Shame filled her. He was right. She had no idea what it was like and it was wrong to pretend like she did. "You're right. I'm sorry. It was insensitive of me."

"Damn right it was," he snapped as he pushed away from the table and stood. "I was too damn scared to go into one of those facilities. Just the thought of being isolated and not having any control was enough to freak me out. I am so relieved Dylan is doing this and no one had to strong-arm him into it."

"Well—"

"Okay, I realize the accident and DUI charges were technically the same thing, but he still could have fought it."

"So what happens now? How long is he there for?"

With a shrug, he paced beside the table. "Not sure. It could be thirty days, it could be more. I think it all depends on how his recovery goes."

"And what about the charges? I'm sure there's going to be a civil suit brought against him by each of the guys in the other car. Will he have to go to court?"

"It's doubtful. He's not going to argue that he caused the accident. It would be pointless. There will be settlements and then…" He paused and shrugged again. "Then Dylan's going to have to stay on the straight and narrow."

"Any word on how badly injured the guys were?"

"Nothing life-threatening, thank God." Seemingly tired of pacing, Matt sat back down. "Broken bones, concussions. Luckily it was a fairly new car and had airbags on all sides. I think it could have been much worse."

"Still. It had to be very scary. And completely pointless—all because of alcohol."

Matt studied her for a long moment. "I know it sounds like an excuse, but it's part of the lifestyle. I know I partied way too much. At the time, I didn't even realize how much. Eventually, it finally registered, and I knew it wasn't how I wanted to live my life. I've seen what it can do to people, what it was doing to me, and that was enough to make me want to quit. But while you're on the road, it's everywhere. Not everyone can resist it. I went on the wagon completely and it was hard to keep saying no when it was being offered all around me. Eventually I learned to drink in moderation, and it's working for me."

"What about Dylan?"

"Dylan drank. It's what he was known for—he was always the partier in the band, and he sort of liked the reputation that went with it." He sighed. "I knew that eventually it was going to come to something like this."

"So it's a good thing he's getting the help," she said

because she didn't know what else to say. It was true she'd never had any unhealthy vices, and for the life of her, she'd never understood how people allowed themselves to become addicted to anything, but she could hear the pain in Matt's voice and knew his concern was real. "Maybe at some point you can talk to Dylan. You can encourage him."

"Maybe," he said and picked up his sandwich. After taking a bite, he threw it back down and looked over at Vivienne again. "I lied."

"Excuse me?" Her stomach clenched at his words, the somber tone.

Shifting around in his chair, Matt rested his arms on the edge of the table. "I really did quit drinking because I didn't like who I had become."

"O-kay…"

"But…it's not the only reason."

Her heart began to hammer in her chest. Vivienne knew that nothing as drastic as what Dylan was dealing with had happened to Matt. She would have heard about it—if not through the media, then at least from Aaron.

His green eyes darkened as he continued to look at her. "I thought I had hallucinated," he said, his voice low and gruff. "After the night you showed up, I thought I had imagined it. Mick wouldn't talk about it and it just seemed like…it never happened. It was there, like on the edge of my consciousness and yet…I couldn't fully remember." He took a moment to take another sip of his drink. "I'd never blacked out from drinking. I'd never forgotten anything—until that night. That's when I knew I'd had enough."

"So you just…stopped?"

He shook his head. "I'm oversimplifying it, but the bottom line is the same. That night was a turning point for me. I stumbled and I screwed up a few times, but in the end I knew I was heading in the right direction."

Wow. Again, what could she possibly say to that? Part of Vivienne was relieved she played some small part in Matt getting sober, but…it did little to make her feel better about the whole thing. She shook her head. It was enough. She had to let it go. They could talk about it and rehash it until they were blue in the face and it wasn't going to do a thing for her. So she did the only thing she could do.

"I forgive you, Matt," she said quietly.

He looked at her in stunned silence and continued to do so until Vivienne started to squirm in her seat.

"The way things happened that night doesn't make me feel particularly proud—of either of us. But there's no point in continuing to hash it out. I think I can say with certainty that I have a better understanding of it all and I'd like to put it behind us." She took a deep breath before saying, "And start over."

Matt continued to silently stare at her.

"Please say something," she prompted nervously, chewing on her bottom lip.

"I…I don't know if I can do that."

A nervous chuckle came out before she could stop it. "What, you mean you don't know if you can say anything?"

He shook his head. "I don't know if I can start over."

Vivienne was completely confused. "Why not? I think it would be a good thing. For both of us."

"I disagree," he said, resting his elbows on the table so he could lean his cheek in the palm of his hand.

"I don't understand why—"

"I kind of like where we are right now. I don't want to pretend the past didn't happen. I'm enjoying the banter we have and the way I find it so easy to talk to you. I think if we ignore that night, that kiss, then we're both denying a part of who we are."

Well, damn. That was a pretty powerful declaration, she thought. "But…it wasn't me that night," she argued. "I honestly don't know why I did any of it. This is who I am," she said, patting herself on the chest. "I'm an introvert who likes things neat and orderly. I hate chaos, and I plan out everything. I hate leaving anything to chance, and I rarely take risks. I like my world to be predictable and organized. I make lists, and I like to check things off. The person you're remembering doesn't really exist."

"Again, I disagree."

"Ugh," she groaned and stood to clear the table. "Do you deliberately go out of your way to make things difficult all the damn time?"

Matt stood and helped her with the dishes. "Viv, I'm not trying to make anything difficult. If anything, I'm simplifying things. You came to see me. We kissed. We didn't see each other for a while. Now we're both here and we kissed again." He placed the dishes in the dishwasher before turning and looking at her again. "And, if we're completely honest for the sake of keeping things simple, we're both still attracted to one another."

Great. She wanted to stamp her foot and tell him to leave, but she would only be proving his point. So now what?

"I…I don't know what it is you want me to say to

that," she admitted. And if she wasn't mistaken, he almost looked pleased.

"What I want is for you to tell me I'm not wrong, that this isn't all completely one-sided." Before she could answer, however, he started speaking again. "But I'll understand if you're not ready to yet. I can be patient, Vivienne, and I believe you're worth waiting for."

And then, in a move that took her totally by surprise, Matt leaned down and placed a whisper-soft kiss on her cheek before stepping back. "I know you have some shopping to do and errands to run. I'm going to go back over to Aaron's and relax and maybe watch a little TV. When you're ready to start working on dinner, let me know, and I'll come over and help."

All Vivienne could do was nod and watch him walk out the door.

—∿∿—

Three days.

Three days since he'd pretty much bared his soul to her and nothing had changed. Well…not really.

There was a bit more ease between them, like they were truly becoming friends, but rather than making Matt happy, he was beginning to feel like he had misread the entire situation. And while he'd had every intention at the time of being patient and waiting until Vivienne was comfortable with admitting she wanted him just as much as he wanted her, he hadn't counted on her hold-ing him to it.

He had figured she'd leave that afternoon and go shopping and do whatever it was she had to do, and by the time they got back together for dinner, she'd tell him she didn't want to wait. He had pretty much visualized the entire interaction right down to taking her up to her bedroom and peeling her out of her jeans and the sweater that had been making him crazy all through lunch.

Black lace.

He'd envisioned her in scraps of black lace under her clothes and he was going to gently, almost reverently, remove her bra—and then tear her panties from her body. And the entire time, Vivienne was going to tell him how much she'd wanted him and couldn't wait any longer.

But had she? No.

They'd made dinner and talked about upcoming menu ideas and how she would present them in the magazine and on the blog. She asked about his favorite kinds of burgers and snacks. Then there was talk about sauces and condiments, spices and drinks. The more she talked about food, the more he began to realize just how seriously she took her job. She wasn't looking at their time together as just for fun and hanging out; it was all business.

And definitely no pleasure.

And Matt was ready to lose his mind.

Patience be damned. Tonight he was going to turn the tables on her. Sort of. They had talked earlier about getting takeout for dinner—one of her writers backed out of an article, so Vivienne was writing it herself—and she wasn't in the mood to cook. Matt had agreed but after coming back to Aaron's, he had rummaged around and found a couple of really nice steaks in the freezer. Not everything Aaron had stocked was for cooking in the microwave, and Matt wasn't a complete idiot. He knew how to grill, and he could easily handle a couple of baked potatoes and a salad.

Hopefully.

A quick glance at the clock showed it was almost five. He knew her schedule fairly well—and knew she was a creature of habit—so he was confident she'd be walking over in the next few minutes to discuss what they were going to order. He looked at the platter on the kitchen counter with pride. He had seasoned the steaks and they were ready to go on the grill. The potatoes were in the oven, and the salad was prepped and in the refrigerator.

And while he knew the saying was "the way to a man's heart was through his stomach," he was kind of counting on it working the other way around. Since Vivienne was a foodie, he hoped he could impress her by cooking a meal for her.

Right on cue, there was a knock on the back door, and he heard Vivienne call out to him.

"In here," he replied, standing next to his surprise.

"So I was thinking Chinese would probably be—" She stopped when she spotted him. Matt couldn't help but grin at the look of surprise on her face. "What... what's this?"

"You've been cooking for me for well over a week now, and I thought it might be nice if I returned the favor." When she started to speak, he held up a hand to stop her. "Now I'm not saying this meal will be anywhere near as amazing as what you can do, but I enjoy making steaks on the grill whenever I'm home or on a break from touring. I thought it might be a nice change of pace for you to let someone else do the work."

He was feeling pretty confident until he noticed the tears in her eyes.

"Oh shit! Oh...Viv," he began nervously. Closing the distance between them, he gently grasped her shoulders. "I...I'm sorry! I didn't mean to upset you. I thought I was doing something nice and... Oh God... please don't cry!"

Vivienne let out a small laugh before leaning forward and wrapping her arms around him and hugging him tight.

"Um...Viv?"

"I'm not upset, Matt," she said and then pulled back to look up at him. "I am so incredibly touched you would do this." Reaching up, she wiped her tears away. "No one has ever offered to cook for me. I think I scare people, and they think they have to compete or something. But honestly, no one has ever done something this thoughtful. Thank you."

For a minute, he wasn't sure if she was being serious or not, but after watching the way her smile lit up the room, he realized she was, and it filled him with pride.

He'd done that.

He, Matt Reed, had made Vivienne Forrester smile.

And it was a beautiful thing.

"Is there anything I can do to help?" she asked, looking around the kitchen.

"Nope," he replied confidently. "No, wait... I'm lying. You can pour yourself a glass of wine and then join me outside while I grill. I know how much you enjoy eating out on the deck and the weather is being cooperative."

"It sounds wonderful." Doing as he asked, she poured herself some wine from the bottle he'd left out to breathe and then followed him outside. Once seated, she took a long sip and sighed.

And then giggled.

Matt looked over his shoulder at her. "What's so funny?"

"I'm sorry. I just can't believe this is happening." She giggled again.

He looked at her in confusion.

"I can't believe Matty Reed, world-famous rock star, is grilling a steak for me!" Another fit of giggles. "It just doesn't feel real."

After adjusting the flame on the grill, Matt put the platter down beside it and turned to face her. "First of all, that's ridiculous. And second of all, I don't want you to look at this that way."

She instantly sobered. "I...I didn't mean to offend you, Matt."

He walked over to her and braced his arms on her chair, essentially caging her in. "I don't want you looking at this like Matty Reed is doing anything. That's not who I am. That guy? He isn't here, and he hasn't been since I showed up here with Aaron. I'm Matt. I'm the guy you grew up with." His expression was fierce, he knew it, and when Vivienne's eyes widened, he almost regretted his little outburst.

"Okay," she said, her voice a little breathless. "That's good."

"Yeah," he said, his voice a little gruff. His gaze zeroed in on her lips and it took every ounce of strength he had not to close the distance between them and kiss her. "Why?"

She swallowed hard and met his heated gaze. "Because I don't want to be with that guy. I can't say I particularly like Matty Reed. But you, Matt? I like being with you."

Damn. Did she have any idea what her admission did to him? Everything in him went hot and he knew it wouldn't be long before she'd notice exactly how her words affected him.

"That's good, Viv," he said. "Because I like being with you. And I want…" He leaned in a little closer. "I need…" His lips were mere inches from hers. A hissing sound came from the grill and Matt cursed. How impressive would it be if he burned dinner? Slowly pushing himself away from her, he walked over to the grill and flipped the steaks over before excusing himself to get their place settings and check on the potatoes.

Once inside the kitchen, he had a brief, yet firm, mental talk with himself. So far the night was going exactly as he'd hoped. Vivienne was clearly relaxing around him and she was enjoying his surprise dinner. And if Matt was honest with himself, he'd have to say he was having a lot more fun making this meal than he'd thought possible. Maybe it was because of all the things Vivienne had been teaching him about food, or maybe it was because he knew he was pleasing her. Either way, he never knew dinner, especially one prepared by him, could almost be considered foreplay.

The oven timer beeped, and he walked to shut it off and grab the foil-wrapped potatoes from the oven. On the counter, he had a tray prepared that had the plates and silverware as well as a basket for the potatoes and small bowls of butter and sour cream. Not wanting to be away from the grill much longer, he quickly picked up the tray, stepped back outside, and placed it on the table.

"Here," Vivienne said as she rose to her feet. "Let me set this stuff up while you check the steaks."

Matt wasn't going to argue. He lifted the lid on the gas grill and saw the steaks looked damn near perfect and he chuckled.

"What's so funny?"

He looked over his shoulder at Vivienne and grinned. "I was just wishing we had your camera. I think these babies look good enough to go on the blog!"

She walked over and nodded in agreement right before pulling her cell phone from her pocket and tapping the camera app.

"Viv," he began even as he laughed. "I was just kidding."

"Nonsense," she said, clicking a few pictures. "They are very impressive and I think this meal should be documented. After all, no one's ever cooked for me, so even if we don't put it on the blog, I'd like to have the pictures for my scrapbook."

That simple statement felt like the greatest compliment in the world. Matt had been revered as a musician, had accepted Grammys and been interviewed by enough reporters—most of whom spent a decent amount of time praising his work and his talents—but knowing Vivienne wanted to put a picture of the steaks he made for her in her personal scrapbook? Yeah, it was better than all his awards combined. And damn if he wasn't getting choked up.

Shaking it off, he quickly turned off the flame and put the steaks on the platter. "I, um…I just need to go inside and get the salad and—"

"I'll go get it," Vivienne said, "and I'll grab the rest of the wine." She looked around at the table. "What are you drinking?"

Normally he would have joined her in a glass of wine, but tonight he wanted to be one hundred percent sober. Not that a simple glass of wine would change that, but if the night went the way he was hoping it would, he wanted to know he was in complete control of his senses.

"Water with lemon, please," he finally said. "There's a pitcher in the refrigerator and I sliced some lemon earlier that's on the shelf beside it. Thanks."

Two minutes later, they were seated at the table. Vivienne's smile was brilliant, and she was practically bouncing in her seat. "Everything looks wonderful, Matt." She rubbed her hands together excitedly. "Can we start? Is it okay if I just dig in?"

He couldn't help but chuckle. "Be my guest," he said, but then quickly added, "just…please don't be disappointed if it's not that good. I mean…I haven't had a whole lot of practice like you with preparing a meal."

She instantly dropped the knife and fork she had just picked up and looked at him. "Seriously? You too?"

"What? What did I say?"

She frowned and sunk in her seat and if Matt wasn't mistaken, she looked…hurt.

"Viv?"

"I told you. People don't like to cook for me or invite me over for a meal because they're intimidated. But you know what? I don't compare! I don't sit down to a meal and critique it or think about how I can make it differently or better or…anything! I just simply enjoy sitting down to a good meal with friends. Do you know how frustrating it is that people automatically assume I'm going to grade them or give them a score on their cooking?"

"Well, I didn't say you were going to score it, but—"

"But nothing," she said, sitting up straight again. Her expression was fierce. "You listen to me, Matt Reed. I am thrilled you wanted to cook for me. And I wouldn't care if the steaks were charred and the potatoes undercooked and the salad was wilted. I love that you did this for me."

And then, without another word, she picked up her silverware again, cut into her steak, and took her first bite.

Matt found himself holding his breath. He heard everything she had just said and part of him began to wonder if the steaks were overcooked or the potatoes undercooked, and he was eyeing the salad suspiciously.

"Holy shit is that good," she moaned. "Wow." Her head fell back and her eyes closed as she continued to chew. "There is nothing like a good steak."

If the scrapbook comment hadn't already tugged at his heart, listening to her moan with delight certainly did that—and more.

———

It was almost midnight and Vivienne could not remember the last time she had laughed so much or had such a good time.

After they had finished eating dinner, they had cleaned up and then gone back inside Aaron's, where Matt had shown off his improved piano skills. She had to admit it, she was impressed. It was obvious he was practicing and taking it seriously, and she praised his efforts. It seemed to be the theme of the night—praising him.

In the years since Vivienne had first started dating, she'd dated her fair share of men. But Matt was definitely the first one who seemed to really hone in on who she was and what would impress her.

And she was the first to admit she wasn't easily impressed.

From the dinner to the conversation and even to the music he had played on the piano, it all just seemed to flow with all of the things she was interested in and enjoyed. She had to give him props—he was clearly very observant.

They were now sitting on the sofa in the living room, and Matt was telling her about the time the band had been on tour in England and met Princes William and Harry.

"Seriously? You got to meet them both?"

Matt nodded. "They were really quite cool. I was expecting them to be a little prim and stuffy, but they were the kind of guys you'd want to hang out with. It was really impressive."

"Wow. So...who's the most famous person you've met so far?"

Raking a hand through his hair, Matt leaned back against the corner of the sectional. "We've met pretty much everyone in the music business it seems. Sometimes it's just a quick greeting and other times it's at shows or events. I think the princes though are at the top of my list."

"Really? So there's no musician out there that you're completely starstruck by?"

"Well, sure. Hell, what musician wouldn't get a little emotional by meeting Robert Plant or Jimmy Page? Mick Jagger? I mean, I've met them all and definitely got a little tongue-tied, but luckily I didn't make a complete idiot out of myself."

"Do you ask for autographs?" she asked teasingly.

"Hell no," he laughed. "You can't do something like that and hold on to your dignity."

She waved him off, joining him in his laughter. "Who cares about dignity? I would love to have something signed by one of those guys!"

He looked at her with disbelief. "Seriously? Page, Plant, and Jagger? Come on, Viv. I picture you being more of a Lady Gaga or Taylor Swift kind of girl."

"Hey!" she said with mock outrage and then started laughing again. "Okay, fine. I pretty much have all of Taylor's songs on my iPod, but I really like classic rock too!"

With a wink and a halfhearted okay sign, he nodded and reached for his glass of water.

"It's true!" she protested.

"It's okay, Viv," he said, his tone playfully mollifying. "I think Taylor Swift is extremely talented, and she's a very nice young woman."

She glared at him. "You're mocking me."

"I bet if I asked you to, you could probably play a couple of her songs on the piano."

Dammit. She could, she thought.

"And I'd also have to say you probably couldn't play one Zeppelin or Stones song." He shrugged and finished his drink. "But that's okay."

"All right, mister," she said, jumping to her feet. "That's it." Storming across the room, Vivienne pulled out the piano bench and sat down before taking a deep breath. It wasn't like her to let herself be challenged into playing music—she'd had enough poking and prodding from her parents while growing up—but right now it was important for her to prove she had an eclectic taste in music.

Doing a quick stretch of her fingers, she gently placed them on the keys and began to play the Rolling Stones classic "Angie." Midway through, and without once looking at Matt to see his reaction, she switched over to the Zeppelin classic "All of My Love." Both were more ballad than hard rock and left her feeling a little uninspired. With very little effort, she segued into a rendition of "Lola" by the Kinks. By this time, she felt like she had made her point but decided she needed a finale.

She went with Taylor Swift's "Shake It Off."

The sound of Matt's laughter made her smile, and with all the flair she could muster, she ran her hands along the keys from one end of the piano to the other before standing and saying, "Good night, North Carolina!"

Matt jumped up and gave her a hearty round of applause even as he continued to laugh. "Holy crap, Viv. That was freaking awesome! Brilliant! Inspired!"

She took her bow, walked over to the coffee table, picked up her wineglass, and finished the little bit that was left in it. "Geez, I don't know how you do that for almost two hours at a shot. I'm exhausted!" She fell back dramatically onto the sofa, sighed, and felt more than heard Matt move closer.

"Imagine doing that with a hundred hot lights shining on you," he said softly, gently combing her hair away from her face.

It felt nice. Soothing. And Vivienne knew if she opened her eyes and looked at him, she'd be completely lost. Why she was still fighting this attraction, she had no idea. It was a lost cause. Every time Matt smiled at her, her heart beat faster. Every time he touched her, her body seemed to go up in flames. It was no longer a matter of if she was going to sleep with Matt but when.

Funny how that all just came to her right then and there.

"I couldn't do it," she forced herself to say, remembering he had sort of asked a question. "My makeup would melt, my hair would frizz—too much stress."

Beside her, he chuckled softly, his hands still caressing her cheek. "And you'd still look beautiful."

"Maybe from a distance," she said, doing her best to keep her eyes closed and not give in to the urge to look at him. Not yet.

"From any distance," he said, his voice going lower, gruffer, and it almost made Vivienne shiver. "And every man in the room wouldn't be able to take his eyes off of you."

It was on the tip of her tongue to protest, but she liked this game—the pretending. The compliments. All of it. "I don't know," she said quietly. "A guy in a pair of ripped jeans who takes off his shirt because he's all sweaty is hot."

He chuckled again, and this time Vivienne could feel his breath on her skin. "Same could be said about a woman whipping off her top. I don't think you'd hear any complaints. Especially if the woman was you and I was in the audience."

"Oh," she said, her voice now almost a whisper. "I couldn't possibly whip off my shirt for a complete audience."

"How about an audience of one?"

A slow smile played at her lips and she gave up the

fight. Her eyes fluttered open and she found Matt to be impossibly close—so close she could see the flecks of gold in his green eyes, could almost count his incredibly long lashes. Vivienne swallowed hard.

This was it.

There was no going back.

And she really didn't want to.

Slowly, her hand reached up and touched the stubble on Matt's jaw. She watched as his eyes closed briefly at her caress. Her name came out as a whispered plea.

There were no more questions and she didn't feel nervous. All she felt was anticipation.

"Matt…"

His eyes opened again and focused on her. Vivienne's hand raked up into his hair as she carefully guided his head down to hers—not that he had far to go.

Breaths mingled, and she moistened her lips right before she felt him stop moving. Confusion threatened to overwhelm her and she looked at him questioningly.

"Be sure, Vivienne," he said. "No one's coming through that door to take you away from me this time, and I don't think I'll survive it if you walk away from me again."

She knew exactly how he felt because there was no way she'd be able to walk away from him again.

"I'm very sure," she said, her voice a little bolder than it had been a minute ago. "Matt?"

"Hmm?"

"Kiss me."

He leaned in and rested his forehead against hers. "Sweetheart, I thought you'd never ask."

Chapter 6

MATT THOUGHT HE WAS READY.

Had been telling himself just that all damn day.

But the reality of it? It didn't even come close.

Their first kiss two years ago had been fairly wild. Their second kiss had been equally frantic—mainly because it was laced with anger. At least on his end. But this kiss? Hell, Matt couldn't remember a kiss ever being like this.

He didn't pounce; he didn't plunder. It started out soft—almost chaste. And then? *Wow*. It was as if he and Vivienne were of one mind as they slowly sank into it. They each moved a little closer, and Matt wrapped her in his embrace, and both her hands now cupped his face. Her skin was so soft, and he knew the stubble on his chin was rough against it, but she didn't seem to mind.

Every time he had let himself imagine this moment— the time when Vivienne would be in his arms and want to be there—he had thought he'd instantly scoop her up into his arms and carry her to bed before she had the chance to change her mind. He imagined it being fast and wild, and it was totally in keeping with the way he tended to enjoy things. But as Vivienne's soft lips moved against his, as her tongue gently swiped across his bottom lip, he knew he would stay right there for as long as possible because it felt that good.

He couldn't help but smile as Vivienne shifted and moved over so she could straddle his lap.

All thoughts of scooping her up and going anywhere vanished. He was pretty content to do whatever it was she wanted right here.

With his hands stroking up and down her back, Vivienne pressed closer to him, the feel of her luscious curves slowly making him insane. He wanted to feel her skin. He wanted to lay her down so he could touch her everywhere.

She let out a sexy little moan when his hands came around to cup her breasts, and the only thing Matt could think of was making her make that sound again.

His lips left hers to travel along her cheek and jaw. Vivienne's head fell back with a breathy sigh as he nipped and licked the slender column of her throat. She tasted so sweet—everywhere his mouth traveled was like a little taste of heaven, and he wanted more.

More skin.

More sounds.

More everything.

Vivienne seemed to be on the same page because she was moving again, doing her best to lie down on the sofa with Matt on top of her. It didn't take long to accomplish, and once she was stretched out underneath him, he groaned at the rightness.

Slowly, he lifted his head, staring down at her beautiful face that was flushed, her eyes slightly glazed, and smiled. "You feel really good here, Viv," he murmured.

Her arms came up around him, and she gave him a sexy grin. "You feel really good yourself."

"As much as I'm enjoying this, I'd like to take this to

the bedroom—stretch you out on my bed and keep you there all night." He bent down and gave her another lengthy kiss before lifting his head again. "What do you say?"

"Only all night?"

Damn. His smile broadened. "For starters."

It was on the tip of his tongue to say he wanted to keep her there much, much longer, possibly forever, but it scared the shit out of him. He stood up, held out his hand to her, and then led her out of the room and down the hall. When she stepped into his bedroom, he shut the door and watched, mesmerized, as Vivienne crawled onto the bed and then turned to face him.

Yeah, forever scared the shit out of him but he was definitely warming up to the idea.

—◆◆◆—

It was still dark when Vivienne woke up. Matt was completely wrapped around her, and it felt glorious. She hated to wake him, but she was thirsty and really needed something to drink. Carefully, she tried to maneuver out of his arms and wasn't surprised when they tightened around her.

He was restless, moving around a little as his head tossed to the side and murmuring incoherently. Was he having a nightmare? she wondered. Should she wake him?

Softly, she whispered his name.

Matt held her impossibly closer. "Don't go," he murmured.

"I just want to get something to drink," she said softly, turning to look at him. Her eyes had adjusted to the darkness, and she reached out to cup his cheek. "I won't be gone long."

"I'm coming with you," he said sleepily right before yawning loudly, seemingly anxious to get out of the bed.

She chuckled. "I think I can make it to the kitchen safely. Stay here where it's warm and cozy and wonderful."

"It won't be any of those things if you're not here with me."

Well, that was pretty damn sweet, she thought. Beside her, he rolled over and she felt him getting up from the bed.

"I'm just going to turn on this light and—"

"No! Don't!" she cried, but it was too late. The brightness was momentarily blinding and she covered her eyes. "Damn."

"Yeah. I know."

When she looked up, he was pulling on the jeans he had discarded earlier, and then he bent down and grabbed his T-shirt and handed it to her. "Thank you."

Matt walked around the bed and reached for her hand and together they went to the kitchen. He handed her a bottle of water and then grabbed one for himself, each drinking deeply before saying anything. In the dim light of the kitchen, his mind raced. This was a fairly new experience for him. For starters, he'd never spent an entire night with a woman and never invited one into his home.

Technically this was Aaron's home, but for the time being, it was his.

Studying Vivienne's face, he saw uncertainty there and he had to wonder if she was thinking about leaving. Putting his glass down, he walked to her, cupped her face in his hands and kissed her until they were both breathless. When he lifted his head, he met her gaze and said, "Stay."

She gave him a small, sexy grin. "I wasn't planning on leaving."

Relief flooded him, a reaction he was beginning to see as a pattern where Vivienne was concerned.

In previous relationships—and he used that term loosely—he had been the one in control, the confident one. But he was finding that now, with Vivienne, she ultimately was the one calling the shots. Matt wouldn't push her; he wouldn't rush her. He'd let her set the pace for where they went from here.

For the first time in a long time, he felt a little insecure, a little vulnerable. For all of his celebrity, right there, in that moment, he was just a man. He already knew that Vivienne wasn't with him because of who he was onstage; it was because of the person he was standing before her. And he had to wonder if that was enough. If he was enough.

"You're looking pretty fierce," Vivienne said softly, reaching up to smooth the creases on his forehead. "You okay?"

"I was just thinking about how amazing you are."

"Matt…"

"And I can't believe someone like you would want to be with someone like me," he said, his voice like gravel.

She took a small step back. "Why would you say something like that?"

Hell. Why had he gone and said something like that?

Without answering, he took her by the hand and led her back to the bedroom. She protested slightly at first, but Matt simply guided her until they were lying back on the bed.

What he was going to say could possibly lead to Vivienne getting dressed and going home, but in his heart, Matt felt like there were things that needed to be said, needed to be addressed, so they could move forward. He didn't want there to be any secrets between them and part of him needed to know that she knew exactly what she was dealing with where he was concerned.

He kept their hands linked together as he began to talk. "I wish we weren't here in your brother's house. I thought about that earlier. I thought maybe it would have been better if we had gone across the yard to your place."

"Why?"

"In my mind, I kept thinking how I wanted this to be perfect—our first time." He gave a small shrug. "It sounds a little ridiculous, I know, but…" He looked up and met her steady gaze. "I never brought a woman home with me. Ever. But you? I wanted to bring you home."

She smiled. "And where is home?"

"Hell if I know," he muttered. "I sold my place in LA and was renting the condo in Manhattan." He rolled onto his back and let out a sigh of frustration. "I guess I was looking for something I can't have. How screwed up is that?"

Without saying a word, she lay down beside him and rested her head on his shoulder.

Matt pulled her close, kissed the top of her head. "I haven't thought about having a home in a while. I mean, I've had houses, and they were places I stopped and hung out while on a break from touring. Then I look at what Aaron's done here and what you did with the guesthouse, and I want that. I've spent a lot of time in this house in the last two weeks, and I see the pictures, the personal touches he has in every room, and then I think about my place in LA. There was nothing of mine there. Seventeen rooms, and someone else decorated it and told me what I'd want to look at while I was there. God, what was I thinking?"

"You had other things on your mind," she said simply. "Not everyone takes to the concept of making a house a home right out of the gate. You never saw where Aaron was living before he built this place."

He chuckled. "No, I didn't."

"It was awful. He purchased a condo in Wilmington, right near downtown. It had a very industrial vibe, and he loved the exposed HVAC and the concrete floors. And I have to admit, when I first saw the place, before he moved in, I thought it had potential."

"So what happened?"

"He pretty much treated it more like a garage than a home. His furniture was all mismatched; he kept his bike in the entryway and had his treadmill in the middle of the living room." She groaned. "It was your typical bachelor pad, and it used to make me crazy to go there. I wanted to move things around and organize it, but Aaron wouldn't let me."

"That sounds about right. The places I've owned were always organized and done beautifully, but they felt very cold and sterile. No personality. I want that."

"Then you should do it." She placed a light kiss on his chest.

"I wouldn't even know where to begin."

Propping herself up on her elbow so she could face

him, Vivienne smiled. "Pictures. That's always a good place to start. Childhood pictures or pictures from your tours or places you've been. Surround yourself with things that make you smile."

He reached up and caressed her cheek. "You make me smile."

She blushed. "Some of my favorite pictures are the ones from when Aaron and I were little. I have a picture in my office of me and my grandfather. I was four, and it was Easter, and I was wearing a frilly, pink dress." She smiled again. "He was a giant to me, my grandfather. I used to love spending time with him. We would have tea parties, and he'd carry me around on his shoulders, and I always looked forward to our Sunday dinners as a family."

Growing up, Matt remembered being envious of Aaron's family, mainly because he had one and Matt didn't. Not really.

Vivienne looked at him, her head tilted as if she was considering her next words. "Tell me a good childhood memory."

His eyes went wide for a moment. That wasn't what he'd been expecting her to say. "I…I don't think I have any."

"Of course you do. It doesn't have to be something big or a special occasion, just something that when you think about it, it makes you smile."

Shit. Why couldn't they have just gotten naked and made love again? There was nothing sexy about this conversation, and if anything, it was making him regret his earlier thoughts of wanting to spend the whole night together. When she softly said his name, Matt sighed.

"Before my mom left, when I was around eight, we used to go on movie dates once a month." He took a deep breath. It had been a long time since he'd allowed himself to think about his past. "We'd go to the local theater—remember the one off of Fairway Oaks?—and she'd make it a dinner date. We'd get hot dogs and popcorn and candy and soda. It was like every kid's dream meal." He chuckled. "And when the movie was over, we'd spend the ride home critiquing the movie like we were Siskel and Ebert."

He could feel Vivienne's smile as she rested her head back on his chest. "That sounds like a lot of fun."

Matt nodded. "It was."

"Do you still like going to the movies?"

"I have no idea. I haven't gone to a theater in years. With Netflix and being able to watch pretty much anything on demand, there really hasn't been a reason to."

"What about just for the fun of it? The experience?"

He shrugged. "Never seemed to be the time."

"Did your dad take you after your mom left?"

"Yeah right," he murmured with a mirthless laugh. "The old man didn't want anything to do with me. He blamed me for all that was wrong in his life."

Beside him, she gasped and raised her head again. "What?"

Now they had crossed the line into a territory he never wanted to talk about. Going for a distraction, Matt maneuvered them until she was beneath him, his hand on her bare hip. "That's a story that is guaranteed not to make me smile, and…" He stopped and gently nipped at her throat. "I'd much rather be touching you and kissing you."

She purred and wrapped her arms around him.

Could it be this easy? Was she capable of letting the topic go that fast? He seriously hoped so. But just to make sure, he ran his hand from her hip to her knee and guided her leg around his hip. The fabric of his jeans was probably a little rough against her soft skin, but he'd deal with that soon enough. Right now, it was more important to touch her and keep touching her until the only thing she could think about was him and how good he was making her feel.

～～～

Exhaustion.

But of the very best kind.

That was Vivienne's first thought when she woke up. She and Matt had slept very little and she wasn't the least bit sorry about it. Normally she was a girl who enjoyed—no, loved—a good night's sleep, but she'd gladly give that up if it meant experiencing the kind of pleasure she'd found in Matt's arms.

Wow.

She had to fight a smile as she realized how lackluster her sex life had been up until this point. All along she'd thought it was good—perfectly enjoyable—but she knew now she'd only been fooling herself. And now it was official—Matt Reed had ruined her for other men.

And as she stretched and came up against his warm body, she didn't even have the strength to care.

There wasn't a doubt in her mind that this was a temporary arrangement—no doubt Matt would be getting antsy soon to return to his regular life back in the spotlight, back with the band and back to touring. Playing music and being on the road and in the spotlight was a large part of who he was. And if that didn't send him packing soon, Vivienne had a feeling that once Aaron was back home, this new turn in their relationship would end.

A sad reality for sure.

Pushing those negative thoughts aside, she decided she would be okay with it. She was a realist if nothing else, and she knew sleeping with someone did not lead to forever and happily ever after. Sometimes relationships simply had an expiration date—some sooner than others—and as long as she didn't lose sight of that fact, she knew she would be all right.

Maybe.

Hopefully.

Rolling over, she snuggled against him and was pleased when Matt's arms immediately embraced her and pulled her close.

"Good morning," he murmured.

"Mmm…yes it is."

He chuckled. "Glad I'm not the only one thinking that way." He kissed the top of her head before looking over at the bedside clock. "Wow…this is probably downright decadent for you. It's after ten."

She playfully smacked his arm as she laughed. "So I'm an early riser. It's not a crime."

"Oh, I know it's not, but I'm just wondering how often you allow yourself to stay in bed and forget about your schedule."

Damn. She did have some things she needed to do today.

"I ruined it, didn't I?" he asked.

"What are you talking about?"

"I reminded you that real life is waiting outside the

door, and now you're worried about all the stuff you have to do."

It was kind of impressive how he seemed to know her so well. Or was she just that transparent?

"I do have some stuff that needs my attention today," she began and then started placing tiny kisses on his chest, "but not my immediate attention."

Matt groaned as he fisted his hand in her long hair, effectively holding her to him. "That feels so good."

Lightly running her tongue over his nipple, she smiled as he hissed. "You taste pretty good too."

"Viv…"

"Shh," she said, moving so she was on top, and then further silenced him with a kiss that was deep and wet and full of promise. When she lifted her head, she smiled at the look of pure pleasure on his face.

One of his hands skimmed down her back until it rested right above her bottom. She liked it—it felt warm, a little rough, and very possessive.

A girl could get used to this, she thought.

Leaning back down, she continued kissing his jaw, his throat, and then she returned to his chest, loving the feel of him moving beneath her.

She should have been sated.

Hell, at the very least, she should be sore and ready for a bit of a break.

But one feel of Matt's arousal pressing against her belly and all Vivienne could think was, *More*.

Matt hissed her name as she moved above him, sliding along the hardened length of him. "What is it you want, baby?" he asked, his voice gruff.

"You," she replied honestly. "I want more of you."

"You have me. All of me."

And right before he slid back inside of her, all Vivienne could think was, *But for how long?*

———

Two days later, Vivienne found Matt sitting on the sofa in Aaron's living room, strumming his guitar. It was almost noon on a Tuesday, and she had a little bit of a surprise for him.

"Hey," she called out walking into the room. "Whatcha playing?"

Shrugging, he put the guitar aside and stood to kiss her. She loved this, the way he was always touching her, always wanting to show affection. It was so new—not just because it was Matt but also because it was just new to her in general—and she found she enjoyed it.

"I was just goofing around. Nothing's coming to me that's sticking. Sometimes it's fun to play gibberish."

"Gibberish? Does that even apply for music?"

He laughed. "It does for my music." And then he kissed her again.

Breathless, she pulled back and smiled. "I'll take your word for it." Stepping away, she looked and noted he was showered and dressed, and if he put on shoes, he'd be ready to go out. Taking a deep breath, she looked him straight in the eye and said, "Get your shoes. We're leaving."

"What?" he cried. "Where? Why? I...I thought we'd make sandwiches for lunch."

The look of panic was almost comical, and she knew she had to proceed very carefully. Reaching out, she took both of his hands in hers and smiled sweetly. "I have a surprise for you."

"Viv…"

"Have I asked anything of you since you've been here?" She didn't wait for him to answer. "Have I made any crazy demands on your time?"

"No," he grumbled with a pout.

"Have I pushed you in any way, shape, or form?"

He sighed loudly. "No."

"So then can you please just trust me on this?"

Matt studied her for a long time and she knew he was struggling with wanting to argue with her some more. His shoulders slumped slightly and he frowned. "Fine."

"That's the spirit," she said brightly. "Now get your shoes or we'll be late."

Without a word, Matt turned and walked to his bedroom. While he was gone, Vivienne walked around shutting off lights and making sure he hadn't left any food out anywhere—it was her own little thing. She liked to know she was leaving the space neat and organized.

Behind her, Matt cleared his throat, and when she turned around, she almost burst out laughing. "Really? That's what you're going with?" she asked. He had put on a pair of sneakers, sunglasses, a baseball hat, a scarf, and a hooded sweatshirt. "Seriously? What is this all about?"

He shrugged and walked toward the back door. "I have no idea where we're going, and I just don't want to be recognized."

She could only stare as he walked out the door. With a shake of her head, she followed, locking the door behind her. "Just FYI," she began as they made their way across the yard toward her driveway, "it's a little overkill. You're not going to have to worry about anyone knowing who you are."

He stopped midstride and turned to her. "How can you be sure? And for that matter, how would I know? You haven't told me where we're going."

She sighed. "I wanted it to be a surprise, and I had hoped you would trust me." As much as Vivienne didn't want to feel hurt, she was. For the last couple of days, they had been closer than she ever could have imagined. They cooked together, spent hours and hours just talking, and the nights? Well, those were something else completely. Every time Matt touched her, it was like she was learning something more about herself and she was having just as much fun discovering him. And just thinking that he didn't trust her…well, it certainly didn't feel good.

"You're right," he said, his voice low. "I'm sorry. I know you wouldn't do anything to hurt me or make me uncomfortable."

They had reached Vivienne's sporty little SUV, and it wasn't until they were seated and the car was started that she turned to him. "Thank you."

Matt was looking slightly more relaxed, but he was still pretty much covered from head to toe. "Can you give me a hint?"

"Let's just say it has to do with food," she replied cryptically.

"Oh great…we're going food shopping, aren't we? We're going to wander up and down the aisles, and you're going to make me push the cart, and I'm going to have to give my opinion on which melon smells better. That's it, isn't it?"

There was no way not to laugh. "Wow. That is quite the scenario. Pretty impressive. I didn't realize you had such a colorful imagination."

He looked at her and grinned. "Really? Have I not been imaginative these last few days?"

Vivienne blushed at all the ways he had been.

"Ah…so you do remember," he said silkily. Reaching over, he placed his hand over hers. "We could turn the car around and I promise to be even more imaginative." Leaning over, he ran his tongue along the slender column of her throat. "I've been thinking about your office."

She looked at him quizzically. "My office?"

Matt nodded. "It's the only room in your house we haven't properly christened. I kind of like the thought of having you in there while you're all in business mode and working at your desk and then…messing you up." He nipped at her earlobe. "Laying you on the desk and kissing every inch of your body. Mmm."

Yes, the man certainly had a great imagination because she could totally picture that scenario pretty clearly now and was having second thoughts about her plans.

No! she chided herself. *Stick to the plan!*

"Nice try," she said, patting his hand. "But I think we're going to do this my way."

"But—"

"Matt!" she quickly interrupted. "You have to trust me."

Vivienne steered the car around town. She had lived there most of her life, and Matt had grown up there as well. She stole a glance at him and wondered what was going through his mind. Certainly things had changed since he'd last been there, but was he remembering what it all used to look like? Did he have fond memories of the places? The people?

Turning on her signal, she turned left and then made

another quick left into the almost-empty parking lot. With so many options, she still chose to park along the side of the large structure, her car almost completely out of view. Turning the car off, she sat back and waited for Matt to say something.

"I...I don't understand," he finally said.

"C'mon," she said, climbing from the car. "Let's do it." By the time Matt met her on the sidewalk, Vivienne was grinning from ear to ear. "I think you remember this place, right?"

He looked up at the side of the brick building and swallowed hard before nodding.

Grabbing his hand, she tugged him around to the front of the building. At the window, she greeted the clerk as she stepped forward. "Two for *Star Wars* please." In the reflection on the glass, she could see Matt had his back to her as he was looking up and down the street. After she grabbed their tickets and thanked the clerk, she reached for his hand again.

They went inside and handed their tickets to the next clerk and then made their way across the lobby to the concession stand. "*Star Wars*?" Matt asked. "From before we were born?"

She nodded. "They turned this into one of those theaters that shows classics during the day. And they have a great menu, and they have more comfortable seating inside the theaters."

The look on his face showed just how confused he was, and Vivienne giggled.

"There are sofas, recliners, and tables and chairs, so you can eat a little easier, plus the usual rows of seats closer to the back. It's kind of funky and different from when we were kids but it makes for a fun movie experience." By now they were standing in front of the large menu board. "And lunch is on me."

"Viv, I can't let you do that," he protested. "I can pay—"

"Nope," she cut him off. "This is my show and the correct response was 'Thanks, Viv. You're the best!'" She winked at him. "Now you try it."

He laughed and repeated her words back to her and then returned his attention to the selection of food. "This is impressive. Mom and I just used to get hot dogs, but that was pretty much all they offered. This is…"

"It's junk food nirvana," she finished for him and was happy to see him smile and hear him laugh. Maybe by the time they sat down in the theater, he'd let go of all the tension and be able to enjoy himself.

"I can't believe you like this stuff. I've been eating with you for weeks, and I have yet to see you indulge in any junk food."

"Moderation. Everything in moderation."

Stepping up to the counter, they ordered two hot dogs, nachos, an order of chicken wings, a large salted pretzel, popcorn, Twizzlers, and the big box of M&Ms. The kid behind the counter looked at them expectantly. "Anything else?"

"Oh, right…drinks," Vivienne said. "We'll take two sweet teas and…hmm…I'm thinking about a milk shake."

"For crying out loud, Viv! You can't possibly eat all of that," Matt said, unable to stop laughing.

"It's not like I'm eating it all on my own. We're sharing it. And, as you pointed out, I've been eating with you for weeks, and I know if I weren't here, you would be able to eat all of it on your own." With a smug smile, she turned back to the clerk. "Two chocolate milk shakes. Please."

"Man, when you go off the wagon, you go all the way," Matt murmured.

"And I won't eat dinner tonight. Trust me. This will give me my junk-food fix for the next three months and then I'll be fine."

"I'll take your word for it."

They paid for their food and told the attendant which theater they'd be in, and he promised to be in shortly with their order. Together, they walked into their designated theater and discussed their seating options.

"Just remember, we can move after we eat if we want to. We're not locked into this for the entire movie."

"How do you know? What if there's no place left to sit?"

She looked at him as if he were crazy. "You're joking, right?" She looked around the room. "It's twelve thirty in the afternoon on a Tuesday. It's a school day. We're pretty much it in here."

And then, it was like all the pieces of the puzzle came together for him and that pleased Vivienne to no end. She wouldn't take him out to a crowded place. She wouldn't overwhelm him by taking him someplace out of his comfort zone. Vivienne had specifically chosen this as his first outing for two reasons—first, it got him out of the house so she could ease him back into public life. And second, it was a place that held good memories from his childhood. Although they'd never finished their conversation the other night about his family life, he realized she knew there weren't too many good memories for him.

Matt led her over to two recliners with a table between

them. He took off the hoodie and his sunglasses and made himself comfortable in the chair. "Wow. This is… pretty damn cool. What a great idea."

She nodded. "I know, right? It's a fun place to come with friends because it's comfortable and not nearly as crowded as the multiplex. I come here maybe once every couple of months with some girlfriends for a night out, and we always have fun. Plus, I don't feel like I ever get to see movies when they first come out, but this way I'm still getting to see them on the big screen. To me, it's a win-win."

"A girl with simple tastes," he murmured approvingly. "Color me impressed."

"What? That surprises you?"

He reached for her hand before bringing it to his lips to kiss it. "Everything about you surprises me. You're not like any woman I've ever met, and I have to admit, I'm liking that fact more and more."

Her heart did a funny little kick in her chest at his admission.

Before she could say anything, there was a waitress placing an overflowing tray of food between them. Vivienne didn't miss the fact that Matt looked away and pretended to be adjusting his seat while they were being served. "It looks like you'll have the theater to yourselves," she said, placing the last of the food on the table and picking up the tray. "Enjoy!"

Vivienne watched the young girl leave before twisting in her seat to look at all their food. "Wow. I mean I know we ordered it all, but now that it's here…"

"Are you saying your eyes were bigger than your stomach?" he teased.

"It's a long movie," she countered. "And I have a feeling there will be nothing left on this table but crumbs."

The room darkened, and the previews started to play.

Vivienne was just about to reach for her hot dog when Matt's hand on top of hers stopped her. "What? Is everything okay?"

A slow smile was her first response from him, and then his eyes welled with emotion. "Thank you."

No other words were necessary. Those two simple ones said it all.

"I didn't remember that part!"

"I can't believe those special effects!"

"I can't wait until the next one is out!"

"I would see it again!"

They bantered back and forth the entire way home, offering up their opinions, praise, and critiques of the movie—just like Matt and his mom used to do.

It was one of the most perfect days he could recall in recent memory.

And it was all thanks to Vivienne.

"So, were you serious about not eating dinner?" he asked. "I mean, you still have leftovers somewhere, right?"

Beside him, she chuckled. He loved the sound of it, loved the way her entire face seemed to light up with it. It made him content to sit and look at her all day.

"You cannot tell me you're even a little bit hungry," she was saying. "You ate your hot dog, all the wings, more than half of the nachos, half a bucket of popcorn, the pretzel, the Twizzlers and the M&Ms, the tea, and the milk shake! How could you possibly even want to think about food?"

He shrugged. "I'm full right now, sure. But later on I'm going to be hungry again. It's a simple fact of life."

Her only response was to shake her head.

"I mean I guess I can heat up something on my own." He sighed. Loudly. Dramatically. "There're some frozen pizzas in Aaron's freezer. I suppose it will have to do."

"Glad to hear you have a plan."

"Maybe I'll even have some ice cream for dessert."

She made a noncommittal sound.

"Hot fudge, whipped cream…hmmm, maybe you'll be ready for some dessert yourself by that time."

When he turned to look at her, she was grinning. Hopefully, it was a grin because she was interested in what he was saying and not just because she thought he was an idiot or something. He decided to test his theory.

"I think I would love to paint your body with hot fudge," he began, his voice low and sultry. "A couple of dollops of whipped cream, placed strategically, of course, would be quite nice too. But the hot fudge on your naked skin?" He hissed. "I can't think of a better dessert than that."

Beside him, Vivienne squirmed in her seat, and Matt was happy to see they were turning into their driveway. She parked the car and calmly climbed out without saying a word. Had he offended her? Shocked her? By the time he looked up, she was already opening the door to her house. He jumped out of the car and went after her, certain he was going to have to apologize or at least backpedal a little bit.

He stepped into the house and heard her footsteps

going up the stairs. Pausing, he shut the door and contemplated his next move. Maybe she had eaten too much at the theater and wasn't feeling well. Although, he thought, she probably would have mentioned it sooner.

"Viv?" he called out.

Silence.

Stepping farther into the living room, he slowly made his way to the bottom of the stairs. "Vivienne? Are you okay?" In the distance, he heard her murmur something, but for the life of him, he couldn't tell what she was saying.

Taking a slight detour, he went into the kitchen, pulled open the refrigerator, and found a can of ginger ale. They had made a chicken recipe with the beverage the other night, and he remembered she had purchased a six-pack. He also remembered it was a great drink to have on hand if you were sick.

Climbing the stairs, he silently prayed she was all right. He hated to think that the great memory they made today would be marred by Vivienne getting sick.

He turned into the bedroom and said, "I grabbed some ginger ale so…" And then he couldn't speak.

Could barely breathe.

Vivienne was on the bed, lying on her side, wearing nothing but two little scraps of purple lace.

And holding a can of chocolate sauce.

Carefully, he put the can of soda down on the nearest surface while kicking his shoes off. Matt had no idea what he'd done to get this lucky. To have found a woman who cared about him enough to make him happy—in both sweet and sexy ways. If he didn't know any better, he'd say she got him because she was his soul mate.

And that thought didn't scare him nearly as much as it should have.

Because if Vivienne Forrester was his soul mate, he would consider himself the luckiest man alive.

―⁓―

"Hey, Viv! How are you doing?"

Vivienne smiled at the sound of her brother's voice. She was used to talking to him almost every day when he was home, but when he was away on business, it tended to be only once a week. "I'm doing good. How about you? How's London?"

"Crowded," he said with a chuckle. "And a little bit rainy. I had hoped for better weather, so I could walk around a little bit and play tourist, but it doesn't look like that's going to happen."

"Wait. You have spare time to play tourist?" she teased.

"Some days I get to leave early because of good behavior."

"Nice." Sitting down on her sofa, Vivienne curled her legs up under her and got comfortable. "So, other than the rain and the crowds, how is your trip going? Are you getting things done that you have to?"

"For the most part. This weekend I'm going over to Paris to see Mom and Dad."

For a second she wanted to ask why. Then she remembered how Aaron had come to grips with their parents' odd take on parenting a long time ago and he saw visiting with them as a pleasant way to spend the time.

As long as that time was brief.

Vivienne had yet to see it that way. In her mind,

parents should be kind and loving and nurturing. Jack and Claudine Forrester were none of those things. Or, rather, they lacked those basic skills. They provided for their children in the most basic of ways—food, shelter, clothing—but beyond that, they left them in the care of nannies as babies, overscheduled them in activities to keep them well-rounded while they were in school, and then completely walked away from them as adults.

"Viv?"

Oh, right. Aaron. "Hopefully the weather will be slightly more agreeable for you in Paris," she said pleasantly. "Are you just going for a day trip, or are you staying the entire weekend?"

"Well, considering it's only a two-and-half hour train ride, I could easily do it in a day, but I'm thinking of spending the weekend."

"With them?" Yikes. A weekend sounded way too long to her.

Aaron chuckled. "Yes, Viv. With them. Our parents. They asked me to stay with them, so I figured I'd jump on the rare invite and see how it goes."

"Oh. Well…good for you. I hope you have a good time."

"Really? That didn't sound even the tiniest bit sincere."

"Aaron…" she sighed.

"I know, I know. I'm sure there's a part of you that really does hope I have fun, but your first thought is how you hope they do something stupid and insensitive, completely keeping in character for them, so you can say I told you so."

"That's not true," she protested. Weakly.

"It's okay. Really. Believe it or not, I'm not holding out hope of this being some grand weekend love fest.

Dad wants to hear about my work, Mom will fuss a little bit—at least in front of her friends—and then I'll leave. More than anything, I think it's a chance for them to show me off."

"Wait…friends? They're having a party while you're there?"

Aaron was silent for a moment.

"Aaron?"

"They've invited some friends for dinner Saturday night while I'm there. It's not a big deal. Trust me, it's more of a buffer so dinner won't be as quiet and painfully stiff as it normally is."

"Oh." She wished they would show her the same courtesy when she went to visit. For all Vivienne knew, her parents had no friends or acquaintances. They never introduced her to anyone on her trips to Paris. "Anyway, at the very least, you know it's a short trip, and you'll get to eat some amazing food. Of that I definitely am jealous."

"I know you are. And if there were a way for me to bring some of it home to you, I would."

"There is nothing like a freshly made croissant," she said, sighing at the memory.

"I promise to eat one for you."

"Such a good brother."

"I know, I know." He paused. "So how is the new job going? How does it feel to be the boss?"

She laughed. "I'm not quite the boss, Aaron. But it has been a little bit freeing not to have to come up with so much content on my own."

He laughed out loud at her comment.

"What? What's so funny?"

"Vivienne—and I say this with love—I don't believe

that you have cut back on your writing. I think you're still writing just as much but are filing it away in case anyone else flakes."

Okay, so clearly she was a lot more transparent than she had ever realized. Why deny it? "Yes, I have been creating backup posts, but that's just being smart! Plus, I've been able to try some great new recipes and Matt has been my willing guinea pig."

For a moment she wished she could take that part back. There was no way to know how her brother was going to react to her spending time with Matt. Maybe he would be against it? Maybe he would warn her to stay away from him? Maybe—

"I cannot thank you enough for including him in your life, Viv."

"Wait. What?"

"I was really worried about him staying alone in the house and having a pity party. I've been talking to him as much as I can, and I can tell he's feeling better about his situation. It was rough that it was Dylan who took the headlines away and how the band seems to be under this black cloud. So I am thankful you got over your initial dislike of him being there and reached out to him as a friend. You're amazing."

Right. If only he knew exactly how she was reaching out for Matt these days.

Naked in the shower.

Naked on her living room floor.

And let's not forget naked and covered in chocolate sauce.

"…now if he would only go out on his own a bit and socialize, I think it would be good for him."

Vivienne missed the first part of that statement and simply answered with "Mm-hmm."

"He told me you guys went to the movies last week. Great idea. Ease him out slowly. Have you gone anywhere else?"

"I haven't tried again. I didn't want to push. After what happened to Dylan, he seemed willing to meet up with Riley and talk to the press and do whatever was needed, but for some reason, he just doesn't want to do anything here in town. I mean, I get it. It's not the most exciting place to be, but still."

"Well, I'm sure he doesn't have a lot of great memories of growing up here, and I kind of think he's afraid of running into his dad."

"What?" Vivienne asked incredulously. "What are you talking about?"

Aaron cursed softly. "It's not a big deal. I'm sure when Matt's ready, he'll—"

"Aaron!" she snapped. "What is the deal with his father?" Her heart began to beat wildly in her chest. Maybe she shouldn't be asking her brother about this, but she had a feeling she wasn't going to get it out of Matt. She certainly wanted to help Matt in any way she could, and the only way to do that was to know exactly what she was dealing with.

"Look," she began, a little calmer now, "I know he and his dad had a lot of issues when he was growing up. I remember hearing something about it. But why is this still such a big deal?"

On the other end, she heard Aaron sigh.

"Please," she softly begged.

"I didn't meet Matt until we were in middle school,"

Aaron began. "By that time, his mom was gone, and it was just him and his dad. At that age, you don't notice a whole lot about people's home lives, but it didn't take long for me to realize Matt never invited anyone over to his house, and he was always anxious to do anything but go home."

Matt's words from their first night together came to mind. *The old man didn't want anything to do with me. He blamed me for all that was wrong in his life.*

"It wasn't until we were a little bit older that I said something to him about it. Looking back I could kick myself. I was like, 'Hey, maybe it would be nice for the rest of us if we ate at your house.' You know, stupid stuff kids say."

She chuckled softly, picturing her brother at that age.

"He looked so damn defeated, but again, it didn't click. So he invited me to sleep over one night. The house was a filthy mess; there was trash everywhere, and his father... Well, let's just say his father's main hobby was drinking."

Vivienne's heart broke for Matt having to live like that. Even at their worst, at least her parents were there and gave them a comfortable home environment to live in.

"It was the only time I ever slept over, and after that, I made sure he came home with me as much as he wanted."

"Was his father...abusive?" she asked cautiously.

"Not physically," Aaron replied. "But verbally? The man was brutal." He paused. "When Matt and Riley started playing around with the idea of starting a band, his dad freaked out. He screamed at Matt that he wasn't going to pay for lessons or for any instruments because he thought Matt was a loser."

"Oh no!"

"Yeah. The only reason I know about that was because we were all hanging out one day after school and we stopped by Matt's so he could pick up a change of clothes."

"So...how did Matt get a guitar, then?"

"It's not a big deal. He just...he got one."

"Aaron."

"I helped him get one," he said softly. "Viv, you have no idea what it is like to watch one of your best friends get beaten down like that. I knew Matt was talented. He used to play around on Riley's guitars all the time, and I hated to think of him never getting his chance because his old man was a prick."

"Wow. I...I never knew."

"Yeah, well... So he got his guitar and they formed their band. It was a great way for Matt not to have to be at home, and it was the perfect distraction. It wasn't until about a year later that he found out his dad had been in a band in high school. He'd thought they'd go on to do something but..."

"They didn't," Vivienne finished for him.

"Yeah. So when Shaughnessy started to get noticed and they were playing small gigs in the area, his father flipped out. I drove Matt home after a show and his father was waiting for him. We only stopped so Matt could grab his overnight bag. I used to tell him to leave clothes at our house but he didn't listen."

"What happened?"

"Matt went in and I stayed in the car. I was waiting and

waiting and waiting and then I heard the yelling. Then I heard glass breaking. I jumped out of the car and ran into the house, and I found the two of them on the floor. Matt had his hands around his dad's throat, and the old man kept telling him he was a no-talent piece of shit. I mean, even as Matt was cutting off his air supply, the old guy was still hurling insults. I stormed across the room, hell-bent on getting Matt out of there. I… It was terrifying."

Tears rolled down her cheeks as she listened, her hand over her heart. "Oh my God."

"It was bad. Really bad. I finally pulled Matt off his dad and I told him to go and pack up all of his stuff, that we'd find a place for him to stay no matter what."

"That was…" she gasped. "That was your senior year of high school! That was why he stayed with us that last month?"

"Yeah. I told Mom and Dad what happened, and they agreed to let Matt stay. He left the day after graduation and hadn't come back to town since—until I brought him back a few weeks ago."

"Aaron," she said, her voice weak and clogged with emotion, "I can't believe that happened. I had no idea."

"He didn't want anyone to know. He was embarrassed."

Well, yeah, she thought. *Who wouldn't be?*

"So where's his father now? Do we even know if he's still around?"

"He is," Aaron said. His voice had a hint of anger to it. "He's cleaned up and gotten sober, gotten remarried. I've run into him a time or two, and he won't even look me in the eye. So many times, I've been tempted to go and knock on his door and give him a piece of my mind, but then…it's not my place. Not my fight."

"How can you say that? Matt's your best friend!"

"We've talked about it, and Matt tells me not to waste my time. I'm trying to respect his wishes."

Vivienne wasn't so sure she'd do the same thing. She'd be more than willing to unleash a little fury on Matt's behalf.

"Matt got out of there and did something amazing with his life," Aaron said, interrupting her thoughts.

"And what about his mom?" she asked, realizing she had no idea. "Why did she leave?"

Aaron stayed silent.

"Does anyone know where she is or what happened to her?"

"She died of breast cancer five years ago," he said flatly. "Matt had hired private investigators to find her once he was making money, but by that time she was sick. He paid for all her medical bills and made sure she was comfortable. It just about killed him when she died."

"But—"

Aaron sighed. "At first, he decided to search for her because he was angry—he wanted to know how she could just walk away from him. He needed to know. But once he found her…"

"And she was sick…"

"Yeah. It took some of the fight out of him."

"Did she ever tell him why?"

"Matt's dad. She wanted a divorce, to take Matt with her, but the guy was a bully and threatened her with physical violence if she left with Matt."

"But…why? From everything you've said, it isn't like he cared about Matt."

Another sigh. "It was just his way of trying to control

her. And the fact that she still left just gave the old man more reasons to take stuff out on him."

She hadn't been crying before, but she was now. "Poor Matt," she sobbed. "God, when I think about our parents and compare them to his? It puts things into perspective. Our parents were cold, but they weren't intentionally cruel."

"Exactly."

So now what was she supposed to do? How could she face Matt without telling him she knew all of this information he clearly didn't want her to know?

"What do I do, Aaron?" she forced herself to ask. "How do I encourage him to start going out when I know his reason for staying in? He's never going to admit any of it to me, about his father."

"I honestly don't know. But I'll be home by the end of next week and maybe I can work on him—if he's still there, that is."

"Wait, what? He's leaving?"

"Not that I know of, but if he's feeling antsy and thinks things are back to normal for him, there's really no reason for him to stay. I can just as easily catch up with him in LA, or wherever he decides to hang his hat for a while."

Dammit. Vivienne wasn't ready to think of that yet. Not that she hadn't—mostly when she was alone or when Matt was asleep beside her—but she just wasn't ready for it to end yet.

"I suppose," she murmured. "So you think I should just let it be for now and keep doing what I'm doing, which is not pushing?"

"Probably."

She nodded even though he couldn't see her.

"So, listen, I better get going. I'll call you after I get back from Paris and we'll talk about my schedule for when I'm coming back. I haven't booked my flight yet—we left it open-ended in case anything came up."

"That sounds good. It probably won't be too hard for me to come and pick you up from the airport—you know, depending on the time."

"You make your own hours, Viv," he teased, "remember?"

"That doesn't mean I can just bail on a conference call or that I want to be parked outside baggage claim at midnight," she countered. "Either way, we'll make it work. Maybe Matt will go pick you up. That might be a good outing for him."

"Hey, that's a great idea! I'll mention it to him when I talk to him."

Just then, Vivienne heard a familiar knock at the door and smiled when she looked up and saw Matt walking in. "Actually," she said to Aaron as she stood up, "why don't you talk to him now? He just walked over to help me with dinner."

"You've got Matt cooking with you?" he asked, his voice laced with surprise.

"I'll let him explain that one to you. It was all his idea."

"This I've got to hear."

"Hang on."

Matt walked over, a sexy grin on his face. Vivienne held the phone out to him. "Aaron wants to say hello and you have to tell him all about the deal you made to get free meals."

Taking the phone from her hand, Matt hit the mute

button. "Do I get to tell him all the ways I thank you?" he asked. Then, leaning in, he ran his tongue lightly against her throat until she was almost panting. He pulled back and then kissed her quickly on the lips. "I'll keep that little bit of information between us."

"O…okay," she sighed and then collapsed back on the sofa.

Matt looked down at her and winked before sitting down at the other end. "Hey, buddy! How's London?"

Chapter 7

OUT OF THE CORNER OF HIS EYE, MATT COULD SEE THAT something was wrong. Vivienne was biting on her bottom lip and seemed lost in her own world. Everything had seemed fine when he came in — she was laughing with Aaron and smiling. But now? Not so much.

He didn't rush his friend off the phone, but he was certainly glad when Aaron said he had to go. Hanging up the phone, he placed it on the coffee table and shifted so he was facing Vivienne on the sofa. "So he might be back by the end of next week."

She nodded but didn't quite meet his gaze.

"And the weekend with your parents? That should be interesting."

Vivienne shrugged. "I suppose."

Yeah, something was off. While Matt knew she was entitled to her private thoughts, he couldn't help his over-whelming urge to take care of her and make her smile.

"And it should be a hoot when he brings them home with him to visit. I told him I'd just move in here with you, and he said that was fine."

"Uh-huh."

Okay. Enough. "Viv?" he said a little firmly and waited for her to look up at him. "What's going on? What did Aaron say to upset you?"

She looked away before coming to her feet and walking to the kitchen. "Nothing. It's…it's nothing."

She pulled open the refrigerator and began rummaging around. "We were going to go for that beer-can chicken tonight, right?"

He was beside her in an instant, shutting the refrigerator door and backing her up against it. "I don't give a damn about dinner right now. I want to know why you're upset."

She looked up at him, her big, brown eyes filled with emotion, and he swore that look reached down into his soul and squeezed. What the hell could Aaron possibly have said to her?

"Like I said, it's nothing. I just...I get this way whenever the topic of my parents comes up."

For some reason, he didn't quite believe her. But why would she lie?

"So you're upset because he's spending the weekend with them?"

She shook her head. "No," she sighed. "It's just...he told me they invited friends over to have dinner with the three of them. They never do that when I visit. When I'm there, it's just the three of us, sitting in awkward silence. I would kill to have some distractions around them. But for whatever reason, they go out of their way to make Aaron comfortable and in the complete opposite direction with me."

He could see why she would find that upsetting. Pulling her into his embrace, he held her tight, kissing the top of her head. "What can I do?" he asked softly. "What can I do to make you feel better?"

"You're already doing it," she replied softly. "I'll be fine. It just...it pisses me off."

"Does Aaron know you feel this way?"

"I'm not mad at him, and I don't begrudge him his

weekend with them. It's just something that's always been this way and neither of us can understand why."

"I'm sorry," he murmured, wanting more than anything to take away all of her hurts and disappointments.

Vivienne pulled back and smiled up at him. "So, come on. I can't believe you've been standing in the kitchen this long without calculating how long it will be until we eat."

Turning them around, he led her out of the kitchen and back to the sofa, where he cradled her in his lap as they sat down.

"Um, Matt?"

"Like I said, I don't give a damn about dinner right now. It's you I'm concerned about." He tucked her head onto his shoulder and simply enjoyed the feel of her in his arms. She let out a shuddery sigh, and he still felt like there was more to her mood than she was telling him, but he didn't want to push. "How about we get takeout tonight? I'm in the mood for Chinese."

"Oh…that does sound good. But are you sure?"

He nodded. "I'll even go with you to pick it up."

Vivienne sat straight up. "Really?"

He nodded again. "I'm not saying I'm ready to go out wearing a 'Matty Reed' neon sign or anything, but I think I can deal with going to pick up food without having to be too incognito."

"You mean you'll leave your Unabomber getup at home this time?" she teased.

"It wasn't that bad."

"Matt? It was more than bad. You wore sunglasses, a hat, and a hood inside a movie theater. It was overkill."

"Fine. It was a little excessive. This time, I'll only wear the hat. And maybe the glasses."

"It's already getting dark out," she pointed out.

"Maybe my eyes are light sensitive. Besides, celebrities do that sort of crazy thing all the time. Wearing sunglasses is acceptable at all hours of the day and night."

"It's weird."

"Says you."

"Damn straight."

He hugged her close. "Let's look at the menu and call it in. I don't think it's warm enough tonight to eat outside, though."

She looked at him strangely. "We haven't eaten outside that much since you've been here. I seem to recall us enjoying quite a few meals right here inside my house. And Aaron's."

He leaned in close and kissed her. "Yeah, but that first night I was here we ate Chinese food out on the deck. I remember looking at you and thinking how beautiful you were."

"You did not!" she said with a chuckle.

He nodded. "I did. I totally did. Then all I could think about was how mean you were to me."

Vivienne elbowed him in the ribs. "That was because I could tell you didn't remember seeing me two years ago. You looked at me like you hadn't seen me since I was a kid."

"I know, and I believe we've already established how sorry I am," he said softly, peppering her cheek with soft kisses. "But I'd be more than willing to make it up to you, repeatedly, if that's what it takes."

"Hmm," she purred. "I may need a little reminding. What did you have in mind?"

"I thought dinner could wait, and I'll show you right

now all the things that raced through my mind when I
first saw you."

"Right here?" she asked breathlessly.

"Right now," he murmured, his breath hot against
her cheek.

"Dinner can wait."

It was after nine when Vivienne pulled up in front of the
Chinese restaurant. Matt looked straight ahead and sighed.

I can do this.

He'd been chanting that to himself since she'd called
in the order.

He wasn't a coward. He was ready to stop hiding, and
this seemed like a safe way to start.

"You don't have to do this, you know," Vivienne said
from behind him. Her tone was light and sweet, and he
knew she was being supportive.

"No one's even in there," he said, noticing the lack
of other customers. One of the perks of ordering late,
he supposed. Turning toward her, he kissed her on the
cheek. "I'll be right out."

With a deep breath, he climbed from the car and
went into the restaurant. The woman behind the counter
barely looked at him as she confirmed which order he
was picking up. In less than two minutes, he was walking back out to Vivienne's car. When he was seated
beside her, he sighed.

"Well that was pretty anticlimactic," he murmured.

"And you were so scared," she cooed.

Matt turned to her and laughed. "Such a smart-ass.
Just for that, I get extra dumplings."

"What?" she cried. "That's no fair!"

"I was the one who was very nearly traumatized here," he said, doing his best to keep a straight face. "I think I deserve a reward."

Vivienne studied him for a moment. "Okay," she said with a sigh, pulling out of the parking space. "If that's what you want to claim as your reward, I guess we're good."

"Wait. What?"

She shrugged. "I mean, I had a whole other option prepared for after dinner to reward you for doing this, but if you're happy with a couple of extra dumplings, who am I to complain?"

"No, no, no, you can't just throw something like that out there. I didn't even know there was a possibility of another reward. I can't be held to a decision I made without knowing all the facts," he reasoned. "So, um, what did you have in mind?"

With a dramatic sigh, Vivienne shook her head. "No, no, no," she mimicked. "I shouldn't have said anything. You seemed perfectly happy with your bounty of dumplings." Reaching over, she patted him on the knee. "They're all yours."

"But...but I don't want them now." He pouted. "I want to know what your reward was going to be. I bet it was going to be something sexy." He looked over at her. "It was going to be sexy, right?"

She shrugged again. "Doesn't matter," she said lightly.

Slouching down into the passenger seat, he stewed. *Me and my big mouth*, he thought. Always thinking of the food, and now I'm missing out on something potentially sexy. Thoughts of Vivienne sprawled out on the living room floor earlier flooded his mind. He felt himself getting hard. Then, images of her on the bed with the chocolate sauce flashed too. He had to shift slightly to accommodate the hard-on he was now sporting.

The remainder of the drive was spent in silence, and Matt forced himself to push the erotic pictures from his mind as he thought about baseball stats and sandwiches and, finally, *Star Wars*.

"Let's just go inside and enjoy our dinner."

Matt looked up and saw they were pulling into the driveway.

He watched Vivienne climb from the car and made sure he was a little more in control before he followed. It didn't take too long, and before he knew it, they were unpacking the food at her dining room table.

"Or would you rather eat in the living room?" she asked. "We could find something to watch—a movie or something if you'd prefer."

Matt studied her for a moment and then shook his head. "No. I don't want to watch TV, I'd rather sit here and talk to you," he said sincerely.

She looked at him oddly. "Really? We talk all the time. All day. Every day. I would have thought you'd be tired of the sound of my voice by now." She chuckled, but Matt could tell it was out of nerves, like she wasn't sure of herself, and it just drew him to her more.

Stepping in close, he wrapped his arms around her waist. "I love the sound of your voice," he murmured against her cheek. "And I love our conversations. I've never met anyone like you before. I love getting your opinion on things, and more than anything, I love how we never really run out of things to talk about."

She seemed to melt against him, and he smiled, pulling her in close. "I love all that too," she said softly.

It would have been so easy to say that he loved her. It was right there on the tip of his tongue. But would she even believe him? Hell, he could hardly believe it himself. They barely knew each other, and yet Matt felt like he knew her better than anyone he'd ever met in his life. And, if he wanted to get technical, they had known one another for years.

"C'mon," she said, pulling back slightly. "Let's eat before this gets cold."

He allowed the distraction, and when they sat down and began opening containers and doling out food, he looked over at her and said, "So where should we go tomorrow?"

―⁓―

The clock on the bedside table said three a.m.

Vivienne sighed quietly and willed her brain to shut up and let her sleep.

But it wouldn't.

Earlier, Matt had gotten restless in his sleep again. She was beginning to notice a pattern. He never talked about it, but if she had to guess, it was a recurring dream that plagued him. It broke her heart to know that something was troubling him so deeply, and it bothered her more than it should have that he wouldn't talk to her about it. She would do whatever she could to take that pain away from him.

Beside her, Matt sighed and snuggled closer. He was wrapped around her, her back against his chest, their legs tangled together. She loved it.

Love.

They had used that word a lot tonight, and lately it seemed like it was happening more and more. There had definitely been…a vibe earlier. Matt's voice was so intense and serious when they had gotten home with their dinner. As he'd held her close and told her all the things he loved about her, her heart had stopped as she waited for him to say that he loved her.

But he hadn't.

And she still wasn't sure if she was disappointed by that or not.

Did she love Matt? Yes. Did it freak her out? Yes. Not so much the loving him part, but loving someone who was clearly going to leave.

It seemed to be a familiar pattern in her life.

Vivienne didn't tend to dwell on it, but if she allowed herself to look at all of her relationships, she saw it. She chose partners—lovers—who were pretty much unattainable. Thinking about it now, it was almost comical. Clearly her parents had done such a number on her that she couldn't have a normal, healthy relationship with men.

And it sucked that she was just coming to that realization now when she wanted one.

But Matt wasn't going to be that guy—no matter how badly she wanted him to be. Everything about him screamed temporary. He didn't own a home; he was always on the road moving from place to place; he didn't seem to put down roots.

Although…their conversation from several days ago came to mind.

I haven't thought about having a home in a while… Then I look at what Aaron's done here and what you did with the guesthouse, and I want that.

Okay, maybe he was thinking about it now, but it didn't necessarily mean it was going to happen or that he wanted it to happen with her. And she really, really, really wanted him to want it with her.

Dammit.

She could feel the sting of tears and willed them away. The last thing in the world she wanted was for Matt to wake up and find her crying. How would she possibly explain her tears to him?

Although she had a feeling it wouldn't take long for her to pour out her heart to him. Seriously, the man had a way of getting her to talk about things she normally wouldn't. Not that Vivienne had any deep, dark secrets, but when she and Matt were together—which was all the time—they really never did run out of things to say. Sometimes, long after a conversation was over, she'd stand back and wonder how it was that they had gotten on to some of the topics they had.

She had shared her feelings about her parents and how unfair it was that they put in more of an effort with Aaron—it was something she almost never talked about. Except with Aaron. Then the other morning, while they were eating breakfast, she had gone and told him about how she preferred working alone and from home because she was insecure about fitting in in an office environment.

Where the hell had that even come from? It was something she had only voiced in her head. And yet, she was getting so comfortable with him that she could simply say whatever she was feeling, whatever was on her mind. And the best—or weirdest—part? He never told her she was wrong for the things she felt. He never told her she was looking at things the wrong way. If anything, he encouraged her to talk even more about things until she felt better.

Damn him. Why did he have to go and be so perfect?

Okay, if she took the rose-colored glasses off for a minute, Vivienne could admit that Matt Reed was far from perfect. For all the sharing she had done, she now knew—thanks to her brother—that there was plenty Matt was keeping to himself. If he had even once shared with her his anger toward his father and why, or his real reasons for not wanting to go around town, she would have felt like they were on the same page.

Clearly they weren't.

They were having fun. She was helping him through a rough time in his life, and when he left—and she knew for a fact he would—she would remind herself to feel good about playing an instrumental part in helping him find himself again.

Right, she inwardly mocked herself. *Like that was going to happen*. The sad truth was, when Matt decided to leave and return to LA or New York or wherever it was he got the urge to go to, she would paste a smile on her face, wish him well, and then hole up in her house in the fetal position and cry for weeks.

Maybe months.

It had taken a long time to get over one silly kiss. How the hell was she supposed to get over falling in love?

—◦◦◦—

"So, you're sure about this?"

"Absolutely."

"There isn't…I don't know…maybe something else you'd rather do?"

"Nope. Not a one."

Vivienne frowned, and Matt thought she looked adorable. She let out a little sigh as she put the car in park but continued to stare ahead.

"Viv, what's the problem? I thought you'd be happy about this. We're out of the house and I'm not dressed in some crazy disguise. I thought it would make you happy." He paused and continued to stare at her, but when she remained silent, he started to get nervous. "Viv?"

"Okay, fine," she huffed, and turned toward him. "Yes, I'm happy we're out of the house. And yes, I'm happy you're not dressed like a weirdo, but—" She stopped and shrugged. "I just wasn't expecting this to be what you had in mind."

Matt looked at the scenery before them. The beach. The sun was shining, it was a little bit cool out, a little bit breezy, but a picnic on the beach seemed like a great idea when he'd come up with it that morning. "It's beautiful here. Me and Aaron and Riley used to surf here when we were in high school." He chuckled. "None of us were particularly good at it, but man did we have fun."

That coaxed a small smile out of her.

"We'd come out here and strut around like we owned the place," he said, smiling at the memory. "Carrying our boards, flexing our muscles—thinking back, I realize what morons we must have looked like because we were all fairly scrawny at the time. Then we'd go into the water, and about ninety-nine percent of the time, we'd wipe out." He laughed out loud. "But the girls were always watching."

"I'll bet," she said with a small laugh of her own.

"Hey, it was every sixteen-year-old boy's dream—girls in bikinis watching us and wanting to be with us."

"When was the last time you surfed?"

Matt thought about it for a minute. "Probably about five years. Riley and I used to go whenever we could while touring. Just the two of us. We would laugh our asses off because we hadn't gotten much better, but it was always a great time."

"How did two of the biggest rock stars in the world go surfing without an audience?"

He gave her a sheepish grin. "I never said there wasn't an audience."

"Ah."

"But most of the time we were at a private resort or had security watching the area," he admitted. "I kind of wish it were warmer out now. I totally would have gone out and tried to show off for you." He winked and leaned in to kiss her on the cheek.

"And I would have no doubt been thoroughly impressed." She grinned and motioned to the basket of food in the backseat. "Come on. Let's go find a good spot to set up."

Together they climbed from the car. Matt grabbed the food, and then they kicked off their shoes and walked out onto the sand hand in hand.

"I'd like to sit closer to the water, but I think we should hang back a bit while we eat because of the breeze." Vivienne looked around and motioned to some large rocks near the dunes. "Maybe over there? It could block the wind a little, so we don't get a lot of sand in our food."

"It's part of the total beach experience," he teased.

"But I agree. Let's set up there and then we can walk along the shore when we're done."

"Sounds like a plan."

Once they were situated, they pulled their sandwiches out. Vivienne had put together some chicken salad on baguettes with fresh fruit on the side. After one bite, Matt couldn't help but moan with pleasure.

"You okay?" she asked.

He swallowed before answering her. "How the hell do you do it?"

She looked at him quizzically. "Do what?"

"Every damn thing you make is amazing. How is that even possible?"

As usual, his compliment made her blush. "You're crazy."

"No. I'm not," he countered. "I have been eating your cooking for weeks, and I have yet to have a bad meal. I have restaurants I go to, favorites, that haven't had this long a winning streak. Sometimes the chef has an off night or sometimes you try something new and it's just not good. That's not the case with you. Everything you make is freaking fabulous."

"Matt—"

"Just take the compliment and say thank you. Okay?"

Her blush deepened. "Fine. Thank you."

They ate in companionable silence, simply enjoying the sound of the waves crashing on the shore. Matt looked around, and since it was still off-season and a weekday, there weren't many people on the beach. It was one of the reasons he chose this particular place to venture out to. There were some couples walking around or sitting on blankets, doing just as he and Vivienne were. There were some families with small children playing. And there were a couple of people jogging with their dogs.

"I always wanted one," he said quietly.

Vivienne looked at him and then noticed where he was staring. "A dog?"

He nodded.

"I guess with your touring schedule it would be pretty impossible."

He nodded again.

She looked at him. "You're not touring now, and from what I can tell, you don't have any plans to in the near future. So why don't you look into getting one?"

Turning his head, it was his turn to look at her quizzically. "Um…because at some point I hope to be back on the road. Then what do I do? I think it's incredibly selfish to adopt a pet and then leave him in the care of others while I'm on the road. I know other people take their pets with them, but I think that's a little hard on the animal. They deserve some stability too."

Her shoulders slouched and she sighed. "Oh. Right. I hadn't thought of it like that."

Matt reached over and took one of her hands in his and kissed it. "It's just one of the downsides of the life, I guess." He watched as two small children ran over to the Labrador that was jogging alongside its owner. They were laughing and trying to pet him, and the dog seemed to love the attention. His heart kicked in his chest at the sight.

Damn.

What the hell was going on with him?

While Matt knew his time off was going to be a time

of reflection, he had no idea it was going to turn into a time of totally reevaluating his entire life. But that's exactly what was happening. What was supposed to be a time to think about the future—his career—was suddenly about something much more personal.

Could he possibly settle down, have a wife and kids? He looked over at Vivienne, who was smiling at the kids playing with the dog and thought, *Yes*. Riley had gotten married, and even though he was touring, Matt had a feeling it would only be a matter of time before they started talking about having kids. He didn't know it for a fact, but Riley came from a big family, and it just seemed like a natural conclusion.

Vivienne laughed beside him, and the sound washed over him like silk.

And it was becoming clearer by the minute that it was a natural conclusion for him as well.

"I cannot believe how sweet that dog is being," Vivienne said, interrupting his thoughts. "I'd always heard Labradors were great with kids, but that whole scene just proved it." She smiled at Matt and then noticed the serious expression on his face. "What? What's the matter?"

He shook his head, unsure if he'd be able to speak. Between the kids, the dog, and...her, emotion clogged his throat.

"Matt?" She reached over and placed a hand on his arm.

Shaking off the heavy pall of emotion, he smiled as he grabbed her hand and kissed it, loving how it always made Vivienne sigh. "That was cool to watch. I wonder if he's that friendly with everyone or just kids."

Looking over as the dog and owner jogged away, she said, "I bet he's good with everyone. The parents were pretty close by and the dog seemed completely at ease." She turned and looked back at Matt. "You sure you're okay? Did...did that upset you? Are you thinking about how you can't have a dog now?"

He shrugged. "No," he said firmly. "I'm thinking— anything is possible."

She looked at him oddly as he rose and began cleaning up their trash. It only took a few seconds for her to join him, but by the time she rose, Matt was already walking over to the nearest trash can and dumping everything. When he walked back to her, she looked at him skeptically.

"What?"

"Care to expand on that last statement?" she asked with a shy grin.

He shrugged again and then bent to pick up their blanket. Together, they folded it up and Vivienne placed it in the basket along with their shoes. When she went to pick it up, he beat her to it. "I'll carry it. Let's walk."

Hand in hand, they strolled closer to the shore. The sand was cold, and they did their best not to get too close to the rolling tide.

"I normally love walking in the water, but it's a little too chilly for me today," Vivienne commented.

"I know what you mean. It still feels good though."

She nodded.

They walked in silence for several minutes before Matt spoke again. "I want to get a dog."

"Okay."

Turning his head, he looked down at her and couldn't

help but grin. She was easily six inches shorter than he was, and right now, he found their height difference to be a little bit comical. He felt as if he was towering over her. He chuckled.

"What's so funny?"

"Us."

Vivienne looked up at him and couldn't help but laugh. "Really? Why?"

"I guess I never really noticed our height difference and it just hit me, and I feel freakishly tall for some reason."

"It's the slope of the sand," she said, still laughing. "It's not like I shrunk or something."

"Okay, that would be funny."

"Back to the dog," she prompted.

Right. "As we were sitting there, I started thinking about what I had thought this break was supposed to do for me—I mean, other than keeping me out of the public eye for a little while."

Beside him, Matt noticed how Vivienne seemed to stiffen a little, but in the blink of an eye, she was back to normal. "And?"

"And…I thought it was going to be a time for me to maybe work on music and think about future projects that I could work on."

"And it's not?" she asked curiously.

"Other than learning to play the piano, there really hasn't been anything inspiring. I enjoy playing with Riley and Dylan and Julian." He paused and simply enjoyed the sound of the ocean. "Anytime I do think about music, they are the ones I want to collaborate with. Maybe I'm being closed-minded or something…"

"I don't think you're being closed-minded at all," she said firmly.

"Really? Because a lot of musicians—"

"Why do you have to be like other musicians? Why can't you just be like you?" He stopped dead in his tracks. Vivienne hadn't noticed, and it wasn't until she was tugging at his arm and almost losing her balance that she turned and looked at him.

She had a point.

A beautiful, brilliant point.

And it was as if the lightbulb got brighter and he had the confirmation he'd been looking for. "So if I opted to take an extended break until Shaughnessy got back together…"

"I'd say that's your prerogative."

He nodded. "I don't want people thinking I'm some sort of pussy who's hiding out or afraid to try something again."

"Are you afraid?"

"No." His tone conveyed his conviction. "I think I'm finally starting to realize my strengths—and my weaknesses. I've been playing with the same guys for all these years for a reason. We're good together. And the hectic schedules, the constant touring, it was all a great distraction from having to think about pretty much anything else. I never thought about what I wanted to do with my life because I was so damn busy with the band."

"And now?"

Matt tugged her close until she was standing in front of him and they were toe to toe. His arms slowly wrapped around her waist. "Now," he began, his voice gruff, "I'm starting to see all the things I've been missing. For so freaking long, I thought I had it all. But I don't."

Vivienne looked up at him, those deep-chocolate-colored eyes going a little wide at his words. He saw her swallow hard as she waited for him to continue.

"I'm ready to start living my life, Viv."

She nodded nervously.

"And that means a house." Then he quickly corrected himself. "A home."

"And a dog," she added.

A slow smile spread across his face. "For starters."

"So…um…" She cleared her throat. "Where do you see yourself doing these things?"

It was on the tip of his tongue to say he wanted to do them right here, with her. Then he remembered why he had stayed away for so long, why he wasn't quite so anxious to be here now. And rather than open that can of worms right now, he simply replied, "I haven't decided yet."

And he couldn't help but notice the flash of disappointment on Vivienne's face.

Dammit.

Before he could correct—or explain—himself, she gave him a smile that he knew was forced. "Well, I guess that will give you something to work on now, researching real estate and seeing where you'll be a good fit. You've traveled so much over the last ten years, I'm sure you're familiar with most of the country. You should probably draw on that experience and see where you can most easily picture yourself. And your dog."

"Viv?"

"Hmm?"

"You're rambling."

"Oh…well…"

Just then, a large wave crashed on the shore, covering them both up to mid-calf. Vivienne let out a loud screech as she jumped to move out of the water. Matt laughed and chased after her, swinging her up in his arms once he caught her. She shivered.

"You okay?"

"Holy crap was that cold!"

Hugging her close, he turned and started walking back toward where they had come onto the beach.

"What are you doing? Are we done already?" she asked.

"It's pretty windy out, and now both of us have wet pants, and I figured it was a good time to turn back." He stopped. "Unless you'd rather stay?"

She shook her head. "No, I'm good. I have a feeling the sand that washed up my jeans is going to get annoying real fast."

Matt picked up the pace.

In his arms, she began to laugh. "Why are you sprinting? Is the sand bothering you too?"

He shook his head. "Hell no. I'm just planning on helping you out of those jeans as soon as we get home, so I'm kind of anxious to get us there."

She laughed out loud, her head falling back. "Yes!"

Two days later, Matt was sitting in Aaron's home office at his desk, looking at real estate.

Local real estate.

There were some amazing options, and yet all he could think about was what an incredible job Vivienne had done on the guesthouse and how much he wanted her to have a blank canvas to do that again on a much larger scale.

He looked at houses that were move-in ready. That was his immediate search. And then he started relaxing a little bit and thinking outside the box, and that's when he started looking at property. They could hire an architect to design a house that met every criterion they had, and then fill it with every wish-list item they had, and everyone would be happy.

And yet it still didn't feel quite right.

Scrubbing a weary hand over his face, he just about jumped out of his skin when his phone rang. Looking down, he saw it was Riley.

"You know, I think we've spoken more in the last week than we have in the past year," he teased. "What's up?"

On the other end, Riley chuckled. "I know, right? And by the way, hello to you too."

"Oh, yeah. Hello. How are you? How's Savannah?"

"We are both fine, thanks. Listen, what are you doing tomorrow?"

Matt frowned for a moment as an unexpected wave of panic hit him. "Um…tomorrow? I…I'm not sure. Why?"

"Oh, for crying out loud," Riley murmured. "First of all, relax."

"I am relaxed."

"No. What you are is starting to have a panic attack."

It sucked when someone knew you so well that you couldn't lie. "Okay, fine. I had a brief flash of anxiety. Sue me. So what's up?"

"Savannah and I are coming to town this weekend

to visit my family. My brother Aidan and his wife just had a baby about two months ago, and they're having the christening on Saturday. We're flying in late tonight and we thought we could see you for lunch or something tomorrow."

"Wow... Yeah. That sounds great!"

"See? Now you sound like your old self," Riley commented. "I thought you were over the worry. I figured you'd be chomping at the bit to get out of exile."

"Funny you should mention that. I'm looking at some real estate sites right now."

"Seriously? Dude, that's awesome! You gonna go back to LA?"

"I'm not sure yet. I'm not tied down to anything right now and..." He paused. "You know what? Why don't we talk about this tomorrow over lunch? You and Savannah can come here, and we can just chill and relax."

"You want us to pick up lunch and bring it?"

"Nah. I've got it covered." Already Matt was thinking of some of the great recipes he and Vivienne had come up with in the past weeks and couldn't wait to make again.

"That sounds great. Text me Aaron's address and we'll see you tomorrow around noon. Will that work?"

"Absolutely. And, Riley?"

"Yeah?"

"Thanks, man. I'm looking forward to seeing you."

"You too, Matt."

Once he hung up the phone, Matt realized he probably should have run all of this by Vivienne first. After all, as much as he wanted to think he was getting more and more proficient in the kitchen, he knew that without

Vivienne right there beside him, he wouldn't be able to make a thing on his own.

And there was no way he was making frozen entrees for Riley and Savannah.

He stood and stretched, feeling a bit excited to hang out with his old friend and be able to catch up with one another face-to-face. It had been far too long and now that he was finally starting to feel like his old self and had a plan—sort of—for his future, he couldn't wait to sit down and get Riley's take on it all.

It was only three in the afternoon, and Vivienne had mentioned a conference call with some of her writers. Matt wondered if she was done or if he should wait before going over. The last thing he wanted to do was interrupt her, but he also knew she'd want a solid heads-up on the plans he'd made for them as soon as possible.

Deciding to take a chance, he walked outside and across the yard to her house and let himself in. The silence hit him first, and he wasn't sure if it meant she was still on the phone or if she was done. Walking farther in, he made his way to her office and stopped in the doorway.

This was one of the looks he loved the most on her—hair up in a messy bun, reading glasses on, head tilted to the side.

"Hey, beautiful," he said softly.

Vivienne looked up and smiled. "Hey, you." She looked down at her computer screen and then slouched in her seat. "Oh, good. I thought I'd lost track of time again and you were here for dinner. Whew."

He stepped into the room. "Sorry. Didn't mean to startle you. Did your call go okay?"

She nodded. "Everyone has their assignments, and we've even gotten a few in the bank besides mine. All in all, I am very pleased."

"Does that mean you can maybe…take the day off tomorrow?"

A slow grin spread across her face as she considered him. "I think that can be arranged. Did you have something…special…in mind for us to do?"

The thoughts that raced through his mind were all X-rated, and he was suddenly sorry they wouldn't be taking advantage of any of them. "Riley just called, and he and Savannah are coming to town for the weekend for a family thing. I invited them for lunch. And I was thinking—"

"That I could make the food?" she asked, her expression going from smiling to neutral, and Matt knew exactly what she was thinking.

"No, I thought we could make the food together."

Her eyes widened for a minute and her lips formed a perfect *O*. "You mean like…together? As in you and me here, like—"

"A couple?" he finished for her and smiled as she quickly nodded. Matt walked across the room and knelt beside her chair. "Viv, I think it's time we faced some truths here—we are a couple. I'm not playing around or killing time. I love the time we spend together, and even when Aaron gets home, that's not going to change. I'm not going to hide it. I want you right here beside me tomorrow when Riley and Savannah come over— and not just because I don't want to make them my sad sandwiches or frozen pizza. I want you to get to know them and for them to do the same with you."

Her eyes were still a little wide, and she wasn't saying anything, so Matt figured he'd better keep talking.

"I know things have been a little...unorthodox. I mean, we've known each other since we were kids and yet we've only been involved for a few weeks, but...I like this. I like where this is going. I want to keep seeing where it can go."

When she remained silent, he started to panic. Maybe he'd spooked her. Or maybe she just didn't feel the same way he did. *Shit*. He was so damn obsessed with the fact that he was growing and maturing and interested in settling down that he never really bothered to think about how Vivienne was feeling about their relationship.

How freaking awful would it be to have her try and let him down easy, just like he used to do to the women he'd been involved with?

Karma at its finest.

"Viv, listen...I—"

"I didn't know you felt like that," she said softly, her voice almost a whisper.

He swallowed hard and nodded. "I do."

"This..." She paused and cleared her throat, speaking a little louder. "This whole thing took me by surprise, and I just figured it was going to be like...a fling. Short-term. I thought certainly when Aaron got back that you'd go back to hanging out with him and we'd just forget this...this side of our relationship and go back to the way it was before."

For the life of him, he had no idea what to make of her comments. They weren't confirming or denying anything.

"What do you think Aaron's going to say when he comes home to this?" she asked.

Hell, he hadn't given that any thought at all because, honestly, it didn't matter. Aaron could be pissed, or he could be happy for them. It wasn't going to change a damn thing. Vivienne was a grown woman, and even though Aaron was her big brother, Matt wasn't afraid of him.

All of which he said to her.

She chuckled. "Yeah, I'm not afraid of him either, but I have a feeling he is not going to be happy. With either of us. And part of me isn't sure which one of us he's going to put the blame on."

"What do you mean?"

"Well, I think the brother in him is going to accuse you of taking advantage of me because I'm so sweet and innocent." She rolled her eyes and laughed. "Then he'll probably laugh just like I did and accuse me of taking advantage of you while you were down in the dumps."

"I can live with that," Matt teased.

"Oh, you!" she said, swatting playfully at him.

He stood and then took a step back so she could get up from her chair. "I probably should have checked with you first before inviting Riley over."

"It's not a big deal. I'm looking forward to seeing him and to meeting Savannah." She stepped around him and walked out of the office to the kitchen. Matt found her staring into the refrigerator. "What do you think we should make?"

"Something that will be done before they get here, so you don't have to get up and cook," he suggested. "Maybe one of your soups or the chili you made last weekend? We could do some salads and bread, maybe those tartlet things for dessert?"

Closing the refrigerator door, she turned toward Matt and clapped.

"What? What's that for?"

"I'm just so proud!" she cried, grinning from ear to ear. "I feel like the student has become the teacher."

He rolled his eyes and grabbed her hands to stop the clapping. "Okay, okay, knock it off."

"What? I'm serious! Not only are you thinking of practical ideas for lunch so I can still get to visit with everyone, but you've also even thought of what will go with it and dessert." She beamed at him. "You've been paying attention."

"Well, of course I have," he said with a hint of defensiveness. "You were taking the time to teach me and help me out. Why wouldn't I pay attention?"

"Okay, okay, I was teasing, Matt," she soothed.

"Oh. All right."

Vivienne looked around the kitchen and then stepped away from him. "I like the idea of the chili if you think they'll like it."

"I know Riley will. I can't speak for Savannah. I don't know her very well."

"Hmm…then I guess I'll make sure we have plenty of side options, just in case it's not something she eats. I'll do corn bread and some of my homemade rolls, a salad…" Walking over to one of the drawers, she pulled out a pen and pad and started making a shopping list. "I'll have chips and salsa and a black-bean-and-corn guacamole out when they arrive. And maybe I'll whip up some chicken tortilla soup just in case. And—"

"Vivienne?" he interrupted, walking over and taking the pen from her hand. "It's only lunch. And there's only four of us. If you make all of those things and the chili and the dessert, no one will be able to move for a week."

"Oh…maybe I am going a little overboard. I love cooking for guests, and it's important to me that there's something everyone will eat." She nibbled her bottom lip. "I just wish we knew if Savannah eats chili and…" When Matt moved away and pulled his phone out, she quickly reached over to stop him. "Don't you dare call Riley and ask him!"

"Why the hell not? It seems like it would save us both a lot of time and anxiety if we just knew the answer."

"But—"

"Viv, relax. It's not a big deal." He quickly typed up a text and sent it to Riley before returning his attention to her. "So I guess we need to hit the grocery store."

"Yes, we do." She sighed.

"Do you have time to do that? Are you done working for the day? Should we go after dinner maybe?"

"I'm good. Like I said, the call went really well, and we're on track with everything. I was just looking over some proposals for upcoming issues and topics to explore. Nothing that can't wait." She glanced over at the clock. "Give me ten minutes to freshen up and change and I'll be good to go."

She was sprinting up the stairs before he could stop her. Then he figured it was probably for the best. If he'd stopped her—or followed her—it would be a lot longer than ten minutes before she was ready to go anywhere.

His phone chimed with an incoming text and he saw it was from Riley, confirming that both he and Savannah loved all kinds of Mexican food—and adored chili. It made him smile, and Matt knew Vivienne was going to be relieved. It was going to make shopping so much easier.

Picking up the shopping list, he began adding the items Vivienne hadn't gotten to and then some things he wanted to get as well, and he had to stop and laugh at himself.

He, Matt Reed, was making a shopping list and going to the store to shop and purchase it himself. It was like he barely recognized himself anymore.

And that wasn't necessarily a bad thing.

Chapter 8

"SO THERE I WAS, THINKING I WAS GOING TO GET TO DO ALL kinds of cool stunts like we'd done on the Exposed tour and Mick was like, 'No. You need to keep it real and personal, like you did at the Hollywood Bowl.'" Riley shrugged. "It's a completely different vibe on this tour. I'm way more relaxed than I can ever remember being when we toured."

Matt laughed. "Well, to be fair, we were largely responsible for all the stress and craziness that followed us around on tour." He shook his head, still laughing. "I'm surprised Mick didn't hire babysitters more often for us."

"It would have been like trying to herd cats. It just wouldn't have worked. The four of us were masters at creating distractions to keep everyone on their toes," Riley said, joining in the laughter. "If you ask me, I wouldn't mind touring like this all the time. If there was a way to keep this kind of level of Zen going and do it with you guys, I'd be a very happy man."

"It could happen," Matt said, instantly sobering. "I think when the time comes, we're going to be a completely different bunch of guys going back into the studio and then on the road."

Riley rested his arms against the back of the sofa as he looked at Matt and smiled. "I agree," he said easily. He studied Matt for a little bit longer. "You're different.

I can see it. I'm not going to lie, I was a little bit nervous about coming here today."

"Why?"

A shrug was Riley's first response. "I wasn't sure what I was going to find. We've been talking, and I knew you sounded good, but I was afraid it was all a show. But now that I'm here, and I see you—and Vivienne," he added with a wink, "I'm really happy for you."

Matt looked over his shoulder toward the kitchen, where Savannah and Vivienne were huddled together talking. As much as he had helped Vivienne prepare food so she wouldn't end up chained to the kitchen, she was still in there, fussing over the meal. Typical of her and just one of the many reasons he loved her.

"It's a good look on you," Riley said, interrupting his thoughts.

"What is?"

"Love."

Matt rolled his eyes but couldn't stop the grin on his face. "Oh, God. Are we going to be those guys?"

"What guys?"

"You know, the sensitive ones who talk about their feelings." He burst out laughing. "Weren't we just talking about how wild we used to be?"

"Used to be—key words," Riley stated. "Look, I don't regret the things we did when we were younger and on the road. It was great. It was fun. But what I have now with Savannah?" His smile grew. "There are no words to describe it. It's just…the best. Every day with her is amazing and…and…and…" He threw out his hands and laughed. "She's everything."

Matt knew exactly what he meant because he felt the

same way about Vivienne. Leaning forward, resting his elbows on his knees, he lowered his voice and asked, "Can I ask you something?"

Riley nodded.

"When did you know? I mean, how long did you and Savannah know one another before you knew she was it for you?"

"The first time she came to the house to start interviewing me. And it was only the second time we had ever seen each other."

"Seriously?"

Riley nodded. "We talked, we had lunch, and the interview got off to a bad start. I already knew I was attracted to her, but I figured that was about it. So we mutually agreed to stop the interview and just sort of hang out and get to know each other. We went down to the game room and challenged each other to a game of ping-pong."

Matt shook his head and chuckled. "Oh, how the mighty have fallen."

"I know, right? If word got out at that time that one of America's hottest bachelors was happily playing table tennis—and it wasn't a euphemism for sex—I would have totally lost my credibility as a sex symbol."

"Boohoo," Matt teased.

"Anyway, we challenged each other, and it was winner's choice. I chose to kiss her."

"Really?"

"Really."

"Damn."

"I knew instantaneously that I was in trouble. And I couldn't wait to see where it would lead."

"But it wasn't all smooth sailing, right? I mean, I remember you being pissed at her over the article."

"I was pissed at her for a lot of things—and they weren't her fault. I was a mess during that time and overly sensitive about everything." He stopped and looked at Matt. "Not unlike how you were feeling not too long ago."

Matt nodded.

"Thanks to me acting like a damn diva having a hissy fit, I almost lost her. It didn't help that we were both stubborn," he said with a chuckle. "But in the end, we made it work." He turned and looked toward the kitchen and then back at Matt. "How does Aaron feel about all of this?"

"He doesn't know yet."

"Uh-oh."

"Yeah, I know," Matt quickly interrupted. "Things sort of got off to a rough start here." He told him about kissing Vivienne two years ago after a show.

"Oh my God! I remember that night! I remember seeing her and helping her get backstage to see you. Wow! I can't believe I didn't put it together until just now."

"Yeah, well…I didn't remember it either. So when I showed up here—"

"She was a little less than enthused to see you," Riley finished.

"Exactly. So the last Aaron saw of us, Vivienne was barely tolerating my presence."

"So what happens when he gets home? What do you think he's going to do?"

"I'm sure he's going to be pissed, although Vivienne and I are undecided on who he's going to be more pissed at." He shrugged. "We're both adults, and I'm not just killing time here, screwing around."

"And how does she feel?"

Matt looked down at the carpet and shook his head before looking at Riley again. "I honestly don't know. I can't get a straight answer out of her, and I don't want to push. Just because I realized how I felt after such a short amount of time doesn't mean she was going to do the same."

Rile nodded. "Okay," he said slowly. "And you're okay with it?"

"I don't have a choice, do I? I don't want to push her away, and I don't have the greatest reputation coming into this. I have to prove to her that I'm serious, that I'm not looking to take off and start having orgies on the road again."

"Look, I know I'm no expert, but can I offer you a bit of advice?"

"Absolutely."

"You need to talk about it before Aaron comes home. Because if you both come at him with differing stories, or if he senses she's not serious about you, I can guarantee you he'll use that to his advantage to try and break you up."

Matt shook his head. "Uh-uh, Aaron wouldn't do that."

"Dude, I speak from experience, as someone with a younger sister. If I even thought for a second that Darcy was involved with someone who wasn't right for her and she wasn't too deeply committed? I would do whatever I could to break them up." He shrugged. "It's the right of the big brother. And no matter how tight you and Aaron are, his sister is always going to come first."

"Shit."

"Exactly."

The sound of female laughter broke into their conversation. Vivienne and Savannah walked toward them. "I'm going to show Savannah my office," Vivienne said excitedly. "I like showing off to a fellow writer!"

Matt watched them walk away before turning back to Riley. "In a million years, I never thought I'd be in a situation like this."

"What? In love?"

"Yeah. And in love with Vivienne Forrester. I mean, she was always around when I was hanging out with Aaron, but she wasn't on my radar at all. She was younger than us and... I don't know. I just never thought of her that way. The night she showed up at my dressing room, I just about had a stroke when I realized it was her."

"So I have to go back to asking: What are you going to do about it? Let's just say you talk to Aaron and he doesn't kill you. What then? Are you going to stay here? Go back to LA? New York? Vivienne has a lot of freedom with her writing, like Savannah did, so it's not like she's tied to this area for her job, but...this is her home. Are you willing to move here?"

"You have no idea how much I've been struggling with that. If she lived anywhere else in the world, I wouldn't even have to think about it. But I don't know if this is someplace I want to live again."

"Have you gone into town?"

"Not much," Matt said with a shrug. "We've picked up takeout, gone food shopping, and went to the beach, but...I do my best to avoid it at all costs."

"Are you even sure he still lives here?"

"Yeah. Aaron's mentioned it a time or two. It pissed me off at first because I was like, 'Why do I need to know this?' but then I realized it's just something Aaron does. He's the same way with Vivienne and their parents."

Riley paused for a minute. "Why? I don't remember Aaron having any issues with his folks."

"Not him. No. Vivienne." He shrugged. "Cold. Distant. Not the warm, fuzzy types at all. And apparently they're even more so with Vivienne than with Aaron."

"I kind of remember that. I know I never felt completely comfortable when we hung out there, but…still. That sucks."

"Yeah. Aaron's one of those guys who thinks everyone should just get along."

"Seriously? He knows better than anyone how much you went through at the hands of your dad. That's just messed up if he thinks you need to be okay with seeing him."

"I've had a pretty good run of it—almost thirteen years since I last saw him. And I have no interest in breaking that streak."

"So no sightings? Not even from a distance?"

Matt shook his head. "And I haven't been looking."

"Okay, let's just say, hypothetically, that you run in to him. What would you do?"

"Honestly? Nothing," Matt replied seriously. "There isn't one thing I have to say to him. I don't particularly care how he is and the feeling is clearly mutual. He hasn't reached out either, and I'm not hard to find."

Riley nodded and then held up his hand. "Okay, let me throw something else out there."

"Seriously?" Matt sighed dramatically.

"Hear me out. What is the worst thing that could happen? Come on. What would you do?"

Straightening in his seat, Matt then leaned back against the cushions and let his head fall back. "I know it's probably hard for you to understand but…I wouldn't do anything. I'd hear him out and wish him well. I don't want him in my life. I don't need him in my life. I needed him when I was growing up. I needed him when I was struggling in school, and I needed my mom there, but he forced her to leave too. So if he's gotten his life together or went and found Jesus, then good for him. But as for inviting him back into my life? It's never going to happen, and I'm okay with it."

Rather than saying anything else, Riley simply nodded.

"Matt?" Vivienne called out from her office.

"Yeah?"

"Can you finish putting the food on the table? Savannah and I will be out in a minute."

"No problem." He was thankful for the distraction, and he latched on to it like a lifeline. Jumping to his feet, he clapped his hands together and smiled at Riley. "Wait until you taste her cooking. I swear to you, it's better than anything I've ever had anywhere."

Riley got to his feet and clapped a hand on Matt's shoulder. "Then let's eat!"

—⁓—

From where Vivienne was sitting, things were pretty much perfect. This was a completely new feeling for her, and she found that it felt…good. She was happy. She was sitting, enjoying a meal with people who were happy. There was no drama, no awkwardness. If anything, she felt as if she had found a new BFF in Savannah Shaughnessy.

It wasn't something that came easily to her.

Maybe it was her upbringing or maybe she was just a snob, but Vivienne didn't bond with many people. Sure she had friends—lots of them. But even with those she'd known since childhood, she didn't feel this kind of closeness.

Besides their careers and love of writing, she and Savannah had similar tastes in food, hobbies, and—obviously—men.

While they had been back in her office, Savannah had grilled her a little bit on her relationship with Matt. Vivienne hadn't been prepared to talk about it—especially not with someone who was essentially a stranger—and yet she had.

In great detail.

And once she'd started talking, she couldn't seem to stop.

By the time she had gone through the whole kiss backstage, the rage at getting thrown out, the embarrassment, and then more embarrassment and rage when Matt had shown up at Aaron's, Savannah was wide-eyed and on the edge of her seat.

"Holy shit! That is crazy."

Vivienne nodded. "I know, right?"

"So how long until he remembered?"

"About a week. Aaron had left, and we were hanging out, arguing a bit, and he kissed me. And it was as if it all came back to him."

Savannah had given her a knowing look.

"What? What did I say?"

"It came back to him because it meant something," she said.

The first thing that came to Vivienne's mind was denial—force of habit—but she knew it would be a lie. And just the thought of all the times Matt had shown her how much she meant to him had her blushing.

"That must have been some kiss."

"You have no idea," she'd replied, giggling like a schoolgirl.

The sound of laughter brought her back to present, and the sight of Matt looking so happy and carefree had her smiling. Sure he'd been relaxed and smiling around her and Aaron, but this was different. Maybe he hadn't been as much at ease as she'd thought because there was a definite difference in his face right now.

As if feeling her eyes on him, Matt turned toward her and winked. Something so small, so simple, and it just tugged at her heart more than anything else. When he reached over and took hold of her hand, it hit her like a ton of bricks.

She was in love.

No maybes about it.

And no chance of her trying to downplay it.

She, Vivienne Forrester, was head over heels in love with Matt Reed.

"You guys should come to the show in Myrtle Beach at the end of the month," Riley was saying. "Come down Friday the nineteenth, the show is on Saturday, and leave on Sunday. We've rented a house for the weekend that is far too big for just the two of us, and it would be a blast to have more time to hang out. What do you say?"

Matt looked over at her, and she could see how much he wanted them to do this. Turning toward Riley, she smiled and said, "That sounds great!"

"Awesome!" Riley replied.

"So what has you here this weekend?" she asked him.

"My brother Aidan and his wife Zoe just had a baby two months ago—a little girl. The first since my sister Darcy, so everyone is just about losing their minds," he said, chuckling. "She is going to be spoiled rotten."

"Well, she should enjoy it while she can because another baby's on the way," Savannah said.

"Wait! What?" Matt cried, looking at the two of them with wide eyes. "Are you two…?"

"What?" Riley said. "Oh…no! No. Not us." He let out a nervous laugh. "My brother Quinn and his wife are expecting too."

"Wow," Matt said with a relieved sigh. "Okay. Whew. I was beginning to think you were holding out on me and that news would have been huge! I couldn't believe we'd been sitting here all this time, and you didn't mention anything about it."

Riley grinned before leaning over and giving Savannah a loud, smacking kiss on the cheek. "We've talked about it, but we want to get through this tour first and then see what we're going to do next."

"What are you thinking?" Vivienne asked, unable to help herself.

"We've only got another dozen stops on the tour, and then we know we're taking a three-month break to go back to LA and stay in our home."

"It's such a freaking amazing home—it has the best views. I couldn't imagine him getting rid of it." Savannah chimed in. "I had a small place, and believe me, it was no hardship to move out of it and in with him."

"And what about after that?" Matt asked, and Vivienne heard the twinge of anxiousness there.

Riley gave another sly grin in Matt's direction. "Why? What do you think I should be doing? Any suggestions?"

A hearty laugh was Matt's first response. Then, shifting in his seat, he said, "I don't know. By then it might be time to get the band back together. What do you think?"

"I've been thinking about it a lot," Riley replied as he reached over and snagged the last piece of cornbread. "But we'll need to see where Dylan's at by then and what Julian's doing. For all we know he's going to still be caught up in Dena's career." He snorted with disgust.

"Or we can hope that he'll have his head out of his ass by then and be ready to come back and play real music."

"We'll see." Riley shrugged. "It's something I'd love to do. But I don't want to do it unless it's the four of us. What about you?"

"I agree. I think I can honestly say that you guys make me a better musician." Matt's voice was deep and serious, and Vivienne knew it cost him a lot to make that admission. She squeezed his hand.

"I think we do that for each other," Riley countered. "Don't get me wrong, I'm loving this new album and the music and the group of musicians who are touring with me, but...it's not the same. Like I said earlier, it's a different vibe. I miss our music."

"Well, whenever you're ready, I'll be ready."

"What about you?" Riley asked cautiously. "What's next?"

Matt sighed wearily, and Vivienne wondered how he was going to answer. She remembered their conversation from the other night, about him wanting a home, but he hadn't talked about what he wanted to do professionally. The fact that he wanted to go back to recording and touring with Shaughnessy was a great thing, but what was he going to do in the meantime?

"You know," he began slowly, "I'm not really in any great rush to do anything. The whole Broadway thing taught me some serious lessons. For starters, I can now safely say that I no longer think I'm infallible. It's hard to believe I can find anything positive with the experience, but it helped me to get a bit of a grip on reality. I'm a good musician, but I'm not great. I know my limitations." He shrugged. "I thought I needed to be doing something different when my life, my professional life, was pretty damn great."

Riley nodded. "I know what you mean. When we put an album together, you, me, and the guys? It's easy. We work together and seem to know what's going to work. I thought I had the talent to do it on my own and it would be easy. But it sure as hell wasn't."

"I guess if nothing else, we can look at this time as a good thing—a growing experience," Matt commented. "Look at us. We're growing!"

"I'm so proud of us," Riley teased.

"You two are idiots," Savannah said with a laugh. She rose and started clearing away plates. Vivienne stood up and started to do the same.

"Viv, everything was amazing. Cooking has never really been my thing. Believe it or not, Riley's the cook in our relationship."

At that comment, Riley groaned. "I set the bar too high trying to impress her, and now I'm stuck in that role."

"Poor baby," Savannah cooed as she leaned over and kissed him. "You know you love it."

"Matt is learning," Vivienne said and then mentioned how they had been working together on meals for the magazine and blog. "The first week he was here, he was making sandwiches and heating up frozen entrées, but it turns out he can grill a mean steak and has been keeping up with me in the kitchen."

"Watch it, man," Riley said, sounding serious. "Next thing you know, you'll be making all the meals while Vivienne's locked in her office writing a novel or something. It happens before you know it."

"Nah," Vivienne said, unable to hide her amusement. "I'm too much of a control freak in the kitchen. I'm unable to sit back and relax while someone's in here messing around with my pots and pans."

"And her organizational system," Matt commented dryly. "I've never seen a space organized with such military precision."

"And yet I know where everything is and never have to waste time rummaging around for utensils or lids or seasonings when we're hungry and want to eat quickly."

"We can save time if we just make a sandwich or a frozen pizza," Matt teased and then looked at Riley and grinned as if to say, *Watch this*.

"Frozen pizza?" Vivienne cried as she loaded dishes into the dishwasher. Muttering curses under her breath, she sighed with exasperation. "So in the time it takes to heat up that…fake food, I can put a gourmet meal on the table. I cannot even believe you would compare the two!

Have you learned nothing in the last couple of weeks? I mean, honestly."

She stopped her rant when she realized how quiet the room had gotten and when she looked up, Matt, Savannah, and Riley were all staring at her while trying not to laugh.

Hands on her hips, she let her gaze settle directly on Matt. "You did that on purpose."

"Guilty as charged," he said, still smiling.

"You won't think it's so funny when you're back to having no choice but to eat frozen pizzas every night," she said, doing her best to sound firm.

"You'd never let that happen," he countered as he stood up and walked over to her.

And then, right there in front of Riley and Savannah, he took Vivienne in his arms and pulled her in close and kissed her. It wasn't a quick peck on the cheek or quick in any way, shape, or form. It was deep and wet and filled with all kinds of promise, and she felt her knees go weak.

Her arms wound around him. Her hands raked up into his hair as she did her best to be as close to him as she could possibly be.

"Jeez, you two," Savannah muttered.

"Shush. It's like free porn," Riley teased.

That was like a bucket of cold water being thrown on them. Vivienne slowly pulled back and looked up at Matt. She knew her eyes were a little glazed, her breathing a little ragged, but she was relieved to see he was equally affected.

With a sly grin, she turned toward their guests. "Don't let him fool you. It's all about the food. And he likes to play dirty."

They all burst out laughing and as Vivienne finished cleaning up the lunch dishes, all she could think was, *Yeah, this is pretty much perfect*.

———

"Oh my God. I'm going to be late," Vivienne huffed as she ran back up the stairs to her bedroom. "I can't find my purse! Where the hell is my purse?"

Matt looked around the living room and saw a purse sitting by the front door. "Is it black?" he called out.

"Yes!"

"It's down here by the door!" He heard her footsteps overhead and then coming rapidly down the stairs. "You need to relax, Viv," he said, tying to sound soothing. "You've got plenty of time to get to the airport. Aaron's going to have to go through customs, and deal with his luggage and all that, so you're going to be fine. It's going to be okay."

She looked at him as if she didn't believe him.

"Do you want me to go instead? I can totally deal with an airport run."

Shaking her head, she reached down for her purse and looked around the room. "No, but thank you. I'm going to be fine. I really am anxious to see him and…" She paused, then added almost reluctantly, "I want the time alone with him to talk about us."

"You're going to do that on the car ride? Why?"

"Matt, it needs to come from me, and I don't want him blindsided when he gets home."

"That's a bit dramatic, don't you think?" he asked, still stunned at her plan. "Why didn't you mention this to me earlier?"

"For this exact reason. I don't want to argue with you about it. We aren't kids, and we're not going to spend our time sneaking around now that my brother is back. I know how to handle Aaron, and it's important to me that I have this time with him."

There were at least a dozen reasons Matt wanted to disagree with her.

But he didn't.

He trusted her. And if she said this was the way she wanted to do this, then he would go along with it. Not happily, but he'd go along with it.

"You're pouting," she said.

"No, I'm not," he said, and dammit, he knew he was pouting.

"Matt," she sighed, taking his hands in hers, "believe me. This is going to be a good thing, and when we get home later, you'll be thanking me."

"I still think we're not giving your brother enough credit. For all we know he's going to be fine with this, and we've been worrying and freaking out for nothing."

She chuckled even as she disagreed. "You weren't around for a lot of years, Matt. My brother has been giving guys—all guys—hell since I started dating. I doubt you'd be excluded from that."

For a minute, all he could do was stare at her. "Okay, fine. Go and get him. Talk to him. Make him see reason." He paused. "And what is it that I'm supposed to be doing while you're gone?"

"You're in charge of the steaks, remember?" Standing on her tiptoes, she kissed him softly on the lips. "All of the side dishes are ready and just need to be heated up. I'll call you from the car, so you can time everything from there. I put a list on the counter so you can follow those instructions."

Looking over his shoulder, he saw the piece of paper sitting on the granite island. His girl was so adorably organized.

"I really need to go," she said and leaned in to kiss him one more time. "Wish me luck!"

Before he could say a word, she was out the door. Matt stood there and watched her climb into her car and then pull out of the driveway. Once the car was out of sight, he realized he was alone for the first time in a long time. Even though he spent a lot of his time over at Aaron's while Vivienne was working, he always knew she was just a few steps away. It seemed odd to be in her house without her there.

A quick glance at his watch showed he had plenty of time to kill before she was going to have Aaron in the car with her. With nothing else to do, he walked out the door and across the yard.

Dinner was going to be a no-brainer—steaks, au gratin potatoes, and salad—and Vivienne had baked an apple pie for dessert. Apparently, this was one of Aaron's favorite meals, and she was hell-bent on going out of her way to keep her brother in a good mood. They had talked about wine, and while Matt knew both Foresters had several bottles on hand, he was really in the mood for a good Bordeaux.

He searched through Aaron's wines and didn't find one and then trekked across the yard to see if Vivienne maybe had one somewhere that he hadn't seen. She didn't. Looking around the room, he decided he would take Aaron's car and head into town.

"Do I want the wine that badly?" he asked himself on his way back across the yard. It wasn't that he *had* to have the wine, but he knew it would go perfectly with the meal, and as Vivienne had done all of the preparations and the shopping, Matt felt he wanted to contribute something other than his grilling skills.

He found the keys and walked out to the garage. It wasn't until he was sitting in the car that he realized he was shaking.

"This is bullshit," he muttered, starting the car. Sure, it had been a long time since he'd driven himself pretty much anywhere, but that was only partially what was freaking him out. For the most part, Vivienne—and Aaron—had kept him sheltered. Whenever they went out, he had on a hat or sunglasses or pretty much did whatever he could to blend into the background. This was going to be the first time since the show tanked that he was going out and being himself.

And the weirdest part was that he felt like he was doing it for the first time.

All those years ago, the last time he had lived in this town, he'd walked around as a rebellious teen and wannabe rock star. Then, his first years in LA were spent with an overinflated ego as they began making a name for themselves. Once the band started touring, he became Matty Reed, who was really like a caricature of himself—a little flamboyant, a little over the top, and always in search of a party.

It was time for the real Matt Reed to stand up.

And it was far more daunting that he would ever have imagined.

He didn't move, didn't back the car out of the driveway

as reality seemed to kick him in the gut. Even he didn't know who the real Matt Reed was anymore.

Throwing his head back against the cushioned headrest, his breath came out in a loud whoosh. Why now? Why did he have to come to this conclusion about himself right the hell now? All he had to do was go out and pick up a freaking bottle of wine and he'd managed to turn it into a life-altering event.

Okay, he told himself. *Breathe.* After a minute, Matt gripped the steering wheel and chided himself for creating so much damn drama. Why did he have to know exactly who he was? Most people go through life trying to figure that shit out. That meant he was no different than anyone else.

He should take that as a good sign.

But he didn't.

Saying he was Matt Reed was easy. Matt Reed, musician. Just because he currently wasn't recording or touring didn't take that identity away. He was a talented performer, no matter what those Broadway critics claimed, and he was looked up to by many of his peers for his guitar skills. And along with being able to play kick-ass guitar, he was an accomplished songwriter. True, he'd done it primarily for Shaughnessy, but that didn't mean he couldn't do it on his own for other projects, other performers.

For the first time in years, he didn't have a plan or a schedule, and rather than letting it make him crazy, he knew he should embrace it. There were endless possibilities out there. Besides the music, there was his personal life.

He finally had one.

One with meaning.

Although he and Vivienne had been struggling with how Aaron was going to react to the news of their relationship, Matt didn't see it as a problem. A future with Vivienne was what he wanted, and if he hadn't been such a damn coward, he would have professed that before she got in the car today.

Or anytime in the last couple of weeks.

Coward.

And the thing was, he had a feeling it was going to be a sticking point when he talked to Aaron later on. They'd been friends for far too long for him not to call Matt out on not making his intentions clear. But in his defense, he knew he had fallen hard and fast, and was trying to give Vivienne some time to see if she felt the same way. He sighed. She hadn't said it yet, but he felt it in everything she did—her every touch, her every word.

Still, it would be nice to hear her say that she loved him and that she wanted a future with him, and not just allude to one.

Okay, maybe he wasn't the only coward in this relationship.

Hell, they both had baggage. Lots of it. But he had faith that together they could make it work and overcome it all. Matt wasn't sure if it was the reality of everything that happened after the show failed or the time alone or the time spent with Vivienne that had had the most impact. More than likely it was the combination of it all, and as much as it pained him to admit it, he was glad the show had failed. He wasn't happy about the public response to the failure, but the failure itself had forced him to take a long, hard look at his life.

And it had brought him to Vivienne.

Back to Vivienne.

The confidence he hadn't felt a few minutes ago filled him as he reached out and turned the radio on. He smiled when the last ballad Shaughnessy had released together, "Suddenly Mine," filled the air.

He'd done that. He'd been the one to write the chorus, the one who had first presented the idea for the melody. And it just proved they were all wrong—the critics, the paparazzi, the press…and his father.

He had talent.

He was someone.

And by the end of the night, he was going to ask Vivienne if she wouldn't mind being someone with him.

Traffic had been a bitch.

She'd already circled the airport three times.

And if Aaron didn't come out soon, Vivienne wasn't going to have any other choice but to park her car and go wait inside the airport.

It was beyond frustrating, and she wanted to wail at the unfairness of it all. She had everything planned out, even made a list. First, pick Aaron up at airport. Second, ask about his trip. Third, get him caught up on her job and how she was doing. And fourth, tell him about her and Matt. It was simple. Beyond simple. She'd had it planned out almost to the minute. But now he was late, and the more time she had to herself, the more her nerves were beginning to act up.

It hadn't been a lie or simply bravado when she had told Matt she would handle this because she knew how to handle her brother. But saying she could do it and doing it were two completely different things.

What if she didn't get around to telling him about her and Matt? What if he talked about his trip for longer than she thought he would, and they got back to the house and Matt wasn't aware of the change of plans? How was she supposed to convey all of that to Matt in a quick text or call with Aaron sitting right beside her? And with all of this traffic, would her instructions for dinner still work or would things end up overcooked?

Dammit! She hated when all of her well-thought-out plans fell apart. If only—

A loud knock on the passenger window had her screaming. When she looked over, there was her brother, grinning like a loon and motioning for her to open the trunk.

"Okay, crisis averted," she murmured as she reached for her phone and quickly sent off a text to Matt telling him Aaron was with her and to wait twenty minutes before starting their dinner.

The car door opened and Aaron quickly climbed in and gave her a kiss on the cheek. "Thanks," he said breathlessly. "I didn't think I was ever going to get out of there."

"All the sites said you landed on time. I was beginning to get worried."

"Sorry about that," he said, leaning his head back on the seat. "It was a crazy flight—loud. There was a crying baby that never seemed to stop. I thought I was going to lose my mind. Luckily they got off the plane in New York. The second flight was better, but it was a small plane and filled to capacity. I was getting seriously claustrophobic."

"That's not a good thing," she said. "I hate flying for those exact reasons. I'm just not good at it. I like my space; I like my peace and quiet. And when I don't get them, I get very cranky."

"Yeah, well, it was definitely getting to that point."

Vivienne eased into traffic to exit the airport as Aaron talked about his successful trip. Between work and the visit with their parents, he was very pleased. "They were asking when you're coming to visit."

"Your clients?" she teased.

"Ha-ha, very funny. Seriously, Viv. I think you'll notice a big change in Mom and Dad when you see them. They've...mellowed."

"Right."

"It's true!" he protested. "And their friends were all incredibly nice and friendly. For a little while there, it felt like I was in some strange parallel universe."

She rolled her eyes. He always did this, made their parents out to be nicer, sweeter, more...parent-ish than they really were. And like an idiot, she'd believe him and go visit them and find them to be the same cool, distant people they always were.

Not falling for that trap again.

But she let him talk. What was the harm? If it made him feel better, she could pretend to consider what he was saying. Merging onto the highway, she felt herself relax. She was back on schedule and barring any unforeseen traffic or accidents, they'd be home on time for dinner—or before dinner was ready, so she could oversee the final minutes of cooking.

"Are we getting takeout on the way home? Maybe it's strange but…eating in restaurants almost every night gets old. Although I did find some incredible new places on this trip that I'll want to go back to the next time, but I have been jonesing for Chinese. Plus, the thought of being home and maybe throwing on sweats and a T-shirt and eating in front of the TV sounds like nirvana."

"Sorry," she began, "no takeout tonight, but we can do that tomorrow. Tonight we're having steak, au gratin potatoes, and salad," she said, sounding very pleased with herself.

"Wow! Okay, I was wrong. That is definitely better than takeout. But I'm still changing into sweats. You've been warned," he teased. "So we'll be eating late?"

Vivienne shook her head. "Nope. The potatoes are hopefully in the oven right now, the salad is already made, and Matt will be putting the steaks on the grill any minute."

Aaron's eyes went wide as he turned his head to look at her. "Matt's cooking? How did you convince him to do that?"

"There wasn't much for him to do, and he grills a fabulous steak. And I wanted to make sure you had a home-cooked meal for your first night back."

"Thank you," he replied, smiling. "And I guess I shouldn't be too surprised. You've both been telling me about him helping you with meals. It still just seems weird how you managed to domesticate the rock star."

She chuckled. "He wasn't too far gone, so it wasn't that hard to do. I think the distraction was good for him, and he's finally starting to see how the life he was leading wasn't making him all that happy."

"Yeah, I'm sure the millions of dollars, world travel, and beautiful women begging their way into his bed were real hardships."

Hell. The reminder of the women who had come and gone before her hurt more than it should have.

"Maybe, maybe not," she said casually. "Either way, there have been some changes." She told him about Riley's visit and some of the things they'd all discussed, particularly the future of returning to the studio with Shaughnessy.

"That's great news," Aaron said enthusiastically. "I think that is the best thing for him. Not that I think it's wrong to want to try something new, but he was at his happiest when the band was together. At least, for a while he was."

"What does that mean?"

"I know he started to get disillusioned toward the end. The drinking, the partying—it was all too much. It would be nice to see him calm down a bit and maybe…I don't know…settle down a bit."

Okay, here was her opening—her brother had segued to it perfectly. "It's funny you should mention that—"

"Although who the hell am to judge?" he interrupted, seemingly unaware Vivienne had even spoken. "I'm settled down and it doesn't seem like I'm any closer to having my shit together than Matt does."

Here was a second hiccup in her well-thought-out schedule. "Why would you even think such a thing? You have a great career, a beautiful home; you travel and have a ton of friends. What's not together?"

Aaron looked at her and gave her a lopsided grin. "Try not to take this the wrong way…"

"O-kay."

"But it would be nice if someone other than my sister was waiting for me when I came home."

"Oh… Well…I, um—"

"It's okay, Viv. I don't expect you to have a solution for me and it's not that I don't love seeing you and appreciate you taking the time to come and get me. It's just that…" He stopped and sighed. "I'm ready to move on to the next phase of life—a wife, kids. I'm tired of being alone."

And there was her opening again. "I know what you mean," she began. "I've been feeling the same way. And I finally realized…"

"I met this amazing woman while I was in Paris!" he blurted out and then sighed. "God. I can't even believe I'm saying this, but…" He twisted in his seat to look at her. "I never believed in love at first sight. I thought it was ridiculous. Then I was walking along the Rue des Barres, and I saw her. Before I knew it, I had turned around and was following her. I've never done anything like that in my life!"

Vivienne was speechless. Aaron wasn't kidding—he wasn't the spontaneous type at all, and she found herself gripping the steering wheel a little harder as she anxiously listened to his story. "So what did you do? Did you go and introduce yourself?"

He shook his head. "Not at that point. But I followed her. I had no idea what I was going to do. Then she stopped and walked into L'Ebouillanté—remember that place? It's a tearoom. Mom's always talking about it."

"I've gone there a couple of times with her."

"I sat down at the table next to hers, and I drank

more tea than I think I have in my entire life." He chuckled. "When I ordered my sixth cup, she finally looked up at me and I swear, Viv, it was like getting hit by a lightning bolt."

She could totally relate to that. Which reminded her... "I know that feeling pretty well myself. Actually—"

"Her eyes were such an unusual shade of blue—almost gray. And her smile—when she finally smiled at me—was so sweet and shy. She blushed. I didn't think women did that anymore." He sighed. "She commented on how I must really like tea, and then I admitted that I was only drinking it because I was hoping to introduce myself."

Clearly she wasn't going to get to share her news anytime soon, so she simply let him finish. "And did you? Finally?"

He nodded. "I did. Her name is Emilie." Just saying the name made him smile. "She's a teacher—elementary school. She was born in Wales but moved to Paris when she was a teenager. Her accent is amazing. We sat in the tearoom all afternoon, and then we left and walked around in no particular direction, and the next thing I knew, it was dark out. I took her to dinner and we sat and talked until the restaurant closed." He laughed softly. "Then we found someplace else to go, and the sun was coming up when I finally walked her home."

Vivienne briefly took her eyes off the road to stare at her brother in shock. "Are you kidding me?"

Aaron shook his head. "If it weren't for the fact we were both near delirious, I wouldn't have even ended it there. I'm telling you, Vivienne, it was amazing."

"So? How did you leave it? Are you going to see her again? I hope you're going to at least call her and go back some time soon. Or maybe she can come here? Did you ask her to come here?"

Beside her, Aaron went silent.

"Aaron?" she asked cautiously.

"Do you honestly think this would be a relationship that had a chance of working? We're on different continents. We had an amazing weekend." He shrugged. "Okay, it was four days. But I don't think I'll ever forget them."

"Wow. I don't even know what to say."

"There's nothing you can say. Sometimes things aren't meant to be." His voice was so sad and so low, and it made Vivienne want to cry.

"Maybe right now," she began, "but you know you're in Paris several times a year. You could always see her on those trips."

He shook his head. "How fair would that be? To either of us? No. It's better this way."

"Better for who? I would think you'd put up a little more of a fight for her if you're really serious." She let out a small snort of disgust at him. "You're being incredibly foolish, Aaron. I can't believe you."

Aaron shot her an annoyed glance. "You're one to talk. When was the last time you fought for a relationship?"

"What's that supposed to mean?" she snapped, completely annoyed how somehow this was becoming an attack on her.

"It means I've watched you date some really great guys, and then you let them walk away. And it never seems to faze you, Viv. How is that possible? Are you so scared of getting attached to someone? Is this all because of Mom and Dad? When the hell are you going to let it go and quit playing the abandonment card? No one did that. They weren't the greatest parents, but you were certainly never deprived of anything. Don't you think it's time you got over it?"

She didn't know how it was possible, but they were pulling into the driveway at home. That scared her because she didn't remember the drive through town. Throwing the car into park, she turned and faced him.

"This isn't about me and it pisses me off how you're trying to make it that way. This is about *you* not taking a risk. You! Not me!" she yelled, stabbing him in the chest with her finger. "You sat there and waxed poetic about this woman and yet you were able to walk away. Seems to me you're also scared to get attached to someone!"

"No I'm not!" he argued. Loudly. "There's a big difference between being afraid of getting attached and knowing when something isn't going to work out! If she lived here in the States or if I lived in Europe, you can be damn certain we wouldn't be having this conversation!"

"Don't be obtuse, Aaron!" she yelled back. "Long distance is long distance. According to your logic, if you lived here in North Carolina and she lived in Oregon, you'd be fine with that. Well, I call bullshit."

"Excuse me?" he roared, unbuckling his seat belt.

"You heard me! It would still be a pain in the ass to trek across the country whenever you wanted to see one another, so don't try and make it out like you'd be okay with it. You fly on business all the damn time. You have more frequent flyer miles than you'll ever use. Take a damn chance! If you ask me, you're more terrified than I've ever been."

"So you admit you do that, that you simply don't

get into relationships that matter because you're inca-
pable of letting yourself rely on someone. Not everyone
leaves, Viv! Not everyone is going to let you down!"

"You don't know what you're talking about," she
hissed and turned to unclick her seat belt. As she was
about to open her door, Aaron reached out and grabbed
her arm.

"You're just like them," he said, and Vivienne knew
that tone—he was trying to be hurtful. It didn't happen
often. Only when they fought. He was bringing out the
big guns, and it was working.

"I am nothing like them," she said, gritting her teeth.
"Let go of me."

"You bitch and moan and cry about how cold and
distant they are and yet you're not doing a damn thing to
make sure you don't repeat their mistakes. What are you
afraid of, Viv? Afraid it wasn't them? That it was you?"

She felt like he had slapped her. Gasping, she pulled
free of his grip and turned for the door. She was stum-
bling out when she realized Matt was standing there,
catching her.

"Vivienne? Are you all right?" He wrapped her in his
arms, and she knew she was trembling, knew there was
no way to explain.

"Take your hands off my sister," Aaron called out as
he climbed from the car. He stalked over and made to
separate them.

As soon as Aaron touched her, Matt shoved him off.
"What the hell, Aaron? What's the matter with you?" He
kept his arms wrapped possessively around her, his hard
gaze never wavering.

"Son of a bitch," Aaron murmured. "Are you freaking

kidding me?" His voice grew louder. "Are you sleeping with my sister?"

"Aaron," Vivienne said as she tried to turn in Matt's arms.

"Yeah," Matt said over her, louder. "Vivienne and I are involved." His tone was defiant and firm, and all Vivienne could do was close her eyes and wait for the fallout.

"I trusted you," Aaron said with a deadly calm that was in complete opposition to his earlier tone. "I opened my home to you, gave you a place to stay when you had nothing, and this is how you thank me?"

"This had nothing to do with you," Matt said, his voice deep and thunderous. "And it still has nothing to do with you. I'm in love with your sister. Do you understand that? I love her."

"You don't know the meaning of the word," Aaron hissed. "You're just using her. You're killing time. Don't insult us both by pretending otherwise."

In the blink of an eye, Vivienne felt herself being spun away as Matt lunged at her brother. She cried out, but she wasn't sure who she was trying to protect. Fists were flying, and she couldn't get close enough without risking getting caught in the crossfire.

"You son of a bitch," Matt snarled as he knocked Aaron to the ground.

"What are you gonna do now, rock star? Who's going to take you in now? Because I want you to get your shit and get out!"

"That's enough!" Vivienne cried, but no one was listening. They were too busy rolling around on the ground, hurling insults at one another. "That's enough!" she screeched and was surprised when they stopped moving.

Matt shoved Aaron away and came to his feet, brushing the dirt off his clothes. He looked at her, and she could see he was doing his best to push his anger aside and not take it out on her. The smile was apologetic, and her heart simply melted. Unable to help herself, she closed the distance between them and wrapped her arms around him.

"I meant what I said, Vivienne," he said against the top of her head, placing a kiss there. "I love you. I should have said it sooner. I was trying to give you time. But it's how I feel. I'm sorry I said it like this—with an audience," he snarled over his shoulder. "But it doesn't change anything." He tucked a finger under her chin until she looked at him. "I love you."

Oh hell, she thought. It wasn't even remotely romantic—something she swore she always wanted—and yet it was perfect. Perfect for them. She smiled up at him. "I love you too."

The sound of Aaron cursing was the last thing she noted before Matt's lips claimed hers.

Chapter 9

"I PROMISE THIS WILL LOOK BETTER TOMORROW."

"I'm not even going to think about it."

"Kind of hard not to. I mean…it's a lot."

"Matt?"

"Hmm?"

"Stop talking." To guarantee that he did, Vivienne leaned over and kissed him. They were lying in her bed, it was well after midnight, and she was mentally exhausted.

After she had told Matt she loved him, she'd helped her brother up off of the ground. They'd had dinner together, but it was strained and awkward. They'd decided that Matt would move in to Vivienne's place, which didn't seem to do anything but enrage Aaron more. He'd been very blunt in his declaration of wanting Matt gone.

But that wasn't going to happen.

He was staying.

With her.

"I can feel you smiling," he said when she lifted her head.

"I can't help it," she replied and then snuggled down beside him. "I'm happy. Very happy."

"Even with my stuff strewn all over the house? I know you hate that kind of thing. I told you I would have hung everything up and put the suitcases away."

"It wasn't necessary. Not tonight. Tonight I just wanted us to come up here and relax and make love."

He kissed the top of her head. "And I believe we did all of those things. Some twice."

She chuckled. "Best part of the night."

Sighing, Matt pulled her close. "I'm so sorry, Viv."

"For what?"

"That it all happened this way. I expected Aaron to be upset, but I never thought he'd react quite like that. I knew I should have gone with you to the airport. The ride home must have seemed like forever."

Realizing that in all the chaos and awkwardness, she hadn't had time to tell him what had happened on the drive home, she told him about Aaron's trip and how it led to the fight.

"So you never even got to tell him about us?"

She shook her head. "Nope. He had no idea until I got out of the car and you were holding me."

"Shit. So really, this is my fault."

"Absolutely not," she said, lifting her head to look at him. The room was dark, but bathed in moonlight, she could still see his handsome features. "The only one at fault is Aaron. I think no matter how we broke the news to him—whether I did it in the car or if we told him together over dinner—he was going to freak out." When she relaxed back against him, she sighed.

"What?" he asked softly. "What are you thinking?"

"What if he's right?"

She felt Matt stiffen beside her.

"About what?" he asked cautiously.

"About me. What if I'm the one who's cold and distant? What if I'm just like my parents? Or what if they're not like that at all and it is just me?"

"Viv, that's not even possible."

"But it is," she cried softly. "Aaron was right—at least partially."

"Vivienne."

"I do end up in relationships that don't matter to me. I choose men who are distant and aloof, and when it ends, I don't give them a second thought. It's like I purposely choose ones who are going to leave. And—"

"Be very careful with your next words," he warned in a low growl.

She raised her head. "Matt, I know you love me. And I know I feel the same about you, but..." She looked at him sadly. "Can you honestly say you're looking for something long-term? What happens when you're ready to go back into the studio or on tour? Do you think you could live here, in this town, with me?"

His silence spoke volumes, and for some reason, it both irritated her and gave her comfort because, in the back of her mind, she knew this always had the potential to be temporary. Maybe getting Matt to admit it now would be the best thing for them both. No need to prolong things further.

Hell. Maybe Aaron was right.

Beside her, she heard Matt's soft sigh. "I tried to kill my father."

Everything in her sagged with relief. He was finally going to tell her.

"Okay," she said softly, but she couldn't seem to make herself move—not to lie back down beside him or to move away. All she could do was continue to watch his face in the moonlight.

"My senior year. He'd been riding my ass for so long, doing everything he could to tear me down and make me feel like I was worthless. For a time, I started to believe him. But then things started happening with the band. We were playing gigs and getting a lot of positive feedback." His voice was low and void of emotion. "I went home one night to grab a change of clothes or whatever. Aaron was with me. I told him to wait out in the car and I'd be right out. But when I went inside, the old man was waiting for me behind the door. Put a gun to my head."

Vivienne gasped loudly and her heart stopped. Was it possible her brother didn't know about this part?

"Oh…Matt…"

"He laughed. The son of a bitch actually laughed. Said it would serve me right, serve my mom right, that the world would be better off without me. And then he laughed even harder. He knew about the band and how things were going, and it gave him a bit of a thrill to think he could take that success away from me by killing me before I had the chance to make something of my life."

She was trembling, physically trembling, as everything in her went cold. For as much as she did complain about her parents, it was nothing compared to this. Her heart broke for the man she loved, the man he was now, and the boy he'd been then. There was no way for her to even comprehend the fear he must have felt in that moment.

"I heard him cock the trigger, and I thought, *This is it*. It's finally going to be over." He let out a mirthless laugh. "And you know what? I was kind of relieved. He'd been beating me down for so damn long that I would almost have welcomed death just so I didn't have to deal with it anymore."

Vivienne shook her head as tears began to fall. Matt's words were in complete opposition to everything she'd ever thought about him. Never in her life could she imagine him being scared or willing to choose death over a situation. Even when he'd first arrived here at Aaron's, when she'd thought he was at his lowest, she could see the fighter in him. It was almost too much to bear.

"Don't…" she began. "You don't have to talk about this, Matt. I'm sorry. I…"

Reaching out, he grabbed one of her hands and squeezed it. "Don't you get it?" he asked sadly. "You need to know this. You need to understand why it is that I feel the way I do."

She almost admitted to him that she already knew, that Aaron had already told her. But the truth was, she didn't know the whole story and maybe Matt needed to tell her—maybe even more than she needed to hear it.

"We'd argued before—knock-down, drag-out fights. Those I could handle because I was bigger and stronger. Not in the beginning, of course. Not right after my mom left. But I remember the first time I fought back, and it felt so damn good. I thought he'd tire of it eventually and leave me alone. Little did I know he was just going to take it to the next level. And that's when I knew it wasn't ever going to end. One of us wasn't going to make it out of there alive, and it was going to be me if I didn't do something."

Wiping away the steady stream of tears, Vivienne gripped his hand harder. "What happened?"

"It was late, and I knew he had been drinking. He was a little unsteady on his feet. There was still a ton of adrenaline kicking through me from the show. I elbowed him in the face, shocked him enough that he dropped the gun. We fought and wrestled to the ground, and I reached out and grabbed it—the gun. And I put it in his mouth." His grip on her was almost painful. "And I pulled the trigger."

Her gasp filled the room as loudly as any gunshot.

"It was empty. The son of a bitch was just screwing with my mind." He muttered a curse. "He laughed like a deranged lunatic, and I threw the gun across the room and just pummeled him until your brother came in and dragged me off of him." He paused, released her hand, and sighed. "I never went back. I grabbed my shit and left."

Unable to help herself, Vivienne leaned down and wrapped herself around him, holding him close. "I'm so sorry," she sobbed. "So, so sorry. No one should ever have to live through something like that."

"I knew what I had to do—I had to leave. But I needed to finish school, graduate. I didn't want him to rob me of anything else. But as soon as the cap and gown came off, I was gone."

She remembered.

"Ever since, I've been afraid to come back. To come home. For all I know that worthless bastard would try to have me arrested. It wasn't a risk I was willing to take."

"But you did finally come home."

He shrugged. "I didn't have a choice. I had no place else to go. And with what Aaron proposed, I wouldn't have to go out or go into town, and no one would know I was here. When you hit rock bottom and someone offers you a lifeline, you tend to take it."

"Matt, I don't think there's even a chance of your father trying to do anything. Don't let him have that kind of power over you. Look at all you've done with your life. You proved him wrong. You're crazy talented, and that's all you. No one did it for you. You went out there and worked hard and have the kind of success most of us only dream of!"

"You just know he was probably freaking giddy when the news hit about the show. He probably—"

"Who cares what he did or what he thought?" she snapped with irritation. "He's not worth thinking about, Matt! What he did to you for all those years is criminal. Charges should have been brought against him."

A shuddery breath was his only reaction.

They lay there, wrapped around each other for a long time.

"Is..." she began cautiously. "Is that what you dream about?"

He didn't answer, he simply nodded.

"I'm so sorry, Matt. For all of it," she whispered, and she held him a little bit closer, the sound of his heartbeat the only thing she heard for a long time.

"I would do it, though," Matt said, breaking the silence.

"Do what?" Her voice was a mere whisper.

"I'd stay here, live here, to be with you." Slowly, he rolled them over until he was looking down at her face. "I would do that for you because you mean that much to me."

"Oh," she sighed, her hands raking up into his hair.

When he leaned forward and kissed her softly on her cheek, then the tip of her nose, her eyes, and then finally her lips, she felt love for him overwhelming her. Never in her life had anyone put her first.

Ever.

And here was Matt, who had more of a reason than

anyone else to hold on to his need to move on, willing to stay in a place that made her happy.

It was humbling.

And terrifying.

And wonderful.

His kiss became more urgent as they began to move against one another, and as Vivienne slowly slid her legs against his and then around him, she knew that as crazy as everything was—that night, their lives, their situations—this man was her future.

———

For two days, it was like there was some sort of stand-off going on. Aaron stayed on his side of the property; Matt and Vivienne stayed on theirs. It was working, but…it was ridiculous. And Matt was seriously done with it.

Vivienne had left to run some errands and go shopping, so Matt figured the timing was perfect. He knew Aaron was home—his car was still in the driveway—and he was done waiting for everyone to play nice.

Even though Vivienne hadn't said anything about it since that night, Matt knew it was bothering her not to be speaking with her brother, and in Matt's mind, they were all at fault here. No one person was to blame. But he was taking it upon himself to make it right. If Aaron had a problem with him personally, then it was time they addressed it and moved on. There was no way he was going to let this kind of thing continue—especially if it was hurting Vivienne.

Pulling the door shut behind him, he stalked across the yard. Aaron must have seen him coming because suddenly the back door opened and he was standing there, filling the doorway and glaring. Matt didn't even break stride. He simply walked up onto the deck and stood right in front of Aaron with the same hard stare.

"We gonna talk about this?" he asked, and was only mildly pleased to see the remains of the split lip and black eye he'd given Aaron.

Without a word, Aaron stepped aside and let him in. They walked into the living room, and each took a seat—on opposite sides of the room. Matt figured he'd be the bigger guy and let Aaron speak first, but clearly he wasn't ready to talk yet.

Fine.

"What do I have to do to prove to you that I'm serious about Vivienne?"

Aaron's eyes narrowed as he sat back in his seat, but he didn't respond.

"Neither of us planned this, bro. We started spending time together, and she was the first woman who ever just wanted to talk to me. She wasn't looking for anything from me and she sure as hell wasn't impressed by me." He chuckled thinking back to how much of a hard time she had given him. "We would sit and talk for hours, and she forced me to look at my life and what a mess I was. I had forgotten what it was like to talk with someone who wasn't trying to kiss my ass."

"And that's how you decided to repay her? By sleeping with her?"

Matt ground his teeth and fought the urge to get up and fight with him again. Silently counting to ten, he shifted in his seat. "This isn't about sleeping with her, and it's none of your damn business. I'm in love with her, Aaron. And that's not going away—no matter how big a dick you try to be. I love her and she loves me."

Finally, Aaron moved, leaning forward and resting his elbows on his knees. "And what about a month from now, Matt? Staying in one place makes you crazy. You know it. I know it. And we both know you're not going to stay here. It took over twelve years for you to come back and you've been hiding out since you got here. Are you going to try and tell me all of a sudden you're okay with being here? With running into your father?"

At the mention of his old man, Matt stiffened. "If this is where Vivienne wants to live, then this is where I'll be."

Aaron let out a derisive snort. "And what? You'll stay cooped up in the house? Never venture into town for fear of seeing your dad?"

"He's not an issue," Matt ground out.

"Bullshit. He's been an issue since you were a kid. I was there, Matt. I remember it all. I know my sister is an amazing woman, one that you don't deserve, but even I know she's not going to be enough for you to overcome your aversion to being here. Eventually, you're going to get tired of looking over your shoulder and then what? Where does that leave Vivienne?"

It had been on Matt's mind from the get-go. Yes, there was going to come a time when he was tired of it, but he didn't know what the solution was.

Not yet.

All he knew was that he was willing to try.

"That's what I thought," Aaron said when Matt remained silent. "You're asking me to sit back and watch you slowly break my sister's heart. I can't do it, man. Not even for you."

"I'm not going to break her heart," he replied defensively.

"You may not think so, but that's what's going to happen. Vivienne's a homebody. She lived in Denver for two years, and it damn near killed her. This is her home. I don't know why she feels such a pull for this town, but she does. Maybe she'll travel with you, maybe she won't mind being in LA or touring with you, but this is always going to be her home base. And I know you, Matt. Like it or not, I know you. I was there," he said emphatically. "This is not the place you want to be—even temporarily."

"In case you haven't noticed, I have been here. For a few weeks now, and I'm fine."

Aaron laughed, but there was no humor in it. "You've been here, but you haven't. You haven't gone into town or—"

"That's where you're wrong," Matt said, coming to his feet. "I haven't walked around town waving a damn flag or anything, but I'm not living like a hermit either. I go shopping with Vivienne. We go to pickup takeout. I went into town alone to pick up wine for the dinner we were supposed to have the night you got home."

"Big deal," Aaron murmured.

"Dude, what the hell do you want from me? You want me to go and stand in the middle of Main Street and let everyone know I'm here? I'll do it! Should I call the local media and invite them over for a press conference? I'll do it!" He stepped closer. "You need to get it through your head that I'm not going anywhere. Vivienne and I may not have all the logistics figured out yet, but her happiness is all that matters to me."

There was nothing but silence again, and Matt had to wonder what he was thinking. Would he possibly believe his declaration, or were they going to keep fighting about this?

"You have to go and talk to him," Aaron said in a low voice.

For a minute, Matt was too stunned to respond.

"It's the only way for this issue to be gone."

"You can't be serious."

Aaron nodded.

"What the hell is wrong with you?" Matt hissed. "Why? Why would you suggest something like that? What have I ever done to you do make you this freaking twisted?"

Slowly, Aaron stood and faced him. "Believe it or not, I'm not doing this *to* you, I'm doing this *for* you. You've held on to it long enough." He put his hand on Matt's shoulder. "Or maybe I should say it's held on to you long enough."

"You have no idea what you're asking."

Aaron looked at him sadly. "That's where you're wrong. I do. But if you're going to stand here and talk about Vivienne and her happiness, you know that living here is a big part of it. And there's no way for either of you to be happy with this hanging over your head. If you are truly serious about my sister, if you love her, then get rid of this ghost from the past, Matt."

"You know what, Aaron?" Matt snapped, shoving his friend's hand off of him. "Fuck you." Turning around, he stalked from the room and out the door, slamming it behind him.

By the time he walked across the yard, he was even madder.

"How dare he!" he shouted to no one as he walked into Vivienne's. "Who the hell is he to try and tell me how to live my life? And what I'm supposed to be done dealing with?" He wanted to pick something up and throw it, but nothing here was his.

Pacing the room, his emotions raged all over the place. Go and see his father? Sure! Why not? Who wouldn't want to go and see the man who got a kick out of pretending he was going to kill you? It had taken years—years!—for that nightmare to start to fade, and it was cruel of Aaron to make light of it.

Okay, Aaron didn't know about the gun. No one did. Until last night, it had been his secret, his own personal hell. Maybe if Aaron knew that, he might not have put the option out there, but there was no way in hell he was going to go back over there and try to make him understand that. He had tried to extend an olive branch, and it hadn't worked. Now he was going to need time to cool down again.

And the worst part was that he didn't want to put Vivienne in the middle, so he would keep this to himself. For now. No need to upset her any more than she already was. They only had four more days until they left for Myrtle Beach to go see Riley and Savannah. Maybe by the time they came back, Aaron would be a little more open to talking realistically and maturely about the whole thing.

Taking several deep breaths, Matt felt himself begin to relax. Maybe by the time Vivienne got back he'd feel normal—or at least not so filled with rage. He couldn't imagine it at the moment; right now, he still felt raw. Betrayed.

Maybe Aaron had a point—it was something a

therapist had said to Matt years ago. He needed closure. He needed to confront his demons. It was easy to say when your demon wasn't flesh and blood and your last encounter didn't involve a gun to your head.

Sitting down on the sofa, he took a few more deep breaths and let them out slowly. Twisting around, he reclined and closed his eyes, put his hands behind his head, and did his best to block out those images. Talking about them with Vivienne had been hard enough. Thinking about them again now was like a fresh wound, and it took all of his strength to make them go away.

"Just breathe," he murmured to himself and pictured Vivienne in his mind.

Her smile.

Her beautiful eyes.

Her sexy curves.

His hands twitched with the need to touch her, to feel her moving with him, over him, beneath him. The sounds she made, the sweet scent of her skin... *Yeah*. It was those images that had him relaxing and pushing everything that was negative in his life away.

And by the time he started to fall asleep, it was with a smile on his face.

—⁓—

With her arms loaded down with packages, Vivienne slowly made her way through the door. She had only intended to go out and buy one or two things—sexy things—for their upcoming trip to Myrtle Beach. But somehow two things turned into four, four into ten, and then someone was helping her carry it all to her car.

Closing the door behind her, she sagged with relief at being home. It was so quiet, and it took a moment for her to see Matt sound asleep on the sofa. Just the sight of him made her smile. The man had boundless energy, and even when he wasn't doing anything, he was bristling with it and always moving. It was nice to see him looking peaceful.

The stress of the last several days had clearly caught up to him. They hadn't talked about it much, but it was there, just under the surface. Something was going to have to give there. She had hoped her brother would simply stop being an ass and apologize, but it was too much to ask for.

From the depths of her purse, her cell phone rang, and she dropped her packages and began to fish it out.

Her mother.

"Perfect," she murmured. "Just perfect." Walking into her office, she sat down before swiping the phone to answer it. "*Bonjour, Mere.*"

"*Bonjour, ma fille.* How are you?"

Vivienne was never sure if they should speak in French or English, but right now she was happy to stay in English. "I'm fine."

"You sound tired, my dear. Are you ill?"

"I'm fine, really. I just got home from shopping and am a little out of breath, that's all. How are you doing? How is Papa?"

"He's fine. He is working in his garden. We had a wonderful visit with your brother. It would be nice if you would both come at the same time, so we could all be together."

And there it was—the condescension that was always sneaking in to their conversations.

"Aaron and I don't have the same schedules," she said, doing her best to sound pleasant. "Plus, I was starting my new position with the magazine and needed to be home working."

"But that's just it, *ma fille,* you work from home. Your work is mobile. You could just as easily work on your computer here."

"It's not quite that simple."

"Either way, we would love for you to come for a visit soon."

It was on the tip of her tongue to ask why. It wasn't as if they made a whole lot of time for her while she was there. And then she decided finally to speak up and get some answers. "Aaron tells me you had a dinner party while he was there and introduced him to your friends."

"Oh, *oui*! It was wonderful. We ate and drank and everyone had a good time."

"I find *that* interesting."

"Why?"

"Because you have never introduced me to any of your friends or had a dinner party while I was visiting. The last I checked, I had impeccable table manners and knew how to carry on an intelligent conversation and yet…you keep me hidden away like a redheaded stepchild." Her heart beat madly in her chest as she waited for her mother's response.

"Vivienne, must you be so dramatic?" Her mother sighed.

"Ah…so I'm the problem. It figures," she murmured.

"I taught you better manners than this. You mumble and talk under your breath to your own mother?"

"It doesn't seem to matter how I speak to you, Mama. You hear only what you want to hear," Vivienne said with a sigh, sinking in her chair. Her head was starting to ache and she wished for bad phone reception.

"What is that supposed to mean? I hear you just fine."

"Do you? Because I'm sitting here trying to tell you it hurts my feelings that you don't introduce me to your friends or make any effort with me when I come to visit, and all you can say is that I sound dramatic. How about answering the question? How about explaining to me why it is that you and Papa go out of your way to entertain Aaron but not me?"

And dammit, she wasn't going to cry!

"I…I don't know what you mean."

"Of course you don't." Vivienne sighed wearily. "You know what? Just…let's forget about it." She reached across her desk for her calendar. "I can probably make time for a trip over after next month. I'll work on my schedule to make sure everything is covered at the magazine. How does that sound?"

"It sounds to me like you are doing it to appease me and not because you want to."

Bingo!

"It's just… It's fine. Sorry. Like I said, I just got home and—"

"Vivienne," her mother interrupted. "Maybe…maybe I could come to North Carolina and see you? Just me— your father finds traveling too exhausting lately."

"Um…"

"I hear you did a beautiful job on the guesthouse, and I'd very much like to see it."

Oh, good grief.

"You don't have to do that. I can bring pictures with me when I come to visit. I know you're not a fan of coming back to the States. 'It lacks the culture of Paris,' I believe you said on your last trip here."

She heard her mother sigh.

"Vivienne, I am trying here. I don't know what it is I'm supposed to do."

"And I don't know what it is I'm supposed to do with you either," she replied. "I come to visit you, and we don't do anything. You come here, and you spend all of your time doting on Aaron and giving my life a cursory glance." And now, dammit, she *was* crying. "Why am I not important enough? Why is it so easy for you to shower him with attention and not me?"

"Oh…oh…*ma belle*, don't cry. Please. I know I'm not the type of mother you have always wanted, but I don't know how to be! I was raised in private schools and boarding schools and by nannies and caretakers. When I married your father and you and your brother were born, I didn't know what to do, but I did the best I could. Sometimes I make mistakes, but if you don't talk to me, how am I to know?"

"I would think it would have been obvious," Vivienne said, wiping away her tears. "Why was it easier with Aaron?"

"Oh, my sweet girl, you and your brother are very different. Aaron goes with the flow. He doesn't make waves—at least he didn't when he was younger," she commented with a small laugh. "But you? You were always emotional, and rather than have temper tantrums, you would simply withdraw and show your disapproval with your carefully chosen words and it was written all over your face. I didn't know what to do with you. And after a while, I realized nothing

I did was working and I simply accepted that I was a failure."

"Oh…Mama…"

"I don't blame you. I should have pushed more when I saw that you were unhappy about something. That is on me. I took the easy way out."

"I could have said something rather than pouting."

"No. As your mother, it was my place to pay closer attention. I made sure all of your physical needs were met, but not your emotional ones. I'd…I'd like to try. Maybe we could have one of those…girls' weekends, yes? Is that what they're called? Where we go to the spa or someplace and get pampered and drink wine and relax? Would you like that?"

Vivienne couldn't help but chuckle as she tried to imagine her and her mother sitting in spa robes with their hair up in towels while they drank wine and got pedicures. It was difficult, but it seemed like a fun way to start.

"I'd like that. A lot," she finally said.

"Really?"

"Yes." And she genuinely meant it.

"Oh, this is wonderful! I want you to find a spa for us and pick a date that works for your schedule, and I will fly over and come and see your beautiful home first, and then we will go away for our weekend and leave your brother behind!" She giggled like a schoolgirl then, and it was the first time Vivienne had ever heard such a thing in her entire life.

"I promise to make it happen soon."

"I'm looking forward to it," her mother said. "Oh, and Vivienne?"

"Yes?"

"Thank you."

"For what?"

"For being brave enough finally to talk to me."

They hung up a few minutes later and Vivienne felt a lightness she hadn't felt in years if ever. And she couldn't wait to wake Matt up and tell him.

—⁓—

These were the kind of dreams that made sleeping more than worth it. He was beyond thankful for it considering his usual options.

Vivienne's hands were roaming all over him—up his legs, under his shirt, and then back to unbutton his jeans.

Yes.

The slow drag of the zipper whispered to him, but it was the sound of her lips kissing his stomach that was the more prominent. So soft. So wet. And moving lower.

Hell yes.

Matt shifted as she tugged his jeans down over his hips, down his legs. Cool air hit his skin and then was instantly replaced by warm, smooth skin. Vivienne's. Her nails raked over him, and she dragged his T-shirt up and over his head, and then he reached up and fisted that gloriously long hair in his hand.

So. Damn. Good.

Carefully, he guided her back down his body—after all, he was just a man and this was his damn dream. Her breath teased and tickled as she moved against him. Her teeth nipped at his abs and then the waistband of his boxers, and he was so hard and so turned on he thought he would explode.

Only Vivienne. She was the only woman who had the

ability to do this to him. When his boxers slid off and there was nothing but warm, naked woman in his arms, he dared to open his eyes.

"I was wondering if you were going to wake up," she said softly, straddling his lap.

Not a dream.

But definitely a fantasy.

In the blink of an eye, he was sitting up, his hand braced on her lower back to keep her intimately pressed against him. She let out a small gasp that he quickly swallowed when he claimed her lips with his.

She writhed against him as his hands moved from her back to her hips and up to her breasts. Vivienne pulled her lips from his as her head rolled back and she sighed his name.

"Baby," he growled, filling his hands with her magnificent breasts. "Feel free to wake me up like this anytime." Then he was done talking. He needed to focus on touching her. Tasting her. Claiming her.

"Yes," she purred, and it was such a damn erotic sound that he knew he would never tire of hearing her say it. "Should we take this upstairs?"

Rather than answer her, he simply continued with what he was doing until she couldn't form a single coherent word. He was almost ruthless in his quest to please her, and by the time he was done, he hoped the moment was imprinted on her mind as much as it was imprinted on his heart.

Closing the trunk, Matt looked over at Vivienne as she was locking up the house. "Is that everything?"

"I think so," she replied, smiling at him. "We're only going to be gone for three days. If we forgot anything, I'm pretty sure they have stores in Myrtle Beach."

He chuckled. "Very funny." Then he saw her look over toward Aaron's. He hadn't shared with her the conversation he'd had with him four days ago. After having her wake him up in such an erotic way, he didn't want to ruin the mood. And then she'd shared with him the breakthrough she'd had with her mom, so he figured he'd keep his argument with Aaron to himself. "Do you want to tell him we're going out of town?"

As was her habit when she was nervous, she chewed on her bottom lip. "Do you think I should?"

Hell, he wanted to say no, but that was just him being childish. So instead he replied, "Sure."

Vivienne studied his face as if she knew he was lying. Then she looked back at Aaron's house before walking over and opening the car door. "I'll text him. I want to get on the road."

Matt certainly wasn't going to argue with her. He climbed in and started the car, happy she was willing to let him drive. Guilt niggled at him a bit, but when he looked over and saw her texting, he let himself relax. They were going to get over this bump in the relationship with Aaron. He just wished it was sooner rather than later.

As they drove, Matt wondered how it was that Vivienne was still single. It wasn't the first time his mind had drifted in that direction. Lord knew he was thankful for the fact, but everything she did just made things better.

Take this road trip—it wasn't as if Matt was

completely opposed to road trips; it was just that any-time he'd done one, he found it boring. In the early years with Shaughnessy, they either drove themselves to gigs or had a tour bus. It wasn't until they got a record contract that they were flying to shows. But those early days on the bus were boring as hell. And now, sitting beside him was a woman who not only put together a fairly amazing playlist for them to listen to, but she was chatting on about license plate games and playing I Spy.

One in a million, that's what she was.

They laughed, he spotted far more license plates from other states than he thought he would, and by the time they pulled up to the private beachside home Riley had rented, Matt was surprised at how the time had flown.

He climbed out of the car and stretched, commenting on it.

"We did a lot of road trips when I was little," Vivienne explained. "My parents listened to a lot of talk radio, so Aaron and I had to come up with ways to entertain ourselves. There is nothing worse than a quiet road trip. You can easily go insane."

That made him laugh. "I don't think kids today would have the same problem. With all of the portable devices, iPads and tablets and even TVs that are built into the cars, this generation will never know the struggles of lack of entertainment."

"Hey, you made good time!" They looked up and saw Savannah standing at the front door, waving. "We just got in a little while ago ourselves. Do you need help with the bags?"

Matt shook his head. "We got them."

A few minutes later, they had their luggage stored in the second-story master bedroom. There was another one on the main floor that Riley and Savannah were using, and both had an incredible view of the ocean.

"A girl could get used to this view," Vivienne said as she stepped out onto their deck. Coming up behind her, Matt wrapped his arms around her waist, kissed her neck. "And this too," she purred.

"That's what I'm hoping for," he said softly, breathing in her sweet scent as he held her close.

Turning in his arms, she smiled up at him. "You are, huh?"

"Absolutely."

She chuckled. "I'm kind of a bed hog."

"I can deal with that."

Vivienne tilted her head and considered him. "I make lists for everything."

"That's good because I tend to forget stuff."

"I can be bossy."

That one made him laugh. "I'm used to being bossed around by my management team. I barely notice."

"Hmm...I've told you all my bad stuff. What about you?"

"You thinking of keeping me?" he teased, but inside, his heart was beating wildly.

She nodded.

"I tend to be sloppy."

"It's a good thing I enjoy cleaning," she said.

"Sometimes when I'm working on a song, I'll sit and play the guitar for hours."

"I love music."

He sighed dramatically. "Well...this last one is pretty

big. I don't know if you'll be able to handle it. It could be a deal breaker."

She looked at him curiously but didn't say a word.

"I enjoy lazy mornings in bed, the kind when we're all wrapped up in one another, making love and never bothering to look at the clock."

"Really?" she asked softly, but it really wasn't a question.

Matt nodded. "Same goes for late nights. Or afternoons. Or really anytime we're together near a bed. That's all I want to do—wrap you up in my arms and love you until we're too tired to move."

"Wow," she sighed. "I totally think I can live with that."

"You do, huh?" he asked with a lopsided grin.

"I really do."

"That's good, Viv. Because I was thinking…"

There was a knock at the bedroom door, and they turned as Riley popped his head inside, grinning. "Okay, good. I'm not interrupting."

"Yeah you were," Matt replied grumpily.

"Nah," Riley said, walking into the room. "You're both fully dressed and on the deck for all the world to see."

Matt shook his head and laughed but kept Vivienne tucked beside him. "So what's up?"

"Savannah's got lunch out, and afterward, I thought you'd like to come to the venue and jam with me for a bit while the girls go and do their thing."

Eyes wide with excitement, Matt looked down at Vivienne. "What do you think?"

She loved that his immediate response was to think of her, but her immediate response was to burst out laughing.

"What? What's so funny?"

"Matt, you don't have to ask my permission. I think it's a great idea, and if it's what you want to do, then you should do it." She kissed him soundly on the lips before turning to Riley. "And what kinds of things does Savannah have planned for us? Do you know?"

"She mentioned shopping and pedicures."

Vivienne's smile broadened, and she playfully pushed out of Matt's embrace. "You two can go and play all day," she said as she walked toward the door. "The women have business to attend to."

When she was out the door, Matt was still smiling as he turned to Riley. With a helpless shrug, he said, "I don't even know what I'm smiling about more—getting to jam with you or just seeing Vivienne so happy."

Riley clapped him on the back and gave him a nudge toward the door. "And it's a beautiful thing when those two things go together." He laughed. "Now let's eat so we can play."

———

"This is pure bliss."

"Mmm-hmm."

"I never knew such a thing was possible."

"It's good to have connections."

"Do you think… Oh God, that's good… Do you think we should…maybe… Never mind. Screw it," Vivienne said as she let her head fall back against the massaging chair. Her foot was being massaged, and she was enjoying the most decadent milk shake she'd ever had in her life.

"If you were going to ask if maybe we should

come back and do this again tomorrow, I'm all for it," Savannah said, sighing with her own pleasure.

"Don't get me wrong. I've had pedicures before, and I've had milk shakes. Just never at the same time. And it's glorious."

Savannah nodded. "We came through here a year ago and discovered the ice cream parlor. I nearly orgasmed after I took my first sip of milk shake. So when I was looking for a spa for us today and saw there was one right next door to that sweet, creamy heaven, I knew it would be perfect."

"From this point forward, I will never doubt anything you suggest."

"Were you planning on it?" Savannah teased.

"No. But this just sealed the deal."

They each took a moment to enjoy the massage and their sweet drinks. Vivienne was so relaxed and happy that she could barely believe it. She turned toward Savannah and smiled sleepily. "So where do you guys go after this?"

"We have about a week off and we're going to visit my parents in Kansas."

"That sounds nice. Does Riley get along with them?"

"Oh, yeah. Our families have become very close. My parents came to North Carolina to see me when I was there interviewing Riley's family, and they became fast friends with Riley's dad and his girlfriend."

"That's very cool," Vivienne replied and then sighed. "I'm sure that would be very nice."

"You don't think it will happen for your families?"

Shaking her head, Vivienne reached for her chocolate shake and took a long sip before answering. "My parents live in Paris and aren't all that social—or at least they never used to be. We're working on that." She had to remind herself that there was a good chance of things getting better and not to have such a negative outlook where they were concerned.

"Do they come back often?"

"Not really. Although my mom and I just talked about her coming for a visit and the two of us having some girl time."

"That could be nice," Savannah said, sounding hopeful.

Vivienne wasn't quite ready to believe it or talk about how complicated her relationship was with her parents up to this point in her life.

"And what about Matt's family? Do you like them?"

"He doesn't have one," she said sadly.

Beside her, Savannah softly gasped. "I had no idea."

Vivienne nodded. "His parents divorced when he was younger and his mom left. His relationship with his dad was extremely volatile, and it wasn't until the band took off that he went and found his mom."

"Are they close?"

"She passed away several years ago."

"Oh man. I don't even know what to say. Poor Matt."

"I know. It's one of the main reasons he never comes home to North Carolina. There's no one here for him. Plus, his father still lives in town and Matt has been fairly adamant about not wanting to see him."

"So what does that mean for the two of you?"

"What do you mean?"

"Well…it's pretty obvious he's crazy about you and vice versa, so how do you make that work? Is he willing to live with you, or are you going to move with him?"

"We haven't talked too much about it," Vivienne

admitted. "He's said he'd stay if it made me happy, but I have to wonder if it's the right thing—the fair thing—to do."

Savannah nodded. "Let me ask you this: How attached are you to where you live? Are you open to living someplace else?"

She shrugged. "It's been my home since forever. Different houses and all, but it's still my hometown." She sighed. "I lived in Denver for two years for a job and I didn't hate it, but…"

"You missed your home."

"Exactly."

"If I could make a suggestion?" Savannah began cautiously.

"Please!" Vivienne replied anxiously. Maybe an impartial third party was the answer.

"No one says you have to live any one place one hundred percent of the time. Maybe you keep a house here but you also have a place somewhere else. Plus, if they start touring again, you're going to be living a mobile lifestyle."

That was something else Vivienne had been avoiding. Her job wouldn't be an issue—she really could do it anywhere, especially now that she was an assistant editor. But the thought of not having a kitchen of her own to cook in? That had the potential to make her more than a little crazy.

"I can pretty much hear you thinking from here," Savannah said. "Don't let it freak you out. We have no way of knowing if and when they'll tour again. Although…"

Vivienne looked at her hopefully. "Although?"

Savannah looked around carefully and then leaned

close to Vivienne, lowering her voice. "I think after this tour is done, it's going to be a while before Riley takes on such a big thing again."

"Seriously? But what about if the band—?"

"He's ready for a break and…we really want to start a family."

"That's great!"

"Shh!" Savannah hissed and then giggled. "We've been talking about it, and we're both excited at the thought of having a baby, but I told him that if we did, he couldn't be gone for months at a time. I refuse to raise a child that way."

"And what did he say?"

"He fully agreed. So what I'm trying to say is… should they get back together, there's a really good chance it's going to be vastly different from the way things used to be. You won't need to be mobile for too long."

That put Vivienne's mind at ease, and she let herself relax again, picking up her milk shake. "I guess that's one hurdle."

"Just remember, you didn't hear it from me."

Making a zipping motion over her mouth, she smiled. "My lips are sealed."

Chapter 10

EXHAUSTION.

That was the only word that came to Matt's mind and clung. The weekend had been a whirlwind and more fun than he'd had in a long time. They'd said good-bye to Riley and Savannah a few hours ago and were almost home.

Home.

Just the thought of it made him smile.

Turning his head, he looked over at Vivienne and saw she was losing the fight to stay awake. Not that he could blame her. They hadn't slept much all weekend, and after the concert last night, they had pretty much stayed up and celebrated until the sun had come up. It was a lifestyle Matt was familiar with, but he knew it wasn't something Vivienne normally did.

When he and Riley had gone to the arena on Friday and goofed around onstage, it had been fun. They jammed, they sang, they talked about how they felt the first time they'd played a venue that large. There was an agenda for Riley that he needed to follow, so Matt had taken a backseat during some of their time there.

When they arrived for the show Saturday night, they had been ushered backstage along with Savannah, and Matt had been shocked when Riley had called him out to play a couple of songs. They hadn't talked about it in advance, and by the time he had taken his final bow, he had felt more invigorated, more alive, than he had in years. He missed it. He missed playing the music he loved with the people he loved. Toward the end of the last Shaughnessy tour, no one had been having fun. They were all burned-out and ready for a break. Playing with Riley again proved that the chemistry was still there, and although they hadn't gone any further in talking about it, Matt had a feeling that once Riley's solo tour was over, the dialogue would be open to the next Shaughnessy album.

Though it would be several months away, Matt tried to picture living back in LA, where they normally recorded. He used to love living on the West Coast. There was always something to do, someplace to go, a party to be found. That wasn't something he was looking for now. Now he wanted to focus on making the music and making a life that was meaningful and not just about having a good time.

Beside him, Vivienne sleepily whispered his name. He reached over and took one of her hands in his while watching the road. "You okay, baby?" he asked softly.

"Mmm...talk to me. I don't want to fall asleep when we're so close to home." She shifted and sat up a little straighter. "We didn't get to talk, just the two of us, about how you felt going out onstage last night."

He couldn't help but grin. When he had walked off the stage last night, he had felt like he was on top of the world. The adrenaline was pumping, and the amazing response from the crowd had felt like total vindication.

He was back!

Before they had gotten on the road, Riley had simply handed him a copy of a review of the show and said,

"We'll talk." When Matt had gotten in the car, he had glanced at it briefly, and his heart had kicked with pure joy. "Riley Shaughnessy Gets a Little Help from His Friend—Matty Reed! And the Fans Want More!" the headline read.

"You saw the review, right?" he asked.

She nodded and yawned loudly. "Oh...sorry. It was amazing, Matt. I know I saw you on the last tour you guys did together, but what you did last night was so much better. There was an energy, a playfulness, that wasn't there then. The crowd was almost deafening by the time you were done."

Exactly, he thought.

"Did you know Riley was going to do that—call you up onstage?"

"We sort of talked about it, but I didn't really think he'd do it. We had so much fun just goofing around on Friday, but I didn't think about doing anything at the show. It's Riley's show, his music, and I certainly didn't want to do anything to take that away from him. But I think the fans loved that we threw some of our old music in there on the fly. Honestly, I was having a great time just listening to him and his band—they sound freaking amazing! Better than I thought they would." He looked over at her and smiled. "Can I let you in on a little secret?"

"Absolutely," she replied, grinning back at him.

"I totally wouldn't be opposed to having those guys with us on the next Shaughnessy album. Even though the four of us sound great and play great together, I think adding a couple more backup musicians could work for us."

"What do you think Riley will say?"

He shrugged. "I have no idea. He seems pleased with all of them, so I can't imagine him being against working with them again."

"And what about Dylan and Julian?"

He shrugged again. "That's anyone's guess. It's a little scary to think about how different we're all going to be when we get back together. By that time, we'll all have done our solo stuff and tried new things and dealt with our own crises, but I have no idea how it's going to change the music. Does that make sense?"

"Definitely. It would seem to me like you were all together for so long that you didn't have a chance to form your own identities. It was the four of you. Now it's going to be four individuals coming together. Are you worried it's going to change the music a lot?"

"Change isn't necessarily a bad thing. But I'd like to think that before we step foot into a studio that we'd spend some time getting to know one another again."

She smiled. "That's a very mature way to approach it."

He nodded. "Clearly I'm growing up." Then he chuckled. "About damn time, right?"

Vivienne squeezed his hand. "I don't know about that. I think you're fine just the way you are."

"You're just biased." His tone was gentle and soothing as he lifted her hand to his lips and kissed it. "Look where we are."

Looking up, she saw they were pulling up in front of her house. "Mmm…home," she purred.

She looked and sounded exhausted, and as much as he knew she was all about being organized and not leaving anything undone, he quickly helped her out of the car and into the house with the promise of getting their luggage later after a long nap.

"But…what if I need—?"

"Shh," he said, placing a finger over her lips before scooping her up in his arms. "The only thing you need is to kick off your shoes, strip down, and climb into bed. We'll deal with the rest later."

The look on her face showed she wasn't completely convinced, but when he put her down next to the bed, she did exactly as he'd suggested and kicked off her shoes and slowly took off her clothes. Matt stood transfixed watching her. Thirty seconds ago, all he could think about was crawling into bed beside her and going to sleep. But as she stripped her black lace bra off and then shimmied out of the matching panties, he was suddenly wide awake.

Vivienne noticed the change in him and gave him a knowing smile. With deliberate movements, she drew the comforter and sheets back and crawled onto the bed, rubbing the spot next to her. "You were planning on joining me, right?" she asked softly, seductively.

He almost swallowed his own tongue as she skimmed her fingers across her breasts and down her belly. His own clothes came off in record time, and before he knew it, he was stretched out beside her, his hands mimicking her earlier movements.

"I thought we were going to take a nap?" she teased.

"We will," he murmured, lowering his head to capture a nipple with his mouth. God, she tasted so sweet. His teeth gently scraped against her skin and Vivienne's back arched off the mattress. "Unless you'd like me to stop."

Her fingers raked up into his hair and held him to her. "No. Don't stop. Never stop."

That was good because he had no intention to.

———

Another week had gone by and things were still tense with Aaron. Granted, he had gone back to work and wasn't home during the day, so that hadn't helped them bridge any gaps. Vivienne had taken on some additional duties with the magazine while one of the other assistant editors was away on vacation, and that left Matt with a lot of time on his hands.

And most of it was spent in his own head.

He hadn't reached out to Riley because he knew his schedule was pretty full and he didn't want to add any more pressure to him as he finished up the tour. But that didn't mean he wasn't working things out in his head—logistics, music, ideas for freshening up their sound without losing their roots.

It was both exciting and terrifying.

He was sitting on the sofa mindlessly strumming his guitar when Vivienne came bustling into the room and went straight for the kitchen. "You okay?" he called out, putting the guitar down.

"Yeah. I just got word I need to be part of this conference call. It's going to be a long one, I can tell already."

Matt looked at the clock and saw it was after four. "This late in the day?"

She nodded and pulled a bottle of water out of the refrigerator. "I know. We're in crisis mode. Janet, the woman who is on vacation, just emailed and said she's not coming back. She's going to work for one of our competitors and she's taking some of our writers with her! Ugh. I hate this kind of stuff!"

"I guess it goes with the territory."

"I know, I know. I guess I didn't realize there would be this kind of stress when I took the position. From where I was before, it seemed like everyone got along. It wasn't until the promotion that I realized there was a lot of animosity behind the scenes. And now I'm getting sucked into the drama."

He stood, walked over to her, and gave her a quick kiss. "I'm sorry, baby. What can I do? You want me to get dinner?"

"Ooo…that would be great. Maybe in about an hour call in an order. I don't even care what you get. It's your call." She looked over her shoulder at the clock and frowned. "Literally. You decide what to get and pick it up and hopefully by the time you get back, I'll be done." She stood on her tiptoes and kissed him before turning back toward her office. "Wish me luck!"

He heard the door close and stood there for a moment. Now what? Glancing back toward his guitar, Matt knew he could pick it up and goof around for an hour until it was time to call in their dinner order, but he had lost his focus.

With a sigh, he walked across the room to the front window and looked over at Aaron's house. He knew he was home, had seen him pull in to the driveway earlier. "This has gone on long enough," he murmured. It was time to let everyone sit down—or try to—and clear the air once and for all.

There was a real chance it was going to all blow up in his face, again, but he was willing to try. He'd call in a dinner order for three and invite Aaron over. It was a simple plan and had a very real possibility of not working, but someone had to make the first move, and it was clear that the Forrester siblings weren't going to do it.

He only hoped Aaron would be agreeable. Matt had a feeling that given the chance, Vivienne would love to have this whole thing over with. And maybe because Matt had no siblings, he didn't fully understand the dynamics, but it almost seemed as if they considered it a weakness to be the one to apologize first. So fine, he'd be the one to do it.

Again.

With a sense of purpose, he walked back to the kitchen and pulled out the folder of takeout menus Vivienne had. Chinese. Italian. Sushi. Burgers. Chicken. He sighed, trying to figure out what it was that he was even in the mood for. He knew Chinese was a favorite for both Aaron and Vivienne, so he opted for that—one less thing for everyone to argue about. So now he knew what he wanted to order and when he had to order it, all he had to do was wait.

He considered Aaron again and wondered if he should go over there first and invite him to dinner, but then thought better of it. Less of a chance for him to get turned down if he showed up with the food already in his hands.

So he'd wait.

With nothing left to do, he sat on the couch and decided to play solitaire on his phone. He had just swiped the screen when it rang—and he nearly jumped out of his skin.

Riley.

"Hey, buddy! What's up?"

"Finally had some time to sit and think and wanted to give you a call and just say thanks for coming and seeing the show last weekend."

Matt laughed. "It was amazing, Ry. Seriously. And thank you for letting me be a part of it. I didn't expect that, but it was great."

"Yeah, well, I knew if I pushed, you'd decline, so I figured I'd better just throw it at you in a way you couldn't turn down."

"I'm glad you did. I had almost forgotten how much I love to play for an audience like that. I still don't think I've come down from the high it gave me."

Riley chuckled. "That's good. That's good. So, listen. What would you think about doing a couple of more shows like that with me as I finish out the tour? We could test the waters, generate some buzz?"

"Are you serious?"

"I wouldn't be asking if I wasn't."

"What does Mick think?"

That had Riley laughing again. "This has nothing to do with Mick or anyone except the two of us. I enjoyed playing with you. I loved having you up on the stage next to me. You always inspire me, and as much as I've been loving this tour and loving the new music, it's not the same. I was starting to feel burned out and just wanted the damn tour to be over, and then there you were and it invigorated me."

"Dude, I felt the same way—invigorated, I mean." Matt sighed, raking a hand through his hair as his heart beat wildly in his chest. It would be amazing to do some light touring, get his feet wet again, and have the chance to start working with Riley again—and laying the groundwork for a future Shaughnessy project was like a dream come true.

"Think about it," Riley said, interrupting his thoughts. "It would be for maybe only ten shows, and it would only be a three- or four-song set, but I really think it could work and be a lot of fun. And you know the fans would love it."

"Can you send me the tour schedule? Let me see the dates and the cities because I'd have to work out my travel itinerary. There would be—"

"We'd have someone handle it on our end so that you were with us. It would just be a matter of you flying out to meet us. What about your guitars? I know we threw this all at you the other night, and you had to use someone else's stuff. You're going to want your own guitars, I'm sure."

"There are so many guitars that I only took the necessities to New York with me," he murmured more to himself than Riley. Then he cursed. "I hadn't even thought about that stuff in so damn long. I'm sure I can get someone to get a couple of them out for me and ship them to the first stop."

"I'm sure Mick can help us out with that. Are you cool with me talking to him about this?"

"I don't have a problem with it. Do you think he's going to? You know, have a problem?"

"Like I said, Matt, it's not his call. This show, this tour, was my baby. And it was starting to feel a little stale, a little flat. I want to inject some life back into it, and that means bringing you on."

"Wow…Riley. I…I don't even know what to say. How to thank you."

"For what? Matt, we've been playing together since the beginning. I wasn't the one who wanted it to end, if you'll remember."

Matt sighed loudly. "No one wanted it to end. We all just needed a break." Then he laughed. "And you can see how well that's worked out for some of us. So feel free to do the 'I told you so' dance when we're all back together."

"You can count on it." Matt listened as Riley started talking to someone in the background before coming back on the line. "Would you be able to meet me in Dallas on Saturday?"

"Saturday?" The last thing he was expecting was a date so soon. "That's only five days from now. I don't know if I'll be able to get all my shit together and shipped out there that fast."

"I know it's soon and if you can't, I'll completely understand. Talk to Vivienne and see—"

"I will, I will, but…yeah. I want to do this. I'll be there on Saturday. No worries. Just send me the calendar and itinerary and all that, and I'll talk to Mick about my stuff in LA."

"Yes!" Riley cried. "You have no idea how excited I am about this."

"I am too. Definitely! This is going to be like old times."

"Only better, my friend. Only better!"

"I'll see you on Saturday," Matt said, grinning from ear to ear. "Let the party begin!" He hung up as he stood up, mentally high-fiving himself. This was more than he'd hoped for because Riley had approached him rather than the other way around.

Looking at his watch, he figured he'd go out and pick up some champagne to celebrate, and he'd call in their dinner order while he was out and about. With a hearty laugh and a definite spring in his step, he walked to the door and scooped up Vivienne's car keys. "I'm back!" he called out, unable to hide his excitement.

And he had no idea Vivienne was standing in the shadows or that she'd heard any of it.

Matt was leaving.

Everything in Vivienne went cold and numb.

Her conference call had wrapped up much faster than she'd thought, and when she heard Matt on the phone, she had tried to be quiet so as not to disturb him. Then she'd heard him talking about leaving and she had frozen in place.

It was almost too much to comprehend. Her heart hurt and tears stung her eyes. All this time she'd been telling herself not to get attached, not to get her hopes up, and yet…he had made her believe. Everything Matt had been telling her made her believe he was staying with her and that they were going to build a future together.

Like a zombie, she walked to the kitchen and poured herself a glass of wine and then went to sit on the couch.

Why? Why would he do this without talking to her? She knew how much he enjoyed playing with Riley last weekend, but was that enough for him to…leave her? It killed her to think his music meant more to him than she did.

Hard to argue with the truth when you were slapped in the face with it, she thought and felt a fresh wave of pain wash over her. She took a long sip of her wine before placing the glass down on the coffee table. The trembling began as she pulled her knees to her chest and wrapped her arms around herself. And then came the tears.

"No," she cried softly. "I'm not ready for this yet." And even as she said the words out loud, she could still hear Matt's in her mind, talking about staying here with her. Talking about them living together. Making plans. "It's not fair." She shook her head and let it fall forward.

She never heard the knock on the door.

Never heard it open and close.

The next thing she knew, Aaron was sitting beside her wrapping her in his arms. "Hey," he said softly. "What's going on? What happened?"

Releasing her hold on her knees, she reached out and launched herself into his arms as she told him about the conversation she'd overheard. When she was done, she lifted her head and tried to wipe away the tears. "I don't want him to go."

Aaron's face was completely neutral. "So you haven't talked to him about this yet?"

She shook her head. "Like I said, I was on a conference call when he got his call, and I guess he didn't want to bother me." She took another swipe at her tears. "Do you...do you think I misunderstood him?"

With a sigh, Aaron pulled back. "Viv, you know this is what he does, right?"

Now it was her turn to put even more distance between them before she jumped to her feet. "Seriously? You're going to start this again? Why can't you just be my brother right now?" she cried. "Why can't you simply try and be supportive? Do you think now is the time to tear Matt down to me?"

Slowly Aaron came to his feet. "What I meant—before you jump to any more conclusions—was that he travels for a living." Then he waited for her to catch on. "He's a musician, Vivienne. In a band. A band that tours. Why are you suddenly so surprised by this?"

She swallowed hard and tried to collect her thoughts. "Because this wasn't on the agenda," she finally said. "We had talked about this being a possibility—down the road! I didn't expect him to pack his things the second he got the call or to do it without talking to me first!"

"You just said he thought you were on the phone," Aaron argued and for a minute he seemed shocked that he was defending Matt. He raked a hand through his hair in frustration and let out a growl to go with it. "Look, maybe he planned on talking to you over dinner but he had to give whoever it was on the phone an answer right away. If you told Matt not to go, I'm sure he'd call them back and cancel." He paused and studied her. "Is that what you want?"

"Yes," she said instantly and then paused. "I mean... no. I mean—"

"Viv," he quickly interrupted. "Stop and think before you do anything. If your relationship with Matt is as solid as you think it is, it should be able to withstand him doing his job. And believe me, it pains me to even say this but...I think you need to hear him out."

She seemed to sag with defeat. "But what if—?"

Aaron shook his head. "I'm not saying you don't have a right to be upset. You do. But you need to talk to Matt and listen to him and find out why he didn't talk to you first." Then he turned and put more distance between them before starting to pace.

"Aaron?"

He turned his head and looked at her, and for the first time, he showed signs of irritation. "I'm trying to do the right thing here, Viv. I'm trying to be supportive."

"But?"

He stopped pacing and slapped his hands down at his side. "What is it that you want from me? You want the supportive big brother? I did that."

"I know you did, and I'm thankful for it, but I can tell you've got more on your mind. I hate how things have been strained the last couple of weeks. I've missed you." She walked over to him and put her hands on his shoulders. "But I also need you to be honest with me. I may not like what you have to say, but we've never lied to one another."

He looked down at her and his expression went from irritated to compassionate to wary. "This is all the stuff I was afraid of."

"What?" she gently urged.

"I know Matt's lifestyle. I know he thinks he's happy right now, but it was only going to be a matter of time before he got restless. It just happened sooner than I thought. When I talked to him last week—"

"Wait. You talked to him last week? He didn't mention that."

Guilt was written all over his face before he looked away.

"Aaron? What happened? What did he say to you?"

"If Matt didn't talk to you about it, there's probably

a good reason. And again, I think the two of you need to talk when he gets back." He paused. "He is coming back, right?"

Panic had her by the throat for a second before she remembered their earlier conversation. "I asked him to go and pick up dinner for us before I got on my call. He's just out getting it. He'll be back."

"Oh. Okay."

It was his quiet acceptance, oddly enough, that made her snap. "I want you to tell me what the two of you talked about last week."

"Viv—"

"No!" she cut him off. "I'm serious. If it had gone well, the two of you would be talking again. But you're not. That tells me you argued some more and I want to know why! Spill it, Aaron!"

He walked over and sat back down on the sofa and looked up at her sadly. "Matt came over to see me. He made the first move to make things right. Only…I wasn't ready to deal with it. I told him he wasn't good enough for you, that I knew he didn't have staying power, and that I particularly knew he didn't want to stay here in town and make a life for the two of you."

She groaned as she listened and sat down on the opposite end of the sofa.

Aaron gave a helpless shrug. "I told him I didn't believe he was serious, so he asked me what it would take to see that he was being honest."

"And what did you tell him?" she asked with annoyance, unable to believe the two men who meant the most to her in the world were being so damn stubborn with one another.

"I told him he needed to deal with his father, that he needed to go and see him and put that ghost to rest."

Vivienne immediately jumped to her feet. "You did *what*?" she yelled. "Are you out of your damn mind? Why would you do that? Why would you even suggest such a thing?"

"Don't you see?" he yelled back. "His father is the reason he never came home! He's the reason he doesn't want to be here. How the hell do you expect to have a life with him here if he can't move on from that part of his life?"

"Who the hell are you to tell him that he even has to? And you of all people, who knows most of what he went through at the hands of that man, should never ask such a thing of him."

"I had…" Aaron stopped and looked at her oddly. "What do you mean I know *most* of what he went through?"

She was beyond furious with her brother. And Matt. It boggled her mind that this had all transpired a week ago and Matt hadn't mentioned it to her. Clearly he wasn't big on sharing things, something she was going to talk to him about when the two of them were alone later.

"Do you remember the story you told me? The one about the last time Matt saw his father?"

"The night of the big fight? Of course I do."

"Well, you don't know everything," she said snidely and picked up her forgotten glass of wine and finished it.

"What are you talking about?" he snapped, his irritation clearly rising.

"It wasn't just a fight that night. His father held a gun to his head and threatened to kill him," she said, pleased by the shocked look on his face. Nodding, she stepped in close to him and repeated the story Matt had told her. "So think about *that*. Would you want to go and make peace with the twisted psychopath who threatened to kill you?"

Aaron paled. "Holy shit," he hissed. "Matt never said a word... That night...I asked him what had happened, but he never said..." Then he groaned.

"He still has nightmares about it, Aaron," she said, some of her anger ebbing. "Not that long ago he told me he'd stay here—for me. But maybe it was all too much. With you pressuring him and all the memories..." She sat back down on the sofa and felt the tears building again. "It's no wonder he jumped at the first opportunity to leave."

She looked over as Aaron sat beside her. Vivienne rested her head on his shoulder.

"You still don't know that for sure," he said softly. "We don't know the whole story."

With a huff, she shifted, pulling her legs up to curl against her. "I hate waiting."

That made Aaron chuckle.

"Yeah. I know. But he's just getting dinner. He'll be back soon."

―᠕᠕᠕―

"Small-town living at its finest," Matt murmured as he scanned the small liquor store for a bottle of decent champagne. It had been a while since he'd had to do this for himself, and now that he thought about it, he had no idea what he was supposed to be looking for. Deciding on the most expensive one he could find, he grabbed the bottle and walked up to the counter to pay.

"Oh my gosh," the guy behind the counter said with a big grin. "You're Matty Reed!"

Panic hit Matt for a second as he realized he wasn't wearing a hat or glasses or anything to cover up who he was. And then it hit him—he didn't need to. He was okay. Everything was going to be okay. The story of him playing onstage with Riley had hit the papers, and there was no mention to his Broadway failure—only praise for the amazing show they'd put on. Putting a smile on his face, he reached out to shake the kid's hand. "Yeah. Yeah, I am."

"Oh man, this is so freaking cool! No one is going to believe this!" He fumbled around for a minute before pulling out his phone. "Would you mind taking a selfie with me?"

"No problem," Matt replied. "Why don't you come around the counter so we can get a good shot?"

The kid jumped the counter and immediately put his arm around Matt and had the camera angled for the shot. Once he was done, he thanked Matt profusely, making Matt laugh.

"Are you sure you're old enough to work here?"

"I get that a lot. I'm Andrew, by the way," he said, still grinning from ear to ear.

"Nice to meet you, Andrew." Matt pulled out his wallet as Andrew rang up the champagne. "Hey, is there still a florist over on Webster Street?"

"Sure is. New people took it over about three years ago, totally rehabbed the place and made it bigger. You can't miss it."

Taking the bag and the receipt, Matt thanked him and walked out, feeling good. He still hadn't called in their dinner order yet, so he had some time to go and pick out flowers for Vivienne. In the time they'd been together, he realized how much she had done for him and how little he'd done for her. That was about to change.

The offer to do the shows with Riley was everything he had been dreaming about—but he wanted Vivienne to go with him. Maybe he should have talked to her first, before giving Riley an answer, but he had been so excited that he hadn't been thinking completely straight.

What if she doesn't want to go? he thought. Hell, Matt had no idea what he'd do then. He would be disappointed, no doubt, but surely they'd come up with a compromise. They had to. They were good together and always seemed to find a way to make things work. Maybe she'd come with him to some of the shows, and they'd go back to her place during the breaks. Matt knew enough about the tour that the dates were fairly spread out, so it wasn't like he was going to be gone for weeks on end.

Okay, they could make this work.

He drove through town and made a left onto Webster and drove past some familiar sights—the dry cleaner, the butcher, and the dentist's office where he'd gone while he was growing up. This was home. Every one of these places had a memory attached to them that made him smile. Turning into the parking lot on the right, he saw that the florist was definitely larger than the last time he'd been here. Back then, it had been a single storefront, but now it was easily three times the size and was called…Reed's Floral Gifts.

His heart squeezed hard in his chest at the same time the rest of him went numb.

It was a coincidence.

It had to be a coincidence.

The smart thing to do would be to simply pull out of the parking spot and leave. No one would know he had ever been here and Matt would simply push it out of his mind.

But he couldn't. Now that he'd seen it, he had to know.

As far as he knew, the only Reeds in town, ever, were him and his parents. His mother was gone, and Matt knew for sure that he didn't own the place, so that could only mean one thing. And he almost laughed at the absurdity of it. His old man, the twisted alcoholic, owning a flower shop? It just couldn't be.

With a deep breath, Matt climbed from the car and stared long and hard at the sign. It wasn't as if Reed was an unusual name. And he had been gone for more than a dozen years. There was a very real possibility that it was just a coincidence. For all he knew, it was a chain and they all had this name.

Still...he couldn't quite shake the unease that was keeping him from moving.

"Do you want to buy some flowers?"

Matt looked down and saw a little girl of about seven or eight years old staring up at him with blue eyes the size of saucers. She had light brown hair and was holding on to the leash of a French bulldog puppy. Crouching down to pet the dog as it sniffed Matt's shoes, he smiled at her. "As a matter of fact, I do want to buy some flowers."

She smiled at him, obviously pleased with his answer. "That's good. We haven't had a lot of customers today."

The comment made Matt chuckle. "So...you own this place?" he teased, and when she giggled her entire face lit up.

"Noooo," she said, still laughing. "My parents do.

But I have to come and hang out here after school and on the weekends. Murphy comes with us too."

Matt looked down at the dog and gave him a good scratch behind the ears. "So I'm guessing this is Murphy."

"Uh-huh. He's a really good dog and my best friend." She glanced at Matt. "Do you have a dog?"

"Nope…but I always wanted one."

"So maybe you should get one," she said simply.

"Carly!" a woman's voice called from behind them.

"Uh-oh," Carly whispered. "That's my mom. I'm not supposed to talk to strangers."

Matt quickly stood up and waved to the woman who was eyeing him warily.

"I'm gonna be in so much trouble…"

Murphy started to whine beside them. "You should probably take him for a walk. I'm going to go buy some flowers." They waved to each other as Matt walked toward the store and the woman. When he was no more than a few feet away, her eyes went wide.

Ah, so she recognized me, he thought. Not a bad thing. He was used to it.

Then she paled.

Okay. That was new.

"You're…you're…" she stammered, and Matt realized she was a lot older than his normal fans. Not that it mattered. He was used to women being nervous around him and a little tongue-tied, but this one looked like she was about to get sick.

"Hey," he said softly, placing a hand on her arm. "Are you all right?"

"I…I need to go inside," she said quickly and all but ran into the store.

Matt followed, but once inside, he began looking around. The place was huge. He couldn't remember ever seeing such a big display of flowers. They were everywhere. Some were real, some were silk, and there seemed to be something for every occasion.

"You've got some great stuff here," he called out. "I'm looking for something for my girlfriend." It hit him that he had no idea what kind of flowers Vivienne liked, what her favorites were, and frowned. "I'm not sure what exactly she likes, but I'd love to do something a little different than just a bouquet of roses. What do you suggest?"

Silence.

She probably was checking on her daughter or getting some water—maybe calling or texting a friend to say that Matty Reed was in her store. He almost laughed at the thought. Now that things were back on track and he wasn't the laughingstock of the entertainment world, it didn't bother him to think of more fans coming out to see him.

Matt continued to browse and came across several displays of lilies. The colors were vibrant, beautiful. He opened the door to the display case and smelled them and thought, *Perfect*. Yeah, these were the flowers he wanted to get for Vivienne. Now all he had to do was find little Carly's mom and—

"Hello, Matt."

The last time he'd heard that voice, it had been in a nightmare two nights ago.

Slowly, he turned around and had to fight the urge to be sick. Matthew Reed Senior. Yeah, he was a junior, but he'd never used it. The face was the same for the most part, but it was older. The hair was grayer. And there wasn't any of the cocky defiance Matt remembered.

For the life of him, Matt couldn't make himself utter a single word. His throat went dry and his tongue suddenly felt like it was the size of his fist.

"I'd heard you were in town," his father said, his voice oddly gentle, almost contrite.

And Matt had to wonder who had tipped him off. Until today, no one had acknowledged him by name. He wanted to know who he'd heard it from, who had ratted him out, but still he couldn't make himself speak.

Standing before him was his every demon. This man was the reason for every bit of self-doubt, insecurity, and feeling of worthlessness he'd ever had about himself. But looking at him now, all Matt saw was a stranger, a shell of the man from his worst memories.

As if sensing the direction of Matt's thoughts, his father took a step forward. "Matt...I..."

Matt took a step back and saw the sad acceptance on his father's face.

"Daddy! Murphy peed and pooped. Can I give him a treat?" Behind them, Carly walked in with the dog. Her cheeks were rosy and she was doing her best to hold on to the dog's leash so he wouldn't take off running around the store. She spotted Matt and grinned. "Did you buy your flowers yet?"

It hit him like a punch in the gut. This little girl was his sister. Well...half sister. And he looked from her to his father and sneered. If this son of a bitch—

"Why don't you get Murphy his treat, Carly?" The little girl scampered off, leaving them alone.

Matt cleared his throat and knew he had to speak.

There was no way he could go back in time and change anything that happened to him, but he could certainly make sure that nothing happened to that sweet girl. He stepped in close to his father—menacingly close. "If I ever so much as hear a whisper that you even *thought* of hurting that innocent little girl, of tormenting her like you did to me, I'll make sure you pay," he sneered.

And right before his eyes, his father seemed to shrink—his shoulders sagged and he hung his head. "Matt," he whispered. "I…I don't even know what to say. Or where to begin." Lifting his head, he looked at his son. "Not a day has gone by that I haven't wanted to die for what I did to you. To your mother."

Rage—more rage than he thought possible—filled him. "Don't talk about her. Don't even think about her!" he hissed.

Matt looked around the store. "Do you do it to them? Huh? Your new family? Do they know what a sadistic son of a bitch you are? Did you tell your wife how you abused the hell out of your first wife? How you put a gun to your son's head?" Then he grunted with disgust. "Of course, you wouldn't. Either that or she's just as twisted as you if she was willing to have a child with you."

He turned to walk out the door, but his father's words stopped him.

"I thought you weren't mine."

Stopping dead in his tracks, Matt slowly turned around and looked at the face that had haunted him for years. "What?"

Matthew Reed swallowed hard as he stared at his son, nodding. "For years…most of your life…I thought you weren't my son."

It felt like he was in the twilight zone and had to wonder if the old guy was drunk again.

"Your mom and I dated on and off before we got married. She was pregnant. It didn't occur to me back then, in the beginning, that you weren't mine. But she said it once, while we were fighting. And it…it stuck."

"You're wrong," Matt said in a near growl. There was no way his mother would play that kind of head game—that was his father's department all the way.

"It wasn't every time we fought, but it was something she'd said and it just… It took root and refused to let go," he said helplessly. "And it killed me. I was already a damn mess, drinking too much, had a lot of bad luck with my job, and then the added stress of a bad marriage… I was slowly coming unhinged. I couldn't stop drinking. I needed the job… You became a convenient target. It was the only way I had of getting back at your mother."

"I was a kid!" He took a step closer to his father. "And you selfishly took my childhood away! Did it ever occur to you to get help? Did you even realize, or care, about all the damage you were inflicting?"

"I… At the time, I didn't. I swear to you, Matt, I wish I did. I…I didn't know how to handle things! And after your mom left—"

"You made her leave," he growled.

His father shook his head sadly. "I know. I realize that." He looked up at Matt, regret marring his features. "And you look so much like her… I…I…"

He was definitely going to be sick. Matt placed a hand over his stomach and willed himself to keep it together until he could leave. All he had to do was turn and…

"I'm so sorry." The words were barely audible.

"And you think that makes it all right?" Matt snapped. "You're sorry? Big fucking deal! You made my life hell! There wasn't a day that went by that you didn't do your damnedest to take away my self-esteem! Every day was misery!"

"I…I know. I realize that now. But I've changed and—"

"There's no way anyone can change that much," Matt interrupted. "You're not capable of it."

"I'm so sorry," his father repeated. "I'm so damn sorry. For all of it."

"You tried to kill me! And all you can say is sorry?"

"I don't know what else to say!" Matthew yelled back, but there was no anger in his voice. "Tell me what I need to do, what I need to say, Matt, and I'll do it."

"There isn't a damn thing you can say," he replied venomously, and when he turned and walked away, he managed to make it all the way to the door. But then he stopped. Dammit, there was one thing he had to know. "Am I?" he asked without turning around.

"What?" Matthew responded in a low voice.

"Am I your son?" *It shouldn't matter*, Matt reminded himself. For years he had sworn that his father was dead to him. Finding out this man wasn't his father would be a relief. Either way, it wouldn't change anything—it certainly wouldn't change the past.

"You are. You're my son. You've always been my son."

It doesn't matter. It doesn't matter. It doesn't matter, Matt chanted to himself.

"Daddy?"

Carly's small voice stopped Matt from walking out the door. Part of him couldn't walk away without knowing his father wasn't repeating the past with this child. One hand had a white-knuckled grip on the door handle as he looked over his shoulder at father and daughter.

His father was crouched down beside Carly, lovingly stroking her cheek as the little girl talked softly to him. Matt had no idea what they were discussing—swore he didn't want to know—and yet he couldn't move.

"He's changed, you know."

Carly's mother—well, his father's wife—was standing beside him. He hadn't seen or heard her approach. Matt turned and looked at her. "I'm Susan," she said, holding out a hand to him. Reaching out, he shook her hand and saw the first traces of a smile on her face. She looked over toward her husband and daughter, and her smile grew. "I can't even imagine what you must be feeling right now."

Matt let out a low, mirthless laugh. "I couldn't even describe it if I wanted to."

She nodded. "I met your father a year after you left. After…what he'd done to you."

He arched a brow at her, wondering how she could know that. He sure as hell didn't believe his father would have admitted to all the stuff that had happened.

"He had finished a year in rehab and needed a place to live," she began. "I had an apartment over my garage for rent that he called about."

Matt glanced over at her and, not for the first time, wondered if the woman was crazy. "And you didn't have a problem renting a place to guy fresh out of rehab?" He didn't quite disguise his disgust.

She met his gaze steadily. "My sister Maureen was one of your father's counselors while he was getting

treatment. She vouched for him. In fact, she was the one
who told him about the apartment."

All he could do was nod. He still thought she was crazy.

"He had lost his house, his job…and you. He needed a
fresh start to get his life back."

"Good for him." His voice was flat, emotionless.

Beside him, she huffed. "There wasn't a day that went
by that he wasn't tormented by the things he'd done."

"Yeah? Well that makes two of us."

"Matt," she said softly, "all I'm saying is that
maybe…just maybe…you could give him a chance to
apologize. To make things right."

"He can't."

She looked dejected. Her shoulders slouched as
she lowered her gaze. "Just…think about it. Please,"
she added softly. "I've begged him for years to reach
out to you, but he was so ashamed. He didn't want to
cause you any more pain and thought that by leaving
you alone and staying out of your life it would make
things better."

Matt looked out the door and willed himself to
move, to leave, but he couldn't.

"You both have so many issues to resolve. I'm not
saying that you have to be close or even friends, but…
you at least deserve the chance to have some closure
with this. Please, Matt," she begged as she placed a
hand on his arms. "Let your father at least have the
chance to make things right."

Yeah, he was pretty much ready to leave. Was this
woman for real? *Make things right?* How was that even
possible? Which is what he was starting to say to her
when Carly made her way over. *Damn.* The kid was all

big, sad eyes, and it just tugged at his heart. When she stopped in front of him, she crooked a finger at him to come closer. He crouched down in front of her.

"Are you my brother?" she asked nervously.

Matt looked over her head to glare at his father.

The man still fought dirty.

With a long, slow sigh, he looked at Carly and saw the hopeful expression on her face. He nodded. "I am."

She gasped and looked at her mother for confirmation, and when Susan nodded, Carly flung herself into Matt's arms and hugged him tight. His heart squeezed so tight in his chest that he could barely breathe. This little girl, this child, seemed to love unconditionally. And Matt had no idea what that felt like.

Except…he liked it.

Wrapping his own arms around her, he hugged her close.

"I always wanted a brother!" she said excitedly and then pulled back. "That's why Mommy and Daddy adopted Murphy for me." She looked over her shoulder and then turned and took off. "Wait right there!" she called out.

Matt stood and looked at Susan in confusion.

"You'll get used to it," she said, chuckling. "Carly's rarely still for long. Chances are she's got something to show you."

He had no idea what it could be, and he noticed his father had moved closer but looked skittish.

"That was a pretty low thing to do," Matt murmured, straightening. "Using Carly to get me to stay."

Matthew gave him a helpless grin. "I knew you wouldn't have any problem walking away from me, but I have yet to find anyone who can look your sister in the eye and tell her no to anything."

His sister.

Holy shit, he really had a sister, and he was standing here talking to his father and feeling…okay. Not great. Not completely at ease. But…okay. Maybe there was a little hope for them.

As if sensing the change in the mood, Susan quietly asked if either of them wanted something to drink. Matt shook his head and thanked her. Once she was out of sight, he turned and looked at his father. "I…I don't know what I'm supposed to do here," he admitted honestly.

"Neither do I. All I know is that I want to try, Matt. There's no way I can change the past—God knows I wish I could." He looked up and gave a helpless shrug. "But I want to try and make up for it, to be the father that you deserve."

Matt shook his head again. "I'm not sure that's possible. I think there have been too many things—"

"I know, I know. But…maybe we could just…take things slow."

"Slow?"

"We're standing here talking right now, aren't we? And no one's yelling or arguing."

Matt chuckled. "That's a definite first for us."

A slow smile spread across his father's face. "I like it."

And the funny thing was, Matt did too.

"Maybe you can come to the house some time. Susan's place—our place—is on the other side of town off of Irish Lane. We're getting ready to close up here if you'd like to come over now?"

"I'm not sure I'm ready for that yet," Matt admitted.

"Oh. Okay."

"I'm supposed to be picking up dinner. I just wanted to stop and get flowers for Vivienne."

"Forrester?" his father asked. "Aaron's little sister?"

Matt nodded and noticed the smile on his father's face. "What? You remember her?"

"She's a lovely woman," he said. "She comes in to get flowers all the time. Come on. I'll show you the ones she favors."

It wasn't much, but it was a beginning. And Matt knew there was a long road ahead of them, but he also knew it was one he was finally ready to walk down.

The room grew darker as the sun was going down, but neither moved to turn on a light. The sound of the door opening startled them both. Spinning around, they saw Matt come in and hit the light switch. He looked around and seemed just as surprised as the two of them.

"Hey," he said, smiling easily. "This is a surprise." Holding up the takeout bag in one hand and a bottle of champagne and flowers in the other, he walked over toward the kitchen table. "I just knocked on your door, man, to invite you to join us."

Vivienne scrambled to her feet and slowly came around the couch. "Are…are we celebrating something?"

Matt grabbed her around the waist and swung her around before kissing her soundly. "I think so," he said as he put her down and then looked at Aaron. "But there're some things that need to be settled first."

"Matt," she began hesitantly. "I think…"

He held up a hand to stop her but kept his arm around her, holding her close as they faced Aaron. "This has all gone on long enough. The last thing I ever wanted to do was to come between the two of you. But you have to know," he said directly to Aaron, "nothing you do or say is going to push me away from Vivienne. I love her. I'm always going to love her, and you are going to have to learn to trust me and deal with it."

Aaron started to talk, but Matt cut him off too.

"Last week, you issued me an ultimatum and it was pretty damn shitty of you, but we're friends, Aaron. At the end of the day, you know me. Better than probably anyone. And I may have been an asshole for a while, but you know who I am deep down, and you should know I would never do anything to hurt anyone. Especially Vivienne."

"I never should have done that, Matt. But she's my sister and—"

"I'll admit I don't know what it's like to have a sister or know that need to protect someone like that, but I kind of do now," he said with a grin, and Vivienne had to wonder if he was talking about her.

"Look, dude, don't listen to me," Aaron pleaded. "It was completely wrong of me to tell you what you needed to do about your life. I do know you, and I do trust you. I can't help being protective of her, but I promise to try to be calmer. This whole thing just took me by surprise and I reacted badly." He sighed. "It's sort of how it's always been—it's the plight of being the big brother. I automatically have this built-in response to any guy who goes near my sister."

Matt walked over and hugged his friend, patting him on the back. "You're my best friend, Aaron," he began as he pulled back. "And I don't want you to change. It's good for you to be here to keep me in line."

"Oh, good grief," Vivienne said as anxiety still had its grip on her. "Don't give him permission to keep being a jerk." Both men laughed, and she had to admit, it sounded like music to her ears.

She studied the two of them as they walked over to the table and began taking their dinner out of the bag. Something was up…different. And she knew there was no way she could sit down and eat even one bite of her food with her own issues still hanging over her head.

"Why were you gone so long?"

Aaron and Matt stopped what they were doing and looked at her. Stepping away from the table, Matt slowly walked toward her and motioned for her to join him on the sofa.

"I think I want to stand," she said defiantly and then rolled her eyes when Aaron sat down.

"I don't even know where to begin," Matt said. He sighed and shifted in his seat and looked from one Forrester to another before he started. "I got a call from Riley earlier. He wants me to join him for the last ten stops on his tour."

"Dude, that's awesome!" Aaron said and then looked at Vivienne expectantly.

She noticed Matt watching her. "I heard."

"You did? When?"

"My call finished quicker than I expected and I came out here to let you know, but you were on the phone. I heard you tell him you'd do it, that you were going to meet him on Saturday." A small sob escaped, and she cursed her weakness. "I can't believe you would just do that without talking to me first! You've been doing nothing but telling me how you were ready to slow down, put down roots, and then at the first opportunity, you're out the door!"

His gaze never wavered, nor did he say anything.

"Maybe I should go," Aaron murmured, coming to his feet.

"No," Vivienne snapped. "Stay. I think we should all be here for this. Don't you, Matt?" Then he grinned, and Vivienne wanted to slug him.

"You are one hundred percent right," he finally said.

Vivienne's eyes went wide. "I...I am?"

Matt nodded. "I should have talked to you about it first. I was completely overwhelmed and spoke without thinking. But Riley had already said I should talk to you first. He knows if you're not on board, then I'm not going."

She let out a huff of agitation and then groaned. "Dammit, that's not how this is supposed to be!" Pacing in front of the sofa, she went on. "I don't want it to be like you have to ask my permission, but I would just like to know what you're thinking of doing, especially if it means that you're leaving me!"

Matt jumped to his feet. "But I'm not leaving you," he argued, even though he was smiling. "I want you to come with me. I want us to get our feet wet with this whole thing. I thought it would be a great way for us each to see if this is where we see our lives—on the road sometimes. Ten shows aren't much, and we can pick and choose when it works with your schedule and it's a place you want to see. I know I can handle it, but that was when it was just me. You've never done this before and I'm excited to share it with you."

In the blink of an eye, he had her in his arms, holding

her close. "You know I loved playing onstage with Riley last week, and I'll admit I had hoped he'd want to do something, but I didn't expect it this soon. But I also meant what I said to you—I want to be here with you, make a life here with you. I've spent this last month learning all about your world—cooking and writing and blogging—and now I'd like you to learn a little bit about my world."

"Oh, Matt," she sighed.

Behind them, Aaron stood and went to finish putting their dinner out. "Can we finish talking about this while we eat? I'm starving."

"Sounds good to me," Matt said.

"Me, too."

The three of them sat, and after they started eating, Matt went back to his story, telling them about the kid at the liquor store and then his trip to the florist.

"Oh my God," Vivienne gasped. "I've been going there for years and never put two and two together!" She glanced at her brother anxiously. "Why didn't you ever tell me?"

He shrugged. "I didn't know he owned the place. Anytime I saw your dad, it was at the home improvement store or the supermarket. I never talked to him or asked about where he worked."

Matt reached out and squeezed Vivienne's hand. "It's okay. Really."

"So what happened?" she asked cautiously. "Did you talk to him?"

Nodding, Matt shared the whole story with them. "I was a little bit pissed how he used Carly to get me to stay, but I'm glad he did. She's amazing. Cute as a button. When she came back, she had the dog with her and put him in my arms and said he was my puppy too. That we could share him." Just the thought of it choked him up all over again. He gave Vivienne a lopsided grin. "I guess I finally got my dog."

Tears rolled down her cheeks before she could stop them. "And what about you and your dad? Where did you leave things?"

He took a forkful of shrimp before he answered. "We both know there's a lot of damage we have to work through. I'm not delusional—and neither is he. We're never going to be best friends, but we know we'd both like to try and maybe build something from here."

Aaron started to chuckle, and both Matt and Vivienne looked at him like he was crazy. "What could you possibly find funny in all of this?" Vivienne asked.

"You have a sister!" Aaron finally said. "I think this is karma at its best right here! Someday, you are going to want to kick some guy's ass for even thinking of touching her!" He burst out laughing again. "And I'm going to be right there beside you, reminding you of this moment."

Matt groaned, his head falling back. "Great. Just great."

Vivienne couldn't help but laugh too. "So...how do you feel about all of that? I mean, it's huge. You have a sister. You talked to your father. You're going on tour with Riley. This is quite the day for someone who's been hiding out for nearly two months."

He straightened in his seat and smiled at her. First, he motioned toward the champagne. "I bought it so we could celebrate. Of course, at the time, I thought we were just celebrating the tour." He reached over and picked up the bouquet of lilies and handed them to her. "I realized I never bought you anything. In all this time, you've been constantly giving to me, and I haven't done anything for you. And for that, I'm truly sorry." His hand caressed her cheek. "I love you, and I promise to stop being such a self-centered idiot from here on out."

"I'll drink to that," Aaron teased, and Matt shot him a look.

"As for the rest of it, I feel…hopeful. I have their number, and they have mine and…" He shrugged. "We're just going to take it one day at a time. It's crazy and scary and stupid and wonderful," he said with a nervous laugh, "and it's my life. And believe it or not, I wouldn't change a thing."

"I'm so proud of you," she said, gazing into his eyes and feeling more love than she'd ever thought possible. "I'm sorry I doubted you and that I acted like a brat earlier."

"You have nothing to be sorry for, Viv. Ever." He kissed her hand. "But if you don't want me to go on this tour with Riley, I won't. If it's too soon for you, for us, then I'm totally fine with it. You mean more to me than a damn tour."

She considered him for a moment and knew he was telling the truth. "Can I let you in on a little secret?"

Matt looked at her and then at Aaron. "Now?"

She swatted at him playfully. "I always wondered what the life of a rock star is like. I think this tour with Riley would be the perfect time to find out."

"Really?" he asked excitedly. "You mean it?"

She nodded vigorously. "I do. I really do."

Hauling her into his lap, Matt kissed her with everything he had—all the love, all the wonder, all the excitement he was feeling—and she met him with the same intensity.

"I think that's my cue to leave," Aaron said as he gathered several of the takeout containers and made his way to the door. "I'll talk to you both tomorrow."

But neither of them were listening.

And it was a long time before either of them even noticed he was gone.

Epilogue

THE NOISE LEVEL BACKSTAGE WAS ALMOST AS DEAFENING as it had been while they took their final bow. Not that it was much of a surprise. The fans always went wild after the encore, always wanting more. But that's how you're supposed to leave them. It guarantees they'll come back and see you the next time you're in town.

Matt Reed wasn't sure that was going to happen.

At least not anytime soon.

Riley walked up beside him and clapped him on the back, smiling wide. "Well? How do you feel?"

"I feel like I'm ready for a vacation. Don't get me wrong. This was great, and I had an amazing time, but—"

"Say no more," Riley interrupted. "I know exactly how you feel. It's a completely different world when you know there's someone waiting for you at home at the end of the night."

"Exactly."

If anyone had told Matt there would come a day when he would be looking forward to going home—or simply back to his hotel room—after a show, he would have told them they were crazy. There was no way the life of the party, Matty Reed, wasn't going to stay out until the sun was up.

That was the old Matt.

The new Matt just wanted a shower, something to eat, and to crawl into bed beside Vivienne and hold her all night long.

As if he had conjured her up in his mind, Matt looked up and saw Vivienne walking toward him. "There you are!" she said, smiling. "Great show tonight." She leaned in and kissed him before looking at Riley. "Savannah said to tell you she'd meet you back at the hotel."

Riley frowned. "Is she okay? Is everything all right?"

Vivienne looked as if she had a secret, but Matt kept that observation to himself.

"She just wasn't feeling well. Nothing serious. Your driver took her to the hotel and he'll be back here to get you in a little while."

"Oh…okay." For a minute nobody spoke. "I…guess I'll go grab a shower and wait for the car."

"Dude, are you all right?" Matt asked. "Vivienne says she's fine. Why do you look so worried?"

Riley shrugged. "I don't know. She's just been a little…off lately. This tour ending tonight is like a huge weight being lifted off of me. We are so ready for a break, and I can't wait to get on the plane tomorrow and fly home." He chuckled. "I can't wait to live with my wife like a normal couple for a few months. We haven't had a chance to do that, and as lame as it sounds, I'm really looking forward to being home, making dinners, and watching TV in our own space."

"Nothing wrong with that," Matt said.

"There you two are!" They both turned and saw their manager Mick walking toward them, grinning like the Cheshire cat. "It's a mob scene back here," he commented.

"What's up?" Riley asked, looking more than a little distracted.

"Great show tonight, boys! The fans loved it!"

Matt could remember a time when they all used to

wait after the show and hang on Mick's praises, but right now, all he wanted to do was get his stuff together and leave. "What's up, Mick?"

"I have news. I was able to talk to Dylan today, and he sounds good. Really good."

Matt and Riley looked at one another and smiled. "That's great," Riley commented. "And how is he feeling?"

Mick made a bit of a face. "He's having a hard time— detox is never easy—but he's got a good attitude, and I think he's going to come out of this thing and be okay."

"I hope so," Matt said, hating like hell to think of his friend and bandmate suffering. "It hasn't been that long though. He still has a long road ahead of him. I hope he realizes that."

"He does," Mick said, shaking his head. "We're already trying to line up some ways for him to give back to the community when he's ready. He's going to need to do a lot more than get onstage to get back in the public's good graces."

"Seriously?" Riley sighed. "Already? Can't you just let the guy get healthy first?"

Frowning, Mick looked at the both of them. "Believe it or not, I'm doing this for you."

Matt's eyes went wide. "Us?"

"Yeah. You saw the way the fans responded to the two of you teaming up on these ten shows! That tells me they're anxious to see Shaughnessy get back together. That's not going to happen unless Dylan's image is cleaned up. I'm just paving the way for it to happen."

"You're a piece of work, Mick," Riley murmured.

"Look, you two let me worry about that while you get some much needed R & R," Mick said, clapping them both on the back. "We'll stay in touch, but I promise to give you at least a month before I start calling."

"Thank God for small favors," Vivienne mumbled, and Matt had to look away to stop from laughing.

Mick smiled at her. "Always a pleasure to see you, Vivienne." Taking one of her hands in his, he kissed it. "Take care of our boy here."

Vivienne smiled but only Matt could see that it didn't fully reach her eyes. He squeezed her hand and they all wished Mick a good night. "Come on, let's go back to the rooms and get cleaned up."

They said their good-byes as they each made their way into their own dressing rooms and promised to touch base in a few days. Matt shut the door and looked at Vivienne, who was checking her makeup in the large mirror. It didn't matter how many times a day he saw her; she always managed to take his breath away.

"I know he's your manager, but the sight of him annoys me."

Matt chuckled. "No worries. We all feel that way about him at one time or another. I don't expect you to be best friends with him. And if it's any consolation, he doesn't seem to notice."

She met his reflection in the mirror and smiled, and Matt felt that familiar tug of arousal.

Reaching behind him, he quietly locked the door and walked up behind her. His hands immediately went to her hips as he nuzzled her neck.

"Mmm," she purred. "That feels good."

"You think so?" he asked, breathing in her sweet scent, watching their reflection in the mirror.

"I do." She wiggled her bottom against him and grinned when she felt his reaction to her.

"Do you remember the first time you were in my dressing room?"

Her eyes went wide. "Do you?" she teased and then let out a squeal of delight when he gently bit her.

"I remember," he growled playfully. "I opened that door to you, and you were so damn beautiful and sexy and everything I had ever fantasized about." His hands roamed up her sides, over her ribs, and rested on the swell of her breasts. "Faded blue jeans, a tight black T-shirt..."

Her blush heated her skin, and she looked away for a minute. "Matt, you've told me this before."

"I know," he said, his voice a low rumble. Slowly, he spun her around and waited until she looked up at him. "Do you know what I wanted to do to you that night? Right there in that dressing room?"

Her blush deepened, and he knew she was thinking exactly what he was thinking.

"How about I show you?" he suggested, lowering his head to kiss and nip at the sensitive skin on her neck.

Vivienne's head fell back as she sighed. "What if... what if someone comes in?"

"The door's locked."

"What about...your shower?" She was panting now and writhing against him.

"It can wait."

"What about—?"

He stopped her line of questioning as he captured her lips and kissed her as he had that very first time—hungrily. She instantly responded to him, and it wasn't long before clothes fell away and his words from that long ago night came true—she was his every fantasy come to life.

Vivienne Forrester's Black Bean and Corn Guacamole

½ red bell pepper, diced

½ red onion, diced

2 cloves garlic, minced

½ (15.25-ounce) can sweet corn, drained

½ (15-ounce) can black beans, rinsed and drained

3 ripe avocados, peeled, pitted, and diced

2 tablespoons fresh lime juice

¼ teaspoon salt

1 pinch ground black pepper, or to taste

½ cup chopped fresh cilantro, or to taste (optional)

· ·

Stir together red bell pepper, red onion, garlic, sweet corn, black beans, and avocado in a large bowl.

Mix lime juice, salt, black pepper, and cilantro into avocado mixture until desired texture is achieved.

Serve with tortilla chips and enjoy!

Vivienne's Chicken Salad Baguettes

- 1 lb. boneless, skinless chicken breasts
- 2 stalks celery, finely chopped
- ⅓ cup mayonnaise
- 2 tablespoons honey
- Salt and white pepper to taste
- 4 crispy French bread rolls

• •

Boil and cool chicken breasts, chop into small cubes, and place in a bowl.

Finely chop the celery and add to the chicken. Season with salt and white pepper to taste.

Add the mayonnaise and honey, and mix everything together.

Warm the rolls in an oven, cut them in half before adding spoonfuls of chicken salad, and enjoy!

Vivienne's Orange-Colored Soup

1 tablespoon extra virgin olive oil

1 cup yellow onion, coarsely chopped

1 Granny Smith apple, peeled, cored, and coarsely chopped (approximately 1 cup)

1 cup turnip, peeled and coarsely chopped

1 cup butternut squash, peeled, chopped, and seeds discarded

1 cup carrot, peeled and coarsely chopped

1 cup sweet potato, peeled and chopped

5 cups vegetable or chicken broth

¼ cup maple syrup

⅛ teaspoon cayenne pepper, or more to taste

Salt, to taste

½ lb. thinly sliced prosciutto

• •

Heat oil in a large stockpot over medium-high heat. Add onion and sauté until translucent. Add apple, turnip, squash, carrot, and sweet potato; sauté 5 minutes. Add the broth, bring to a boil, then lower the heat to simmer, stirring occasionally, about 30 minutes or until vegetables are tender. Cool slightly.

When cooled, puree with a handheld mixer, food processor, or blender. Pour the pureed soup back into the pan and reheat until warmed. Add syrup, cayenne pepper, and salt to taste.

In a separate pan, fry prosciutto on medium heat until crispy (like bacon). Remove from pan and place on paper towels to cool.

Serve soup in bowls, crumble the prosciutto on top, and enjoy!

Matty Reed's Grilled-to-Perfection Steaks

4 1¼ to 1½-inch-thick boneless rib eye or New York
    strip steaks (about 12 ounces each), trimmed
2 tablespoons extra virgin olive oil
½ teaspoon kosher salt
½ teaspoon fresh ground black pepper
½ teaspoon onion powder
½ teaspoon garlic powder

· ·

About 20 minutes before grilling, remove the steaks from the refrigerator and allow to reach room temperature.

Combine salt, black pepper, onion powder, and garlic powder in a bowl.

Heat grill to high. Brush the steaks on both sides with olive oil and season liberally with seasoning mixture. Place the steaks on the grill and cook until golden brown, 3 to 5 minutes per side, until desired doneness.

Transfer the steaks to a cutting board or platter, tent loosely with foil, and let rest 5 minutes before serving.

Keep reading for a sneak peek at

A Sky Full of Stars

Book five in the beloved Shaughnessy Brothers series by Samantha Chase

---

There was a girl in Owen Shaughnessy's class.

A. Girl.

Okay, a woman. And she wasn't a scientist and she wasn't awkward. She was…pretty. Beautiful, actually. Though he had no idea if she was awkward or not. She had walked into the lecture hall minutes ago and there were only five minutes left in his talk so…why was she here? Maybe she was the girlfriend of one of his students?

Looking around the room, he ruled that out. He seemed to be the only one taking note of her presence. He chanced another glance her way and she smiled. He felt a nervous flutter in the region of his belly, and as he continued to look at her, her smile grew.

And now Owen felt like he was going to throw up.

He immediately forced his gaze away and looked at the notes in front of him. "Next time we'll be discussing dust trails and dust tails—which represent large and small dust particles, respectively. Please refer to your syllabus for the required reading material." Lifting his head, Owen scanned the large lecture hall and noted the almost universally bored expressions staring back at him.

Except for her. She was still smiling.

He cleared his throat before adding, "Class dismissed."

There was a collective sigh of relief in the room as everyone stood and began collecting their belongings. As the students began to file past him, Owen did his best to keep his eyes down and not react to the words he was hearing.

Geek. Nerd. Weird. Awkward.

Yeah, Owen not only heard the words being murmured, but knew they were being used to describe him. It was even worse considering the students in the room were all interested in the same subject he was— astronomy. So even in a group of his peers, he was still the odd man out. He shrugged. He'd learned not to let the hurtful words land—to fester—but sometimes they stung a little.

Okay, a lot.

Packing up his satchel, he kept his head down as the class of two hundred students made their way out. Or escaped. Maybe that was the better word for it. He didn't make eye contact with any of them—he simply went about his task of collecting his papers and his belongings so the next instructor could come in and set up on time. He was nothing if not polite and conscientious.

His phone beeped to indicate a new text and he couldn't help but smile when he pulled up his phone and saw it was from his twin brother, Riley.

Skype. Tonight. 8 your time.

Refusing to acknowledge how once again he and his brother were in sync with each other—Riley loved to say it was because they were twins—Owen couldn't help but be grateful for the timing. There were just times when the need to talk to someone—or more specifically, Riley—and there he was.

And the more he commented on it, the more Riley would go on about twin telepathy.

It was ridiculous.

As a man of science, there was no way Owen could accept the phenomenon as fact. Coincidence? Yes. Fact? No. His phone beeped again with a second text from Riley.

Whatever you're stressing about, we'll discuss.

He read the text and chuckled. "Nope," he murmured. "It was just a coincidence."

The last of the students exited the lecture hall as he slipped the phone back into his satchel, and Owen relished the silence. This was how he preferred things— quiet. Peaceful. He enjoyed his solitude, and if it were at all possible, he'd stick to speaking at strictly a few select conferences and then spend the rest of the day doing research and mapping the night sky.

"Excuse me…" a soft feminine voice said.

His entire body froze, and he felt his mouth go dry. Looking up, Owen saw her. Up close, she was even more beautiful. Long blond hair, cornflower-blue eyes, and a smile that lit up her entire face. And that light was shining directly at him.

She wore a long, gauzy skirt with a white tank top. There was a large portfolio case hanging over her shoulder, along with the sweater she'd obviously chosen to do without in the too-warm classroom, and multiple bangle bracelets on her arm.

Gypsy.

No. That wasn't the right word. Gypsies were more of the dark-haired variety and wore a lot of makeup. This woman was too soft and delicate and feminine to meet that description.

Nymph.

Yes. That was definitely more fitting, and if he were the kind of man who believed there were such things, that's what he would have categorized her as.

He couldn't form a single word.

Her expression turned slightly curious. "Hi. Um… Dr. Shaughnessy?"

She was looking for him? Seriously? Swallowing hard, Owen tried to speak—he really did—but all he could do was nod.

The easy smile was back. Her hand fluttered up to her chest as she let out a sigh of relief. "I'm so sorry for showing up so close to the end of your class. It was inconsiderate of me. I meant to be here earlier.

Well, I was supposed to be here for the entire lecture, but I lost track of time talking to Mr. Kennedy." She looked at him as if expecting him to know who she was talking about. "He's the head of the art department," she clarified.

Again, all he could do was nod. He cleared his throat too, but it didn't help.

"Anyway, I'm supposed to meet my uncle here— Howard Shields. He suggested I come and listen to you speak. He thinks very highly of you and thought I'd enjoy your lecture."

Seriously? Howard Shields thought someone would *enjoy* hearing him talk about meteor showers? That wasn't the normal reaction Owen received from his talks. Informative? Educational? Yes. Enjoyable? Never.

Not sure how he should respond, he offered her a small smile and felt a flush cover him from the tips of his toes to the roots of his hair. She was probably regretting listening to her uncle. As it was, she was looking at him expectantly.

"Anyway," she said, her voice still pleasant and friendly, "Uncle Howard talks about you all the time, and when he told me you were in Chicago doing several speaking engagements, I knew I had to come and meet you. My uncle thinks very highly of you."

Owen finally met her gaze head-on because her words struck him. It was no secret that Owen looked up to Howard Shields—he'd been a mentor to Owen for as long as he could remember—but to hear it wasn't all one-sided? Well, it meant the world to him.

Most people in his field looked at Owen a little oddly. It wasn't because he didn't know what he was talking about or that he wasn't respected, it was because of his social skills. Or lack thereof. It seemed to overshadow all of his fieldwork, research, and teachings. He was more well-known for being painfully shy than anything else. He was filled with a sense of relief—and pride—to know that Howard Shields had said something nice about him.

And now he also knew he was going to have to speak.

"Um…thank you," he said softly, and felt like his mouth was full of marbles. When he saw her smile broaden, it made him want to smile too.

So he did.

But he had a feeling it wasn't nearly as bright or as at ease as hers.

"Ah, there you are!" They both turned and saw Howard walk into the room, his white lab coat flowing slightly behind him. "I was on my way here and was sidetracked talking with Dr. Lauria about the waiting list for the telescope." He shook his head. "Students are up in arms over the lack of availability."

Owen nodded but remained silent.

"I see you've met my niece, Brooke," Howard said before leaning over and kissing her on the cheek.

"We haven't been formally introduced," she said shyly, smiling at Owen.

"Well, let's rectify that," Howard said, grinning. "Owen Shaughnessy, I'd like you to meet my niece, Brooke Matthews. Brooke, this is Dr. Owen Shaughnessy."

Brooke smiled—a genuine smile—as she held out her hand to Owen. "Feel free to make fun," she said.

Owen looked at her oddly. "Fun?"

Her head tilted slightly. "Yeah…you know. Because of my name."

Now he was confused. "I'm sorry," he said nervously, "is there something funny about the name Brooke?"

Howard laughed out loud and clapped Owen on the shoulder again as he shook his head. "Don't mind him, Brookie. He doesn't get pop culture references."

Pop culture references? Owen looked back and forth between the two of them for some sort of explanation. Then he realized Brooke's hand was still outstretched, waiting for him to take it. Quickly wiping his palm on his slacks, he took her hand in his and gave it a brief shake. He murmured an apology and averted his gaze before stepping back.

Tucking her hair behind her ear, Brooke continued to smile. "Our parents named me after Brooke Matthews — the model." When he still didn't react, she added, "She's also an actress." Still nothing. Looking at her uncle, she shrugged and let out a nervous chuckle. "Well, anyway…um, Uncle Howard, I'm afraid I was late to Dr. Shaughnessy's class."

Howard placed an arm around her and hugged her. "I knew pointing you in the direction of the art department was going to be a problem." He chuckled and turned to Owen. "Brooke is an artist and looking to intern either here at the university or maybe get a lead on a gallery where she can work and perhaps get her paintings looked at." He smiled lovingly at her. "She teaches painting classes during the summer semester at the community college, but she's far too talented to keep doing it."

"Uncle Howard…" she said shyly.

"What? It's true!"

Owen still couldn't quite figure out why Brooke was here or why Howard had thought she should come and hear him lecture. He was just about to voice the question when Howard looked at him.

"Brooke's specialty is painting the night sky."

For a moment, Owen wasn't sure how to respond.

Brooke blushed and then looked at Owen to explain. "I know most people would say the night sky is simply dark—or black—with some stars, but I don't see it that way. I see the way the stars reflect off one another and how it causes different hues in the sky." She gave a small shrug. "Most of the time my work is a little more…well, it's not abstract, but it's more whimsical than a true portrait."

"Don't just tell him about it," Howard suggested. "You have your portfolio with you. Why don't you show him?"

"Oh!" Brooke turned and took the leather case from her shoulder and laid it on the desk in front of her.

Owen watched in fascination as she worked—noting her slender arms and the music that came from her wrists as her bracelets gently clattered together. Her long hair fell over one shoulder, and it was almost impossible to take his eyes off her.

"I hope we're not keeping you, Owen," Howard said, stepping closer. "I probably should have asked you earlier about your schedule before we both sort of bombarded you like this."

He shook his head. "I… I don't have anything else scheduled for this afternoon. I had planned on heading back to the hotel and doing some reading before dinner. I'll talk with Riley later." Howard and Owen had known each other for so long that he didn't need to specify anything regarding his family—Howard knew all about them.

"How's he doing? Is he back in the studio yet?"

"Not yet. He didn't want to do another solo project, but getting the band back together isn't going as smoothly as he'd hoped."

Hands in his pockets, Howard nodded. "That's too bad. Still...I'm sure the time off is enjoyable. How is Savannah doing?"

Owen smiled at the mention of his sister-in-law. "She's doing well. She found an agent and she's submitting proposals for a book she's been working on."

"Wonderful! Is it based on her work interviewing rock stars?"

Beside them, Brooke straightened and gasped.

"Are you okay, my dear?" Howard asked.

But Brooke was looking directly at Owen. "You're Riley Shaughnessy's brother," she said. It wasn't a question, but a simple statement of fact.

A weary sigh was Owen's immediate response. This was how it normally went—not that it happened very often. At least not to him. But he heard from his other brothers what usually occurred when a woman found out they were related to Riley. And it wasn't as if Owen knew Brooke or was involved with her, but he braced himself for the disappointment of knowing that from this point on, she was probably only going to want to talk about his famous brother.

And for the first time in a long time—possibly since high school—he resented his twin.

Might as well get it over with...

Clearing his throat, Owen nodded. "Um...yes. Riley's my brother."

Brooke nodded, her smile just as sweet as it had

been since she walked into the lecture hall. "How fascinating! I mean, I think it is, anyway, to see such diversity in a family."

And here it comes, he thought…

"You're both so talented but in such different occupations. Your parents must be incredibly proud of you both!" Then she turned and straightened her pictures.

Wait…that was it? She wasn't going to obsess or go on and on about how talented Riley was or how much she loved his latest song?

"So let me ask you," she began as she faced him and Owen braced himself again. Now she was going to do it. Now she was going to gush. "What colors do you see when you look up at the night sky? Do you just see black or do you see different shades of blue?"

He stared at Brooke.

Hard.

And his jaw was quite possibly on the floor.

About the Author

New York Times and *USA Today* bestselling author Samantha Chase released her debut novel, *Jordan's Return*, in November 2011. Although she waited until she was in her forties to publish for the first time, writing has been a lifelong passion. Her motivation was her students: teaching creative writing to elementary age students all the way up through high school and encouraging those students to follow their writing dreams gave Samantha the confidence to take that step as well.

When she's not working on a new story, Samantha spends her time reading contemporary romances, blogging, playing way too many games of Scrabble or solitaire on Facebook, and spending time with her husband of twenty-five years and their two sons in North Carolina.